I0817751

THE MONSTER HUNTER FILES

VOLUME 2

BAEN BOOKS by LARRY CORREIA

THE MONSTER HUNTER INTERNATIONAL SERIES
Monster Hunter International
Monster Hunter Vendetta • *Monster Hunter Alpha*
The Monster Hunters (compilation) • *Monster Hunter Legion*
Monster Hunter Nemesis • *Monster Hunter Siege*
Monster Hunter Guardian (with Sarah A. Hoyt)
Monster Hunter Bloodlines
The Monster Hunter Files (anthology edited with Bryan Thomas Schmidt)
Monster Hunter Fantom (anthology edited by Marin Fajkus & Jakub Mařík)
The Monster Hunter Files, Vol. 2 (anthology edited with Jason Cordova)

MONSTER HUNTER MEMOIRS
Monster Hunter Memoirs: Grunge (with John Ringo)
Monster Hunter Memoirs: Sinners (with John Ringo)
Monster Hunter Memoirs: Saints (with John Ringo)
Monster Hunter Memoirs: Fever (with Jason Cordova)

THE GRIMNOIR CHRONICLES
Hard Magic • *Spellbound* • *Warbound*

THE SAGA OF THE FORGOTTEN WARRIOR
Son of the Black Sword • *House of Assassins*
Destroyer of Worlds • *Tower of Silence*
Graveyard of Demons • *Heart of the Mountain*

DEAD SIX (WITH MIKE KUPARI)
Dead Six • *Swords of Exodus* • *Alliance of Shadows*
Invisible Wars (omnibus)

NOIR ANTHOLOGIES (EDITED WITH KACEY EZELL)
Noir Fatale • *No Game for Knights* • *Down These Mean Streets*

Gun Runner (with John D. Brown)
Target Rich Environment (short story collection)
Target Rich Environment, Vol. 2 (short story collection)
Servants of War (with Steve Diamond)

BAEN BOOKS by JASON CORDOVA

THE BRONZE LEGION (WITH MELISSA OLTHOFF)
To Tread Obsidian Shores

Mountain of Fire
Monster Hunter Memoirs: Fever (with Larry Correia)
Chicks in Tank Tops edited by Jason Cordova
Dancing with Destruction edited by Jason Cordova

THE MONSTER HUNTER FILES

VOLUME 2

Edited by
Larry Correia &
Jason Cordova

THE MONSTER HUNTER FILES VOLUME 2

This is a work of fiction. All the characters and events portrayed in this book are fictional, and any resemblance to real people or incidents is purely coincidental.

A Baen Books Original

Baen Publishing Enterprises
P.O. Box 1403
Riverdale, NY 10471
www.baen.com

ISBN: 978-1-6680-7317-9

Cover art by Alan Pollack

First printing, March 2026

Distributed by Simon & Schuster
1230 Avenue of the Americas
New York, NY 10020

10 9 8 7 6 5 4 3 2 1

Printed in the United States of America

To everyone in the Monster Hunter nation.
You made this second volume possible. Thank you.

CONTENTS

THE MONSTER HUNTER FILES

VOLUME 2

INTRODUCTION

The following reports have been compiled from the archives of Monster Hunter International, as well as items which are believed to have leaked from the United States Monster Control Bureau, the Oxford University Supernatural Archives, the Blessed Order of Saint Hubert the Protector, Special Task Force REDACTED, other miscellaneous monster-hunting organizations, and individual records.

Though I can't verify all of them, I believe that these accounts are for the most part accurate and should be useful for all of our Hunters in the field. But as always, when dealing with unearthly forces it is best to tread carefully. Like Earl Harbinger says, keep a flexible mind.

—Albert Lee
MHI Archivist
Cazador, Alabama

Okay...this is awkward. I've compiled a lot of stories over the years, from other Hunters, from various organizations—both rival and friendly—from witnesses, and even some accounts from the very monsters we hunt, but I've never written one myself based on my own experiences. I've read thousands of records like this, but telling the story about one of my experiences is different. I'm a librarian, not a writer.

—A.L.

Albert Lee and the Scroll of Doom

Larry Correia

I suppose I should do an introduction. I'm Monster Hunter International's archivist, Albert Lee. Not to toot my own horn, but I'm likely one of the world's leading experts on monster lore. I don't claim to be a brilliant scholar or anything like that, it's just that the more academic types who do what I do for a living keep ending up cursed and insane, so I've outlasted the competition. It's all that insatiable curiosity, delving into forbidden mysteries thing. It gets them every time.

Oh look, here's an ancient Sumerian tome of rituals bound in human skin and inked in blood. Most paranormal archivists would be pumped at such a find and immediately read it. Me? Though tempted I'll take a quick look, make a note about the contents for the catalog, and then toss it in the safe with the rest of the haunted crap that whispers it wants to be read, to be saved for a rainy day if/when MHI runs into something pissed off from ancient Sumeria. I'm pragmatic like that.

It's not that I'm incurious. On the contrary, I love this stuff.

It's that I've seen firsthand the costs of curiosity when it comes to certain haunted subjects, and that price is way too high for me to mess around with that sort of thing willy nilly. That's how you get your Martin Hoods and Ray Shacklefords. Specifically, Julie's dad, not the several other Ray Shacklefords who turned out sane and uncursed, but that family does love to recycle their names through the generations.

One downside of becoming the de facto company historian is learning that guys like that—who got corrupted or driven crazy—aren't that big of an anomaly in this business, and some topics are forbidden for a reason.

Generally speaking, knowledge is good. As we were taught by the greatest philosophical work of all time, *knowing is the half the battle.* There's nothing more satisfying than pinning down the details that allow us to banish or kill the latest evil beastie.

But when it comes to magic, oh hell no. Do not screw with that shit. Humans messing around with magic is like giving a toddler a stick of dynamite to play with.

As company archivist, I'm basically the guy who hands out that dynamite. Well, I guess it's more like metaphysical dynamite. Milo Anderson's the one who hands out the real dynamite. Not that I'm a slouch in that department either. When I was recruited by MHI I was working as a county librarian, but before that I was a 1371 Combat Engineer, United States Marine Corps. Books and bombs are my favorite things.

But anyways, back to the evil magic stuff.

Long story short, MHI has accumulated a lot of wicked, nasty, possibly haunted, sanity-devouring tomes over the last century. When you off some necromancer or mad scientist, you can't just leave their grimoire or lab notes lying around for normies to mess with. And we can't just get rid of them either, because, as we've seen repeatedly, those things can be super useful. So part of my job is to make sure dangerous knowledge is only used responsibly in the proper circumstances. It's like don't drink and drive, don't take this medication and operate heavy machinery, don't commune with the wrathful spirits of the dead and open portals to hell, that sort of thing.

Years ago when my leg got badly injured and I had to go off of field duty, I volunteered to fix the MHI archives. Back then the place was a disorganized mess. It was more of a fire hazard than a proper library. Arguably the third or fourth best collection of monster lore in the world looked like something off a reality TV show about mentally ill hoarders. The state of the MHI archives offended me to the core of my librarian soul.

It took years to get the place up to my standards, with everything properly labeled and cataloged. What used to take weeks of combing through dusty tomes to find some nugget of monster trivia, now takes minutes. Hunters call in, wanting to know about some odd creature they're up against, and I can send them copies of everything we have fast. I might not be out in the field, kicking doors and blowing shit up anymore, but I still help save lives.

Nowadays I've got a pretty good system. Regular records on the shelves. Creepy books under lock and key. Since if you let just any random Hunter dick around with sensitive information, there's going to be bad results, I'm extra careful with the forbidden knowledge. Barring a few unforeseen complications early on in my career, I've managed to keep those particular scary records accounted for, to only be checked out in case of emergency—with MHI leadership approval—and brought back and stored safely as soon as the crisis is averted.

Everything was organized, accounted for, and in its place.

Or at least it was, until Owen Z. Pitt held a giant fucking gunfight in my library.

I've put up with a lot of indignities since joining Monster Hunter International. On one of my very first hunts, my buddy Trip left his tomahawk buried in a master vampire's head, and the vampire returned that tomahawk by throwing it *through* my leg. More recently, I caught a .357 Magnum bullet to the chest, fired by some poor bastard who'd been possessed by an Adze.

Surveying the damage to my beloved library was worse.

As broken glass crunched underfoot, I saw that there were spent plastic shotgun hulls everywhere. Shelves had been knocked over. Books had spilled in every direction. Some of them had been turned into confetti from buckshot. The ghostly projectiles fired by the army of Drekavac had started several small fires, but at least their corpses had dissipated upon death. Tiles had gotten knocked out of the ceiling and most of the lights had been broken. The walls were puckered with bullet holes and scorch marks. The glass wall was in ten million jagged pieces.

I'd stacked a bunch of Drekavac monsters myself during the battle, but I'd had the decency to do it out in the hallway like a civilized man. Z had gotten chased in here, hosed the place down with a full-auto shotgun, and even tossed some grenades for good measure, like a *barbarian.*

Z was a good friend, teammate, had saved my life upon multiple occasions, the entire Earth at least once, and in his defense had been trying to protect a girl from the hell-spawn clone army of an undead witch hunter... and even considering all that if he'd been here right now I still would've beat him over the head with my cane *because look at this place.* He was lucky he'd gotten teleported to Brazil.

News on that front was still spotty, but Earl Harbinger was leading a quick reaction force of Hunters to South America. We didn't really know what was going on down there, but apparently millions of lives were at stake. So, the usual. Those injured in yesterday's battle—and there were *a lot* of those—and those of us who weren't physically up to fieldwork anymore, were left here at the compound cleaning up and waiting to be called on for our expertise. Which was supremely frustrating, but again, the usual.

My bad leg was really bugging me, and I would have sat down to take in all the destruction, but a spectral sword had sliced my nice office chair in half, which was just adding insult to injury at this point. Rather than stand there angry, I went to the closet and got out a broom and dustpan. Somehow even the dustpan had a bullet hole in it.

I'd spent the last day helping to put out fires and ferrying the wounded to the orc healers or the hospital. Between Silas Carver's dark magic and Milo's defense system, we'd torched or blown up half the compound. This had been the worst monster attack on our headquarters in MHI history.

But now that the immediate damage control was done, there was some unholy threat out in the jungle, some of MHI was on the way to deal with it, and in the process they might need me to look up some useful lore on whatever they encountered. I wouldn't be able to do that very efficiently with all our original reference material lying on the floor covered in broken glass, so I got to sweeping.

It was after a few hours of righting shelves and restoring books to their proper homes that I found the secret compartment.

That particular bookshelf was some early 1900s, Bubba Shackleford-era furniture. Which still worked great because they built things to last back in those days, and all the new shelves I'd built from Ikea were flimsy in comparison. The sturdy old shelf covered one entire wall and had caught a Drekavac ghost bullet in the top corner. I had to stand on a ladder to inspect the damage, and it pissed me off to find that some of the original Professional Monster Killer journals had gotten hit by flaming shrapnel.

Hannah Stone had been the most prolific writer of the Hunters from that early period of the company's history, and it pained me to see one of her journals had gotten shredded by splinters. That was over a hundred-year-old, irreplaceable, historical document, obliterated in an instant by some undead asshole Puritan. That really pissed me off.

Except when I started pulling out the burned chunks, the wall behind it shifted. At first I thought it might just be a loose brick, but when I poked at the edges with my pocketknife, I discovered a hinged mechanism had been holding it place. It was well concealed and had been plastered over sometime in the distant past, but the Drekavac's bullet had cracked it open.

Finding a long hidden compartment wasn't too strange, as there were secret doors and tunnels all throughout the MHI compound, which is what happens when a bunch of militant paranoids do renovations. But when I used my flashlight I saw the hole was small, and the only thing inside was a sealed metal tube.

"What're you doing?" someone asked from below.

I looked down to see Trip Jones standing there. "I found a secret compartment or something."

When you see Trip, the first thing you think is *tough guy*, because he's this really buffed black dude, who was a high-level athlete and still carries himself with that kind of physical swagger that only really confident jocks have, but Trip is one of my favorite coworkers because he's just genuinely an all-around nice guy. Except right that moment he looked weary and in pain.

"You're limping bad as me, Trip. What happened to you?"

"I sprained my ankle really bad during the battle fighting a succubus."

"Huh . . ." Things had been so chaotic that night I'd not even known there'd been a succubus involved. "Succubi are mind-controlling demons who attract their prey by seduction and feed on their life force. How'd you sprain an ankle?"

"This one was less sexy, more punchy. It's a long story."

"That's nonstandard monster species behavior. You need to update that for the records ASAP."

Trip sighed, because my coworkers weren't as zealous as I was about proper documentation. "I just got back from the hospital, Al."

"You didn't go to the orcs?" Magic and humans didn't mix, but it worked fine for the tribe of orcs MHI provided shelter for, and they had some fantastically good healers. They were why I was hobbling around on a gimpy leg, instead of an artificial one.

"Gretchen and her girls are exhausted and been working non-stop since the fighting stopped." Trip shrugged. "There's a lot of Hunters who were worse off than me who needed their attention more. I just had to make sure nothing was broken."

Putting others first was just Trip's nature. "I've got some ibuprofen in my desk if you need it. Assuming Owen didn't shoot that too."

"I'm good. What's in there?"

"I'm not sure. I was just checking it for booby traps first. It looks clear."

"Should I go put my helmet on?"

"Naw." I was pretty sure it was safe. The hole was plain and from the dust this thing hadn't been disturbed for a really long time. When I poked the metal tube with my knife nothing happened, so I reached in and pulled it out. It was just an old lead pipe with a cap screwed on each end. "That's a lot of effort to hide plumbing supplies. I bet there's something inside."

Trip held the ladder while I climbed down. "Anything in your notes about this?"

"Not that I can think of." I held the pipe out to Trip. "You want to do the honors?"

"In case it's black magic or radioactive?"

"What are the odds of that?"

"Around here? Greater than zero. Naw, man. I'm good. I'm just going to stand over here while you open it." Trip hobbled back a few feet. "You know, in case ghosts come out and melt your face like the Ark of the Covenant."

"Now you're just being dramatic." I had to wrestle the cap because it was really on there. I was thinking about going to find a wrench when it finally came loose. Rather than face-melting ghosts, the only thing inside was a tightly rolled-up sheet of paper. "Hello, beautiful. What do we have here?"

I took it back to my desk so I could put on my white librarian gloves and get a pair of tweezers. If that pipe had been in there since the Bubba days, the paper was over a century old, and was likely to be extremely fragile. Now that I knew the contents were paper I was really kicking myself for suddenly exposing it to air and humidity. At least the main building's central air-conditioning had survived the attack so it wasn't too bad here in the basement. I put on a surgical mask anyway.

Trip followed me back to my desk and watched as I worked. "Why the mask? Do you think it's got anthrax or something?"

"Anthrax? For a guy who fights disgusting slimy creatures for a living, you are so nervous about germs, I swear... The mask's not to protect me, I'm trying to protect the paper from my breath." I eased it out of the pipe with the tweezers and laid it on my desk.

"It's a scroll."

"Just because it's rolled up doesn't make it a scroll," I explained as I gently began to unroll it, and the first thing I saw was that the title at the top read *Scroll of Doom.* "Well, shit. My bad."

"What is it?"

"I don't know yet." Despite the ominous title, it didn't *feel* dangerous. I'd dealt with thousands of old records, and the ones we knew to be legitimately tainted by evil tended to give off an icky vibe. Other than the unorthodox storage method, this one seemed perfectly normal. Plus, this was just a single handwritten sheet of paper. All the haunted tomes I'd ever messed with had some heft to them. They had *gravitas.* This was probably nothing.

What's the worst that could happen?

I got the whole thing opened up and saw it was in cursive English. The message wasn't very long, so I started reading, got through the entire thing in a few seconds because I'm a natural speed reader... and immediately regretted it.

"Shit... Stay back. Don't look at it. It's a curse."

"I knew it!" Trip was brave, but he took another couple of steps back, because he'd had some bad encounters with voodoo before. "You sure?"

It could just be a hundred-year-old prank, except it had been hidden in the basement of one of the world's best monster-hunting companies, so I sincerely doubted that. "I think it's legit."

"Then don't just stand there looking at it. Burn it or something."

I thought about the warning in the message I'd just read. "It's more complicated than that." I had no choice but to read it again to make sure I understood the ramifications. The first part I can't write down here for reasons that'll become apparent as the story goes on, but it concluded with *By reading these words the contract is voluntarily entered into and the ritual begins,* which of course I didn't see in time because that was at the *end* of the damned thing.

"What's it say?"

"I can't tell you. If I do, or read it out loud, you might be bound too. I've got to think about how to paraphrase this..." I hate to admit it, but I was kind of freaking out right then as the ramifications begin to sink in. "You remember how there used to be those emails, where it was if you forward this message to someone else, you'll have good luck, but if you don't, you'll die?"

"Yeah. Before that it was chain letters. Make copies of this and mail them to ten other people or else. Some guy in Canada named Fred didn't mail this letter and a piano fell on his head."

"Exactly."

"Then it's probably nothing." Trip seemed relieved, but then he noticed I was sweating profusely. "What's wrong, Al?"

Rather than reply, I flipped the Scroll of Doom over so Trip couldn't read it and endanger himself, grabbed my keyboard, and typed in the name from the signature at the bottom of the scroll. It had been signed by one Orson K. Pangle, Professional Monster Killer.

SEARCHING.

"I'm looking to see how the guy who wrote this chain letter died." I was really hoping to find that he'd gone peacefully in his sleep at a very old age. The results came back, and... nope. Orson Pangle had been suddenly devoured by a horde of imps, a few days after the date beneath his signature, *exactly* like the Scroll of Doom promised. "That's not good."

My computer screen Trip could read safely, so I swiveled it for him to see.

"Who's this Pangle dude?"

"A Bostonian lawyer, recruited to be one of the earliest of

Bubba Shackleford's Professional Monster Killers from before the company changed its name to Monster Hunter International, and the alleged author of this Scroll of Doom."

Trip skimmed the end of the file. "It looks like this OG was just standing on the corner minding his own business in front of some other Hunters, when a bunch of little carnivorous mutant-bug demons appeared from out of nowhere, and were on him like piranha on a cow. In a few seconds all that was left of him was just a bloody mangled skeleton, they didn't attack anyone else, then poof, those creatures vanished without a trace, no explanation, never to be seen again."

"Since I can't tell you specifically what's on the scroll, let's just say that fate is pretty spot on with what Pangle foretold in that note, and he'd read the curse exactly seven days prior."

"Oh..." Trip said as he truly grasped the enormity of the situation. "I'll go find help."

"Thanks." After Trip had limped off as fast as he could, I rolled the scroll back up and returned it to the tube. I'd been so damned careful for so long when it came to this sort of thing, that I was really kicking myself. One of the rules of handling ordnance is that you never, ever get complacent, because even the smallest mistake can kill you. Evil writing worked by the exact same principles and I'd been sloppy.

Now I had seven days to figure out how to break the curse, curse someone else to take my place, or die horribly.

I found myself in a difficult position. It's my duty in life to document everything I can about monster hunting, only I got cursed with something that if I were to write it down, that would risk passing that curse onto someone else. I can't even write it here without putting the lives of whoever is reading this into danger.

I looked up everything I could about Orson K. Pangle in the archives, and by all accounts he was a charmer, a ladies' man, and a great card player, but he was also a very intelligent and courageous Hunter, as well as a decent, honorable man. I was pretty sure that last part was accurate, because when he'd found himself in the same situation as me, rather than take the easy way out and pass the curse on to some other sucker, he'd kept it secret to not endanger his friends, and instead tried to lawyer his way out. He couldn't destroy the message without dying and inflicting the curse back upon whoever had given it to him, so he'd written it down and sealed it away somewhere it *might* eventually be found, believing that would be a sufficient technicality to count as passing the curse on. Since he'd gotten ripped to pieces shortly thereafter, clearly it had not.

I don't know if Pangle was the one who'd hidden it in the wall, or if it had been put there by somebody else after his death. Whoever had done that had probably been hoping that future Hunters would be better equipped to deal with the curse. The problem was, I didn't know if we were.

The help Trip had sent me so far were some of the smartest Hunters MHI had. Milo Anderson had been on MHI's primary team forever and seen a lot of craziness. He's a bona fide mechanical genius. Ben Cody was a much older Hunter who had come out of retirement to help with our recent situation, but before that he'd been the leader of our New Mexico team that specialized in mad-science issues, and Cody collected doctorates like I collected Funko Pops.

Unfortunately, Milo had just punctured a lung and Cody was still suffering from a concussion. Like I've said, that had been one hell of a fight against the Drekavac. Our orcs had gotten them tuned up, but they were still obviously hurting.

The three of us were sitting around my desk, and I was still bitter that I was using a cheap metal folding chair instead of my eight-hundred-dollar office chair that had gotten cut in half. Z owed me a new chair.

"So how'd you get your skull cracked?" I gestured at the bandages around Cody's big shaggy head.

"Succubus." He muttered the word while squinting like he had a bad hangover.

"The same one who clobbered Trip?" When Cody nodded, I laughed. "You guys are really ruining my image of succubi. I thought they would be more of a 'death by snu snu' sort of thing."

"She tried to get in my head like that, but I love my wife way too much for that nonsense to work on me. When I resisted her charms, she just body-slammed me instead." Cody massaged his temples with his fingers. "Can we please focus on your mysterious death curse?"

"Good idea." Milo was sitting behind my computer, reading the Pangle file, and making a wheezy noise as he breathed. He'd told me the healers had reinflated his collapsing lung with some orcish device that looked like bagpipes, and that yes, that was as painful as it sounded. "Just don't tell us anything that'll get us cursed too. MHI's kind of swamped right now."

I glanced around my shot-up library, and sarcastically said, "I'd not noticed."

"What do you have so far?" Cody asked.

I'd been doing my research, skimming through records as fast as I could. Which made me glad for all the work I'd put in scanning documents. "Chain-letter curses go back a longer time than you'd think—sixth-century Europe even, but those records are super spotty, and we'd have to go to Oxford to see the originals. Then in the Edo period in Japan there was a rash of these, with legit monster activity involved, something about an oracle with the body of a cow but with a human face, only the translations are spotty."

"I've fought Japanese monsters before," Milo said, "but no cows with people heads. Though come to think of it, I do know a minotaur, which is pretty much the opposite. Just don't call him a minotaur. They think that's racist. The polite term is Texas Bullmen."

"Okay." To the uninformed it might seem like Milo had a hard time focusing, but it was just that his brain worked on a different plane from the rest of us mortals. Sometimes you just needed to let the man cook. "I'll keep that in mind."

"What's the ratio of real curses to hoaxes and scams preying on social anxiety?" Cody asked.

"Actual magic ones are exceedingly rare. But it turns out there have been some capable assholes and creatures who've done this sort of thing from time to time, using everything from handwritten letters to VHS tapes as the delivery method. I've printed off the shelf a number of everything in the archives that's got any sort of reference to those cases." I handed both of them a sheet of paper. "I'm thinking we should start by checking for any examples of thwarting or breaking this sort of curse."

That was when Trip returned with one more expert in tow. Cody groaned and Milo grinned when they saw her. Cody was too sciency to put up with what he referred to as *elven nonsense*, but Milo thought she was great. "If it isn't Tanya, princess of the elves. Hey, Your Majesty."

"Good to see you too, Red Beard. How y'all doing?" she asked as she flounced in, wearing Daisy Duke cutoffs and a tank top in proper trailer-park-royalty fashion. It looked like MHI's token elf employee had made it through the battle unscathed.

"We're okay except for the part where Lee's probably cursed and about to get carried to hell by a swarm of hungry, vicious little demons," Milo said.

"Yep. Trip told me 'bout that. Bummer. This ain't my usual area, but I can maybe still help."

Humans can't do magic without it coming at some great cost, but that rule didn't seem to apply to our supernatural cousins. Even if she did look like any other hot, slutty redneck girl—only with pointy ears—if I knew anybody who could break a curse, it was Tanya. "Happy to have you aboard."

She scowled at me for a long moment. "Hoo-boy, Al, you're like super cursed. It's all over your aura. Whatever you attracted is downright *nasty.* I bet it's promising all sorts of fancy reward if you do something evil to put another link in the chain."

I couldn't tell her about the vague promises of immortality for any bearer of the curse who was selfish enough to pass it on to someone who was so righteous they would willingly sacrifice themselves to end the curse once and for all. "Yeah. That's in there. And the way it's written I suspect that whoever cursed Orson Pangle might still be alive."

"Oh, we can remedy that!" Milo declared with great and murderous enthusiasm.

"Even though you can't speak specifically on what the scroll says, I feel safe assuming time is of the essence." Cody wobbled, dizzy, as he stood up. "Let's get to work."

Six days, twenty-three hours, and forty-five minutes after reading the Scroll of Doom, I rudely walked into a wealthy investor's study, unannounced. The man of the house was standing behind his desk, looking out the window at his majestic estate, contentedly surveying his kingdom. According to my research he was two hundred and ten, but he didn't look a day over fifty.

He heard the door open, but didn't bother to turn and look. "Leave my supper on the table and go," he said dismissively.

"I didn't think to bring any food, but we could probably order a pizza if you want."

I'm not good at the one-liners under pressure like some of my wittier teammates, but that was pretty good for me.

Vernon Gastelon glanced my way and saw a stranger, holding a suppressed .300 Blackout carbine aimed at his face. Despite my obvious willingness to shoot him dead, he remained calm, and gave me a slow nod of greeting. The dude was cool. I'll give him that.

"Where are my guards?"

"Your human employees are alive. Zip-tied, duct-taped, and tossed roughly into the back of a van which is now departing the grounds of your mansion, but they're alive. Your inhuman employees, not so much." Keeping the gun on him, I slowly hobbled into the room, and then nudged the door closed behind me. "We'll be filing the PUFF on those to offset the costs of this little expedition."

"I have no idea what you're talking about."

"Don't play stupid, Vernon. It doesn't suit you. I know who you are. So you can probably figure out who I'm with."

He looked me over, took in all the tac gear and weaponry, before he saw the green smiley face with horns patch on my vest, and smiled. "Ah . . . Monster Hunter International. I suspected this confrontation would come someday."

I'd seen that smile on TV before. Hell, I owned stock in some of his companies. It was just that nobody had ever realized that Vernon Gastelon the Fifth was actually Vernon Gastelon the First, and he'd just turned himself functionally immortal through a blood-magic-fueled chain curse.

"So how's it work? You make up a kid, and send him off to some imaginary boarding school so nobody ever sees him. Fake your death when you can no longer hide the fact you don't age. Inherit your own riches. Repeat for five generations. That's how higher-level undead do it." He was standing in front of a sunlit window without catching on fire, and his reflection appeared just fine in the mirror on the wall, so he'd not turned himself into a vampire. "I wonder with the immortality curse if the adjuster will declare you count as a subtype of lich, or if you'll just be categorized as a predatory sorcerer."

"Why does it matter what I am?"

"Because we get paid more for liches."

"Is there good money in that?"

"It pays great." But then I looked around his office, which was decorated with a bunch of sculptures and paintings that each cost a lot more than my house. "Well, relatively speaking, of course."

"Of course... If you were here to simply kill me, you would have shot me already. Your leg appears to be troubling you. Would you like to take a seat?" He gestured toward the couch.

Comfy as that looked, I said, "I'll stand."

"Would you care for a drink?"

"I'll pass."

"Too bad. This is three thousand dollars a bottle. It's rather good." I believed that, but I was already cursed. I didn't need to get poisoned too. When I shook my head in the negative, he picked up an empty glass for himself. "Do you mind if I have one?"

"Go ahead. Just do it slowly."

As Vernon poured himself a glass, seemingly unworried about me and my bullets, he asked, "So what do I owe the pleasure of this unexpected visit, Mister...?"

"Lee. Albert Lee."

"I've never heard of you. Not many people know about MHI, but as a student of the illicit arts, I pride myself on keeping up with potential threats. I know of the Shacklefords. I've met the lovely Julie at a fundraiser once. I've heard tales of the legendary Earl Harbinger. And what's the large one? Pitt? But you, I've never heard of."

"You wouldn't have. I usually work in the basement." I checked my watch. Assuming demons were punctual, my time was short. "I'm the guy who's been cursed by your stupid chain letter."

"Splendid." Vernon pulled out his chair and sat down. "I wondered what happened to that branch. It dropped off forever ago. I never know the specifics, but I can always tell when there's a new link added to the chain, as that's one more useful life—or death—for me to draw energy from."

"Like a non-sexy succubus... There's a lot of that going around lately."

He clearly had no idea what I was talking about there. "How did you figure out it was me?"

"It took a bit of effort." I still needed to kill a few minutes. "Can I tell you a story, Vernon?"

"You're the man with the gun, Mr. Lee. Do as you see fit."

I lowered the carbine to my waist, to let the sling take most of the weight, but I kept it casually leveled at his chest. "I was born here, but my parents were immigrants. You know those stereotypes about Asian parents, right?"

"No. I do not."

"Well, anyways. One time when I was in high school, in this advanced placement math class—which by the way, I am not good at math—one Friday our teacher screwed up, and handed out the wrong homework assignment. This was something we hadn't covered yet, and wouldn't get to for months. It was way too advanced. But we didn't know that. So I go home, and I am stumped. There's no way I could figure this out. I tell my parents this has to be some kind of mistake. But my mom and dad were like, oh no, you lazy ingrate bum, your older brother's in med school, you're going to get back in there and figure that math homework out or else. We don't care about *fair*. But oh yeah, make sure you do your piano practice first. Man, I hate the piano to this day."

"I do not understand where you are going with this."

"I'm getting there. So I practice the piano, then I spend the entire weekend trying to crack this math homework. This was pre-tutorial videos on the internet too, so we had to do it the hard way. So I get with my friends from class and we went to the library, and we racked our brains and tortured ourselves, but we got it figured out and basically taught ourselves calculus over the weekend—which, keep in mind, I'm bad at math. Monday morning, the teacher goes, I'm so sorry I gave you kids the wrong homework. I sure hope none of you wasted your time trying to do something that was way too advanced for you. Who did the homework? And guess what happens."

"I have no idea," he said, bemused.

"Every Asian kid in class raised their hand."

He stared at me for a long time. "What?"

"I'm trying to tell you that you picked the wrong nerd to fuck with, Vernon."

I wasn't going to explain it all to this asshole, but after gathering the smart Hunters, we'd gone to work, done the research, learned how this type of curse operated, tracked down similar events, built a map and timeline, looked up all the known and suspected wizards from that period and region, and then found a painting of one particular dickweed who happened to look exactly like his great-great-grandson, who we already had a file on for being a known trafficker in black magic.

Just like back in school, we'd been given an advanced homework assignment, but we had brains, a work ethic, a really well-stocked library of monster lore, and a powerful lot of incentive to get this done. MHI had bigger fish to fry and I really didn't want to get ripped apart. Though that was still preferable to piano practice.

"A lovely story, Mr. Lee, but the clock is ticking. As a Monster Hunter, surely you must understand what's at stake. You need to find someone to trick into reading or listening to the curse or you will die rather horrifically. When you spread the curse, you'll be blessed with extra years taken off their life. There's no need to feel sorry for them, though. All they have to do is continue the cycle. It's a win-win. But you need to hurry. This is a limited time offer."

"Wow. I've seen you on *Shark Tank*, but you really *are* a good businessman."

"With this spell I created a product which must be forever propagated to escape great personal harm. There is no greater motivator than that. I didn't invent multilevel marketing, Mr. Lee, but I perfected it."

Even without the curse part I would've shot him, just for that. "You're a prick, you know that, right?"

"So I take that to mean that you will not be participating in my program?" Vernon looked past me, to where the door was closed. "What is that noise that I am hearing? Is that your friends talking outside?"

"Nope. It's just me. They're waiting a safe distance away."

"I find it curious that you came to face me—an opponent of unknown capability—alone. I was under the impression that Monster Hunters were smarter than that, working in teams whenever possible."

"We do."

"Then threatening me in my own home all by yourself was a very foolish thing to do." Vernon blinked, and now his eyes were gleaming purple. Even as he was just sitting there behind a desk, he seemed to puff up, becoming bigger and more dangerous. His previously baggy silk shirt was stretched by instantly generated muscles, like he was on supernatural steroids. We still weren't sure what exactly playing with dark magic had done to him, but Vernon went from kindly to profoundly fucking intimidating in an instant. "My mortal bodyguards were just for show. I am more than capable of defending myself from the likes of you."

"I figured that, but I didn't want to put my team in danger when the horde of whatever kind of extradimensional beings you enslaved to enforce your curse show up here." I looked at my watch again. "In about three minutes."

Vernon blinked, this time in surprise, and his eyes flipped back to normal. "You're bringing the blood swarm *to my home*?"

"Party at Vernon's house! I bet it'll be a rager."

Despite being momentarily shaken by that idea, he went back to fearsome real quick. That transformation must have helped his hearing too, because the faint voice he'd been hearing earlier was now loud enough that he stuck one finger in his ear and wiggled it around. "Though insane with a desire to kill, the swarm will not lay a claw on me. When they come into this dimension they only attack those who have been cursed."

"Yeah . . . about that. A bit of bad news for you. You're cursed too."

"Impossible. I've seen no letter."

"No, but we hacked your computer and pretty much everything you've looked at for the last couple of days, the Scroll of Doom has been crammed in there somewhere. Subliminal messages, audio *and* visual, not to mention we snuck it onto some of the documents your secretary had you sign, white print on a white background, and those two times you clicked yes on a user agreement, that was all from Melvin, MHI's internet troll. He's still regrowing his legs from when they got blown off last week, so he was bored and got creative."

"Surely such low trickery doesn't count!"

"Take it up with my elf. She said that should be close enough for an Irkallan blood swarm and that when you play with Fey fire you deserve to get burned. And just in case . . ." I reached into my pocket and pulled out the speaker that had been playing a recording of me reading Orson Pangle's Scroll of Doom out loud, on a loop, at ever-increasing volume the entire time I'd been here. I turned it all the way up.

"No!" Vernon rose, flipping his heavy desk end over end. It crashed into the couch and knocked the stuffing out of it.

Thankfully he couldn't attack me, because he was too busy mashing his now gigantic hands over his ears to try and block the sound of my voice.

Milo must have been watching the window through his scope for any sudden movement, because a hole appeared in the glass and one of Vernon's hands exploded into a cloud of meat and bone fragments. Flesh barely slowed Milo's .338 Lapua bullet, which kept on trucking along to smash one of the marble statues at the far end of the room into dust.

Cody's bullet hit a split second later. This time the whole window shattered and the big .50 tore Vernon's other arm *clean off.*

He might have turned himself immortal, and would probably heal from even that, but he sure couldn't plug his ears anymore!

The message on the recorder ended, and my voice started over again.

Vernon turned to me, purple eyes bright as LEDs now, shrieked, "You bastard!" and started my way.

The carbine's selector was already flipped to full auto and I let it rip. I'd been using subsonic projectiles to get past the guards, because those were ninja quiet, but for my meeting with the big man himself, I'd loaded a mag of full-power, high-velocity, ruin-your-afternoon rounds. Even with the silencer on the end of my gun these were a lot louder, but thirty of them in one continual burst did a real number on his pelvis.

We didn't want him dead. We just didn't want him getting away quite yet.

With his bowels falling out his taint, Vernon slid, stumbled, and fell against the wall. Unfortunately for him, he could still be seen through the window, and another big bullet from outside exploded his collapsed right leg. Milo was so brilliant it was easy to forget that he was also a really good shot.

According to my watch, we'd gone slightly over time, except then there was a rumble, and the whole mansion shook. A red glow began to gather around one wall. It was time to go! Since we'd not damaged Vernon's ears, I dropped the speaker on the floor so it could continue condemning him on a loop, and limped for the door.

"Lee, wait! Don't leave me. I'll give you anything." Vernon looked at the red fog that was quickly solidifying into a gate and began to panic and flail. His curse was so potent—powered by so many lives—that I could see he was already healing. Purple light was shooting out of the stumps where his arm and hand had been, and the flesh was bubbling and reforming, but even then he wasn't going to come back together before the blood swarm arrived.

The red wall bulged, like hundreds of baby-sized hands and lobster pincers were straining against a layer of plastic wrap. It was really gross.

"You want money? Power! Magic! Name your price!"

Z probably would have thought of some really cool thing to say as he walked out, but honestly, I wasn't a hundred percent sure if I'd successfully transferred the curse or not, and was scared to find out, so I just yanked the door open and started down the stairs. Thank goodness there was a safety rail to hold onto or I might have fallen and broken my neck.

I was halfway down the steps when I realized that Earl Harbinger would've played it even cooler and picked up that really nice bottle of bourbon on the way out, but that's why Earl is the leader and I'm the librarian.

Behind me there was a tearing sound as the blood swarm erupted into our world. It was like boiling, hissing, and ten thousand cicadas screaming and clicking. Vernon was wailing and begging for their nonexistent mercy, when they lit into him with a noise like electric knives carving a moist turkey combined with a dentist grinding your teeth, and somehow despite all that horrific racket, I could still hear my recorded voice, calmly reciting the promises of the Scroll of Doom.

Trip and Tanya had been waiting for me right outside in our getaway vehicle, parked next to the truck with the gigantic homebrew ammonium nitrate bomb they'd parked there while I'd been talking to Vernon. I'd hopped in the back of the van, we'd sped off, and once we were at a safe distance, set off the truck bomb. Popping a pseudo lich—or whatever the hell Vernon Gastelon would be declared to be by the PUFF adjuster—was great and all, but eradicating an entire extradimensional blood swarm too? That would make for a fantastic PUFF bounty. We'd even provided the MCB a convenient cover story. According to the Monster Control Bureau, thousand-gallon home propane tanks blow up by themselves *all the time*. I'm pretty sure we got the swarm too, because when I looked back at the mansion, blood had still been spraying out the broken office window like it was going through a lawn sprinkler.

Being the one who'd been cursed, I'd gotten to do the honors with the detonator, and it had been a rather pretty explosion. That was satisfying.

As the mushroom cloud had risen into the sky, we'd pulled over, I went off a ways by myself just in case, took out the Scroll of Doom, and set it on fire. With both the originator of the curse and his blood-swarm enforcers dead, nothing appeared to punish me for that act of defiance, so the spell was broken. Then we picked up Cody and Milo from where they'd been sniping and the five of us headed for the airport so we could get back to Alabama.

During the drive, I checked my messages, and there were fifteen new ones from different Hunters asking me questions about monster lore. Earl needed to know how to fight a monster made out of colors. Now that sounded fascinating.

It would be good to get back to the office.

Sloppily getting cursed taught me a valuable lesson about hubris. But that's a good example of why I started compiling these records, so that today's Hunters can learn from those who came before us, whether it be from our mistakes or our triumphs. I hope that the other entries in this volume will prove helpful and educational. And most importantly, if you ever find something labeled something ominous like the Scroll of Doom buried in your wall, don't read the damned thing!

—A.L.

The Perpetual Unearthly Forces Fund (PUFF) is the bounty system where Hunters get paid by the government for eliminating monsters. Some creatures, hybrids, and humans who've been touched by the other realms can earn PUFF exemptions through good behavior.

Eyes Like Mine

Melissa Olthoff

It would've been nice to go to college.

Go to classes and earn a degree during the day, get a little wild and a lot stupid at night.

Instead, I was stuck in nowhere Indiana in a life I didn't want. All because of a curse. A real curse, one that had wound its tendrils through my family tree like kudzu. Pretty, deceptively powerful, and eventually deadly.

My mother had called our Fey-touched sight a gift.

I called it the reason I no longer had a mother.

Regardless, the end result was the same—glamour didn't work on the women in my family. Ever since a distant ancestor had managed to spectacularly piss off a Fey, we could *see* past the illusions monsters used to hide from humanity. And because my great-whatever-grandmother was an overachiever, the Fey hadn't just cursed her. He'd cursed her and every female descendent until the end of time—or until our line died out, whichever came first.

So normal had never been an option. But it would've been nice to pretend . . . even if it was just for a few years. Ball State, the number-one party school in the country, was less than two hours away, but it might as well have been in a different country.

Because I wasn't a college student.

I was a monster hunter.

"You know, Taylor, I could be at a party right now," I muttered.

I kept my rifle low, finger lying along the trigger guard, and carefully stepped over a flattened section of cornstalks, dirt crunching faintly under my boots. Something had crashed through this part of the field, but it was too large for what we were hunting. Likely deer or maybe bored teenagers, though even teenagers probably had better things to do than mess around in Dirk Kessel's back forty on a Friday night.

Unlike me.

I sighed and kept walking, breathing in the earthy, slightly musty scent of corn and dirt with every step.

"I could flirt with a hot guy, jump on the back of his bike, get drunk under the stars and make fun life choices. But nooo." I shot my brother an irritated glare as he matched my pace in the next row. I only caught glimpses of his broad frame through the dried stalks, but I could see enough to note the matching irritated expression on his face. "Here we are, spending another Friday night cleaning up a mess. No, not a mess. An infestation."

"An infestation of *monsters*, Essie," Taylor said in a low voice, pointedly speaking quieter than me. "And you're supposed to be working on making *smarter* life choices, not fun ones."

"God, you talk like you're fifty, not twenty-four."

"And you talk like you're fourteen, not twenty," he shot back, still keeping his voice low.

"Well, I've been doing this since I was fourteen, so . . ."

"Grow the fuck up, Essie," he said gruffly. "Focus."

I rolled my eyes and ghosted deeper into the field, towering stalks rustling in the persistent breeze. The night sky was cloudless, a smattering of stars and a sliver of a moon providing more than enough illumination for my Fey-cursed eyes. As chilly as it was in late fall Indiana, there was enough humidity in the air for fog, mostly rising from the farm's stock ponds. The mist snaked along the ground, wound through the fields and pastures, combining with the stupid cornstalks to limit our visibility. Add in the cover of rustling leaves, and it was no wonder we'd already been out here for over an hour with nothing to show for it.

"Taylor, we're hunting *dard*," I said dryly as I raised my Ruger 10/22 rifle in emphasis. Perfect for taking down small game. Or small monsters like the dard, an invasive species from France that glamoured themselves as harmless cats. The farmers welcomed them because cats kept the mice population under control, while in reality, the dard were helping themselves to the farmers' livestock. "We might as well call ourselves Pest Control."

A flicker of a smile finally cracked the granite of Taylor's face. "You have to admit, O'Connell's Pest Control has a nice ring to it."

"We'd probably make more money too," I grumbled, thinking about how expensive even online college classes were, and how few I could afford to take each semester.

While dard could in very rare cases be dangerous to people, they were considered so low a threat you had to search *way* down the government's PUFF table to find them. Even if we took out the whole nest tonight, they were worth barely enough to restock the fridge, let alone pay for an extra class. At the rate I was going, I'd graduate in the next decade or so with a boring degree in finance I'd probably never get to use.

We cleared the latest field without finding a trace of the little assholes, concealing stalks falling away between one step and the next and leaving us standing out in the open. Taylor flexed his broad shoulders and scanned our surroundings with sharp but perfectly ordinary eyes.

A flicker of motion caught my attention, a flash of a reptilian tail with a faint blur around it, as if it were slightly out of focus. Gone by the time I'd finished turning, rifle stock pressed firmly to my shoulder. I took my finger off the trigger, sighed, and tilted my head toward the decrepit building visible above the swaying brown stalks of the next field.

"Wanna check out the creepy barn next?"

"Not particularly, no. But if it gets the job done..." Taylor grimaced. "You're not the only one who'd rather be somewhere else tonight, you know."

I snorted. "Is it a recliner? Maybe a lawn chair so you can sit in our front yard and yell at everyone to 'make smart choices'?"

"Focus, Essie," he ground out, taking the lead, his rifle up and ready.

We'd already searched the main barns and outbuildings closer to the farmhouse, but this one was tucked out of sight of the main road and didn't look like it'd last another winter. Leaning against a rusted tractor like a drunk hanging onto his buddy after one too many shots at the bar, the metal roof was more rusted hole than actual roof, and there was a gaping opening where a door should be.

Nope, not creepy at all.

Cautiously, we crept up to the entrance. The thick scent of carrion and copper coated the back of my tongue, and cracked bones littered the dirt. I eased one last step forward. More flickers of motion, more blurred outlines—and eyes glowing in the dark shadows.

I flicked on the Trinity 1000-lumen LED flashlight mounted beneath the barrel of my rifle and swept the beam across the interior of the barn, getting a rough count of a dozen of the cat-headed, gray lizards. Spiky brown manes rose up along their spines, and they hissed like vipers, flinching away from the harsh light.

"Jackpot," I crooned, trying not to spook them into running. "They're all dard."

Once Taylor had confirmation that none of the creatures crawling all over the rusted machinery or perched on rotted straw bales were actually cats, he began picking them off, one controlled shot at a time. I was less precise, but I carried extra ammo for a reason, and I made up for my lack of precision with enthusiasm. It helped that the dard were partially stunned by the flashlight, one of the reasons we'd hunted them at night. Only two managed to dash past us into the foggy night, and we trotted after them as soon we'd cleared the barn.

We ran straight into Dirk Kessel.

Oops.

"Drop the peashooters," the old farmer growled, rheumy eyes glinting with steel as he stared at us down the barrel of an ancient shotgun. His lanky frame was stooped from age and years spent working his land, but his hands were steady and that double-barrel shotgun didn't waver an inch.

Farmers were tough bastards. Even farmers closing in on their eighties.

I glanced sidelong at Taylor and took my cue from him, pointing my rifle at the ground but not dropping it.

"Sorry, sir," he said respectfully. "We didn't mean to trespass."

"Well, you did," Kessel snapped, outrage stamped on his weathered features. "The fence should've been a goddamned cluebird. What in heck are you doing on my property?"

Taylor slid forward half a step, trying to keep the farmer's attention focused on him rather than me. "We were tracking a coyote."

The farmer grunted, unconvinced, and flicked on a flashlight every bit as powerful as the one I carried. There must have been a sale at the local gun shop, because in the instant before I was blinded, I swore it was the same brand as mine. Hissing in discomfort, I squinted at the bright light and fought back the urge to shield my eyes. I didn't want to get shot by accident.

And then Kessel cursed, the flashlight focused squarely on my face.

Damn it. I should've risked being shot.

The chain around my neck seemed to grow heavier, the metal exemption tag beneath my shirt cold against my skin. Too bad it wouldn't mean shit to this old man.

I'm human, but my eyes are decidedly not. Human eyes could be bright emerald green, but they sure as fuck didn't reflect a golden color at night the way mine did. The technical term was tapetum lucidum, a reflective layer that made seeing in low light easier and somehow tied into my ability to see through glamour.

I can't imagine what I looked like to Kessel, but for the first time his shotgun wavered, hands shaking. He panned the flashlight from me, to Taylor, and stopped on all the little furry bodies lying in the dirt behind us in the barn.

"What in God's name . . ." The old man trailed off, horrified at what looked like a massacre. The dards' glamour hadn't faded in death, and it very much looked like we'd just slaughtered a bunch of cats for funsies. "What are you, some kind of devil worshippers?"

"It's not what it looks like," Taylor said, desperately trying to salvage the rapidly deteriorating situation. He faltered, cleared his throat, and I jumped in the gap.

"It was um . . . the coyote." I smiled hopefully at Kessel, and he flinched at my eyes before he did what most people would do—he came up with a rational explanation to explain the eye shine away.

"Crazy kids and their stupid contacts." He shook his head, hands steadying. "Unless that coyote's name is Wile E., he didn't shoot a bunch of innocent cats. Get the fuck off my property. I see you again, I'll sink a load of buckshot into your backsides."

Cautiously, Taylor sidestepped around him, but I didn't move. Dards weren't worth much, but without samples to back up our claim, they weren't worth anything at all. And I had a feeling the farmer was the type to take care of the not-cat bodies before we could sneak back.

Kessel followed my gaze, and his expression hardened.

"Sick freaks." He fired a blast into the air. "I said get!"

We ran.

Rather that stick to the dirt path, Taylor made a beeline for the closest fence and the county road beyond it. A wild laugh bubbled up at the ridiculousness of running from an old farmer like a pair of teenagers. I peeled one white-knuckled hand off my rifle and threw up a pair of devil horns.

"Hail Satan!"

Taylor shot me an incredulous look as Kessel fired another, much closer warning shot. "Really, Essie?"

I cackled like a lunatic and ran faster.

If I couldn't make fun life choices, I could at least make the life I was stuck with a little more interesting.

"I still can't believe you did that," Taylor muttered as he pushed the grocery cart down the brightly lit aisle.

I strolled along next to him, scanning the dozens of cardboard boxes for my preferred cereal. "I still can't believe you're surprised."

After escaping Kessel's property without getting peppered with buckshot, we'd secured our gear in Taylor's pickup truck and headed to the grocery store.

Just another glorious night for Batesville's premier—and only—monster hunters.

We might have lost out on the PUFF for those little pests, but at least we still had enough in the checking account for *some* food. Wincing at the price tag, I bypassed the cereal I really wanted and grabbed the off-brand version. My steps slowed when we reached my favorite aisle. Dinner had been a sad peanut butter sandwich, and I could think of no better reward for a mostly successful hunt than chocolate.

My lips curled into a smirk. No better reward that I could find at a *grocery store*, anyway.

I turned my attention back to the extensive chocolate selection, ignoring Taylor's increasingly impatient huffs. I'd picked out two chocolate bars and was debating if we had enough money for a third when his patience finally snapped.

"Would you hurry up?" Taylor called over his shoulder, trying to beat an old grandmother to an open checkout lane. He lost. "I've got someplace to be."

"Got a hot date?" I teased as I sauntered after him, clutching my *three* chocolate bars to my chest like a dragon with new treasure.

When Taylor avoided my gaze, giving far too much attention to unloading our cart for checkout, my eyes widened. I dropped my prizes onto the belt and grabbed his arm.

"Wait, do you really have a date? It's Lizzy Hallstrom, isn't it! Oh! Or Nora Kensington! Or—"

"Becca Thomas." His face reddened and he swiped a hand through his dark hair, messing up the short waves. "It's just a first date at Ducky's, no big deal."

His nervousness said it *was* a big deal. I took a good look at his clothes, but outside of a few scuffs of dirt on his boots, he looked presentable enough for the local pool hall.

"Tell you what, why don't I just drop you off? I can bring the groceries home."

"You sure?"

I pointed at my chocolate bars. "Trust me, I'm sure."

It took longer than either of us wanted for the bored teenager to ring up our groceries. My attention wandered to the old TV blasting the local news. Another suicide. The fifth one this month.

Trying to ignore the newscaster's terrible attempt at sympathy, I grabbed the bag with my chocolate bars and wandered over to the corkboard near the exit to see if there were any part-time jobs posted. The internet had been a thing for*ever*, but folks around here still preferred to advertise the old way. All I could find were far too many missing person posters, and I turned away from the bleak images to dig through my grocery bag.

A wan-faced woman shuffled toward the exit, hands clenched tight around the handle of her cart and shoulders hunched. I took a step back so she could pass when a chill snaked down my spine. My head snapped up, and my gaze locked onto the spectral figure hovering next to her.

Motherfucking ghosts.

I didn't know if they were really a person's spirit or just an echo left behind by their passing, but most were harmless remnants, imprints that lingered in the cracks of grief and heartache. Some were a little more than that. Judging by the way the woman subconsciously flinched away from her hitchhiker, this particular ghost was strong enough for some part of her to hear the hate he was spewing. Vague, middle-aged features were contorted into a snarl as he silently berated her. I fought back the urge to snarl back, but only because the asshole couldn't hear or see anyone other than the person they'd fixated on.

My nails bit into my palms, the sharp sting an outlet for the familiar frustrated anger curling through my chest. There was a reason there wasn't any PUFF for ghosts. We couldn't kill them, couldn't affect them, couldn't do a damn thing to stop the dead from being assholes.

But sometimes I could do something for the living.

Before the woman could scuttle by, I whipped my hand onto an abandoned cart and jerked it into hers. The clash of metal startled her into actually lifting her gaze from the scuffed linoleum, and I winced at the dark circles beneath pretty brown eyes.

"Oh my gosh, I'm so sorry. I was distracted by my chocolate." I lifted my bag sheepishly and gave her a warm smile. "I love your hair, by the way. I can never get mine that straight."

Her whole face brightened at my genuine compliment, and the ghost faded just a little. Small things helped. The chocolate bar I slipped into her cart while she was distracted would help too. Not because it was magic, but because it was delicious.

"Thanks." She smiled shyly, and I realized she couldn't be more than a few years older than me. "And your curls are gorgeous."

"Thank you!" I tucked a dark auburn lock behind my ear and grinned, loving the way her tormentor faded even more, features growing indistinct as the woman's own spirit strengthened. With a little luck, he'd continue to fade until he was nothing more than a bad memory. "Hope you have a great night!"

Taylor frowned at the woman as she walked away, shoulders just a little less hunched than before. "Someone you know?"

I smiled. "Nope."

Our town was small, but not *that* small. A few minutes later, after paying *far* too much for groceries, we headed to Ducky's. An upbeat song popular over two decades ago drifted out on the chill night air, a few rough notes here and there telling me it was a live band, and a pretty good one at that.

Taylor pulled down the visor and checked himself in the tiny mirror, smoothing his hair down. "Do I look okay?"

Biting my lip to hold back a grin, I brushed off the dried corn husk clinging to his sleeve and gave him a thumbs-up. He slipped out of the passenger seat and shut the door, but I rolled the window down and hollered after him.

"Remember to make smart life choices!"

A handful of people smoking outside laughed, and he shook his head. "Grow up, Essie."

"Never!"

I drove out of town, a pretty crescent moon sailing high overhead. As I turned onto the overpass that would take me over I-74 and toward the ramshackle old farmhouse we called home, my headlights flashed over an animal near the middle of the bridge.

Abruptly, I slammed on the brakes.

That wasn't an animal.

A young man, barely more than a boy really, stood next to the guardrail, staring down at the highway traffic below. Throwing on my emergency flashers, I pulled over as far as I could on the narrow bridge and slipped out of my truck.

"Hey!" I called out, desperately wishing Taylor was here with me. "Stop!"

Every line in his body tensed, and I lifted empty hands as I eased closer. A spectral haze floated next to him. Between one blink and the next, it solidified into an ethereal woman, so distinct I could see the golden hue of her eyes and the inky black of her flowing hair. She whispered in his ear, a sweet melody that raised the hair on the back of my neck.

Resting one hand on his arm, she caressed the guardrail with the other. An invitation.

He climbed over it.

And then she looked at me. She *looked* at me.

Golden eyes ensnared mine, and my steps stuttered to a halt. She could see me. It was an effort to look away, but she wasn't important right now. The trembling boy on the other side of that guardrail was.

"Hey, you don't really want to do this."

"You're wrong." He glanced over his shoulder, despairing

expression backlit by the bright headlights of the semi-trucks barreling past. "I really do."

"No!" I leaped forward, hand outstretched, but I was too far away to stop him.

One second, he was perched on the edge. The next, he was gone. A horn blared and brakes squealed, but there was no stopping that kind of tonnage on a dime. Even if he'd survived the fall, the semi-truck had surely finished the job.

I pressed a hand to my mouth to swallow my cry.

The spectral woman tilted her head. Smiled at me. And vanished.

Goose bumps raced down my skin, and cold fear belatedly washed over me. Ghosts couldn't see random people. But she'd seen me, and she'd been cognizant enough to enjoy my reaction to her victim's death. Stumbling and shaking and two seconds away from vomiting, I stepped up to the guardrail. Four slash marks had cut through the metal exactly where her hand had caressed.

Like a knife through butter. Or claws.

Definitely not a ghost, then. So what the hell was she?

By the time I made it home, the groceries were warm and I needed something stronger than chocolate.

I'd called 9-1-1, waited on the side of the road just beyond the overpass, and told the county sheriff what I'd witnessed—minus the not-a-ghost part. Every time I blinked, I could still see red and blue lights flashing, still see the despair on that young man's face, still see those beautiful golden eyes.

And when I drove home, it felt like something watched me the entire way.

Floorboards creaked under my boots as I stomped inside, carrying all the groceries in one trip. I'd go back for our hunting gear after I got some food in my belly and my hands stopped shaking.

"I'm home!"

My voice echoed in the big house, bounced off dust-cloth-covered furniture and empty rooms. It was too much space for just the three of us, but we were too sentimental to let the place go. Also, with the way the housing market was, we wouldn't get nearly what it was worth. My nose wrinkled at the pile of dishes in the sink, the new cobwebs in the corners of the ceiling, and the muddy tracks across the kitchen, and then I decided it was a problem for Tomorrow Essie.

The squeak of wheels on hardwood announced my Uncle Will's arrival. "Hey, kiddo. How'd the hunt go?"

"Well, we didn't get shot by Kessel for practicing the dark arts, and we got all of the dard except for two . . . but we couldn't get samples so we lost out on the PUFF." I buried my head in the fridge, searching for something other than chocolate or alcohol. In an attempt to distract my uncle from the lost income, I added, "Hey, you ever hear of a spirit that can see the living? Not just their victim, but other people?"

Silence.

I kept rummaging. I was certain I'd put my leftover Chinese in here but I couldn't spot the white container. Damn it, if Taylor had stolen my food again, I was going to stab him with chopsticks.

"Ha!" I reached all the way in the back, where the container had gotten shoved behind a gallon of milk that may or may not have expired a month ago. "Found it."

"Essie."

At the grim note in my uncle's voice, I pulled my head out of the fridge, Chinese food clutched possessively in one hand.

Will O'Connell had been a big man once, but he'd slowly wasted away, useless legs shriveled and twisted. He'd been wheelchair-bound ever since the Monster Control Bureau team that killed his wife nearly beat him to death for daring to try to protect her.

Some days, I think he wished they'd succeeded. Most days, he remembered he was all we had left, and he endured when I think he otherwise would've eaten a bullet.

"If it saw you, it couldn't have been a ghost," he said as I grabbed a set of chopsticks and dug into my second dinner. "You steer clear of whatever it was until we figure it out, then you can go hunting."

"Got it," I mumbled around a mouthful of cold noodles.

My uncle disappeared into the depths of the house and came back half a container of Chinese later carrying a stack of leather-bound books balanced in his lap. He never smiled anymore, but his expression was bright with interest as he wheeled himself to our battered kitchen table and gently set the old books on the scarred surface.

"Tell me everything you remember, and we'll do some research."

It wasn't exactly how I wanted to end my Friday night, but

it beat curling up in a ball and remembering the way that barely grown boy had just . . . let himself fall.

By the time Taylor got a ride home from his date, it was past two in the morning, and we were deep into the old family journals and Uncle Will's favorite bourbon. Taylor's long stride faltered at the edge of the pool of light illuminating the kitchen table, and he visibly braced himself before he took a seat and poured himself a drink.

"What happened?" Taylor finally asked, hand tight around the glass.

I took a deep breath, the air heavy with the scent of savory pork lo mein, sweet gun oil, and musty old paper. Decided it wasn't enough, took another . . . and told him what happened after I'd dropped him off.

"Shit." He took a long swallow of bourbon, draining half his glass before he set it down with a quiet *clink*. "What've you got?"

"We're still not sure." I slumped in my chair, eyes burning from reading the widely varied styles of handwriting in those journals, some barely legible. "It could be a White Lady or a lamia. Maybe even a banshee variant we haven't seen before."

Uncle Will shook his head. "Golden eyes. You're sure it had golden eyes?"

The flashing lights and the fatal despair had faded away, but I still saw those eyes every time I blinked. Beautiful and wicked and cruel.

"I'm sure."

He laid a thin hand on the oldest of all the journals. The one we only brought out of the safe when everything else had failed us. Great-whatever-grandmother's journal.

"I think it's something that's been Fey-cursed."

I stilled. "Like me."

My eyes reflected gold because of the curse, but I'd never been able to see what they looked like. Were they wicked and cruel like hers? And how badly had she been cursed for her eyes to be *solid* gold?

"No, not like you." Taylor gripped my shoulder. "Whatever that thing is, it's a monster."

"A monster we're going to hunt down." I forced a smile. "Maybe the PUFF will be enough for me to take extra classes next semester. Or finally replace the roof. Oooh or a vacation."

But Taylor shook his head firmly. "No, Essie."

I sat up straight, frowning. "No? What do you mean *no*?"

Uncle Will ignored us, carefully stacking the journals and setting them aside in favor of my beat-up old laptop. The screen had been cracked for years and half the letters on the keyboard had worn off, but it did the job.

"No, we're not..." Taylor frowned at our uncle. "Since when do you know how to use a computer?"

"Essie taught me," he said absently as he pecked at the keys with his index fingers.

"I tried to teach him for years," Taylor grumbled at me.

I gave him a slow smile. He didn't need to know that the screen had an extra crack in it from when I'd slammed it shut in frustration after hours of beating the basics into our firmly old-school uncle's thick skull.

Another few minutes of painfully slow tapping and Uncle Will stopped, sighed, and looked at us. Nights like this, it was hard to remember he was only in his fifties. He looked damn near as old as Dirk Kessel and nowhere near as strong.

"I took a look at the public county death records. The number of suicides has steadily increased in the past decade. Officials blame it on cost of living, lack of job opportunities"—he waved a dismissive hand—"you know, the usual when they don't know why people are dying but need to give some kind of explanation. Those numbers aren't completely terrible until you combine them with the number of missing persons reports. Mostly vagrants passing through that nobody would miss."

Flashing back to the grocery store corkboard, I hoarsely added, "Most, but not all."

Taylor leaned forward. "Is there any pattern?"

Uncle Will nodded and turned the laptop so we could see the cracked screen. He'd pulled up a local area map and added pins color coded by year, with red being current. There was a lot of red. All of it centered on Batesville.

"Something's been feeding here for years, right under our damn noses," he said grimly. "And it's stepped it up in the past month."

My gut tightened, certainty sinking into my bones. "She's getting ready to do something big."

Taylor reached over and firmly shut the laptop. "Which is

why we need to call it in to someone who has the firepower and training to take whatever it is on."

Something ugly burned in our uncle's eyes. "Boy, if you mean the MCB—"

"I'm talking about the Chicago MHI team."

Uncle Will relaxed, but my hands tightened into fists. "Taylor, no. What can they do? They can't even *see* her."

"You said it clawed the guardrail. That means it can go corporeal. That means they can see it and kill it."

"We need the money," I snapped.

"We need to be smart."

I rolled my eyes. "Smart life choices are *boring*, Tails."

"Boring is better than dead, *Esther.*" Taylor swayed back just far enough to avoid my fist, an amused smile on his tired face before he sobered. "I'm calling it in tomorrow."

Hours later, when both men were asleep, I crept back downstairs and opened my laptop. The map was still up, and I looked for a pattern to the kills. A triumphant smile danced on my lips when I found one.

"Jackpot," I crooned as I zoomed in on the blank spot in the center of everything.

Three possible locations jumped out, three places that Fey-cursed bitch might be nesting. Three chances to hunt her down before the stupid MHI team arrived. If they even decided it was worth their while. They might not. From what I'd heard, they'd been busy lately.

So I made one of those smart life choices Taylor was always harping about. After a brief stop in the guest bedroom we'd long-since converted to an armory, I went back to bed. Exhausted and slightly inebriated was no way to start a hunt. I might want to have a little more fun, make things a little more interesting, actually earn enough money to not be poor—but I wasn't stupid.

Unfortunately, neither was Taylor.

He kept me busy the next day. First on the shooting range running drills to improve my shitty aim, then on the endless home improvement projects needed to keep our house from completely falling apart. The sun was setting by the time I managed to escape, and only because Taylor got a phone call. Gaze sliding toward mine, he muttered something about Becca Thomas and dinner, snapped at me to stay with Uncle Will tonight, and took off in his truck.

Perfect.

I changed into sturdy hunting clothes and loaded up what I needed in my old Mustang, but I didn't climb in the driver's seat right away. Instead, I tilted my face up to the sky and breathed in the twilight, the air crisp and earthy with the scent of my favorite season. Something wild in my soul settled into calm focus.

Everyone has their pregame rituals.

"Essie!"

My head snapped down, and I found my uncle on our front porch, hands white-knuckled on the push rings of his wheelchair. His expression twisted, lines deepening on his craggy face.

"Be careful, kiddo."

I gave him a teasing smile. "I promise to make smart life choices."

"If we were smart, we wouldn't be in this business." He wheeled himself down the ramp and toward his beloved garage. "Don't be smart—be better than the monster you're hunting."

A casual salute, and I slid behind the wheel and started the car. The rough purr of the engine vibrated through the leather steering wheel, urging me to go fast, but I kept my speed nice and controlled all the way into town.

Out of the three possibilities, the old cemetery seemed the most likely on the surface, but it was at the edge of that cleared space on the map. I parked the car under a burned-out streetlight in the middle of Batesville's derelict downtown and smiled at the old marquee with its broken lights and faded posters.

The abandoned movie theater, on the other hand, was dead center.

The locks had been broken by bored teenagers ages ago. After checking my gear one last time, I pulled open the door and slipped inside. The scent of stale popcorn slapped me in the face, and silence filled my ears. Flicking on my flashlight, I swept it across the lobby. Unimaginative graffiti marred the rotting wallpapered walls, and debris was scattered across the once beautiful travertine floor, no different from the last time I'd snuck in. Definitely not like some kind of Fey-cursed not-ghost was nesting here.

I swept my gaze across the space one more time before focusing on the closed double doors leading to the one and only theater room. Glass crunched under my boots as I crept across the lobby, flashlight in one hand and the single-edged knife I'd grabbed from the armory in the other. I'd spent far too much time sharpening it, but if Uncle Will was right, it was going to be far more useful than the Sig Sauer P365 holstered on my hip.

My fingers tightened on the leather wrapping the hilt and protecting my skin. The Fey curse that twisted through my soul didn't react well to the metal, and while the pain wouldn't kill me, it would certainly distract me.

My heartrate increased the closer I drew to those doors, a thundering roar in my ears, and sweat trickled down my spine. I'd gone on solo hunts before, but never after something quite this . . . nebulous. There was a whole lot of wiggle room in "Fey-cursed not-ghost," especially one who could claw through a steel guardrail. Resisting the urge to tug on the stab-proof vest under my button-up shirt, I let out a slow breath, tucked my flashlight under one arm, and reached for the door handle.

"There's no need for that," a sweet voice whispered in my ear.

I whirled around knife-first, dropping my flashlight in the process. It bounced and rolled across the floor, light cutting across the lobby wildly before it fetched to a stop against a broken chair. That was fine. I didn't need a light to see my quarry, her entire body lit up in a spectral light only eyes like mine could see.

She'd drifted back out of reach of my strike with unearthly speed, inky black hair moving gently in a breeze I couldn't feel and golden eyes burning past my every defense and peering straight down into my terrified soul. Up close, she was strange and beautiful in a way humans simply *couldn't* be.

Because we'd been wrong.

"I've been watching you," she crooned. "Ever since you *saw* me."

So very wrong.

"If you wanted to talk, Fey-touched child, all you had to do was ask."

She wasn't Fey-cursed.

She was *Fey*, and so far out of my league it was laughable.

My grip tightened on my knife. At the time, cold iron had seemed like a smart precaution. Now, I was pretty sure it was the only thing keeping her from attacking. That, and a curiosity she didn't bother to hide as she drifted around me, gliding more than walking with that unnatural Fey grace.

I licked dry lips. "Who are you?"

"A bold question."

Icy cold slithered down my spine at her tone, and I offered her a polite smile and an apology. "I'm sorry, lady. My Fey etiquette is rusty."

"That's quite all right." Her head tilted, smile deepening as she drew in a deep breath. "Your fear smells delicious. Flavored with bravery, impetuous youth, and . . . a touch of the Twilight Court. How long it's been since I walked their forest paths beneath purple dusk and soft starlight. For that treat alone, I'll offer you a story."

Oh goody. The urge to ask for safe passage instead of story time danced on the tip of my tongue, but I held the unwise words back.

Look at me making smarter choices already, Taylor!

My breath shook and I risked a casual step toward the door. She blocked my path, her golden eyes gleaming with mischief and malice.

"I will not give you my name, but know that I am a Lady of the Wild Hunt. Unjustly cursed." A hand flashed out, caressed the side of my face before I could jerk back, the touch at once impossibly gentle and icy cold. "Not cursed to *see* like you, but cursed to *stay*."

Warmth trickled down my cheek.

"I am being punished by the Hunt Mistress for allowing prey to escape. He was far too pretty to die . . . until I was done with him." She lifted one shoulder in an elegant shrug. "For ruining the hunt, I was sentenced to fifty years anchored to this place."

There was real frustration and longing in her voice, and I felt unwanted sympathy stir. I was tied to this place by my heritage and lack of money, nebulous chains just as real as hers.

"How long have you been trapped here?"

The question slipped out before I could stop it, but she didn't seem offended this time.

"Long enough." A slow smile, elongated canines gleaming white in the spectral light. "The Mistress left me a loophole, a way out of my snare. If I can amass enough power, I can break the geas that binds me and be *free*."

Power . . .

"The suicides, all those missing people." Cold fear gripped me, any urge toward sympathy dying. "You're feeding off their deaths."

"Oh no, sweet child, no." She laughed, a chiming, light sound that raised the hairs on the back of my neck. "I'm feeding off their *souls*. And after this evening's feast, I only need two more."

She glided closer, and I retreated, holding my knife crosswise in front of my torso. My back slammed into the theater door, and I couldn't *breathe* for the fear. But my hands were steady and my blade didn't waver, a flimsy shield between us as her voice slid into a satisfied purr.

"This latest soul tasted like aged wine. Pain and guilt, grief and sorrow, all flavored by sweet relief. Delicious." Her tongue flicked out, tracing her sculpted lips. "I give thanks to the good fortune of our paths crossing, child."

Her head titled as if she could hear something I couldn't and her smile turned catlike with anticipation. My heart thudded in my chest.

Once.

Twice.

Two men burst through the front door, guns leveled at my face. A flashlight blinded me, and a fresh spike of fear shocked through me. Those were MHI patches on their gear. And my eyes had just reflected gold like the monster they were hunting.

"Drop the knife!"

"I can't," I gritted out. It was the only thing keeping me safe.

The chain around my neck grew impossibly heavy, a reminder that it could've helped keep me safe too. I was a fucking idiot. I knew Taylor had called MHI. I should've pulled it from beneath my shirt so it hung in plain sight before starting this hunt.

"Last warning," the older man barked. "Drop it or we will shoot."

My gaze flicked from the armed Hunters to the spectral Fey standing between us. They couldn't see her.

Fuckfuckfuck.

Death by Fey bitch or death by Hunters. Either way I was dead.

She breathed in my terror with a satisfied expression. "I'll see you soon, Fey-touched child. You know where to find me."

She closed one golden eye in a wink and vanished from even my sight. She was gone.

I dropped the knife.

"I have an exemption!" I shrieked over the sharp clatter of metal hitting the dirty floor.

My voice was easily an octave higher than normal, and my

hands were shaking so badly that I probably would've dropped the blade even if they hadn't ordered it.

This was how my Aunt Matilda died.

The really shitty thing was if it wasn't for the MCB showing up to "help" during the zombie outbreak that took out my parents and most of our company, my aunt would've survived. And maybe my uncle wouldn't have been broken in both body and spirit. But they'd seen her reflective eyes and shot first and asked questions never.

Thank fuck these guys weren't MCB.

"Let us see it," the older Hunter snapped out, voice hard and unyielding.

My hands were shaking so hard it took long seconds before I was able to pull the exemption tag from beneath my shirt. The gold-and-red seal of the MCB glinted in the harsh light, PUFF Exemption stamped in bold letters beneath. There was a whole litany on the back that could be summed up with, "If you shoot me you might go to jail."

Cold comfort if you were dead.

The older Hunter jerked his chin at the younger one, a rugged guy around Taylor's age with a long scar cutting down the side of his face and his arm in a sling. "Check it, Lawrence."

Lawrence holstered his sidearm and approached. There was a smooth competence in the way he moved, in the way he kept the other Hunter's firing line clear. Professional and deadly.

Also stupid hot, but that wasn't relevant right now. Maybe later.

"It's legit." Lawrence raised a brow at the tiny metal dog tag my uncle had insisted I add to the chain since exemption tags didn't have names. "*Esther?*"

"It's an old family name," I growled, still shaking from my near miss. "I go by Essie."

"Aw fuck." Lawrence sighed as he read the rest of the dog tag, that simmering promise of violence disappearing between one blink and the next. "You're O'Connell's sister. He's going to be pissed—"

"You're damn right I am."

My eyes widened as my brother stalked into the lobby with a third MHI Hunter following on his heels. I spared the newest Hunter a quick glance—noting the walking cast on his left foot, the recently broken nose, and the intelligent dark eyes—before glaring at Taylor.

"I thought you were on a date with Becca!"

"*Because that's what I wanted you to think!*" he roared in exasperation. His gaze narrowed on my face. "Are you okay?"

I swiped my bloody cheek, hissing at the sting, but it felt like a tiny cut. "Fine."

"Thank fuck." He sighed, some of his anger fading away. "How did you even find this place?"

"Uncle Will's map." My chin lifted. "There was a pattern—"

"Yes, Essie," he said dryly. "I saw it too. And the cemetery and the junkyard. Remember who trained you?"

"Apparently not good enough, O'Connell," the oldest Hunter growled as he stalked up to me.

He looked like he was in his forties, and he moved carefully, favoring his right side. In fact, all three MHI Hunters looked like they'd been on the losing end of a recent fight. Or maybe that was what winning looked like. They were still breathing, after all.

He stooped and picked up my knife. When I reached for it, he pulled it back, a dangling carrot to get what he wanted.

"Why didn't you drop it when I told you to?" he demanded, an irate glint in his faded blue eyes. I had a feeling if he *had* killed me, he might have felt bad about it, but he wouldn't regret doing whatever was needed to keep his team safe.

I held his judgmental gaze. "Because I was holding off the bitch threatening to eat my fucking soul."

"It was here?" Lawrence glanced at the older Hunter. "Did you see anything, Mac?"

"Just a stupid girl with cat eyes refusing to drop her knife," Mac grumbled.

"They're not cat eyes," I grumbled back, deliberately mimicking his voice.

"They're green and reflect gold."

"Yeah, and they see things ours can't," Taylor jumped in.

"Yeah, *Tails*, they do," I snapped, angry all over again. "So why the *hell* did you leave me out of this when you know damn well I'm the only one who can see her when she's incorporeal?"

The intelligent Hunter in the walking boot propped his shotgun over one shoulder and arched a thin brow. "I'm guessing it's because you pull shit like go after a Fey-cursed spirit alone?"

"Fuck you..."

"Alphonse," he supplied helpfully.

"Fuck you, Alphonse," I finished, a brief smile tugging at my lips before my mirth fell away. "And she's not a spirit. She's Fey."

Taylor dragged a hand through his hair and cursed viciously. Quickly, I briefed them on what she'd told me. It wasn't until I reached the end that I faltered.

"She said I'd know where to find her, but I don't—"

Ice sank into my bones. She'd come dangerously close to thanking me, avoiding the taboo by the thinnest of margins by expressing gratitude to our paths crossing.

And the soul she'd described...

I felt the blood drain out of my face and swayed. "Taylor! Call Uncle Will!"

Taylor paled and whipped out his cell phone. Seconds ticked past, each an eternity where I silently blamed myself. I'd felt eyes on me the entire way home last night. I'd led that bitch straight to our *home*. And then I'd left my crippled uncle alone.

Slowly, he lowered the phone. "He's not answering."

Oh, God. I knew where she'd been, where she'd gone *back* to. "I know where to find her."

Lawrence and Alphonse exchanged a loaded glance, silent words passing between the men in a flicker of expressions. Then they looked at their team leader. Waiting.

Mac flipped my knife in his hand, catching it by the tip and extending it to me hilt first.

"Lead the way."

I didn't remember the drive home. Didn't remember racing down the driveway, gravel spitting behind spinning tires. Didn't remember bypassing the house in favor of my uncle's garage. The one where I'd spent an entire summer "helping" him restore my old Mustang but mostly just getting in the way and providing him with beer.

But I'd always remember the feeling of my knees hitting the oil-stained concrete in front of his wheelchair. Remember how his hand was still warm... remember the way his blood and brains still oozed down the drywall, copper and worse thick on my tongue and a scream trapped in my throat.

Too late. I'd known we'd be too late, but hope had refused to die until I knew for sure.

Vaguely, I was aware of Taylor and the MHI team searching the garage, half the overhead fluorescent lights burned out and leaving pools of shadow between the partially disassembled Chevy truck and the half-rebuilt Suburban. I'd already *looked* before I'd fallen next to my uncle, seen nothing, but now I rose to my feet and drew my knife.

I felt eyes on the back of my neck and turned a slow circle.

"Boys," I murmured.

Instantly, I had everyone's attention. Hands tightened on weapons. They felt it too, even if they couldn't see her. She'd said if I wanted to talk . . . all I had to do was ask.

"Hey, bitch! I want to talk to you!"

A phantom hand slid down my arm in a gentle caress.

"I'm no longer interested in talking," she crooned in my ear.

She'd eaten my uncle's *soul*. Maybe killing her would set him free, maybe it wouldn't.

My smile was all teeth. Either way, she'd be dead.

I spun around, iron knife leading the way, but she flitted out of reach and laughed. Judging by the reactions, the men heard *that*. The beautiful sound bounced off the walls, the concrete, the cars, coming from everywhere and nowhere, impossible to pinpoint, impossible to track. But the scrape of metal on concrete was, and I spun around in time to see her go corporeal with a freaking *tire iron* in her hand, the chrome-plated steel no danger to her flesh.

"Down!" I bellowed at Alphonse.

The lean, intelligent hunter *moved* and the tire iron whipped through the space his skull had been a fraction of a second earlier. Alphonse kept moving, clearing the line of fire with impressive speed considering the walking cast on his foot. Thunderous gunfire filled the garage. My ears rang in protest, but that didn't stop me from shifting my knife to my off-hand, drawing my Sig, and adding my own bullets to the mix.

I think she stayed corporeal to taunt us.

Because none of us managed to hit her.

Fast, she was so damn fast as she glided across the garage, feet barely seeming to touch the floor, as if she was too good, too *pure* to sully herself by touching the oil-stained concrete. An impression entirely at odds with the length of chrome-plated steel elegantly gripped in one fine-boned hand.

In a heartbeat, she'd crossed the length of the garage and lashed out with the tire iron again, catching Mac a glancing blow to the side. The tough bastard roared in pain and unloaded his Remington 870, pump-action, 12-gauge shotgun in her face.

She didn't like that.

"Rock salt's a bitch, ain't it?" Mac growled over her piercing shriek, sidestepping and pumping the action, muzzle tracking her as she clawed at her skin.

Another thunderous roar, another piercing shriek... and then she dropped the tire iron and lashed out with her bare hands. Claws sliced through the barrel of the shotgun. If it wasn't for Mac's quick reaction, those claws would've sliced through his forward hand as well. Blood still sprayed, and he stumbled back, clutching his shredded arm.

She spun and lashed out at Lawrence, but the rugged hunter was faster than he looked. He avoided the first strike and the next, emptying his handgun as he dodged. The slide locked back as he fired the last round, but she didn't let up for even an instant, giving him no chance to reload.

A barked "Down!" and Lawrence dropped without hesitation. A thunderous roar, and Alphonse managed to tag her with rock salt again. The Fey bitch shrieked, the sound almost as full of rage as pain.

She went incorporeal and I called out her location to Taylor, armed with another iron knife. It wasn't the first time he'd fought blind, and we trained for hunts like these, where I could see and he couldn't. Grim-faced, he struck with controlled violence and the tip of his blade scored her arm. Her scream nearly dropped me to my knees, and she jerked out of reach of his next strike, some of her grace lost to agony.

She'd been playing with us before, but the iron had really pissed her off.

And so had I.

Golden eyes found mine, burning with rage and pain. She moved, insubstantial form blurring across the space between us. I darted back. Not fast enough. A flicker and she was solid once again. My Sig was torn from my hand, a tiny *snap* and a shock of pain announcing at least one broken finger. Clawed fingers flashed toward my belly, canines gleaming in a wicked smile. I twisted away. Cloth tore and fire scored my side, but the stab-proof vest beneath my shirt deflected her claws just enough that my intestines didn't end up on the ground.

Snarling in frustration, she backhanded me, and I tumbled across the floor, fetching up against the Suburban with bone-jarring force. She smiled at my pained cry, licking my blood off her hands before she went incorporeal again as bullets tore through the space she'd been standing. A high-pitched whine filled my ears, and everything seemed just a little skewed.

"Where'd she go?" Mac barked, turning a slow circle, injured arm cradled to his chest and a large sidearm in his hand.

I sucked in a shaking breath, metallic copper and smoke heavy in the air, and pressed my hand to my side. Risked a glance down and found only shallow cuts.

"Essie, where'd she go?" Lawrence and Alphonse shouted in overlapping voices.

A sharp shake of my head, and the world finally snapped back into focus. I staggered to my feet, swept my Fey-cursed gaze across the garage, but I didn't see her. Frantically, I stalked toward the center of the garage, trying to see everywhere at once, and then Taylor let out a hoarse cry behind me. I spun toward my brother as his knees hit the dirty floor, gun pressed to his own temple.

"I'm sorry, Essie."

The Fey bitch was wrapped around him. Her inky hair floated on a spectral breeze, and her golden eyes turned to molten honey as she crooned sweet venom in his ear. Taylor's expression twisted, a familiar guilt in his eyes, one he'd always tried his best to hide.

"So sorry I couldn't give you the life you deserved."

"Taylor!" I dove for the bitch, iron knife leading the way. She vanished even from my sight, and I flew past my brother.

Bang!

"NO!"

My heart stopped as I tumbled across the floor. Somehow, I managed not to stab myself, but in that moment, I couldn't have cared less. Because it was my fault, all my fault.

I should've gone for his gun.

I whipped around, so convinced he was dead that for the first time in my life, I almost didn't believe my eyes. Taylor was alive, restrained by Lawrence and Alphonse and struggling like a madman, but he was *alive*. I nearly vomited from the relief.

A frantic heartbeat later, sanity returned to his eyes. My brother slumped in their hold, panting as if he'd just run a marathon.

"Fuck that bitch." Taylor gave me a wild grin before tugging on Lawrence and Alphonse. "I'm fine. Let go."

Metal scraped concrete.

My head snapped to the side, eyes widening, mouth stretching open in warning.

Too slow.

The Fey darted toward the three men, discarded tire iron in hand. She swung so fast, the chrome-plated steel blurred into a shining silver arc—and she broke Taylor's skull as easily as if she'd crushed a watermelon.

I'll never forget the sound. Never forget the blood and worse that splattered all three men. Never forget how my brother fell, dead before his body hit concrete.

My warning cry twisted into a scream, denial and rage and agony all tangled together. She attacked the other Hunters, but I couldn't look away from Taylor, lying on the floor. Desperate shouts rose when she vanished again. I caught a flicker out of the corner of my eye, cold brushing the side of my face before sorrow and grief tried to drown my soul.

Sobbing, I crawled toward my brother's body, knife clenched in one hand like a safety blanket. Laughter chimed in my ear, and then bullets were flying just over my head, so close I swore a round tugged at my hair.

I didn't care.

Cared less when cold coated my skin and despair splintered my heart.

Time stuttered around me. Gunfire and shouting, then cold despair so thick I couldn't *breathe*. More gunfire and a bellow of pain, then agonizing loss sapping the strength from my limbs. Stutter-stepping time, gunfire then grief, over and over until I reached Taylor.

And then there was no more gunfire, only grief.

My iron knife clanged against concrete, safety blanket slipping from numb fingers as I collapsed at his side. A keening cry hurt my ears, and I only vaguely realized it came from *me* when fresh pain tore at my throat. I couldn't look at my brother's face because it was *gone*, couldn't even collapse on his chest because of the thick coating of gore and gray matter soaking his shirt.

So I picked up his hand. Clean, unbroken, whole. Pressed it to my forehead and rocked.

"Essie, where'd she go?"

My fault, all my fault.

All your fault.

He'd wanted me to stay out of this, wanted me to make smarter choices. We stuck to small things for a reason and a Fey was anything but small... just like my ego. I'd thought I was good enough, thought I could earn us enough to climb out of the hole, and I'd gotten Taylor killed. A man no amount of money could ever replace. My brother, who'd been almost a surrogate father since our parents died.

"Fuck's sake, Essie! Snap out of it! Where is she?!"

Cold shivered through my skin, guilt pulling me down beneath dark waves.

My fault, all my fault.

Yes, your fault. All your fault.

Our parents wouldn't have even been there the night of the zombie outbreak if I hadn't *seen* the monsters skulking in the dark. My mother had been distracted, hadn't noticed. If I'd just kept my mouth shut they'd still be alive.

"Essie, get the fuck up and fight! We need you!"

I deserved the guilt, deserved the icy cold creeping through body and soul.

My fault, all my fault.

All your fault, the sweet voice agreed. *So many mistakes, so much to pay for.*

All I did was get the people I loved killed, and now they were all gone.

"ESSIE!"

I wasn't cold anymore.

My fault...

Yes, but you can see them again. They're waiting for you. Go to them.

The sweet voice was right. It was only fair that I joined them. How else could I apologize for everything I'd fucked up?

My hand dropped to my holster, but of course it was empty. A rictus of a grin twisted my lips. I might have lost my gun, but I still had my knife. Clumsy from grief and despair, my fingers missed the wrapped hilt and brushed against the iron blade. Pain shocked up my arm, hit between my eyes like a freight train, cold agony that burned murky thoughts clear.

My eyes snapped open—when the *fuck* had I closed them?—and found ghostly fingers caressing the side of my face, gripping my shoulder.

That fucking bitch was in my ear, crooning sweet poison.

Terror and rage shocked me the rest of the way awake. If I'd still had my gun I would've blown my own brains out. Instead, I had my knife. And she'd done me the favor of snuggling up real close to ensure the kill. My hand tightened around the hilt, the only part of me I moved. Muscles coiled tight, tighter, and then I exploded into motion, turning and stabbing the blade into her chest.

Her scream was like an ice pick straight to my brain, and warmth trickled out of my left ear. Cold iron forced her to turn corporeal, and she struck at my face with those deadly claws. I jerked back, but again I was too damn slow, and fiery agony tore across the side of my face. Blood and maybe worse blinded my left eye as I scrambled away from her.

My eyes, she'd gone for my *eyes.*

Gunfire in a continuous roar filled the garage, and another piercing scream threatened to burst what was left of my eardrums. I clamped my hands around my ears, flattened myself to the cold concrete, and desperately hoped I wasn't going to get hit.

I didn't want to die.

Long seconds later, the gunfire stopped.

Silence—and then a very real, very corporeal body hit the floor.

For a moment, the only sound I could hear was my pulse pounding in my ears, and I just lay on the floor shaking. I wasn't sure how long, but I blinked and Lawrence knelt in front of me with the med kit my uncle had kept on one of the workbenches in his hands.

"Let me see." Strong fingers gripped my jaw and tilted my face up to the light. He let out a slow breath and helped me sit up. "Hold still."

As he examined the shallow, bloody cuts beneath my ruined vest, I saw Alphonse tending to Mac's shredded arm on the other side of the garage. Then Lawrence cleaned my face, and there was pain, nothing but pain. More pain when he cleaned and bandaged my side and splinted my broken finger. I didn't mind.

Better to lean into the pain than stare at my brother's mutilated corpse or my uncle's slumped body.

"You're okay, Essie." Lawrence's voice was low and gentle, like he was speaking to a wounded animal. "You need stitches, but she missed your eye."

I tried to summon the ability to care. The desire to die had been nothing more than the Fey bitch's manipulation, but the guilt? That was all mine.

My whole family was gone now.

I was alone.

And nothing anyone could say would ever convince me it wasn't my fault.

Weeks passed, and the weather progressed to my least favorite part of autumn—constant damp and cold rain. It was the middle of the day, but I was surrounded by gray. Gray skies, gray gravestones, gray rain... black clothes.

I'd laid fresh flowers on my parents' grave markers, and my aunts' and uncles', their stones all weathered by eight years of Indiana winters. I placed a flower on top of Uncle Will's gleaming marker, a bittersweet smile tugging at my lips at the thought of him finally being reunited with his beloved wife. I'd decided that killing the Fey bitch had released all those stolen souls, and I wasn't interested in learning otherwise.

A shaking breath, and I moved on to Taylor's fresh grave. My hands crushed the remaining flowers, and my heart faltered at the pain raging through me, bright and sharp and breath-stealing. My brother, my fucking *rock*, the person I'd relied on to keep me from making too many stupid choices...

"I'm so sorry, Tails." My voice cracked, broke. "So sorry."

A stupid part of me waited for him to call me Esther.

But he was gone, and I'd never hear his voice again.

I had no idea how long I stood there. Long enough that I was soaked to the skin and numb with cold.

A footstep behind me, a polite scuff against wet grass to let me know someone was there. I looked up as a familiar monster hunter stopped next to me, but I didn't bother wiping away my tears. The rain did a good enough job of hiding them. Also, this was *Lawrence*. I'd already sobbed all over the poor man on a dirty garage floor when my shield of physical pain had finally broken that awful night. What were a few tears mixed with rain compared to that?

"You lost the sling." I'm not sure why it was the first words to tumble out of my mouth, but Lawrence flexed his arm.

"And your stitches came out," he said with a crooked grin.

I'd been right, all those weeks ago. The man was stupid hot. I wished I cared. My fingers tangled with the chain around my neck, playing with the links to give myself something to fidget with other than the red and tender scars on the side of my face.

"What are you doing here?" I finally asked when it was clear he wasn't going to volunteer the information.

"I knew today was the funeral." Lawrence stared down at the freshly turned soil. "Taylor was . . . maybe not a friend, but an acquaintance. A good man. Didn't seem right to let you stand alone."

"The funeral was two hours ago."

"Ran into some trouble on the way."

I noted the split knuckles and the fresh bruise on the side of his jaw. A few weeks ago, I would've demanded details about the monster he'd fought, but I was emotionally drained. All I could muster was a nod and a vague sense of gratitude that the other hunter was okay.

"I also came to give you this." Lawrence held out a card with MHI and a green happy face with horns on one side, and way too much text to read in a glance on the back. "There's a new training class starting in a few weeks. Thought you might be interested."

I stared at the card for a long moment before I finally accepted it. "Why?"

"Because you can blame yourself for the loss of your family"—he tapped calloused fingers against the scars on his own face in emphasis—"or you can do something about it. Your choice."

He didn't linger.

I was grateful for that, too.

Carefully, I tucked the card away to protect it from the rain and stood in front of Taylor's grave until the gloomy day gave way to twilight. Then I knelt, kissed my fingertips, pressed them to the cold stone . . . and walked away without looking back, that card burning a hole in my pocket.

If I couldn't make fun life choices, maybe I could make better ones.

Though we have worked with their hunters on several occasions, the Vatican's Blessed Order of Saint Hubert the Protector remains a very secretive organization. If this leak is accurate I can see why.

—A.L.

Psalm of Vengeance

Steve Diamond

Psalm of Vengeance: The Gift—Part 2

With a gout of flame and a stone-rattling roar, the reinforced door to my safe house exploded inward. Blown completely out of the frame, the door slammed into the inner wall opposite it, shattering drywall and splintering the wooden studs beneath. Had I been standing in the way of the massive projectile, not even my ability to heal quickly would have saved me from becoming a red smear.

Fortunately, I sat calmly at my kitchen table, expecting this moment. I kept my hands placed flat on top of the table, none of my weapons within visible reach. Not that it mattered much. Had I truly wanted to kill these invaders, weapons wouldn't have been needed.

Being faster and stronger than any human had its advantages. So did being able to shrug off wounds that would have a normal person in a hospital bed for months.

But then, my attackers weren't normal.

They were all Knights of the Secret Guard of the Blessed Order of Saint Hubert the Protector. Once my comrades. Once my friends.

Or so I thought.

They didn't scream at me as they breached the front door. They flooded in, silently fanning out to search every room of my home while several entered the kitchen, rifles trained on me. Even in this state, I still could have taken them and escaped. But what good would that have done? That wasn't the plan.

How could I save the Order and get the answers I needed if I ran?

Behind the black-garbed soldiers entered a man, older in appearance, dressed in a scarlet, full-length cassock. A cardinal of some sort, but I didn't recognize him . . . and I knew all the commanders within the Order.

He strolled into the kitchen, ignoring the destruction caused by his men, and appraised my humble accommodations.

"We've been looking for you for months, Fidele. Imagine my surprise to have you snitched out by a demon of all things?" His eyes took in my place, and registered . . . disappointment. "Interesting. Safe house or not, I expected something more ostentatious for one of your reputation."

I said nothing. That wasn't the goal here, and I'd never been one to spout witty catchphrases or retorts. That was the purview of Hunters—like the group in Alabama—and I was more than a Hunter.

Or maybe less. I suppose it depended on the day.

But a reputation I *did* have. One of blood and righteousness. At least that had been the case once upon a time before discovering the curse of my existence.

"Somehow it seems you were expecting us," the man said. I couldn't place his accent, and in my centuries of life, I've heard nearly every style of English the world has to offer. He nodded, and his thin lips spread into an imitation of a smile. "No matter. I've long wanted to meet you. After that . . . incident . . . in Mexico, I figured it was time. My name is Cardinal Augustus Fontaine. I doubt you've heard of me, but I certainly have heard of *you*."

The cardinal smiled again, and in his eyes, I caught the barest flicker of putrid yellow.

Two Days Earlier . . .

The legion of demons screamed, overshadowing the single voice from the body they possessed. A good, old-fashioned torture session with one of the damned. My prisoner—he'd once been an IRS auditor, an easy mark for possession—sat strapped and manacled to a dental chair.

My captive wailed again, its shrieks splitting the air and filling it with an anti-melodic chorus that would drive the average person insane. The sound was no picnic, even for me. Thankfully, I had a soundproof room in the basement of this safe house for such occasions. I couldn't have neighbors or passersby calling the local authorities every time I tortured some form of demon or supernatural creature. It would have rather defeated the purpose of being off-grid.

"Mercy! Please have mercy!"

To hear the demonic choir beg while weeping would once have made me chuckle. But since discovering the true origin of my abilities, joy and laughter eluded me.

Patting the possessed man on the shoulder in mock understanding, I increased the drip rate of the intravenous bag of holy water feeding into his arm.

"No... No! Please!" Hundreds of demons wailed their pointless protest. "Mercy, we beg of you!"

Mercy. A popular theme in the Gospels. A necessary trait for those who would enter Heaven's Gate. But knowing the perversion I was, I knew I had no hope of entering into the Divine's presence. I was already damned.

Mercy. No... there would be no mercy from me. Only violence and vengeance.

Looking down at my arm, my old scars tried convincing me of their old lies. The falsehood that my bones had been grafted with those of saints and angels. I'd believed that story for centuries and had allowed it to carry me forward in exterminating evil after evil. Century after century. Witches in Salem. Supernatural serial killers in a gaslit London. Cultists in Mexico. Any manner of wetwork for the Vatican. All because I believed I had been made a holy vessel of judgment.

So what was I to think when I discovered those bones beneath the scars littering my body were not the bones of saints... but of old, evil gods and creatures from other realms?

I turned the drip rate on the IV bag even higher, letting the demonic screams wash over me.

Letting the holy water consume the demon seemed like the prudent choice. For a moment. Maybe a longer moment than I would have allowed in my younger days. With a sigh, I reduced the drip rate to a minimum. Killing the legion of demons and the host they inhabited wouldn't make things better. At least, not right at this moment.

"Are you ready to answer my questions?" I smiled, knowing the expression didn't reach my cold eyes.

After a few heavy breaths, the demons answered by having their meat suit nod frantically.

"Good. Good. Do you know who I am?"

A terrified nod.

"Do you know *what* I am?"

Pure fear rippled across the man's face. In it I saw the visages of a dozen of the dark spirits hiding within. But the legion didn't answer. I reached for the drip switch.

"Wait! Yes, we know. You are one of *His* creations."

"Of God's?"

The man shook his head. "No. You are just a slave to that God. A puppet. Nothing more than—"

Before I realized what I was doing, I hit the man as hard as I could in the abdomen. Air *whooshed* out of him. Not that the demons cared about having the wind knocked out of their host. But they felt the pain and screamed in protest even as the host gulped for air.

"If not God's," I asked, "then to whom do I really belong?"

"You are the Herald's."

The Herald? I reached into my pocket and pulled out a drawing of the hook-nosed man that had spliced my bones all those centuries ago. The same man I'd seen during the Mexico incident. "Him?"

My prisoner recoiled in fear and again nodded.

Interesting. The Herald. I'd never heard anyone—much less my apparent creator—referred to by that title.

"Who is this man the Herald for?"

"Not who. *What*."

I didn't like the sound of that at all.

When the demons seemed reticent to continue their explanation, all I had to do was make a small move to the switch on the IV drip.

"Alright, alright! It's not complicated. The Herald has been trying to get an Old One to wake up for a while."

"Which one?"

"How would *we* know? Are you *kidding* us right now? We don't associate with those psychos."

"Don't pretend your kind are any different." Evil always tried to pretend they weren't as bad as the other brand of evil. Just another way to seduce the masses.

"You don't get it. We want souls and bodies for our own. We want hosts so we can walk the earth again."

"I know what you want. I've been exorcising your kind for centuries. What's your point?"

"Our point?" The man looked at me like I was an idiot. "Our *point* is that we can't do that if this world ceases to exist. Do you understand, now? These Old One cultists don't want control. They want destruction. They revel in annihilation."

I didn't speak for several minutes, pondering the legion's words. Though I hated to admit it, they made a certain amount of sense. So what was my role in all this? I stood and paced around the small room, my fingers aimlessly brushing against the sound-deadening panels. I nearly asked the legion of devils if they knew why this Herald had made me, but any answer to such a question would either be a lie, or filled with only enough truth to lead me astray. Ask a demon its desires, and it won't shut up. Ask it for truths outside itself, and it would sooner be exorcised into oblivion than give a straight answer.

The trick is to cater to their sense of selfishness and self-preservation.

"I think I understand your point. It's a perversion of order and light, but I can at least understand your evil nature. It's predictable to a point. You say you don't have any contact with these 'cultists.' But do you know where they are?"

My prisoner looked down at the rune-marked restraints that not only bound him to the dental chair, but prevented the demons from vacating the meat suit. He followed the snaking IV line from where it pierced his vein up to the bag of blessed water. Finally, his incredulous glare locked on to me.

"Do you honestly think we'll *help* you? You abducted us and tortured us."

I shrugged. "Maybe we can make a deal."

This time the man's eyes narrowed in suspicion. "You are known by all our kind. There are centuries of stories about you. No mercy for our kind, or for the other monsters of the world.

You trade in violence and death. Your commitment to your faith... as your name suggests.

"But not once," the devils continued, "have we heard a story about you making a deal with us."

I shrugged again. "In case you haven't noticed, times have changed. For me. For you. For this world. I can deal with you and those like you. But I can't do that if the world doesn't exist. In all those stories you've heard about my supposed exploits, how often did you hear of me lying?"

The demons didn't answer, but obviously considered my words. Using their own words against them had seemingly stuck a nerve. And I *hadn't* been lying. At this point, striking a deal with the devils I knew seemed like the best bad choice left to me.

The alternatives? Run around blindly? Walk into the Vatican and ask the pope if he'd kindly help me figure out my purpose as a damned soul? Ask the Order of Saint Hubert to execute me as the abomination I was?

The Order had always kept me at arm's length anyway, only calling on my abilities when something particularly heinous needed investigating and putting down. I'd spent years—closer to centuries, really—hunting the most powerful creatures in this world without the Vatican's help or approval. And these days they'd largely ignored my existence.

The Lord helps those who help themselves.

If I wanted answers to my existence, and the ultimate goals of this so-called Herald, I'd have to rip them out of this falling and failing world myself.

"What kind of deal?" the legion of demonic voices asked in near unison. Cautious curiosity. It had been a while since I'd heard that tone from scum like this.

"What do you want?"

More suspicion on the stolen, dead face. "To... leave?"

Nodding in agreement, I sat down in the metal chair across from the prisoner. "I think I can accommodate that."

"You swear you'll let me leave if I help you? This isn't a trick?"

"Again, in all those stories you've heard, how often have I lied?"

"Never."

"Never," I agreed.

The demons considered the proposition for several minutes. During that time, I intentionally never even looked at the IV bag.

I couldn't have the demons thinking this deal was done under threat. They had to think I offered them a real way out. Which I did . . . after a fashion.

"Deal," they hissed at me. "What do you want?"

"I want to know where these cultists are plying their trade."

With a sly grin the demons replied, "Why, all over the world."

I smiled along with them, still pointedly not looking at the IV bag of holy water I wanted to drown the demons in. "Obviously. Let me be more specific. Do you know where this Herald and his followers are located? You might not associate with them, but surely you all know where they are? If for nothing more than to avoid them."

Confusion spread across the vessel's face, followed gradually by the shifting of some of the legion into amusement. Howls of laughter followed. The body's face contorted into a hundred versions of maniacal glee. To my supernaturally attuned eyes, the face bulged under the pressure, barely able to contain the laughing devils within.

I wanted to flay the skin from this abomination.

But then . . . given that I was made from the grafted bones of Old Ones, was I truly any different of a monster from the creature before me?

So I held my tongue and let the demonic mirth before me subside. By the time the legion quieted down, his face was wet from laughter-induced tears. But in this case, they were tears of blood.

With a red-streaked face, and a wide smile laden with madness and glee, the demons asked, "You don't already know? Surely you've figured that out by now? You don't need me to answer *that* question."

I opened my mouth to ask what they meant, but it all crashed home at once.

"They are already in the Order."

My eyes pried themselves open, crusted closed by sleep and dried blood. When had I last actually slept? I'd been put into a magical sleep back during the Jack the Ripper events. I couldn't remember a time since.

"Well, well, well," a familiar voice came from nearby. "Sleeping on the job, Fidele? I know things were rough in Mexico, but sleep? You? Frankly, I didn't even think you knew *how* to sleep."

Despite the unaccustomed grogginess, I smiled. Blinking away the sleep, I pushed myself up into a sitting position and took in my surroundings. I knew my location immediately. I put more than a few people and monsters into these very cells over the decades and centuries.

The prison below the headquarters of the Order of Saint Hubert.

Vertigo briefly took me as my vision swam, but my perception stabilized with a quick shake of my head.

Across from my cell, on the bare cement floor of another barred room, sat my old friend, Michael Gutterres.

He looked terrible. Dried blood covered half his face. The cut from which all the blood had spilled had already mostly closed. After all these years, I still didn't know what manner of creature he was, or what type of power he had that allowed him to heal like he did. To move as fast as he did. I'd never met a regular human who could take down a master vampire . . . except Gutterres.

Which meant he wasn't "regular."

He looked to have been pulled from bed. He still wore rumpled plaid flannel pajama pants along with a bloodstained and torn T-shirt. The shirt had the word "VOLA" on it. Likely some band he listened to. I'd never been able to give much care or attention to modern music. When you'd been friends with Wagner, it was hard to care too much about whatever was considered "music" these days. Slashed in multiple places, similar healing gashes were visible across his torso beneath the ruined garment.

"Did you get taken while asleep?" I asked. "You're slipping."

"Some of us actually require sleep, old friend. Besides, you hardly have room to talk. How on our Lord's green earth were *you* captured? And with only a small bump on your head?" He stared my way for a minute, then grinned. "Ah. I think I understand. When did you figure we'd been infiltrated?"

"I suppose it depends on what day it is," I answered. "How long have I been here?"

"Only a day."

"Then . . . three days."

"It took you that long?" Gutterres winked. "You're slipping."

I waved a tired hand at him. Whatever that cardinal had done to me had me feeling more tired than . . . well, ever. "I was busy."

"The hook-nosed man from our jaunt to Mexico. I see. And that led you here. Which means they are connected."

"Indeed." I stood slowly and leaned against the iron bars of my cell to stretch and get my blood moving. "I captured a man inhabited by a legion of devils. Made him a deal for information."

"You made a deal? With demons? Fidele, that seems extreme even for you."

"What else could I do?" I twisted my upper body, feeling my back pop in response. "After Mexico and discovering the damnation in my bones... well, I figured it was best to hide until I figured out the extent of the issues plaguing us. I just... I just didn't account for it all being as bad as *this*." I waved a hand the prison around us. "Besides you, I didn't know who to trust. And when I tried reaching out to you through the more discreet channels, I got nothing."

"I understand, old friend, and I'm sorry. I wish I'd been there for you. I was sent from hunt to hunt. Mission to mission. No breaks, no time to even breathe. But the missions didn't make sense, and the orders were from some cardinal I'd never heard of. So I began asking questions. It all came to a head a week ago."

"The cardinal visited you?"

Gutterres pointed a finger and made a shooting motion at me. "Bull's-eye." He rubbed his shoulder and grimaced. His beating must have been on the heavy side. "But tell me, Fidele. What kind of deal did you make with the legion?"

"I promised to let it go free if it told me about the hook-nosed man. He's known as 'the Herald.' Leads a cult of Old One worshippers who want to summon—"

"Who want to summon their dark god to destroy the earth." Gutterres rolled his eyes. "You'd think these cultists would be a *little* more original. Still, it makes sense based on what we fought in Mexico. That Herald had serious power. The kind that could actually make good on waking up a sleeping Old One."

"The demons told me the Herald had already infiltrated the Order. Or rather, they made me realize and recognize that I already feared the Order was compromised." My legs had begun trembling, so I lowered myself to the cold floor. "After that, I told him I'd keep my promise and set him free."

"Well, I can obviously see where this is going. You made a vague, shifty deal with a legion of devils, and they didn't catch the phrasing? I swear, we don't even get good demons anymore."

Shrugging, I replied, "Devils don't like to be tortured any more than mortals. After a certain point, they'll agree to anything to make it stop. So when I began exorcising the legion, they were rather upset. I told them if they didn't like it, they could tell the Herald how to find my safe house. I'd send them to Hell just like I was about to do to the demons."

"Devils. So predictable. And here you are."

"Here I am."

"So what's the plan?"

"Violence and vengeance."

Gutterres' ever-present smile turned feral. "Some of my favorite words."

Lights flickered above my head as power surged in the subterranean prison. Gutterres cocked his head to the side, brow furrowed in concentration. He'd finally noticed it too.

"Fidele, is it just me, or is there a pattern to the lights dimming? But it almost seems like—"

"It's getting faster."

We'd been locked in the Order's cells for two days now, and for the last twenty-four hours, the lights had regularly softening and dimming before pulsing back to full brightness. It happened nearly every two hours on the dot. Nearly.

Living as long as I have offered a unique perspective on the passage of time. I didn't need a clock to know how many minutes, hours, or days had passed. Every two hours, some sort of power drain caused the fluorescent tubes above to fade out for a moment. Except every time the surge occurred, it happened faster and faster. Like clockwork.

"The lights dim just a little faster each time," I continued. "Whatever is pulling power is slowly speeding up."

"The power drain must be immense." Gutterres pointed up at the lights. "I've never seen surges down here. It shouldn't even be possible given the dedicated section of the power grid we've been allocated in Vatican City. What could be causing it?"

"Nothing good. Which means we need to get out of here sooner than I'd planned."

"What do you mean 'sooner'? How long were you planning on taking to lull the guards into complacency before getting a stupid one to come close enough to choke out?"

"As long as it took."

Gutterres rolled his eyes. "Look, just because you're basically amortal doesn't mean the rest of us get to lollygag our lives away. How much longer do you estimate we have before the surges start blending together?"

"A day. Likely less."

"Great." He stood up and pointed a finger through the bars at me. "Your plan—or lack thereof—sucks. Leave this one to me."

"What are you—"

"*Shhhhh*," he interrupted. It had been more than a century since the last time a person shushed me. I'd beaten them into a coma. "Just be ready. I know you aren't in top shape, so try and get your"—he waved a hand vaguely at my sitting form—"*all that* in order."

It was my turn to roll my eyes, but I didn't argue. I still hadn't recovered from whatever hex or spell the cardinal had put on me. My abilities weren't gone. I still felt the regenerative properties of my body working away, struggling against the supernatural smothering blanket that had been draped over my shoulders.

My body just felt so heavy and stiff. Since I don't normally sleep, I'd stood and stretched every hour during the two days of our imprisonment.

But more than that, I felt oddly *drawn* to something above our heads and to my left. I'd caught myself staring in that direction multiple times.

I'd never felt this sensation before: of my body *longing* to run to the source of whatever it was calling to me. I'd never been much of a romantic. Living as long as I did rendered romantic relationships pointless. But the idea of being irrevocably and undeniably drawn to someone—of that raw magnetism pulling you into someone's orbit—was the only sensation I could compare my current feeling to. I knew it wasn't a romantic or lustful feeling, but every minute that passed made the sensation deeper.

Like it was in my bones.

No... it *was* in my bones.

Which meant catastrophically bad things were in the process of descending upon us.

My fear and suspicion were confirmed when, at the next power surge, the pull on my body grew markedly stronger. Every moment passing by made the desire stronger. I also felt the lethargy lessening, but at a slower pace than my wish to head to the source of the power above.

I had no idea what Gutterres had in mind for a plan. My plans tended to lean toward long stretches of patience punctuated by merciless violence. But my friend was right. We didn't have time to wait things out and take advantage of some guard's inevitable mistake. They all made them, it was just a matter of being ready for it. The ever-quickening pulsing power somewhere above us made patience a virtue we couldn't exploit.

"Guard! Guard! Hey, get over here!"

Gutterres' shouts pulled me from my thoughts. How long had I been zoned out, consumed by the need to find the source of energy pulling at my bones and my soul?

One of the Order guards walked slowly into the cell block, Sig SG 552 held ready. I didn't recognize him or any of the other soldiers I'd seen. I hadn't recognized any of the guards up to this point. They all did their jobs with trained precision, being a specialized elite subset of the Pontifical Swiss Guard. But something in their expressions—or better stated, something in their utter *lack* of expression—rubbed me wrong.

The approaching guard carefully stayed in the center of the aisle between our cells. Like I said, well trained.

Gutterres had his arms through the bars, waving the guard over. "Hey! When are you going to bring us our daily meal? It's at least an hour late." When the guard shook his head and began walking away, Gutterres changed his tone from outrage to pleading. "Hey, come on. Don't be like that. Look, we're just tired and hungry. We've been cooped up in these cells for days now. No mattresses, no blankets. Nothing. I'm one of the highest-ranking members of the Order, and no one will even tell me what is going on. I don't even know your *name*."

The guard let out a long sigh and tilted his head side to side, eliciting loud *pops*. But he said nothing. Again the guard started to leave, and Gutterres held out one hand, stretched out as far into the aisle as he could.

With his other, I caught his subtle signal to get up.

What was he planning?

I pulled myself noiselessly to my feet just as the lights began to dim again from the next power surge. The guard, already slightly leaning back away from Gutterres' frantically waving hand, never saw me stand.

The instant the light faded completely out, Gutterres gripped the bars of his cell, screamed, and began shaking like he was being electrocuted. The charade looked absurd. Back before the truth had been revealed, I'd have laughed.

The suddenness of the movement, especially with the timing of it against the light momentarily going out, caught the guard by surprise, and he did the one thing he shouldn't have.

He backed away from the screaming, writhing form of my friend...

...and right into my waiting arms.

I yanked him back, slamming his head as hard as I could into the metal bars of my cell. His helmet saved him from the worst of it, but it dazed him enough for me to pull his rifle around and through the bars so he couldn't use it. Then I wrapped my arms around his neck and squeezed and pulled until I felt his neck snap. I dropped him like a broken puppet.

"Did you have to kill him?" Gutterres asked. "For all we know, he was under a spell, too."

"Maybe. Maybe not. I haven't seen a familiar face since we arrived. I have to assume they are all compromised. From here on, I'm not taking the chance. Not with the Order. Not anymore."

Was that the moment I decided to leave the Order permanently? Perhaps. Or maybe it had been brewing over the last hundred years. Being a tool for a group that only used me to end the existence of monsters on *their* terms. Until that moment, I hadn't realized how truly tired I was of blindly following the Order's edicts.

I'd always looked down a little on the Hunters around the world...but maybe some had the right of it. Not waiting for an assignment to take down evil, but seeking it out proactively.

With the dead body slouched against the bars to my cell, I went through its pockets until I found a key to open my jail's door. As I pushed my way into the hall, I tossed Gutterres the key and bent down to pull off the corpse's useful gear and weapons.

Gutterres unlocked his own cell, then stretched as he exited. "See," he said patting me on the shoulder. "The plan worked perfectly. I should have taken my acting talents to Hollywood."

"You'd have exterminated the whole industry for their evils."

"Win-win?"

Despite everything, my friend's quip made me smile. I held up the rifle for him to take, but he waved it off.

"Don't think I've ever seen you refuse a weapon."

"Normally I wouldn't, Fedele. But you still look like a reanimated corpse. I think I'll let you be the trigger man for a bit." He squatted down next to me and took the guard's long-bladed knife and collapsible baton. He flicked the baton to extended it, then held up the weapons and grinned. "I'll be just fine."

I looped my new rifle's sling over my head and shoulder and stood . . . then almost fell over. Gutterres hadn't been wrong. For a moment, my vision darkened at the corners and I had to reach out to grab the bars of the cell I'd just vacated.

"You're going to need more ammo." Gutterres pulled one of my arms around his shoulder and steadied me until my eyes cleared. We took a several steps down the long hallway before Gutterres paused to stare at me.

Free from my prison, the urge to run to the source of surging power grew, bubbling up inside me like boiling water that threatened to spill over the sides of my soul.

"What's going on with you, Fidele? I've never seen you like this."

"I think that cardinal—or whatever he really is—put some sort of spell on me. Haven't felt this way since Salem." I pointed up above us and to my right in the direction of the eldritch energy. "And whatever is causing these power surges is adding to it, I think."

Gutterres didn't speak immediately. His eyes followed the direction I'd pointed. "Fidele, can you tell exactly where the source is?" When I nodded, he asked, "Should I assume you're connected to it somehow?"

"Seems like an easy assumption to make." I tapped one of the visible scars on my arm. "I feel it here, in my bones."

He opened his mouth to reply, but the sound of bones cracking and flesh tearing and squishing made him close it with an audible *click*. In horror-movie unison, we both looked over our shoulders at the corpse we'd left behind us.

The dead Order soldier's body twisted, rending its own flesh and snapping bones. Blood sprayed in all directions, coating the jail-door bars, ceiling, and floor. Fleshy, spindly appendages ripped their way free of the body as it reconstituted the corpse's pieces into a new, blasphemous form. At the thing's center was a fleshy, dripping mass—almost a meaty tumbleweed. From it sprouted three spiderlike legs on one side, with four on the other. The only piece still recognizable as vaguely human was the hand that reached out toward us from the tumbleweed's front.

A fist at first, the hand extended out our way, then opened its palm to face us. An eye opened in the hand's center, regarding us with an expression I could only interpret as *hunger.*

Gutterres looked at the knife and baton he held and let out a sigh. "I need a new career. I'm getting too old for this shit."

"Amen," I said.

I pushed away from my friend, turned and shouldered the rifle. I put a three-round burst into the monstrosity's center, the first of which took it in the glaring eye. It didn't scream or squeal, but it did flinch and skitter backward, spike-ended feet slipping on the blood-slicked floor.

Being weaker than normal wasn't going to impact my accuracy with a rifle.

The flesh spider jumped straight up, its legs reversing instantly in their joints to drive the pointy feet into the ceiling for purchase. The eyeball hand hung limply down below it. Whatever power leaked into this world from the happenings above us didn't seem to be fixing the damage I'd done.

That was something I could work with.

Concrete fragments fell to the ground as the creature walked slowly to us, seemingly feeling its way forward. I put ten more rounds into the spider's body, then another five into the joints where the legs met the body on the side with only three legs. The bullets tore through the intersections of dripping flesh, and tore two of the legs free. Under the sudden strain of weight, the remaining third leg on that side popped out of place and ripped away.

The center mass of the body swung down and the thin joints on the four-legged side shredded in wet spouts of blood. The tumbleweed hit the ground with a fleshy smack, blood fountaining out from it as the meaty sack ruptured.

"That's one of the grossest things I've ever seen," Gutterres said. He pointed at my rifle. "I think we both need more bullets. And I need some shoes."

"Good thing we know where the armory is."

"No place like home!" Gutterres grinned and began walking down the hall, bare feet moving soundlessly on the cold concrete. We waved at me to follow. "Come on, old man. Let's get out of here before that thing sprouts any more legs."

The halls of the Order's headquarters lay empty. Our footfalls echoed in the coolness of the halls. The stale air itself exuded a stillness only present in tombs, and in that air I faintly detected the beginnings of a peculiar smell reminiscent of the old condemned husks of forgotten buildings. Even though it couldn't have been long since the hostile takeover of the Order's headquarters, the walls had already lost their luster and holiness. This place was now a mausoleum dedicated to the absence of righteousness now facing the organization. How deep did the rot sink? If we survived whatever we'd find above us, would the Order survive? Could it be rebuilt? Did I want it rebuilt?

In my heart, I knew I found myself at a moral crossroads. Serve a group that only used me for the jobs they didn't want to subject their rank and file to? Help them rebuild and hope they wouldn't see me as the abomination I truly was—a man possessed not of the bones of saints, but of Old Ones? A monster no better than the spider thing I'd just killed. At least, that was how I saw it. And even if they did accept me, could someone—some*thing*—like me help them in doing good?

Occasional stains of old blood marked the floors and walls of the Order's once hallowed halls. Our headquarters were not made with marble and opulence like many of the Vatican's other buildings. We—*they*—had always stuck to a stark utilitarianism. The bloodstains seemed to betray that simplicity.

Their age also suggested the Order, as I knew it anyway, was dead.

Gutterres stopped to stare at one of the larger darkened patches of concrete. Filling a huge section of bare wall, and then spreading out to cover dozens of square feet of walkway, the number of bodies once spilling blood here must have numbered in the dozens.

"I haven't been here in months," my friend said quietly. "They kept me moving from mission to mission. If I'd been here—"

"You'd be dead," I interrupted. "You'd have made this stain a little larger, is all."

Anger twisted Gutterres' face and he pointed an accusing finger my way. "You know nothi—"

I quickly stepped in close, batting his hand aside, and gripped his shoulder. "Stop. They took you with little effort while you were asleep. They would have done the same here. Your grief—however justified—can wait. I understand your anger, believe me. For today, its only purpose must be toward stopping the evil above us. Perhaps God has plans for you that don't involve you as a nameless bloodstain."

His shoulders relaxed and he nodded. "Perhaps you're right. I forgot my faith for a moment. I'm sorry, my friend."

I patted him on the shoulder and moved around the bloodstain, avoiding stepping on it. Just down the hall, the door to the armory hung open. As we'd walked, my legs grew steadier. I couldn't tell it if was from walking and getting the blood flowing, or if it was because of my growing proximity to the eldritch energy pouring into our world. The power surges continued, happening ever quicker. We no longer had a day.

We had hours, at most.

The armory door easily swung open the rest of the way on well-oiled hinges. I barely had to push. At least that much of this building hadn't fallen into decay. Inside, we found it mostly intact. Standard-issue Sig SG 552s and their longer-barreled 550 sisters hung nestled in racks on the walls. Drawers filled with loaded magazines rested beneath the weapons, and I knew pallet upon pallet of ammo containers would fill the room behind this one. To the right of the rifles, the wall held dozens of halberds with razor-sharp edges glinting in the fluorescent lights. No swords, to my dismay. Normally I'd have taken a halberd along with the rifles, just as the Order recommended and issued. But not today. I couldn't count on my stamina lasting, and swinging one of those around—no matter how satisfying—would tire me out quicker than simply pulling a trigger.

Gutterres found a pair of boots, but no pants. He tucked the legs of his flannel pajama bottoms into the boots. We both put on vests, loaded them down with magazines for the rifles, and grabbed the nearby Glock 19s. No matter how much ammo I shoved into pouches and pockets, it didn't seem like enough. The image of the flesh spider kept crawling in my memory. Good thing I didn't sleep or dream. I didn't relish the thought of having that thing haunt my nightmares. Even thinking of that monstrosity made me grab a couple grenades for good measure.

More than anything else, the empty armory unnerved me.

Unattended weapons left in perfect order. No one had made it here to resist the apparent purge we'd missed. A single dark splotch on the floor marked where the room's guard had died. I hoped, for his sake, that he'd *just* died. The thought of some righteous, fresh-faced soldier turning into an eldritch abomination turned my stomach.

"To the emergency staircase?"

Gutterres had already walked to the door while I'd been lost in thought. I nodded and followed after him. I'd have loved taking an elevator, but knowing our luck today, the *ding* of it reaching the main level would draw an Elder God to crush us like ants.

We moved through the silent halls and up several flights of stairs to the main administrative level of the Order's HQ. This section of the building held mainly offices and conference rooms. The building, much like cathedrals of old, had been built in the shape of a cross following a standard cruciform plan, just a little larger to account for the extra offices, conference rooms, and indoor gun ranges. Most importantly, at its center was a chapel built for prayer and worship.

Which is exactly where my bones directed me.

I pushed the door from the stairwell to the main floor open quickly, letting Gutterres lead us out into the main level of the building. We found ourselves in the right arm of the headquarters' cross at its very end.

Like an eldritch god's discarded, bloody, broken toys, soldiers of the Order of Saint Hubert the Protector lay rotting in the halls. Appendages and heads torn from them lay scattered about in pools of dried blood. They hadn't just been killed, they'd been exterminated to the man.

No movement. No life.

Perhaps no hope.

The only positive thing I could rest my hat on was that they'd been dead for some time, and weren't transforming into monsters of flesh, hatred, and evil.

To my side, Gutterres let out a long breath. Normally such a happy example of God's creation, to see and hear him in this amount of emotional pain saddened me more than anything I'd witnessed in the last century.

We walked forward wordlessly, keeping our footsteps as quiet as possible. Shadows cast from the pulsing lights stalked us in wavering forms as we crept to the chapel. While the lights below had been in bright fluorescent white, up here none worked. The only light in the gloom originated ahead of us, in sickly green. A green that made the rotting colors of putrid Louisiana swamps look the picture of health.

The pulsing of that bloated, corpse-like green light had become a continual pattern. An emergency light that warned me not to safety, but drew me to damnation. To destruction. My bones howled for it. Longed for it. Begged and pleaded for me to run to it with open arms.

So I was attuned to evil after all.

No surprise, but I still felt the last grip I had on the lie of my holiness slip away. I was left only with anger and the need for vengeance. They would have to do.

We passed the corpses of our once comrades, a few of which I still recognized despite their state. Gone, but not forgotten. Not by me, and certainly not by Gutterres. As we approached the open, massive wooden double doors that marked the entrance to the chapel I noticed a rank breeze outward toward us. It smelled of centuries of hate, and somehow of impending destruction.

I slipped through the door heading left, knowing Gutterres would go right.

Inside the chapel were piles of bodies—Swiss Guard, civilians, clergy. Benches had been thrown to the side of the chapel to lay as kindling.

At the front of the chapel, rather than the normal religious trappings and iconography, stood an immense doorframe. It appeared to be made of some dark stone, of the like I'd never seen before. When the green light pulsed, it seemed to absorb it, drinking it in like a greedy vampire.

That green light emanated from within that doorway as a churning mix of liquid and mist. Laced within that green were swirls of eldritch, putrid yellow the same as I'd seen in the cardinal's eyes when he'd taken me.

I'd been in this room countless times over the centuries—usually at night, when standard services were long over. It had always provided comfort. I'd loved seeing bright moonlight streaming in through stained glass, and seeing the night belong to God in such a peaceful setting.

Now the windows were blacked out, like they prevented the Lord's mercy from touching this once holy place. The whole of it now despoiled. Even if we managed to drive back the encroaching evil, this place would never be the same. It was now unhallowed ground.

From the darkness near the swirling abyss, a figure in scarlet robes emerged. From the way shadows played, I couldn't quite tell if he came from beyond the portal, or just from behind it. His eyes glowed with yellow fire in the gloom.

Cardinal Augustus Fontaine.

"I'm pleased you could make it." The dread cardinal's voice boomed in the fallen chapel. "I should have known better than to keep only a single guard on you at the end. I'd have used more"—he waved at the piled corpses—"but they were rather indisposed. I'd planned on sending one of my god's servants bring you here at the appointed time, but you delivered yourselves. I appreciate it."

Neither Gutterres nor I spoke. I raised my rifle level with Fontaine's chest while flicking my eyes side to side looking for movement.

"Have it your way," Fontaine said. "Though I find it odd you ask no questions. I know you have them. If you won't ask them of me, perhaps you will to an old friend."

An old friend. Surely he meant the hook-nosed man. The Herald. My glances into the shadows became more frantic at the prospect of seeing the man who'd made me the abomination I was today.

Instead, Fontaine dropped to one knee, screaming in pain. It was first one scream, then two, both issuing from the same throat. Just like the legion of devils I tortured only days earlier, Fontaine was possessed by something...

...or some*one*.

His back stretched and another figure seemed to push up and out from him. This new figure straightened, absorbing a thin line of green-and-yellow mist that stretched out from the doorway to an Elder God's realm. The vile mist and shadows roiled in midair, then coalesced into the familiar shape of the hook-nosed man.

The cardinal stood, his eyes without the yellow flames. His face had gone slack, and drool trailed down his chin in a thin line.

"Hello, my son."

The voice issued from the cardinal's mouth without it moving. From behind him, the Herald's mouth moved in perfect synch with the words.

A puppet, then. No different from the possessed devil's own I'd dealt with for centuries. I felt oddly let down.

Behind the two servants of an Eldritch God, the doorframe drank in more of the green light, and the pulsing subtly sped up.

"Screw this." Gutterres lifted his rifle and pulled the trigger, sending a stream of 5.56 at our enemies... or so I thought. Instead, the rounds pinged off the black doorframe. From here I couldn't tell if any damage had been done, but after the echoes faded, I thought I head the faintest sound of a tiny piece of stone hit the ground. I hope I hadn't imagined it.

"Useless," the Herald said through his proxy. He looked back at the green-and-yellow portal and gestured to it like an old stage magician. "My God comes."

The mist pushed outward as something tested its boundaries. An appendage of some sort, maybe. It wasn't humanoid. I didn't like the idea of anything like that coming into our world.

At that same moment, searing agony and ecstasy rippled through me. Rifle falling from my hands, I dropped to the floor.

Then I felt myself float gently into the air and be slowly dragged toward the portal.

Distantly I heard Gutterres firing his rifle, all while the Herald laughed. As I passed under one of the stained-glass windows, the shadows covering it dripped down. Moonlight pierced the darkness, illuminating those shadows as dozens of the flesh monsters like the one we'd killed earlier. No two looked alike, and they blurred together and separated into new forms as they scrambled over each other to reach my friend.

I couldn't do much of anything. My hands moved so slowly when they could move at all. I tilted my head back as far as I could, and saw I was already at the portal.

I hovered there, next to the black stone. I'd never seen anything like it. Smooth black glass, yet in the moonlight I caught what looked like the grain of wood just beneath the surface. Some sort of petrified wood, then? It was funny what pulled my attention when I was about to have my existence ended.

The Herald materialized over me. Though everything else around me seemed to be in a muffled haze, his voice sounded in my head with perfect clarity.

"*It was only a matter of time*," he said. "*You were built for this moment. For the perfect confluence of stars that mark this time. Made on their first conjunction, and now sacrificed on their second to mark the coming of a new age.*"

Below my face, marring the perfectly smooth doorway near where it met the ground, were the tightly grouped marks from Gutterres' earlier shots. Left arm dangling, I pointed as best I could, praying to a Lord who would likely want nothing to do with me. Praying that he would let Gutterres see what I was doing.

For a long moment, nothing.

"*I will spread your soul on this doorway as a final offering to my God,*" the Herald continued. Looking down on me, images of the past and present collided in my mind. Him cutting on me, surrounded by chanting monks . . . or, rather, cultists, I supposed. It had all come full circle.

The hook-nosed man raised a hand above his head, and a thin stream of the green mist floated to pool in his palm. It spun around in his hand, then slowly took shape into a long knife. The same knife I remembered him using on me all those centuries ago.

Next to me, pieces of the doorframe's surface exploded outward as a hail of gunfire from Gutterres' rifle poured into it. The Herald flinched, and his gaze lifted from me to look for the cause of the interruption.

I don't know if it was the diverting of the Herald's attention, or the damage done to the frame keeping the eldritch portal in place, but a bit of the weight smothering me lifted.

Clawing at my side, I drew my Glock, lifted the muzzle up under the Herald's chin, and pulled the trigger three times as fast my numb finger would allow.

Shadow and yellow mist sprayed upward out the top of his head instead of brain matter and blood, but my nemesis reeled backward, the sacrificial knife ripped from his grasp by the thin otherworldly stream of mist. Like a tether had suddenly snapped.

I dropped to the ground hard, cracking my head against the stone floor, and rolling down the steps from where the holy altar should have been. I pulled the rifle up from where it hung from me on the sling, aimed, and dumped an entire magazine of 5.56 into the same spot Gutterres had shot.

As I ejected the empty mag, I risked a quick glance over my shoulder and saw my friend weaving between the ruins of the chapel, shredding flesh creatures with lethal accuracy. He moved so fast. Wraithlike. Pure, cold fury etched a snarl on his face as he moved faster than I'd ever seen from him. No, he wasn't normal. Some sort of blessing maybe. A legitimate one, unlike the perversion of my own.

A dual-voiced shriek filled the chapel, arresting my attention.

The two shapes of the Herald and the cardinal strained at each other, fighting for stability. They soon steadied, and then Fontaine's back bulged and strained again. This time the audible sounds of cracking bones accompanied the movement.

The back of his rib cage ripped outward, stretched, morphed, and unfurled into blood-dripping, fleshy wings.

An evil eldritch angel.

Just great.

I slammed a new mag home and immediately dumped it into the new threat. Nothing happened. Then the sound of the clinking of spent rounds as they hit the ground short of their target.

Gutterres spun around slashing appendages, shooting monster after monster, but he wouldn't last forever. Our weapons wouldn't touch the Herald or his puppet in this state. We were running out of options. Maybe his own dagger would have done some damage, but it had been yanked back in the vortex.

The vortex.

It spun like a hurricane, pushing outward every few moments as the Old One tested the firmness of the veil between our worlds. I could have used a nuke at that moment. After all, it had worked for the Hunter in Alabama. But all I had was a couple grenades.

An idea hit me. Call it centuries of preparation, or divine providence given to me by a god that hadn't quite forsaken me, but these moments of inspiration had rarely led me astray. As fast as I could, I pulled a grenade and hurled it at the damaged base of the doorframe.

I dove for cover behind a pile of damaged benches, reaching safety just as the grenade detonated.

The double scream from the Herald and the cardinal returned, this time in agony and fear. When I poked my head around the side of the benches, the side of the doorframe buckled, and collapsed under itself like a controlled demolition.

Without the doorframe to keep it contained, the swirling green-and-yellow portal shuddered and began falling in on itself. As it did, thin, ethereal lines of the mist stabbed out, hitting the flesh monsters where they chased Gutterres. One by one they were grabbed and sucked into the void.

With a thunderous *crack*, the doorframe crashed to the ground. A lash of yellow energy swung outward in an arc, slicing through the cardinal. Two halves of Fontaine fell to the floor in wet pieces as blood splashed outward. Green tethers reached out and grabbed the pieces, vanishing them into the eldritch realm.

The Herald was caught by the same tethers that pulled his host through the portal. As he disappeared, the last image I had of him was one of fury.

In my head, his voice came through clear before being cut off.

"This is far from over. You will see me ag—"

The unstable mist bulged outward, then completely collapsed in on itself, winking out of existence.

"So what will you do now?" Gutterres asked me.

We sat in a small café several blocks from the headquarters of the Blessed Order of Saint Hubert the Protector. Fire engines flew by, sirens blazing. The conflagration of our old home illuminated the night sky. No amount of water would put out this blaze. We'd made sure of it. Once it had burned everything to the ground—and the subterranean levels had been suitably destroyed from the explosives we'd carefully set—the pope would have to see about reconsecrating the ground. If he could.

"I'm unsure," I answered. "I think I need to do a little soul-searching. Figure out what these cursed bones truly mean." I self-consciously rubbed at one of the scars.

"Makes sense."

"And you?"

My friend shrugged. "Buy a new motorcycle. Travel a bit."

"Lying doesn't become you."

Gutterres smiled. Not his normal mischievous grin, but one of a man who had the weight of new responsibility heavy on his shoulders. "You're right. I don't expect to be traveling any time soon. Too much to do. You're positive you won't stick around? Help me rebuild the Order?"

"There's no place for my kind there."

"There's always a place as my brother. I'd see to it."

I smiled. "I know. And I appreciate the offer." A small laugh escaped me. "You know, it's ironic."

"What is?"

"My name. It means 'faithful,' but now I certainly lack that virtue."

I made to leave but Gutterres pulled me back down into my chair. His usual carefree expression was absent, replaced by pure seriousness. "You lack nothing, Fidele. Nothing. You simply face a moment of doubt. I mean this in the nicest way, my friend, but that trial is not special or unique to you. All us humans face it at one time or another."

"Am I even human, Michael?"

A smile crossed my friend's face. Not his normal mischievous one, but an expression of pure kindness. It had been a long time since I'd seen the like. For the first time in over a hundred years, I felt tears well up at the corners of my eyes.

"Look, Fidele. All this"—he waved in the direction of the burning Order headquarters—"is bigger than you or I. This is God's work. His design and direction. I am the way I am because of God, and I'm grateful for it. I see your doubt, brother. Since Mexico you've worn it plain for all to see. You think you are damned, but you are *not.*"

"Gutterres, I—"

"I'm not finished. Whether you like it not—whether you believe you are worthy or not—you are a Knight of the Cross. A Knight of the Order. You are my brother. You think you are lost and damned because of what the Herald did to you. And yet you've only used that *gift*—yes, I still consider it a gift—to help this world. That is not damnation, but *service.* I know it might not feel like you can right at this moment, but you need to trust in your faith. And if you can't do that right now, trust in *my* faith in you.

"At the very least, look at it this way, Fidele." His normal sly smile returned. "If something like that Franks creature can be saved by our Lord, surely you can too."

His words swept away a weight from my shoulders. I reached up and pretended to scratch an itch by my eyes so I could catch the tears before they fell. This time, when I stood to leave, Gutterres didn't stop me.

"I think you're right, Gutterres."

"Obviously."

"I think it's time to find myself again. To look for that faith you say I need to trust in."

"I agree. So what will you do?"

"I think I'll go freelance for a while I figure things out."

"I'll be here, waiting for you when you are ready to return. But you'll keep in touch, yes? In case I need assistance from a brother?"

"Sure. I'll even give you the friends-and-family rate."

Gutterres laughed as I walked away. But he called out to me one last time.

"Fidele, your name means something else. It also means 'hope.' There's nothing ironic in that meaning."

Waving goodbye, I turned and left him to watch the distant flames while I thought on his parting words.

Hope.

Something I could hold onto.

The veracity of this recounting is difficult to gauge. Could it merely be an exaggerated war story, or is there more truth to this than any of us prefer? As noted once before, the implications are disturbing.

—A.L.

Teddy and the She-Beast

Brad R. Torgersen

Santiago de Cuba, July 1898

"Why are they all looking at us so strangely?" Lieutenant Colonel Roosevelt asked, spying the faces peering out windows up and down the filthy boulevard. "Haven't any of these people ever seen an American before?"

Brigadier General Leonard Wood—field-promoted to command of the Second Brigade, Cavalry, United States Fifth Army Corps—motioned around him with his hand.

"That's what I need you to find out, Teddy. The Spanish capitulation hasn't put an end to the trouble. Not in this part of Santiago, at least. Wheeler sent me to check, because he thought it was yellow fever or malaria flaring up. I'm a doctor, after all. I know about those kinds of things. But I've not seen any sign to make me believe disease is what's happening here. Something else is going on."

The lieutenant colonel continued to look around at the two-story and sometimes three-story plaster-walled dwellings that lined both sides of the boulevard. In other parts of the city, the locals were already coming out to make nice with the US regulars and volunteers who were bringing the place under American control. But not here. Here, the Cubans remained almost entirely buttoned up behind doors and glass.

"These poor people look like they've got barely two *centavos* to rub together," Roosevelt muttered.

The gutters stank, and were cluttered with detritus from the departing Spanish troops, who hadn't exactly tidied up during their organized surrender two days before. Though none of the United States officers present were allowed to call it a surrender per se—on direct order from Major General Wheeler, who had himself once been captured by General Sherman's men, in Georgia, over thirty years earlier.

"Better than what I saw in the field with Lawton for the Geronimo campaign," Wood said. "At least some of these homes have *some* kind of sanitation. Though, little of it's liable to be up to New York City standards."

Roosevelt *tsk-tsk*ed his tongue against his prominent front teeth, then frowned at his boss. Teddy's spectacles cast peculiar circles of light and shadow on his damp, round cheeks. The sun was high overhead, making the July humidity even more uncomfortable than normal. Roosevelt and his men had somewhat acclimated during their training in Texas, prior to departing for Florida. But nothing could adequately prepare them for Cuba, with its tropical climate, persistent mosquitos, and three-digit temperatures. Challenging conditions for even some of the tougher cowpunchers recruited from Oklahoma and the Dakotas.

"Winning the peace can be trickier than winning the war," said the pepper-haired sergeant who'd accompanied Roosevelt from his headquarters.

"You'd know better than most, Potter," Teddy replied.

Like General Wheeler, Deke Potter was of Civil War vintage, having marched under General Grant's officers at Vicksburg. And like a lot of the presently deployed First Volunteers, Potter had come out of the American West, drawn by the promise of glory and adventure. Signing on with the aggregate of men whom both Wood and Roosevelt had kludged together for the American effort to end Spain's despotic rule over this largely rural island country.

Most importantly for the specific task at hand, Potter knew how to talk to Mexicans, which meant he got on with the Cubans better than most of Roosevelt's men, though the older noncommissioned volunteer still occasionally struggled with the differences in dialect—Cuban Spanish versus Mexican Spanish.

Now that the Rough Riders were in the city, men like Sergeant

Potter were vital to establishing good order and relations with Santiago's inhabitants.

"What I'm seeing," Potter continued, "ain't as peculiar as what I *ain't* seeing, sir."

"How do you mean?" Roosevelt asked.

"Where are the youngsters?" Potter asked. "Plenty of older folk about, though they're peeping at us through their shutters. But no children."

"I'd keep my kids inside, too," Wood said, "if someone else's army was newly occupying my streets."

"Naw, sir," Potter drawled. "It ain't that."

"Well," Wood said, "this is why I need you men on the job. Teddy, you've got my say-so on whoever or whatever you need. Just keep me appraised, you understand? Wheeler wants answers, because the last thing we can afford—with the Spanish departing—is for this city to go to hell under our watch. If there's something criminal going on, we need to spot it, and stamp it out. Or, if it's something else, we need to spot *that,* and stamp it out, too."

"You needn't worry about my ability to perform the chore," Teddy said, his neck straightening as he looked his friend directly in the eye. "Remember who was New York's police commissioner? There can't be anything here that I didn't see there. You've picked the right man."

Wood smiled, and put out his hand to the lieutenant colonel. "Exactly what I told General Wheeler when he asked me who'd be best."

Roosevelt shook his boss's hand strongly, then Wood—his own retinue of junior officers and noncommissioned officers in tow—left the boulevard, and went two blocks up to where their horses had been temporarily tied.

Potter's and Roosevelt's horses remained at hand, along with the horse belonging to Roosevelt's adjutant. Who'd not said a word since their arrival.

"I saw a bit of city like this back in Chicago," Sergeant Potter said. "But these people here are frightened instead of curious. You can feel it."

"We'd best start with whatever passes as the constabulary," Teddy said. "If we're going to get to the bottom of it, they'll be involved—one way, or another."

The three men mounted their horses and took them slowly

north. Teddy's mildly crumpled, dusty, and sweat-stained campaign hat provided his eyes some relief from the oppressive midday sun. In another time and place his partial blindness would surely have prevented him from volunteering to lead men in the field. But he'd never taken "No!" for an answer on anything he'd set his mind to. And his bad eyes certainly hadn't stopped him from going up Kettle Hill before taking San Juan Hill. It had been an audacious charge that had done much to convince the Spanish that keeping Cuba—under the present circumstances—was not in Spain's best interest.

Stern faces and wide eyes continued to peek out at them from windows and doorways. There was almost no horse nor wagon traffic, as Teddy would have expected in any similarly sized American city. Just the refuse and debris from the Spanish army's hasty departure, mixed with the usual trash that inevitably piled up if people weren't actively street-sweeping.

"The Spanish brutalized these wretched souls," Roosevelt remarked.

"I reckon," Sergeant Potter said speculatively, his own eyes shaded by a rather tall, wide-brimmed prairie hat that had come with him all the way from Salt Lake City. Where he'd also picked up the adjutant—a young, red-haired volunteer by the name of Anderson, who had himself come down from Idaho when he got word about Roosevelt's call for men to join him.

"Makes you appreciate what we have at home," Corporal Anderson said, his voice almost sounding like that of a teenager's compared to the adults he rode with.

"That it does, young man," Teddy said. "And I used to tell people in the East the same, after I got done running cattle in the West. It's good for any man to know what he's got, but you generally don't learn that sitting at a desk or working behind a counter in the city."

The trio rode around a corner, and there were the open doors of an eating and drinking establishment. The first sign of hospitality the three Americans had seen so far. With a dirty-aproned Cuban man standing outside, looking at them intently.

He didn't smile.

"Buenos días," Lieutenant Colonel Roosevelt said from horseback, attempting the lingo.

"You have an accent like an Italian," the man in the dirty

apron responded, in English that sounded much too American to be an accident.

"I know some Italian," Roosevelt said, containing his surprise. He stopped his horse, causing the two US troops with him to stop theirs. "I also know Latin. You, meanwhile, clearly know my manner of speech better than I know yours."

The man grunted and continued to just stare up at them.

"Say, *amigo,*" Roosevelt continued, with a slightly crooked smile on his lips. "You couldn't tell us who the local *gendarme* is around here?"

"I don't know that word," he said.

"Sorry, using my French this time. It means policeman."

"Ah," the man said and aimed a thumb over his shoulder back into the eatery. "He's got his nose in a mug when he ought to be out finding whoever's been kidnapping our sons and daughters."

All three Americans stiffened in their saddles.

"Beg pardon?" Anderson said, his young voice cracking.

Roosevelt looked over his shoulder at Sergeant Potter, nodded his head once, and then all three of them were dismounting, tying up, and walking through the eatery's front doors, their US Volunteer uniforms contrasting against the civilian clothing of the few Cubans inside. Most of whom were sullenly staring at plates on tables, or the bottoms of mugs and glasses. Teddy thought it uncouth that any man—to say nothing of a woman—should be tilting a drink at this time of the day. But something had clearly happened to these people. And at the mention of *kidnapping* and *children,* the lieutenant colonel instantly became determined to find out what.

Teddy frowned. The *Orden Publico* cop at the bar was half out of uniform, with his neglected topcoat draped carelessly over the empty stool to his left, and his white undershirt stained by old sweat. His leather belt with pistol and saber were draped across a stool to his right, and the redness of his eyes told Teddy that he hadn't slept off drinking from the night before. He also didn't speak English, and slurred his answers to Sergeant Potter's questions as Roosevelt asked them, English being combobulated to Spanish, then back again.

"Esteban here says he doesn't know anything about no kidnapping," Sergeant Potter said, his raised eyebrow expressing his skepticism without needing to utter a word.

The half-drunk Cuban constable looked to be of mixed ancestry—islander with Spanish—and glumly kept his eyes on the bar while he talked. His voice was whispery, like the man were deathly tired. And he occasionally paused between responses, as if he were fighting to cohere his thoughts. Everyone else around them had stopped cold and were watching intently as Roosevelt—through Potter, with Anderson as scribe—continued the interrogation.

"Now, I don't know what the Spanish did to you, or anyone else in this city, during their tenure, but if there's a child-slaving ring at work, by God I'm going to do something about it!"

Teddy's raised voice was punctuated by him slamming a fist on the bar.

The Cuban constable just put his forehead in both hands and seemed almost on the verge of tears.

"He can't tell you what it is," said a woman's voice from over Roosevelt's shoulder.

The lieutenant colonel turned, and was near awestruck by the image of a remarkably beautiful woman who practically glided through the eatery's entrance. Her gown and gloves were high society, but somewhat outdated. Like something Roosevelt would have seen some of his mother's friends wearing when he was just a young teenager. Her complexion and features were unblemished. Pristine. Her cheeks strong and distinct, with just a hint of makeup. Like her lips, which were full. And almost suggested ancestry beyond the bounds of Europe. But she wasn't a Cuban, that much was sure. Nor did she have the accent of an American. Plus, her eyes captivated him. Like no woman's eyes the lieutenant colonel had ever seen. Teddy could only stare at her while his young adjutant dropped his pencil to the tile floor with an embarrassing clatter.

"Madame," Teddy said, reflexively bringing his hat to his chest. "As I was saying to this rather forlorn fellow, if someone's slaving the children of this city, I'm absolutely going to do something about it. You don't know me, but back where I am from, I've got some experience with that sort of thing—cleaning it up!"

"I actually do know who you are," she said, her voice smooth, and in the lower feminine register, such that it filled Roosevelt's ears like a mouthful of fine brandy.

The lieutenant colonel snapped at his clumsy adjutant to pick up the pencil, then Teddy took a couple of steps forward.

"I apologize, my dear, but if I'd previously met someone of your remarkable quality, I am quite sure I'd remember it."

"I talked to your wife," the woman said, also taking a few steps into the eatery. Now the attention of the Cubans in the eatery promptly shifted from Roosevelt to her.

"If I recall," the woman continued, "you were much too engaged in conversation with the senator from New Jersey. But your wife? She was pleasant enough. I liked her."

"You know Edith?" Teddy blurted.

"Alice," the woman corrected him.

At the mention of his late first wife's name, Roosevelt froze. His mouth formed a thin line that trembled just for an instant, before a sigh like a gust of wind went out of him.

"I lost Alice when Baby Lee was born," he managed to say, while his eyes momentarily brimmed with restrained tears.

"I'm very sorry to hear that," the woman said. "I only spoke with her for a few minutes. You know how New York uptown parties go—everyone swirling around each other, laughing gayly, while saying little of consequence. But I do remember the way Alice beamed in your direction while we talked. I think she loved you very much."

"And I, her," Teddy said, still managing to restrain his tears. "And now Baby Lee is a teenager. My oldest at home, with Edith, my second wife, and our other children."

"Why then are you here, covered in war's glory, Mr. Roosevelt? So far away from your family."

"What business would it be of yours?" Teddy replied, feeling his neck and face grow hot.

"Nothing, nothing," the woman said. "Just noting that the priorities of an ambitious man don't always abide mundane obligations."

"Edith's more than woman enough to run our home," Teddy said. "And before our conversation goes any further, miss, I think I deserve to know your name."

"I've had several in my life," the woman said, stepping forward a few more paces until she was face-to-face with the lieutenant colonel. Her almost unnervingly perfect eyes didn't blink, nor did she shrink from Teddy's gaze. Which had grown somewhat hostile at the insinuation he might be shirking more important responsibilities.

"Then out with it," Teddy demanded. "Whatever you go by now. And what do you know about what's supposed to be happening to the children of Santiago?"

"In this city I'm known as Eva," she said, putting out a gloved hand. But not to be kissed. To be shaken, like a man's. "And I am reasonably certain that the people of Santiago are being preyed upon by El Coco."

"Who?" Deke asked, trading glances with Anderson the adjutant.

One of the Cuban women in the eatery wailed, then stood up, crossed herself hurriedly, and rushed out of the door through which Teddy and his two men had entered only a few minutes before.

"*¡No puedes decir su nombre!*" the cop at the bar exclaimed, slamming his mug down with such force, it shattered. "*¡Cúando dices su nombre, los niños sufren! Él se los toma, directo de las sombras, y de vuelta. Hace tres días que no lo veo a mi hijo. Y solo se me queda mi hija, desde que falleció su madre. ¡No tienes ni idea de quíen o de qué te has metido!*"

Teddy opened his mouth to ask what the hell the man had just said but stopped when Eva held her unshaken hand to her face, and touched her full lips with the tip of a poised finger.

"I've been in Cuba longer than you have, Theodore," Eva said.

"Edith might call me that," Teddy growled, "but my friends call me T.R., and sometimes Teddy. *You* are not my friend, despite the fact you know something of my family, and claim to have at least spoken to my late wife. You might be beautiful, Miss Eva, but that doesn't excuse your overfamiliarity with a man who's not granted you the right."

"Your pardon, sir," Eva said demurely, her voice remaining smooth. Teddy couldn't tell if it was guile or if the woman was simply that rare example of a female who couldn't be made to fluster. She looked at Teddy with her unnaturally symmetrical and penetrating eyes, and the entire establishment seemed to hang on her every word.

"Let's talk," Eva said, motioning her hand at a round table in the back.

The four of them quickly sat down. Teddy noticed that the

proprietor specifically did not come around the bar to ask any of the four if they wanted anything to drink, despite the heat.

"Alright," Teddy said. "Someone tell me what the constable was on about just now."

"He said he hasn't seen his son in three days," Deke replied. "Something about being taken by the shadows, and now all he's got left is his daughter."

"Good Lord," the redheaded Anderson said, his eyes watching the Cuban policeman. He'd slumped against the bar, and was quietly sobbing into a bloodied palm.

"That explains the man's distraught state," Roosevelt said. "But that doesn't explain—"

Eva cut him off.

"The creature you're looking for has a legendary history in this country, with roots going all the way back to the Iberian Peninsula itself. El Coco is . . . it is the monster under the bed, if I understand correctly what many American children grow up fearing?"

"No monster's mean enough to scare a bullet," Teddy said, patting his leather holster where his Colt M1892 No. 3 revolver was kept loaded.

"If pistols and rifles were good enough," Eva said warningly, "the people of this city would have dealt with the problem before you got here."

"And what," Teddy asked, pushing his glasses up his nose, "is a woman of your breeding doing in Santiago? Especially the day *after* the Spanish Army's abandoned it? Don't bother telling me you're from Spain, I can already tell that you're not. I hear hints of an accent in your voice, which I cannot quite place. Not British. Not Russian. German, maybe? I can speak and read German."

"I can speak and read a dozen languages," Eva said. "But that won't help me defeat my enemy, any more than cartridges in a carbine will help you defeat yours. And if I am right, our foe is the same."

"What the hell is this *El Loco* supposed to be, anyway?" Deke asked, his hands curled over each other beneath his chin. The old noncommissioned volunteer had become genuinely worried. Teddy could see it in Deke's eyes.

"Not *Loco,* Coco," Eva corrected him. "Easiest to think of the monster like something that hides in the shadows, until you blow out a candle. Then the darkness comes, and El Coco comes with it."

Deke scoffed. "Sounds like a bad, ol' spook story for scarin' kiddos. You believe this, sir?"

Teddy's eyes didn't blink. He simply stared at the woman across from him, and replied, "I might, Sergeant. Wood wanted me to handle this because of my time cleaning up New York. But what even he doesn't know—and I've not told anyone in the First Volunteers before now—is I had to clean up more than just the cops, or the crooks. I ran into something a lot worse, once. *Much* worse. Miss Eva, please continue."

"You're right," Eva said, turning to look at Deke. "El Coco *is* a tale often used to scare children. By generations of mothers and grandmothers especially, who needed to frighten unruly boys and girls into doing their chores, and going to sleep when told. But what the people of Santiago have learned these past two weeks is that El Coco is all too real."

"You said the constable at the bar couldn't tell us who this is," Deke said. "So how come *you're* able to tell us?"

"I have never married, and I can never have children," Eva said matter-of-factly.

"An extraordinarily lovely lady such as yourself, not married? Ever?" Teddy said, his disbelief plain on his face.

"No, never." Eva said. "And that insulates me, because El Coco will hunt the children of any adult foolish enough to utter its name. Which is why no one at this table can utter it. Not even under your breath."

"Well?" Teddy said, looking Sergeant Potter straight in the face. "You told me earlier that you had a bad feeling. And now I think I know why. It's the same thing making all these people stare at us like we're the coming of a plague. They think the war's done it, somehow. It brought this thing."

"Yes," Eva confirmed. "The locals are sure the war has conjured El Coco. And when children kept being taken even after the Spanish Army marched out, the Cubans of this city began to lose hope that El Coco would march out with them. At least in this particular part of town. Which is the poorest of any you'll see. No rich men suffering here. Just people already down on their luck."

"When I went to New York's worst boroughs," Teddy said, "I

saw people down on their luck like you wouldn't believe. And I made a damned difference. I'm going to make a difference here again, too."

Convincing the constable to lead Lieutenant Colonel Roosevelt to where the constable claimed his son had disappeared took no small effort on both Deke's and Eva's part. The two of them had to plead together—in emphatic Spanish—for the man to listen. And only Roosevelt paying the constable a sum in American silver dollars finally got them all moving. Out of the little eatery, many blocks southeast, and finally to a side street where chalk had been used to draw on the pavement, and the plaster was peeling from the walls.

English-to-Spanish translation—Teddy, to Deke, then the policeman, then to Deke, and back again—was tedious. But the Cuban cop seemed to have sobered a bit during their walk, and was now talking more clearly, his eyes moving rapidly, and his hands pointing this way and that.

"He says his son and his son's friends played here," Deke said. "Every day. With regularity. Now they're gone. This El Co—"

Eva's hand slapped over Deke's mouth before he could finish.

The old veteran gently pulled her hand back.

"Sorry," he said. "The monster got them. The boy's father panicked. Tried to bring a Catholic priest to undo what had been done, but it was too late."

"El . . . the monster took the kids out here?" Teddy asked skeptically. "I thought this thing hunted in the shadows."

The Cuban cop almost tore his hair out by two fists, then pointed to a doorway in the alley where it was so narrow it looked like the sun never touched. He said several more sentences in Spanish, then sat down at the spot and hugged his knees to his chest, his eyes looking terrified.

"He says his son was taken inside."

"This was his home?" Roosevelt asked.

"Yes," Potter translated. "And still is. He sent his daughter to be with his sister and her family, in a different part of the city. In case the . . . thing made a return visit."

Teddy grimaced, looking at the poor Cuban father.

"One thing I don't understand," Roosevelt said, turning to Eva. "How come this thing suddenly starts taking children now?"

"Someone opened a *portal*," she replied. "Using black magic, perhaps? El Coco was *called*. Once El Coco stepped through into this place, it was here to stay. Waiting for anyone to utter its name."

"You know far more about this legendary Spanish monster than any Brooklyn socialite should," Teddy observed.

"New York's a fascinating city," Eva said. "But I don't live there anymore. And I'm not just familiar with this legend, I'm here to *stop* El Coco."

"If guns can't stop it, what makes you think a woman can?" Deke asked bluntly.

"I'm not like any woman you've ever met, Sergeant," Eva said, and the tone in her voice told Teddy that she was quite serious. "I've been dealing with things from the other side since before any of you were born."

Now it was Teddy who scoffed. "You can't be a day over thirty."

"I suppose I should be flattered," Eva said. "But if I told you how old I really am, you'd never believe me."

"What did you mean by 'the other side'?" Anderson asked, continuing to take notes in his little travel ledger.

The Spanish cop muttered another couple of sentences, punctuated with the name *Diablo*.

"Beelzebub," Potter said gravely.

Eva tapped a gloved finger at the side of her nose.

"Very good, Sergeant."

"You mean we're dealing with literal *Satan*?" Anderson said, incredulous.

"Not Lucifer Morningstar himself, no," Eva replied, "but a servant of the darkness just the same. It prefers to take children because they're easy prey, and it additionally feeds on the anguish from the adults who're left behind. Every parent who's lost a child. Their sorrow is part of El Coco's sustenance. That, and the fear-soaked souls of the children."

"Have you seen it?" Teddy asked.

"Yes," Eva said. "At least twice."

"What does it look like?" Deke asked.

"It's very difficult to describe. You'd have to see for yourself. Also, you should see what it's done."

Eva said a few Spanish words to the Cuban cop, and he collected himself, stood up, then hesitantly opened the small door.

At two inches shy of six feet, Teddy had to stoop as he entered, as did Potter and Anderson, who came with him. The small hovel of a home looked to have not been lived in for several days. And there was tipped-over furniture in the tiny parlor, which also doubled as a kitchen. The Cuban policeman took them back to the two small bedrooms, one of which was clearly the father's, and the other belonged to the children. Or had, before being demolished from the inside. The two child-sized beds had been flipped, and smashed. As had the single side table. Dried wax was splattered where the candles had fallen. And there were long marks on the tile, and through the plaster on the walls, the sort Teddy couldn't associate with any animal he'd ever seen.

"A bear took this place apart," Anderson said, staring around the little bedroom with wide eyes.

"Even a grown yellow-backed grizzly couldn't do that," Sergeant Potter said, stooping. His sun-browned hand was somewhat wrinkled with age, and he passed his palm experimentally over the marks, letting his fingertips trace them while Roosevelt looked out the only window through which the light of the afternoon streamed. The glass was surprisingly intact.

"Didn't come in this way," Roosevelt said, testing the pane and latches.

"The marks start *and* end at the closet," Anderson said, pointing to the small, darkened entrance opposite where the beds had been—the door of which hung partially unhinged, with a huge crack down the middle.

"Ask him *exactly* what happened," Teddy instructed Deke.

The Cuban policeman spoke back and forth with Sergeant Potter for a couple of minutes.

"He said his daughter woke up in the middle of the night," Deke related in English. "Bad dream. She came to crawl in with Papa. They both fell asleep again. Then, some time later in the night, they both woke up to hearing her brother scream. An unholy sound, according to the father. He got a lantern going and brought both it and his revolver to bear, only to find his son gone, and..."

"Well?" Roosevelt said, noting Deke's pause, with a hard swallow.

"The eyes, sir. All he saw were the *red eyes,* looking out at him from the closet. He shot three times, and the eyes disappeared.

But when he threw what was left of the closet door wide, nothing was there. Not his son. Not the monster. Just three bullets lodged in the plaster."

Roosevelt tested the walls by slapping his palm on them several times.

"Brick, I'd guess," he said. "Not hollow."

Potter asked the policemen, then said, "Yessir. Solid brick all the way around. And the floor, too. Whoever—whatever—came to take his son, it got the boy. And left. Without so much as leaving a trace of itself. Except those *claw* marks."

"You claim to have seen this thing," Teddy said, turning his attention back to Eva, who'd mostly been spectating the proceedings.

"Yes," she said.

"*And?*" Teddy demanded.

"Like this man, in both cases I was too late. I only caught a glimpse. Yes, the red eyes. A demon's eyes."

The Cuban policeman began to weep uncontrollably and begged them all to leave his home. Once outside he slammed the door shut, and locked it.

Twice more that afternoon Lieutenant Colonel Roosevelt allowed himself to be led to the homes of the victimized. And in each place, the signs were the same, with similarly traumatized parents. All of whom seemed to assume—as the policeman had—that their children were lost, and that the parents themselves were to blame for having inadvertently invoked El Coco. Who came in the night to steal their sons and daughters, never to return again.

As the sun began to drop in the western half of the sky, Roosevelt and his group found themselves back where they'd started, though everyone in the place had departed. Save the proprietor, who kept glancing out the doorway at the slanting rays of the sun, and muttering unhappily under his breath.

"Why would these parents call for you?" Teddy asked Eva. "You said earlier that you considered this thing to be an enemy. There was a familiar quality to that pronouncement which needs explaining."

Eva looked squarely at Roosevelt and asked, "Why are *you* in Cuba, sir?"

"The *Maine*," Teddy replied defiantly. "When she went up in Havana harbor, it was my duty to act."

"But you weren't under orders from President McKinley."

"No, ma'am, I resigned my position under John Long, and along with Colonel Wood—now Brigadier General—set about rallying our men."

"Let's just say," Eva replied, "that we're both volunteers in our own separate wars, sir. You felt moved to take up arms against the tyranny of colonial Spain, I've taken up arms against another kind of tyranny. Purely of my own mind and by my own will."

"Your pardon, ma'am," Anderson said, "but you're a *lady.* The prettiest any of us have seen since leaving the boat. What business does a lady have in war? Especially if it involves monsters?"

Eva breathed deeply, then slowly exhaled.

"You three have to swear on your honor as Soldiers of the United States, to not utter a word about me to any of your superiors. If news of my existence got to the wrong people in your government, it could result in catastrophe. For you three. For many others, too."

"How do you mean?" Teddy demanded.

"Just swear it," Eva insisted again. "Then I'll tell you why I'm here."

Teddy looked from Potter, to Anderson, then back again, and made them both do it. Followed by himself.

"Thank you," Eva said, then her mesmerizing eyes took on an especially keen-edged quality, "I'm more dangerous than you can imagine. In some ways I'm actually *worse* than El Coco."

"Explain why," Teddy pressed her.

"I was made, not born," Eva replied. "By a man living and working in a country very far from here. I was his client's slave, for a time. Then, I was made the slave of others. Until finally I became free. Your man Franklin arranged it."

"Franklin who?" Sergeant Potter asked.

"Benjamin, to be exact," Eva said without flinching. "Intelligent old man. Part statesman, part physician, part philosopher, and part tinkerer."

Lieutenant Colonel Roosevelt wanted to call her a liar, but somehow her gaze upon him had a chilling effect. She was being completely and thoroughly serious, and the lack of a smile on her lips told him that there was no jest in her statement.

"Can you kill El... it?" Anderson asked, fascinated by the beautiful older woman's story.

"I don't yet know," Eva admitted. "Every time I set myself to hunting something from the other side, it's a new challenge. War in the mortal world has an unfortunate tendency to stir up the war with the nether world. So, when the Cubans began rebelling, I made my way here, through the Spanish embassy, learning after I'd arrived that an alarm over El Coco had already started among the working poor. I promised the Cubans I could help stop this demon. Twice, I was too late. Then, I heard that the Americans were sending an experienced officer to investigate El Coco's activity. So, I knew I had to find you. To try to talk you out of tackling the monster all on your own."

"We've already proven we're no cowards," Teddy stated firmly. "Even young Corporal Anderson here was with us going up San Juan Hill. And we're not about to show ourselves yellow now. Major General Wheeler won't tolerate the peace being broken so soon after United States forces have begun to garrison the city. Especially not by some evil *thing* taking tots from their mothers."

As if on cue, the shrill scream of a woman was heard outside.

Eva moved so fast, Teddy and his men were barely out of their seats by the time she had cleared the door and was out in the street. Her long dress seemingly unable to hold back her strides, which were Olympian, considering the distance she covered in so short a time.

A grandmotherly old Cuban woman was shaking and shouting. Her hand aimed to a front stoop just a few doors down. Teddy found himself huffing as he tried to keep up. He was more accustomed to the saddle than a foot chase, and he let both Anderson and Potter get ahead of him while they followed Eva into the home.

What Lieutenant Colonel Roosevelt saw after finally crossing the threshold almost made his knees wobble. At the top of the little Cuban home's single staircase, a truly unspeakable phantom dangled two small children by the neck. They were each squealing with fear, while their mother and father cowered at the bottom of the stairs, pleading in Spanish.

It had no shape like any man nor beast Teddy had ever encountered. Rather, the darkness itself seemed to have come alive of its own accord. The coal-black appendages that held the two children seemed like articulated gouts of oil, and two bright points like burning stove coals glared down at Teddy. As if he were being eyeballed by the Evil One himself. A hideous burst of what Roosevelt would forever remember as the most wicked laughter he'd ever heard rang down at them all like the Spanish bullets from San Juan Hill. And for a brief moment Lieutenant Colonel Roosevelt forgot himself, forgot the mission, and even forgot the war—struck dumb by the sight of something that at once could not be seen, but which also promised to haunt Teddy's nightmares until the end of his days.

Only Eva seemed to be able to withstand the monster's palpably terrible presence.

When she opened her mouth to speak, the language that came off her tongue wasn't like any Earthly language of men. It hissed and sizzled like red iron hitting the trough at Hell's own forge. An ear-breaking string of words that could have been a challenge, or a curse. Perhaps both?

The black and formless demon seemed to shudder and recoil, almost dropping the two children from its clawlike clutches. Then another burst of that awful, pounding laughter battered every human ear. Followed by what could only be a fiendish rebuke—directed at Eva in particular.

For the first time since coming ashore, Teddy Roosevelt was scared stiff. Going into the teeth of the Spanish guns at the top of San Juan Hill had been a thing of joy by comparison. He'd experienced the zeal of battle. Carrying him completely past any sense of his own mortality or danger. But this? This was something else altogether. Worse by far than what Teddy had faced in New York. El Coco's presence was so hateful it almost seemed to make the air vibrate with malice.

"Fool!" Eva spat back at the black shape, this time in English. "I haven't served the Master in well over a century, and will not answer the Master's demand for allegiance—least of all that which is spoken by *you!* Unhand the mortals, and face a proper challenge from one who knows the Master's spawn!"

Out of the corner of his eye, Teddy saw Eva's arms pulled back and outstretched, her fingers taking on the appearance of talons. How a woman so lovely could suddenly assume the guise of something so ghastly was another image Teddy would remember for the rest of his life. She'd ceased to be a lady and become something else.

The air was concussed by another exchange of Hellish dialogue between Eva and her foe, the children flailing helplessly in the monster's grip.

Finally, Teddy dragged his body from its momentary paralysis, snatching his revolver from its holster. He aimed at the eyes of the thing—and away from the two children suspended to either side—then pulled the double-action trigger four, quick times. Shots that would have doubled up any normal man and sent him plunging lifelessly down the stairs. Just like the Spaniard Teddy had boasted over, when the fight to take San Juan Hill was concluded.

But Roosevelt's revolver seemingly did nothing except fill the stairwell with sulfur-smelling smoke, while leaving a bad ringing in Teddy's ears.

When the monster laughed this time, it was practically volcanic in quality. And the creature leaned itself out over the stairwell, at once threatening the mortals crowded at the bottom, and taunting them with the still-suspended children, who flailed about like little rag dolls, their shrieks piteous and awful.

Eva launched herself at the monster, flying up the stairs as if her feet never touched the steps—the expression on her face becoming one of total rage. She slashed both of her arms at El Coco, her clawed hands coming away with what appeared to be tar-filled globs of blackly smoldering ichor.

The yowl of pain from the thing shook the entire residence.

This time, the children were dropped. And Teddy just barely had the reflexes to dive to catch the little girl, his spectacles barely hanging on while Anderson caught the little boy.

More pistol shots. Deke Potter's gun. An older Colt Single-Action Army .45-caliber sidearm. Whether Deke hit or missed, Teddy could not tell, as he rolled partially back down the stairs, with the little Cuban girl shielded by his body. He came to rest with a *thump,* then Anderson *thump*ed next to him, and there was a banshee's wail like nothing any mortal ear could imagine.

Before, suddenly, quiet.

Then sobs. Little, terrified sobs.

Lieutenant Colonel Roosevelt uncurled himself from around the Cuban girl, and allowed her mother to reach down and pick her up. Both of them were bawling hysterically while the father rolled Anderson over, to retrieve his son.

Teddy got onto his hands and knees, and was horrified to see

Anderson's face. The young corporal's eyes were locked open in a moment of supreme surprise, and his lips were almost white. Trembling.

"I... I think it got me, sir," the young volunteer whispered.

Teddy immediately splayed Anderson out, his hands searching for the wound, as he'd trained to do back in Texas. But there was no saber gash. No bullet hole. Teddy flipped Anderson onto his side, and saw the long, black mark cleanly splitting the young trooper's uniform shirt down the back. It traveled through skin, muscle, and bone. Almost like a white-hot scythe cauterizing as it went, across spine and ribs alike.

"My brothers," Anderson gasped. "Tell my brothers in Idaho, sir. Tell 'em I done it *right.* Tell 'em..."

And when he went limp in Roosevelt's grasp, Teddy knew it was over.

"Gawddammit," Deke Potter drawled, getting to his feet, and looking down at the dead young volunteer. "Seen too many kids like him go over the years. Way too many."

The mother and father fled out their front door, letting it hang open. A large crowd of Cubans had formed in the street. Some holding lanterns. A few holding torches to light the way, against the gloaming.

Teddy reverently let the lifeless Anderson's head down onto the floor, and stood up. Then he and Sergeant Potter looked up to the top of the stairs, where Eva knelt, her arms still spread wide, fingers aimed forward like the natural weapons of a hawk, and a strange, unsettling growl coming from her throat. There was no sign of the monster. Teddy took an oil lamp from the bottom landing, before he and Potter proceeded cautiously up the stairs. Teddy gently reached out a hand to touch the woman on the shoulder.

She spun around so fast the human eye could scarcely register the movement, revealing the front of her dress torn asunder. And a wound not unlike that which had killed Anderson tracing from her left collarbone down across one breast, through her stomach, to end at a hip. Except, unlike Anderson, she was still alive and well. Or at least as well as could be perceived, given the unnerving expression on her face—like someone or something possessed.

There was not a trace of El Coco.

"What in hell happened?" Deke asked. "Ma'am?!"

Teddy reached out a hand to touch the beginning of the wound at her collar, and she slapped him away with stinging force.

"Forget it," she barked. "It will heal. In time. I *always* heal. Part of Dippel's genius."

"No blood," Deke Potter observed.

"How—" Teddy started, but sound from outside interrupted him. Voices of the crowd. Shock and fear beginning to transform into rage.

"Please, Deke, tell me you can talk to those people," Teddy asked, helping Eva get to her feet while she sashed up the front of her gown.

"They won't dare attack us," she said sternly. "As long as you're with me, you won't be harmed. Either of you."

"Anderson's body—" Deke said.

"You can give him a hero's burial later," she said unceremoniously. "Right now? We have to get to El Coco's lair."

"How do you know where that thing hides?!" Roosevelt asked.

"I didn't know, before tonight," Eva said. "But we've exchanged blows at last. I've held El Coco's essence in my hands. *Now* I know. And I can tell you the children it's taken aren't dead, either. Though they're likely in a state some might consider worse than dead."

The cemetery was old. Crypts and mausoleums of the formerly wealthy mixed with the headstones and simple wooden crosses of the formerly poor. All made equal in the sight of God, once the great leveler of death had come. Except, tonight, something very undead had chosen the cemetery for a home, and Roosevelt and Potter had ridden like mad—Eva holding onto Roosevelt's waist as she clung to his back, telling him which avenues to take—to reach it.

She'd not even let Roosevelt stop to give proper greeting and attain recognition at two different US checkpoints, which had thankfully been manned by other Volunteers. If those posts had been Regular Army under Major General Shafter, the men might not have recognized Roosevelt's high-pitched cries for them to hold their fire.

Now dismounted, the two men kept their sidearms drawn as they followed Eva through the cemetery. Moonlight cast eerie shadows among the graves, giving the place a ghostly quality that made Teddy's hair stand on end. There'd been nothing in his Reformed Dutch church experience to prepare him for coming face-to-face with the otherworldly El Coco. Much less a woman who seemed in some ways to be El Coco's equal. Enough to hurt it.

"I'm not sure we need to be quiet," Eva spoke normally. "A stealth approach may not matter."

"The patrols of Volunteers who're sure to follow us here will matter one hell of a lot," Teddy promised. "It won't take long for word of our charge through the streets to stir the men. They know me. If they think I'm onto some action, you won't be able to hold them back."

"Which is why we need to finish El Coco before they get here," Eva said grimly. "Or you'll be putting more young men like Anderson into their graves by daylight."

"How is it possible my bullets can't touch the damned thing," Teddy asked, "but you can do it harm with your bare hands?"

"I told you who I was," Eva replied. "No woman's womb birthed me. I was *made*. Johann Konrad Dippel created me before your country even existed, sir. And I remain a made thing—though more than a few of the Adversary's children have tried to unmake me since that time. El Coco being just the latest. The Adversary's children do hold a hell of a grudge."

"You talk like you were a demon yourself," Deke said.

"I was one of the third who became Fallen," Eva said. "We were denied bodies, on account of Lucifer Morningstar's war with God. And I'd have stayed that way, except for Dippel's experiments. Seeing an opportunity for a body, I took it. Dippel thought he'd made the Landgrave a perfect spouse. Then, when I proved far from perfect, they made me into a slave. To be used as a weapon against men and empires."

"Until Benjamin Franklin," Teddy said, still somewhat unbelieving.

"Yes," Eva said, walking carefully, but with determination—turning this way and that through the cemetery, as if by invisible dousing rod. "Old Ben gave me my liberty."

"Liberty to do what?" Teddy asked.

"Anything I wanted," Eva replied. "And, at first, I wanted nothing to do with men, nor wars, nor anything at all. But that kind of isolation gets boring. And I could feel that the world was changing. Events were multiplying. When the Confederate States of America fired on Fort Sumter, I knew I had to come out of hiding—though I couldn't come *too* far out. There is another one like me. Who, if he learned of my existence, would seek to destroy not just me, but all he suspected of aiding and abetting me."

"You have a brother?" Deke asked.

"A *predecessor,*" Eva replied, being specific with her wording. "He actually works for your government. I decided to devote myself abroad—where there was much less chance of his path crossing mine, but I could still do similar work. Freelance, if you will. The arcs of mortal and immortal history are bending closer and closer together, such that labor like this is becoming plentiful. Once El Coco is dispatched, I will move on to the next."

"Hell of a way to make a living," Teddy remarked.

"Not a living, sir," Eva said. "A recompense. Hopefully. If God truly is merciful."

The crypt at which they arrived was a particularly large one. With large stone doors barring their path.

"Now we'll *have* to wait for our men to catch up," Teddy said, looking the place over more by feel than by eye. "It'll take several strong boys to dislodge the rock."

"And then what, sir?" Deke asked, putting his revolver in its holster. "Neither your shots nor mine seemed to touch that thing. I am not sure what more good we can do."

"The children," Eva reminded. "If I am right, they're here."

"Sure, we try to rescue the kids. But if the monster kills you before you can kill it?" Teddy asked, stopping her with a hand before she could get her fingertips into the crevice between the crypt's doors.

"Dippel did his work almost too well," Eva said. "*Nothing's* killed me. Not men. Not evil things that put terror into the hearts of men."

With that, she applied her full strength. Impossibly, the stone doors slowly, grindingly swung open. Revealing absolute and total blackness within.

Teddy almost expected El Coco to strike. If the thing throve in darkness, few places in Cuba were darker than this. But no monster came. Indeed, there was no sound at all. He'd managed to retain the oil lamp from the residence where El Coco had attacked, and with the strike of a match, he relit it. Giving them a dim view of the stone stairway that led down into the ground below.

"I've had mountain cats half about to eat me, scare me less than that," Deke remarked, aiming his finger down the stone steps.

"You and me both, Sergeant," Teddy said, and held out a hand—offering for Eva to lead the way.

She reached to her knees and forcefully ripped away the tattered lower half of her dress, then used a scrap of it to re-sash the front where she'd been struck prior. Also, her golden-blond hair was now out of its pins, and badly tousled by the ride, its broad curls going every which way. And her otherwise immaculate skin merely scuffed, where it should have been badly bruised.

They went down three stories and were met with an underground series of hewn passageways. Where the topsoil had given way to the rock of the hillside on which the cemetery had been placed, back when the city was first founded.

"El Coco could not have created these," Eva said, reaching out a hand to grasp Teddy's wrist, and bringing his lamp close to one of the walls. A series of carved and painted symbols were on the rock, looking not too unlike the tribal etchings Teddy himself had seen when he went West as a younger man. Except what they depicted—ritual sacrifices—made him curl his lip and turn away.

"They worshipped and made human offerings to the damned thing," Lieutenant Colonel Roosevelt spat.

"The mortal societies you call pagan often did," Eva said matter-of-factly. "Though El Coco is not a devourer of bodies. It would have wanted the *emotions* of its ritual victims. Like spices and sweeteners. Fear, terror, anguish, these are all potent 'flavors' for El Coco's ethereal diet."

"Is this what it's doing to the kids?" Deke asked, looking at the carvings.

"I think El Coco has a different use for the young ones. If we can find them soon enough, it might not be too late. El Coco may not have drained them past the point at which they become the living dead."

"Christ protect us," Deke breathed, as they moved deeper into the passages.

"Yes," Eva simply replied.

They stopped short of one corner, around which a very faint light seemed to be coming. Teddy motioned with his hands for Eva and Deke to wait. He then extinguished the lamp and waited for their eyes to fully to the dark. Then they all carefully spied around the edge of the rock, and got a full view of the ritual chamber beyond.

Half a dozen grown men and women were arrayed around a stone altar, the likes of which Teddy had never seen described in any antiquarian's text. A faint, nondescript, cold glow emanated from the altar, around which bleached bones were piled. Above the altar, floating like a visible miasma, was an inky, amorphous cloud. The half dozen people around the altar were audibly moaning something that sounded like gibberish to Teddy's ears. Not English, nor French, nor Spanish. Not even Latin. Each man and woman was bare to the waist, and each was caked with mud-painted pictograms from neck to navel.

"Now we know who brought El Coco forth," Eva whispered to her allies. "The Catholic church did a lot to stamp out pagan practices on this island. But a few of the old cultists kept their traditions alive. Probably passed down through families. They've decided to put the old ways back into practice."

"Oh my God," Deke breathed. "Look."

Without needing to be pointed in their direction, Teddy instantly saw the problem. Over a score of young Cubans were standing motionless on a grid carved into the chamber's rock floor. The same strange, cold light from the altar also seemed to emanate from the lines of the grid, and each child appeared frozen in place. Eyes rolled up into the backs of their eye sockets. Little mouths twisted into cries for which there was no sound.

"Behold," Eva whispered. "El Coco *feasts*."

"Gawddammit," Deke drawled for the second time that night.

"Yes, I think He does," Eva breathed.

The three pulled back from the edge of the rock, and there in the blackness they deliberated in tones so hushed, Teddy could barely hear.

"It's making sense now," Eva whispered. "El Coco's cult is reborn. They not only gave him an entrance to the mortal plane, they also serve as his anchor in this world. He feeds on the children, but the cultists give him status. We kill them, El Coco's cord may be cut. He will no longer be able to travel the shadows of Cuba, taking the children of those who speak his name."

Teddy pulled out his revolver by feel—having reloaded upon their initial arrival at the cemetery—and reached out with an opposite hand to tap Deke's shoulder.

"Six shots apiece," Teddy said. "Even with misses, we oughta be able to get 'em."

"Yessir," Deke said, and pulled out his own revolver. "But I'm sure after the first shot, El Coco's going to notice."

"Leave that to me," Eva replied.

The three of them peered back around the corner, and Deke crouched to aim, while Teddy braced himself directly above Deke, also aiming. In the dim light, it was almost impossible to see the front sight post, especially with his bad eyes. But Teddy slowed and then stopped his breathing, gradually brought back the hammer on his revolver, then gently applied pressure to the trigger.

Two gunshots rang out simultaneously, but only one of the cultists fell.

Again, Teddy's ears were ringing.

After that, everything was a literal blur. Cultists diving and scampering. More gunshots. Teddy walking directly out into the opening, with one fist on his hip and pistol raised so that he was sighting straight down his arm. *BLAM! BLAM! BLAM!*

A fluttering of cloth whirled past Roosevelt's shoulder, and Eva was half flying at the swirling ink blot suspended above the altar—the coal-glowing eyes of which had at once spun around to face the two US Volunteers, and then Eva herself as she came on. It reached out tendrils of itself to try to ensnare her, but her fingers were once again curved like sabers, and as the monster tried to slash her, she slashed it.

Meanwhile, Teddy's cylinder went empty. *Click, click, click!*

"Reload while I cover!" Deke yelled, and his boss took a knee to upend the No. 3 and slam the ejection rod, pouring the empty .38-caliber casings onto the stone. Then he reached to his cartridge box on his belt.

Deke's shadow advanced forward, until his .45-caliber Colt also went dry. *Click!*

"Aw hell," Deke said, and suddenly two of the cultists were tackling him.

"Sergeant!" Teddy bellowed, and snapped his pistol's cylinder shut before he could get all six chambers full. Two cartridges clattered uselessly to the ground. But Teddy came to his feet and advanced on the two mud-painted people raising knives over their heads to strike down at Potter's exposed chest.

Click, click! Then, *BOOM! BOOM!*—chest, head—*BOOM! BOOM!*—chest, head.

Forever after, Teddy would recount that he hadn't consciously chosen the sequence. Knowing he didn't have a full cylinder, he'd simply aimed and pulled the trigger at almost point-blank range, wanting to incapacitate each of his enemies with assurance they wouldn't get back up again.

Teddy then reached out his free arm and grabbed Potter's extended hand. Helping the sergeant to his feet.

Five mud-painted bodies were on the rock, now. Pools of blood spreading from their fatal wounds. Where the sixth cultist had fled, Teddy couldn't be sure. The light from the altar seemed to be sputtering and guttering. Almost like an electric bulb back home, when it was nearing the end of its usable service life.

The scorching language of the underworld—which Eva and El Coco had exchanged between them before—was heard once more. As a wounded Eva clutched at both her side and leg, while the also-wounded monster bore the full force of its hateful gaze down on her. Spewing hellish invectives, the likes of which no mortal ear could decipher—until at last an anguished, deafening scream went up from the thing, the altar beneath it went dark, and then it simply winked out of existence.

It was pitch black. Teddy couldn't see a thing, though he could hear both himself and Potter breathing heavily.

"Did we do it, sir?" Potter asked, gulping for air.

"I don't know yet," Teddy admitted, also gulping for air.

Then came the sudden cries and shrieks of children, disorientated and terrified. Deke barked for quiet—with as much stern care as he could muster in Spanish—but it wasn't any good. The children were panicking, and following the voices of the two grown men until Teddy and Deke were surrounded by desperate, grasping little hands.

"Gotta get back to that lamp!" Teddy shouted.

"Yessir," Deke said. "But these tykes won't let go!"

Blessedly, several lamps presented themselves at the entrance to the ritual chamber. The Rough Riders had come.

"It's Colonel Roosevelt!" one of them shouted. "Sir, are we glad to find you. And Deke! Dammit, Deke, when we found Anderson dead, we thought the worst."

"How many men did you bring with you, Bill?" Teddy asked, remembering the identity and voice of the young captain of Volunteers who now greeted him.

"Just a squad with me, sir. But a platoon up top. And more coming."

"Help us get these kids out of here!" Sergeant Potter barked. And then remembered himself, with a quick, "Sir."

One by one, the terrified, hungry, parched children were peeled off of Roosevelt and Potter, then taken back the way the Rough Riders had come. Until it was just Roosevelt and his noncommissioned friend left to examine the scene.

Five of the six cultists had been shot. Teddy and Deke's handiwork. While the missing and final cultist had been strangled to death just beyond and to the side of the ritual chamber's entrance—a long piece of cloth torn from Eva's gown, wrapped several times around the man's neck like a noose, and his eyes bugging out of his skull.

Eva was nowhere to be found. And when Teddy called her name, he was answered with only silence.

Lamp still in hand, they went back to examine the dead.

"We'll take them far from this place, and burn the bodies," Teddy determined. "Scatter the ashes."

"Yessir," Deke said. "Meanwhile, what about the she-beast?"

"She-beast?" Teddy said, raising an eyebrow.

"Not sure what else to call a gal who can garrote a man with a scrap of her ballroom best," Deke said, pointing back at the man who'd been strangled.

Teddy allowed himself a bit of a smirk.

"Deke, I would not place bets on us seeing her again. Sounds to me like she's eager to not be found. However, she's taught us about a much bigger fight I'd not—to this point in my life—been fully aware of. We owe her for that. Just as we owe her our sworn silence."

"What about El Loco?" Deke asked. "The men will want an explanation, as will General Wheeler."

"That's a different matter," Teddy said confidently. "You leave the official story to me. Then I'm going to talk to some people in the War Department when we return to the States. Maybe I'll even take it up to the President himself? This is the second time in my professional life I've had to deal with what I'd call unearthly trouble. I have a feeling Washington, DC, might be in for more of the same. You heard what Eva told us: events are multiplying."

I despise vampires. They're the worst. —A.L.

Friday Night Wights

LawDog

Angela

We staged ourselves at the only truck stop that served decent coffee in a twenty-mile radius. Officially, we were standing by, waiting on a pair of Newbies to arrive from the Lubbock International Airport. Unofficially, we were on a break from an ongoing vampire hunt, and I wasn't stupid enough to have my team out in the field before the sun came up.

The residual heat from the day before still radiated gently off the cracked concrete as the faint carmine blush of Before Morning Nautical Twilight lightened the eastern horizon. I sat on the trailer next to the Bobcat S450, sipping my extra-large, extra-sugar, extra-creamer, extra-everything coffee.

Beside me, Miggy maintained his usual phlegmatic look as he sipped meditatively from an ancient convenience store mug the size of a wine butt.

Ten feet away, Tully swore under his breath as he checked the tie-downs in the ordnance trailer. I appreciated his caution: something coming loose back there would be a headache we'd probably never notice until we'd spread half our gear across the desert.

I'm Angela Wainwright, Team Very Large Mammals, and I do a fair bit of business for MHI. We don't suck at it

Luis

"Damn it, Danny, quit squirming!"

Danny Hudson had the grace to look abashed. He gestured at the cramped confines of the car. "Sorry, Luis, but..."

We had specifically requested the largest vehicle the rideshare program had—Danny and I were both over six foot tall—and of course, they sent a Toyota pocket rocket.

I sighed and looked at my marine brother. True to form, his boot ass looked around in delight. I sighed again. That man wore the same expression as when I'd first seen him on the bus to MCRD Parris Island, and very little—not Marine Corps training, not deployments to the Sandbox, not fighting a hyena-ghoul-demon-thing in Iraq, and not Newbie training at Cazador—ever dimmed that sunny outlook.

Our driver, a sleepy-eyed college kid, looked dubiously at us in the rearview mirror. "You want me to take you from the airport...to a truck stop?" I could see questions flit across his face. We were in Texas, and he probably recognized the smell of gun oil from the duffel bags in the trunk. And in the cases across our laps, and the carry-ons...

"Yes, please," I said, trying to be polite. "About how long?"

"Maps app says nineteen minutes. At this time of the morning, closer to fifteen."

Thank you, God.

Beside me, Danny elbowed me in the ribs as he fished through his pocket. He pulled something out and ran his fingers across it. I frowned. It was a small PVC patch, round and white, with a hot pink border, and pink details. Lettering across the top of it said "MHI 1895," and across the bottom: VERY LARGE MAMMALS. In the center was a cheerful *chibi* T. rex, with a bow on its head and a cheerleader skirt, holding one of those old cartoon round bombs with the lit fuse.

I had known there was very little chance that we would get assigned to Harbinger's team, and I'm not against women, but choosing a pink cartoon character for the team patch didn't seem to indicate to me that the team leader was serious about monster hunting. And damn it, part of me had hoped that Harbinger would pick us. I'd been hiding my disappointment ever since

Z had handed us our Team assignments and patches, but I was pretty sure Danny was perceptive enough to pick up on it.

Beside me, Danny watched the stars gradually fade as the eastern horizon brightened. At fifteen minutes on the dot, we pulled into the parking lot of a truck stop. "Ayo," grunted the driver, somewhat more sleepily than I'd like. "Main building, or what?"

"Give us a sec," I murmured, fishing in my pocket for my cell phone. Then Danny nudged me and pointed with his chin at two big Ford pickups pulling trailers off on the far side of the lot all by themselves.

A big guy wearing MHI armor hopped out of the trailer and stretched his back. I tapped our driver and pointed. He blinked at me a couple of times before he pulled the Corolla across the lot and stopped by the trailer carrying what looked like a little bulldozer. Danny whacked me on the shoulder and bailed out like a golden retriever in a human suit, bouncing up to the guy before I could squeeze out of the cramped back seat.

"Y'all the Newbies?"

"Yes, sir! Danny Hudson! That's Luis Sevilla, reporting!"

The man in the armor shook his head, gently. An older guy, with thick gray hair and a thicker white beard, he was slimmer than us but tall. Tall enough to look me in the eye, and I stand at six and a half feet in my socks. "I'm not a 'sir.'" His pale eyes flashed behind reading glasses. "I'm Tully. Tully Roberts. Grab your gear."

As Danny and I unloaded the duffel bags and gear bags from the trunk of the Corolla, Tully knocked on the driver's window and handed him a folded-up bill. "Why don't you head on back into town and go get yourself breakfast for a couple of hours?"

Behind Tully, another man and a rather petite woman, both wearing armor, walked up. The rideshare driver looked at the armor and the guns, slowly took the fifty from Tully, nodded, then drove quickly out of the lot.

The other man stood every bit as tall and as old as Tully. He had the heavier build of a strength trainer, with a firm handshake to match. "Miguel Gonzalez. Call me Miggy." He gestured to the woman beside him. "This is the boss."

I blinked. Team Leader Angela Wainwright was freakin' tiny.

Angela

I looked at the new kids and sighed. Earl Harbinger is one of my oldest and dearest friends, but nobody can run a joke into the ground like he can. Of course, both kids were gorillas. Earl hadn't sent me a Newbie under six-foot-four since he stuck me with a team, because, you know, it's funny to surround your five-foot-tall Team leader with kaijus. Identifying all my team members by staring up at their nose hair was getting old.

The blond one, Danny Hudson from Kentucky, bounced up and gently took my hand, almost vibrating with excitement. His buddy, Luis Sevilla from Florida, wasn't quite as enthusiastic, and held back. Ah, well.

"Ma'am, I have read all of your reports, and it is a pleasure to meet you." Danny shook my hand with all the enthusiasm of a Labrador puppy. "It's an honor to be on your team." Luis just gave a hesitant nod.

"All right, boys." I gently pried my hand loose from Danny's giant paw. "Bathroom is in the truck stop—get coffee and something to eat. We've got water, so don't worry about that. Use the trailer to change into your gear and arm up. We'll do a quick brief when you're ready."

The Newbies looked at the stop. Then the blond kid grabbed their gear and bounced into the ordnance trailer. Luis moved with considerably less urgency. Miggy looked impassively at me over his glasses. I raised my eyebrow at him. "I know, Miggy."

"A five-man team against two baby vampires is a bad idea, *Doña* Angie. Especially when two of the team are Newbies."

I reached up, way up, and patted his Kris Kringle beard. "What do you want me to do, Miggy?"

Behind me, Tully cleared his throat. "S3 is dealing with a chupacabra outbreak in Phoenix. TALON has a luska down by Corpus. The Los Alamos team . . . I didn't understand half the words they used, but they sounded pretty flustered. And we're still on hold with MCB."

I put my thumbs in the armholes of my armor and shifted my shoulders. "Burke's still got six months of rehab after the surgery on his busted leg, and Rogneby's ribs have him down for at least a month. Earl is not going to let LaForce back into the field until Gretchen figures out why his nose keeps falling off, and the only folks he can spare are those two Newbies."

I smiled gently at Miggy. "We play the cards that we're dealt, old friend."

He snorted at me in frustration, and then the Newbies climbed out of the trailer, the blond kid smoothing the team patch down on the front of his armor, smiling. The other one, I noticed, hadn't put his patch on. Not that I blamed him—what red-blooded marine monster hunter expected a hot-pink-and-white patch with a cartoon dinosaur on it? But it was a gift from boys long dead.

"Okay, guys, bring it in. About four months ago, MCB rolled up a vampire nest just outside of Minneapolis, only it looks like they missed one of the babies. About a month after the op, a baby vampire hit a small town down I-35. About every two weeks or so, he hits another small town, and he stayed on I-35 until Oklahoma City. Then he pulled a sneaky on us and switched to I-40. At Amarillo, he did it again and hooked south on I-27."

Luis frowned and narrowed his eyes. *Sharp, that one,* I thought, and nodded at him. "Yeah. This one has a distinctive pattern."

I took a deep breath, let it out slowly. "Every two weeks, he goes to a small-town high school. Once there, he finds a girl student, either a junior or a senior, who is an outcast."

I took a slow sip of my coffee, not thinking about what we had been finding.

Tully cleared his throat. "Once he finds his victim, he turns her. Then he sets her loose on the popular kids. And, apparently, watches the slaughter."

I shook my head gently. "Night before last, we took a scientific hairy-assed guess and crashed a high-school barn party. Turns out that we're pretty good at guessing, because we got there just as the screaming started."

I shivered, remembering the screams, and I noticed Luis the Newbie frown at me before he turned his eyes to Tully. I ignored the look and went on. "We know that the newest vampire was there, and we're pretty sure that Vampire Prime was there to watch the butchery, but both of them got away in the fight. Fortunately, we got a drone on one of the surviving wights. Unfortunately, the one we tagged was pretty badly wounded, so it took until dark last night for it to go to earth in what we think is the newest nest."

I rapped my knuckles softly on the fender of the Ford. "We do not take on a vampire nest—I don't care how young they are—during the night. Not unless we absolutely have to."

I nodded to the east. "Sun's coming up. Time to go to work."

Luis

Tully Roberts drove quietly. After showing me where to stow my gear and offering me a water, he didn't say much for the rest of the trip. Tall, skinny, with a close-cropped gray beard and longer hair, he didn't look like my mental image of a veteran monster hunter.

Without any conversation, I watched the Texas landscape pass by the window. The pickup ahead of us kicked up an odd pale gray dust that lingered in the air. It damned sure wasn't Florida-flat—flat enough that you could stand on a tuna can and watch your dog run away for three days.

Finally, we came to a break in the sagging barbed-wire fence, and the truck thrummed as we drove over a pipe cattle guard before Tully came to a stop in the middle of the road behind the other truck. Ahead of us, the road went another two hundred yards in a gentle curve to the left, before ending up in front of a dilapidated one-story farmhouse.

Tully took a last swig from his travel mug. "Caliche road," he grunted. "You'll see if anything is under it, but take a good look at anywhere you want to put your feet, especially when you step out of the truck. And don't step off the road unless you've got a buddy with you." He unholstered a 1911, opened his door, and with the pistol aimed at the dirt, stepped gingerly out of the truck.

That seemed a little extreme and I rolled my eyes. I got out and followed him up to the lead vehicle. As we got there, I heard the buzz of a quadcopter drone taking off. Ms. Wainwright and Danny were looking at a tablet mounted to the center console of the truck as Miggy deftly moved the joysticks on a game controller, and the shifting video feed on the tablet showed that he was controlling the drone. Ms. Wainwright ran her finger across the tablet's touchpad, clicked an icon, and altered the feed, causing thermal signatures to appear on the screen. In the back seat, I heard Danny take an appreciative breath. Wainwright tapped the screen with a closely trimmed nail. "That's one."

Where she tapped was showing as rough oval. Danny and I both squinted at it. It looked for all the world like a . . ."Is that a grave?" asked Danny quietly.

"Of a sort. That's probably a wight hiding under a thin layer of dirt. It's an old vampire trick for guarding a nest. Miggy, do a slow circuit."

With the thermal overlay, it was quite easy to see three more graves.

Miggy made a thoughtful noise. "Nine missing from the school. Eight wights, one baby vampire, and Baby Vampire Prime. Not the worst we've seen, *Doña* Angie."

She looked at him over her sunglasses, then turned to Tully and me. "They put two veteran Hunters in the hospital last night. Be careful. And remember your eyes and ears."

Tully nodded, jerked his head at me, and we went back to our vehicle. Tully pulled around Miggy's truck and we drove up the road, toward the bright orange drone hovering gently in front of the house. Miggy's truck pulled up to our right, and Ms. Wainwright climbed out through the passenger side window onto the roof of the cab, AR-style rifle in hand.

Tully reached into the back seat and retrieved a black Cordura case, unzipped it, and began screwing the shaft of a spear together. I recognized it from Newbie training: eight feet long, with a cross guard just under the broad leaf-shaped blade and a battery-powered UV light on the cross guard, it was designed to keep things off you. A sudden memory of desert heat, screaming Iraqi children, and charnel breath hot on my face forced my eyes closed for just a second. I opened my eyes from what had just been a long blink, and Tully was looking at me with calm eyes.

"You okay?"

I nodded.

"Let's go to work. You see the dirt under the drone?" I looked, and where he was pointing, the dirt was darker, less settled. I nodded again, unzipped my gun case, and took out my AR-10, slotted a magazine home, and released the bolt. Tully grinned, surprisingly fierce under the beard. "I'll poke it. You do what comes naturally." Remembering what Tully had said earlier, I kept the rifle pointed at the ground as I got out of the pickup, then rotated the muzzle up and fell in just behind Tully as he advanced toward the disturbed ground under the drone, spear held firmly in an on-guard position.

It was a space of six breaths and Tully paused, looked at me. I nodded, and he drove the spear blade into the dirt.

The shriek was . . . unreal. The almost ultrasonic peal shut down the amplification in my MHI-issued earplugs, and then the ground just . . . exploded. I had a brief glimpse of a shredded blue letter jacket and blond hair before Tully cursed and slipped sideways. A boy, obviously a football player, just . . . scuttled . . . out of the grave, crabwise, with his back and butt to the dirt, and crouched. He looked at Tully, then at me, and his mouth opened . . . and kept opening, going past ninety degrees, showing a jaw full of teeth that didn't belong in the mouth of anything that didn't have a dorsal fin.

The green dot in my sight appeared on his chest, followed by a couple of distant thumps, and the wight abruptly sat down, looking confused. Tully lunged and drove the spearhead through its chest up to the crossbar. Between the spear and the two rounds of silver-tipped .308, it didn't have anything left to scream with, but it bucked like a landed fish. Tully leaned his weight onto the spear, looked at me. I let the green reticle drift onto the thing's face, and a stroke of the trigger sent it to peace.

Tully woofed a big breath of air and yanked the spear loose. I brought the rifle back up, snapping a quick look toward the pickup. Ms. Wainwright was still on the roof, looking through the sight on her AR-model carbine, and Danny knelt on the roof of the trailer above her, scanning the windows of the house through the scope on his AR-10.

"One down," grunted Tully. "Day isn't getting any longer."

I scanned the area. The blaze-orange drone was surprisingly easy to spot under the early Texas sunshine as it bounced merrily above a second patch of darker dirt. We stepped carefully toward the probable hiding spot. As Tully was about to stick the dirt, I heard two dull thumps that had to be Danny's .308, interspersed with several higher cracks, and more of that ultrasonic screeching. I pivoted, rifle coming up, and the green dot settled on a prom dress. I blinked.

Beside me, Tully swore viciously, and I felt the slap of dirt as another wight came out of the disturbed patch eight feet in front of us. I tracked, slow, slow, finger into the trigger guard, the rifle jouncing firmly against my shoulder, and the blue letterman jacket that had appeared in my optic spun. Quick movement beside me, and Tully pinned it against the ground, more rifle fire distant as I put another one out of its misery.

"Good, kid."

Closer to the house, Danny pinned the flailing undead in the prom dress with another spear, and Ms. Wainwright precisely and clinically shot it in the face. Then both Hunters stepped back from the house, rifles up and covering the windows, before scrambling up on top of the truck to scan with their rifles.

I took a deep breath, nodded at Tully, and we moved carefully to where the drone was bobbing impatiently above more disturbed earth. All of the gunfire must have woken them up, because the dirt erupted, and another one in a blue-and-white jacket scuttled toward us, limbs rotating like windmill vanes, impossible. It took way too many rounds before I finally got one into the brain case, dropping it less than ten feet in front of me.

I tried to hide my shaking as I dropped the magazine and fumbled another one out of my vest. Beside me, Tully dropped his spear, and another one just appeared around a corner from behind the house. It came at a full sprint, much faster than it should have been. I slammed the magazine home, thumb going for the bolt release. Then Tully came up with his FAL, and we both hammered rounds into the gibbering nightmare, driving it to its knees before the insurance shot.

Dragging deep gulps of air into my lungs, I scanned left and right. Inside the house, something yowled. It sounded like a leopard on one of those old Animal Planet shows, only angrier, and the sound sent cold, clammy chills up my spine.

"What the hell was that?"

Tully cleared his throat, spat. "That, Hunter, is a pissed-off vampire."

A whistle, clear and silvery, cut through the chills. I shook my head and looked back toward the pickups. Ms. Wainwright took her fingers from her mouth and made a circling motion over her head.

Angela

When the vampire woke up, I called my boys in. Even for experienced Hunters, a vampire squalling is unnerving. For Newbies, it can be a real gut check the first time they hear one. Danny had a fascinated expression on his face, and it reminded me of a kid in a museum. That boy wasn't right. Luis, on the other hand, had a countenance that said he was three-parts angry because of the one-part scared. Good. Miggy, as ever, looked unflappable, and Tully was, well, Tully.

"Okay, boys..." This was more for the Newbies than my veterans, but a little reminder never hurt. "The vamps can't come out into the sunshine, and the wights are wimps. Everyone hydrate, and then Danny? Back up on the truck and watch for anything coming out of the house. Luis, help Miggy get the skid-steer off the trailer. Tully and I will get the targets ready."

Luis

Miggy thumped me on the shoulder and jerked his head. On the rearmost trailer sat a little bulldozer with wheels instead of tracks, and he started undoing straps. I hurried around the end to pull them loose, coiling them out of habit. Miggy came around the end of the trailer, saw my neat pile of strapping, and nodded in approval. We walked around to the ramp, up to the machine, where Miggy patted it fondly. "Bobcat S450. Handy little thing. Used for construction—and demolition. *La Doña* talked a reclamation company into giving us this one after we helped them with a nest of ahools they uncovered in an old cotton gin."

I blinked. Ahools? He grinned.

"Indonesian monkey-bat thing. Got to Vietnam in the 1960s and South America in the '80s. Been heading north since then." His grin turned vicious. "Think of a smelly twenty-five-pound flying piranha." He unwrapped a stick of peppermint and jammed it into his mouth.

"*Mira.* Joystick here. Bucket control here. This little beauty is a zero-turn, diesel-powered Black-and-Decker Monster Wrecker." He hopped into the driver's seat and quickly backed the little machine down the ramp. Ms. Wainwright and Tully came out of the closed trailer, carrying four plastic torso targets and some coils of silvery tube; Tully hopped into the bucket, and Ms. Wainwright handed him the targets.

"Luis." Her red hair was braided and wrapped around her head like a crown. "Into the bucket with Tully. Listen to him and keep things off him, please."

I nodded. This was not the monster hunting that Danny and I had talked about over beers, and it wasn't the monster hunting we saw during Newbie training, but it had the *Chaos But Overwhelming* element that was familiar to me from the Marine Corps. "Yes, ma'am."

I stepped into the bucket, and Tully handed me two little green cylinders. "Here, put these in your pockets. Don't step on the targets, you'll bend the det cord."

I froze.

Ms. Wainwright looked at Tully over her sunglasses, and he grinned back. She sighed. "Luis, it's perfectly safe, but if you crimp the det cord, we'll have to remake the breaching charges."

Oh. I stepped carefully into the bucket and shot Tully a discreet middle finger. From the cab, I heard a soft snicker, and the skid-steer lurched forward toward the house. The bucket raised gently, and we stopped just short of the eaves. Looking around, I was impressed—we were about eight feet off the ground, and there was solid steel between us and anything that might try to get at us from the ground. Behind us, Danny and Ms. Wainwright were lying on top of one of the pickups again, scanning the house through their optics.

"Okay." Tully handed me one of the plastic targets. One side was sticky with a thick layer of something—grease?—and four strips of military-grade det cord around the edges. "Lay this on the roof, and then gently slide it as far as you can up the slope." Reaching out, I used my rifle muzzle to slide the charge almost up to the ridgeline.

"Perfect." Tully took the end of a silvery tube and inserted it into the end of one of those little green cylinders, crouched below the lip of the bucket, and firmly pulled on the ring.

The *whomp* was impressive, but the yowling shriek and thuds as something slammed into the rafters and crashed through the ceiling was even more so. At once, my rifle was up and I was focused on the green dot.

Tully cleared his throat and spat. "Guess what? We had a vampire in the attic."

I blinked at him, and he snorted. "And that, Hunter, is why *Doña* Angie is team leader of Very Large Mammals. We don't kick in doors and take on monsters on their own turf—that's for Earl and the others. She cheats with explosives and power equipment."

The older man looked at me over his glasses, hauled himself to his feet, and showed a thumbs-up to Miggy. The skid-steer pivoted and started rolling along the house away from the hole, letting the sun in. "Get out one of those igniters, Hunter. Your turn."

Pretty quickly, we had four three-foot diameter holes blown into the roof, and I discovered that I really, really liked igniting shock-tube.

We used angle iron-shaped cutting charges, ran a Kevlar snatch strap hooked to the Bobcat and yanked the roof clean off the house, then started methodically taking the place apart. As each wall came down, the yowling got louder, and angrier. The wight attacks got more and more desperate until Miggy used the bucket of the Bobcat to turn the last one into a goo-filled, wight-shaped dent in the clay soil of what had been the backyard.

Finally, all that was left of the farmhouse was a debris-covered wooden floor. Miggy backed the Bobcat away, turned off the engine, and jerked his head at me. "Now we earn the PUFF, Hunter."

I hopped off the side of the little bulldozer, landed awkwardly, and swore. Pain from the titanium replacement hip flared, and for a moment I was lying flat in the Iraqi dust, Danny standing over me, SAW snarling, as he went cyclic on something impossible swarming out of an Iraqi cemetery.

I blinked, shook my head, and met Miggy's eyes. He nodded, briefly, reached into his vest, and handed me a stick of peppermint.

Ms. Wainwright was standing beside where the front door had been, staring contemplatively at the floor, Danny hulking at her back, and Tully crouched, casually throwing rocks onto the flooring. Under it, something growled, yowling angrily every time a rock thudded onto the floor.

Ms. Wainwright turned to look at Miggy and me. "Well, boys, crawlspace or basement?"

Danny looked quizzical. "What's the difference?"

Tully rose and dusted off his hands. "Crawlspaces suck marginally less than basements."

"Oh."

We carefully slid breaching charges on the floor, being absolutely sure not to get onto, or even close to, the floor where something with fangs and bad breath might yank us through, then sheltered behind the trucks as Tully finished setting up. Then he winked at me and pulled the ring on an igniter. Six charges going off was considerably louder than the single charges we had been using, and bits of floor were still raining down as I came around the end of the truck and crouched, rifle pointed at what was left of the house.

I waited the space of several deep breaths, but no smoking

fang face came up. Then motion to my left, and Ms. Wainwright, behind her little pistol-caliber AR, Miggy and Danny flanking her, advanced on the house.

Tully and I likewise advanced until we were looking through holes into what turned out to be a crawlspace, about three feet deep, now filled with plenty of good Texas sunlight, but no sizzling vampire carcass. I began scanning, and spotted a spray of fresh dirt thrown out from the base of the foundation wall just ahead of where Ms. Wainwright was moving, and tracked it back to . . . yep. It had burrowed into the dirt wall.

I stopped and waved my hand until Ms. Wainwright saw me, pointed to my eye, and then pointed to the burrow. She nodded, then backed up and came around the foundation to my side, where she blew an exasperated breath. "I hate it when they do that."

"That's one, *Doña* Angie." Miggy was still scanning the rest of the crawlspace. "Where's the other?"

The tiny woman shrugged. "Mayhap they're both in the same hole?"

Miggy looked at her over his glasses. "Uh-huh."

"Let's find out. Tully, take Danny and get the stuff, please."

"Yes, *Doña*."

"The stuff" turned out to be a mirror and Kevlar strapping. Working quickly, we made a noose out of the strapping and hung it like a snare around the mouth of the burrow, looping the free end twice around a floor joist. Then Ms. Wainwright slung her little carbine across her back, took the mirror and just . . . hopped into the crawlspace.

Miggy shifted his grip on the spear he was holding, murmured, "I swear to God, that girl—Luis, be ready."

I saw what she was doing an instant before things went . . . kinetic. The spot of sunlight on the wall of the crawlspace from the mirror shifted, tracked along the wall, and disappeared into the burrow. An instant after the sunlight vanished, the yowling increased in pitch and volume, and the vampire burst out of the burrow.

The joist the snare was wrapped around was a solid two-by-eight chunk of good American wood, and when she hit the end of the noose, it cracked. Down in the crawlspace, Ms. Wainwright was scrambling backward. The vampire was at the end of the tether, sizzling and smoking, and I tracked the green reticle up its back and emptied twenty rounds of silver-tipped 7.62 into her, Danny and Tully doing the same.

When our rifles ran dry, Miggy ran the spear into it, and then leaned on the shaft as the undead flopped and burned, before Tully dropped between floor joists with an entrenching tool and took its head off.

Damn.

I heard my empty magazine bounce off a floor joist, and I slammed a new one in, covering the hole it had come out of. Down in the crawlspace, Ms. Wainwright blew out a big breath of air and gave a thumbs-up. Miggy wiped his forehead with a rag. "Well, that's one."

We didn't find the other one.

After a couple of hours of searching, we came back to the trucks. Ms. Wainwright was sitting on the edge of the floor, looking at the vampire's body down in the crawlspace, her expression sad and exhausted.

"*Doña.*" Miggy's voice was soft. "He's not here."

She sighed, closed her eyes. "Of course he isn't."

"We should go. The evening comes."

"I know." A pause, then her voice, quieter. "She couldn't have been more than sixteen, Miggy."

"Yes, *Doña* Angie. And she killed how many at the dance?"

"I know, Miggy."

Tully cleared his throat, spat again. "She put Burke and Rogneby in the hospital, and would have killed them if we hadn't gotten lucky. She would have pulled your arms and legs off this afternoon and not been bothered a bit."

A soft sigh. "I know."

"Come, *Doña*: let us go back to the hotel. We can start the chase again in the morning."

"Okay."

Angela

I thought about that poor girl, and the four previous girls, all the way back to the hotel. I was so tired. Tired of the cruelty. Tired of the death. Tired of being one step behind. I should have been frustrated by being outwitted by one idiot teenage vampire, but I was just... cold, and tired.

At my suite, I called the boys in. "All right, gentlemen, we missed him again. If he's true to habit, he's already on the road, probably heading south."

Tully huffed. "And if he's not?"

I loved these overprotective knuckle-draggers, even the two Newbies. "He hasn't broken that pattern in sixteen weeks. I think we can be pretty sure it's his habit."

Tully looked frustrated. Miggy was phlegmatic, and the two Newbies... well, looked like Newbies.

"We need some downtime. Everyone go do something that isn't hunting monsters. Go dancing. Have a drink. Whatever. Just go do it out of my room. Shoo!"

Miggy raised his eyebrow, not moving from where he had perched a ham on the mass-produced sideboard in my room. "*Doña*, you have your phone?"

"Yes, Miggy."

"Do you have everyone's number—even theirs?"

"Yes, Tully."

"*Bueno, Doña* Angie." He stretched and popped his neck. "Do not forget it, please."

"Yes, Miggy."

Tully snorted and then made shooing motions, following the other three out of my room. Hopefully to blow off some steam.

I took a long shower, treating myself to some of the luxury bath products that came with the room, and put on the slinky Little Green Dress, added some warpaint, and stepped into the pair of sky-high tan Christian Louboutins that I had splurged on. What looked back at me from the mirror didn't look a bit like a veteran Monster Hunter. Good. Lastly, a Ruger LCR, loaded with silver wadcutters, went... well, a lady has to keep her secrets.

In the lobby, I checked my wallet. Driver's license, handgun license, speed-strip, some cash, a credit card, and my smartphone. I wrinkled my nose at it, and it dinged, announcing that my rideshare had arrived.

The driver was an older gentleman—with a ring, damn it—and he still gave me a very male look as one of the valets helped me into the back of his four-door Ford pickup. It felt good. "Are you sure you want to go to Walmart in that getup, Miss?"

I laughed. "Actually, I need some advice."

He gave me a Tullyesque look over his glasses. "I just drive, Miss."

"If I wanted to go somewhere safe, where unattached gentlemen might be found who might want some company, where would you suggest?"

A long look in the mirror, and he gave a slow nod. "Bad week?"

"You have no idea."

"Ah. I would suggest the Marriott. It's a convention hotel with lots of people cycling through. Good security so a young lady of the nonprofessional variety might feel safe."

"Excellent."

"It's two blocks away, Miss. Not really worth . . ."

"Have you seen the shoes I'm wearing?"

A long pause. "Good point. Seat belt, please." I couldn't help myself—I stuck my tongue out at him before buckling up.

The Marriott bar was pretty much standard: too loud, too bright, people moving through too quickly. But it had a giant window out to the pool, and the bartender made a perfect dirty martini. I contemplated many things: Should I get another cocktail? Should I retire from monster hunting? Should I send a beer to that tall drink of water at the end of the bar?

I nibbled on the olive as I pulled my phone out of my clutch to check the time, and someone flopped down on the barstool beside me. Mentally betting on whether he'd have an untanned band on his ring finger, I glanced over. Oh, great. There must have been some kind of school function at the convention center, because the skinny little geek who smirked at me from inside his blue-and-white letter . . .

. . . deep in his eyes, red sparks glittered, and my thumb frantically bounced on the power button of my smartphone. Once, as a pink cotton-candy feeling invaded my mind. Twice, while thoughts became . . . slow . . . unimportant. The third time was . . . difficult . . . but it was . . . for some reason . . . important.

"Hey, shawty. Why don't you just go ahead and give me that phone, hmm?"

I handed him my phone.

Luis

"Well, dumbass." Danny lofted a bag at my head. "If you'd actually read the case studies they gave us in training, this wouldn't be a surprise."

I opened the bag to find two steaming sleeves of deep-fried gas station burrito goodness. Danny flopped down on the other bed in our room and pulled a beef-and-cheese out of his bag, took a big bite. "That snallygaster outside of DC ten years back? MCB went in its cave, and it tore them up? Somebody else did the same thing and got wiped?"

He took a big gulp of Dr. Pepper. "Earl sends Ms. Wainwright, and the first thing she does? Packs a remote-controlled toy truck full of ANFO and nails. Runs it into the cave, blows that thing to bits. She and her team go in, it's still trying to put itself back together, they pick through the pieces until they find the heart, torch it. Bam! Problem solved, problem staying solved. Twenty minutes."

I chewed slowly, swallowed. "Yeah, but..."

Danny's phone on the nightstand abruptly sounded the Star Trek Red Alert noise. At the same time, mine gave a bosun's whistle, then both external speakers kicked on. "*... Well, kitten, let's take a look at your contacts, hmm?*"

I blinked, the realization hitting Danny a split second ahead of me: "Oh, shit! That's the vampire!"

I dove for my phone. On the screen, a nerdy little kid was peering at me, geeky and harmless... until I saw the red glitter in his eyes. Shit, shit, shit.

"*Ah, here we go.*" A finger appeared, the nail too long and filthy, and made poking motions. The view switched from his face to a close-up of a too-pale ear, and bounced a moment, then his voice:

"*Hey, is this Earl? I'll bet this is Earl, isn't it? Hey, brah, got to tell you, I never saw the attraction of redheads, but man, I have to say, this one is changing my mind.*" A long pause. I frantically thumbed the Maps icon on the SOS screen. Come on, come on... "*Yeah, no shit. You might actually be as smart as people were telling me.*"

Another pause. Damn it... "Danny! Two blocks west. Looks like the Marriott we passed on the way in, probably the bar..." Danny was gone, door slamming off the wall behind him. Goddamnit.

"*Naw, naw, brah. Not a hair on her pretty little head. Matter of fact, I figure I'll wrap her in a ribbon and send her back to you. Like a present you can open.*" I snatched my armor and my AR-10 off the chair, and ran after Danny, cursing the dull, tired ache in my wrecked leg that slowed me down.

Angela

In the depths of the trance, my grandmother's whisper cuts through the saccharine pink cloud suffocating my thoughts. *You are of Appalachia. Your mother's people were Cunning Folk, going back to before the world changed. You have danced in caves older than bones and sung for beings who watched the rings of Saturn form.*

The cotton-candy numbness in my mind cleared, somewhat—enough that my own voice snarled, "My grandfather was Valentine Sackett, the warrior scion of a warrior line, who taught me the ways of fire and steel as a young girl. I am *not* going to show up in Valhalla and tell that old man that his granddaughter has been bested by *some horndog teenage vampire*."

At the last, the fog of the trance twisted, and then evaporated like darkness before the dawn.

He was eyeing me like a Pennsyltucky tweaker eyes a catalytic converter. I reached up and slowly pulled the hair-stick out. His eyes dilated as I slowly shook my hair loose, and he started licking his lips... ignoring the needle-pointed length of bog-oak I held in an icepick grip, my hand laying close to him on the bar. "Holy shit, Earl, how have you not had a taste..."

I slammed my fist into his chest, the bog-oak stick, passed down from mother to daughter from the time the Old Country was ours, sizzled as it popped through his leathery skin. The air-horn shriek told me that I missed his heart, and then an explosion of pain and glass as he backhanded me off the barstool and through the glass window into the pool area, my left arm going numb when I hit the concrete. Moving impossibly fast, the vampire blurred out of the bar area and I was hanging in the air, his hands around my throat.

"You little bitch." His eyes had gone fully red, and his canine teeth were making his words hard to understand. "Let's take some of the fire out of you." The world blurred, and I hit water. I was struggling to the surface when he landed, grabbing my right hand—my good hand, and standing on my hair. Thrashing, my scalp flaring with pain, I tried to reach my thigh with my broken arm, but it just wouldn't move.

Well, shit. Sudden distant concussions, then the vampire rocked, letting go of my hand, and I grabbed for the Ruger snub-nose holstered under my skirt, ran the barrel up his inseam until I hit squishy stuff, and squeezed all five rounds into his taint. The pressure on my hair vanished, and I breached the surface, coughing, trying not to throw up, looking for the vampire.

And then I saw his handiwork. Danny Hudson, the big blond Viking Newbie, the weight of his armor holding him to the bottom of the pool. Though the water, I could see his calm, composed expression—and his missing throat.

The world went red, and I staggered up the stairs. Over by an Ikea tiki bar, the vampire jerked and flopped erratically. Silver through the heart probably didn't feel good, but it wouldn't put him down permanently. I limped into the bar, spotted my purse, and popped open the cylinder of the Ruger, using the bar top to push the ejector rod and empty the gun. I knelt, put the revolver behind my knee, grabbed a speed-strip out of my clutch, and flexed two rounds into the cylinder. Standing up, I closed the revolver and limped out to the tiki bar.

The vampire saw me coming, his eyes huge and startled. I knelt next to him, placed the muzzle of the Ruger on his chest. He feebly batted at my hand. I looked him in the eye, pulled the trigger twice, blowing a nice hole through his chest.

He arched, let out an explosive breath, then gasped, "Bitch. I'm a vampire. You think a little bullet is going to stop me?"

I stood up. "No."

I put the heel of my stiletto pump in the gunshot wound, already healing in his chest. "I don't."

I drove my weight down, shoving the steel-reinforced oak stiletto of my Louboutin heel right through his rotten heart.

"Fuck you and just die."

Luis

If I'd had a doubt, the persistent annoying clamor of a fire alarm at the Marriott pretty much told me Bad Things had happened. At the side, a high stucco wall surrounded the pool. In the center, an ornate wooden gate hung half on its hinges. Like a 220-pound white boy marine had crashed through it, but I didn't hear any more gunshots. Fuck.

I took a deep breath, getting ready for a quick, quiet entry, then remembered: it's a vampire. He probably heard me two blocks down the street.

"Danny! Danny! Talk to me, bro!"

Nothing. Another deep breath, and I button-hooked the gate, both eyes open, the green circle of my sight hovering in the air, sweeping over . . .

There he was: prone, on his back, the blue-and-white letter jacket stark against the gray concrete. I didn't even realize my finger had slipped into the trigger guard until I heard the faint distant crack of the rifle, and its head snapped to one side.

I continued the sweep and came off the weapon when I found Angela Wainwright. She was sitting in the pool, on the steps, drenched, her eyes huge and terrible and weeping. In her lap . . .

Oh, Danny. No.

Her left arm, just below the shoulder, had an obvious fracture, but she had pulled him into her lap and was stroking his forehead. His throat was gone, to the point I could see his spine. *Fuck, Danny.*

"Luis." Her voice was raw, ragged with pain and loss. "There you are." She nodded toward the vampire. "Would you be a good boy and bring me that bastard's head?"

"Yes, ma'am." I brought the sight back up on the vampire's body and quick-stepped over to him. On his chest sat a dainty stiletto heel, almost like she had . . . she had. Stabbed him right through the heart with a high heel. Damn.

I slung the rifle, brought out my grandfather's smatchet, and quick and sure its head came off. I picked it up by the mullet, walked to the pool, knelt on one knee, and placed it where *Doña* Angela could see it.

"Thank you, Luis." Her calm voice was a stark contrast to the madness lurking behind her eyes, and I could see her teeth starting to chatter. Post-combat adrenaline shakes, most likely, but the cold water probably wasn't helping.

"*Doña* Angela, let me help you out of the pool."

"I'm not leaving him. The water is cold, and I'm not leaving him."

"Yes, ma'am. Let me . . ." There was a crunch behind me, and I spun, green dot coming back up, to see Miggy and Tully coming through the shattered door from the bar, moving with the smooth precision that spoke of years of working together. Tully's eyes were cold and calm behind the FN-FAL, sweeping the pool area. Miggy—one hand on Tully's back—covering the rooms overlooking the pool area. A quick thorough scan, and both men slung their weapons and trotted over to the pool, Tully dropping to one knee and smacking the vampire's head into the pool. "*Doña* Angie . . ."

"I'm not leaving him alone, Tully."

A splash as Miggy jumped into the water and waded over to the tiny woman. "Come, *Doña*—Luis and I will get our brother out of the water. Let Tully see to your arm, yes?" She looked at him for a long time, then nodded. I reached out and gently took her good arm, helping her up until Tully could slide his arms under, pick her up and carry her to a cushioned chair still standing amidst all the wreckage. Then Miggy and I picked up poor Danny Hudson and carried him out of the pool.

We laid him on a lounge cushion. If you didn't look at the gaping hole where his throat should have been, he looked for all the world like he was sleeping off a twelve-pack . . . but there was no sleeping this one off.

"Damn it, Danny." It wasn't fair. Three deployments, never touched. Held off a pack of hyena-whatthehellevers, not a scratch on him. One idiot puberty-stricken vampire . . .

Across from me, Miggy picked up Danny's hands and laid them on his chest. He reached up, gently closed Danny's eyes, and made the Sign of the Cross.

"Eternal rest, grant unto him, O Lord, and let perpetual light shine upon him."

He looked at me, calmly. "She doesn't see this part."

Miggy inclined his head to where Tully was fussing over *Doña* Angela's broken arm. "Ever."

Tully looked over her shoulder and gave a slight nod. Miggy pulled a long slim kukri from a sheath at his back and took a deep breath, but I reached out and touched his arm.

He looked at me with eyes too old. "You sure?"

I nodded, drew the smatchet again, then struck, as quickly and cleanly as I could. And my marine brother was at rest.

A breath I didn't know I was holding slipped out, and I tried not to think of what I had just done. On his armor, the Team Very Large Mammals patch had been stained with his life's blood, a faded rusty orange streak running down the center of it. I peeled it loose from the Velcro and held it in my hand. He had been so very excited about this silly little patch.

"Now what?"

"Now we go back to Cazador and mourn our brother. We will teach and play gopher until *La Doña* heals." He gave me a measured look. "You did well. She will recommend you for another team, should you still wish to hunt with others."

I pulled my intact patch from a pocket on my armor and smoothed it onto his. To bury him without it seemed . . . wrong. I slapped his stained patch onto the Velcro of mine. "I need to learn how to run the Bobcat."

Miggy's grin was approving. *"Bueno."*

This record is a leak from the Secret Government Task Force That Shall Not Be Named, and as such I cannot confirm the details. However, it appears that code name "Fluffy" is the son of MHI member Chloe Mendoza, who was the subject of *Monster Hunter Memoirs: Fever.*

—A.L.

The Ghost of Bogotá

Jason Cordova

In the endless war against evil, the Monster Control Bureau is considered the shield, and Special Task Force Unicorn the sword. And the eyes and ears... and when needed, the assassins.

As was the case at this particular moment. Jorge Quintilla Cabrera, aka Jorge the Goat, had pissed off someone high up in the Colombian government... or more than likely, missed his scheduled bribery payment and needed to be made into an example. Or both. One never actually knew when it came to the order of things down here. Colombia is *wild.*

Information changed hands, calls were made, and I'd quickly found myself parachuted into Colombia less than twenty-four hours after. There hadn't been many details as to what had driven my boss to such an extreme response, only that the low-level drug lord needed to be handled without either the US or Colombians being fingered for the deed.

And by handled, good old Mr. Stricken meant splattered across the walls in a message that no language barrier could possibly mistranslate.

"Fluffy in position," I murmured into the throat mic as I continued to scan the compound. When it came to STFU ops, nothing was ever as it seemed. And this one practically screamed "bad shit is going to happen" to all of us.

Intel said that Jorge was supposed to be nothing, a low-level narco on his best of days, yet he'd quickly climbed the ranks since the fall of the Cali Cartel. However, neither the DEA, CIA, nor even Search Bloc—the Colombian antidrug task force—had any idea just *how* he had pulled off this miraculous feat. Nor were there any bodies left in his wake. For the most part, people who went against the Goat simply vanished in the night. No trace, nothing. It was if they'd ceased to exist.

A Search Bloc team had been sent in to apprehend him. They were hardcore and used to fighting the cartels. They went in, heavily armed and motivated as hell. Nobody found a single trace of them afterward. Looked like Jorge the Goat had some additional hired muscle, one who knew how to handle men with guns and how to dispose of them after. People started talking about his top bodyguard, someone nicknamed the Ghost of Bogotá. Of course there were no pictures, or even a tentative ID on them. Or confirmation they were even real.

It was suspicious as hell and practically *screamed* supernatural.

Jorge the Goat's compound was well guarded, which was to be expected. The '80s had been a wild time for coke dealers in Colombia, but ever since Noriega up in Panama had been ousted, things had gotten a little tougher for them to move product. The bribes of judges and politicians weren't as readily available as previously, and the US had finally started being proactive toward the narcos. The result? A serious dent in their business stratagem, a loss in profits, and some pissed-off but well-armed psychopaths looking for someone to blame.

In the deep jungle on a moonless night like tonight, I'm all but invisible. Thanks to this I was, as usual, out in front to find any traps or ambush sites. My kind were one of the rarest monster hybrids in the world, with me being only the second to ever make it to adulthood in recorded history—if just turning twenty counted as being an adult. Sitting still, in the shadows of a tree line just north of the compound, nobody would be able to see me. If they had those newfangled thermal scanners I'd be nothing like what a human body should be showing.

Satellite intel had said that there were at least two dozen guards with AK-47s along the walls, and once again the images provided to us had been correct. Everyone gives the CIA and NSA all the credit, but those of us out in the field knew that it was the men and women buried deep within the dark bowels of the NRO who were the true workhorses behind out success. They were my favorite agency that did not exist.

"Samurai is in position," a raspy voice came over the radio. I smiled. Kenta Sato, a Japanese *tokuromubi* who had just joined the team two months before, was probably the closest thing to a friend that I had these days. *Tokuromubi* were resilient, tough fighters who could actually extend their extremities beyond what normal people could. They were very similar to *rokurokubi*, only far more dangerous thanks to their almost-indestructible skin. He was also trained in some sort of kung fu and was about as fast as I was. With his katanas he was a deadly assassin who could slip in almost anywhere and chop someone up into pieces in no time. He was also like me: in it only for the PUFF exemption, and then back to trying to live a normal life.

The rest of the team checked In. Stricken was with overwatch, of course. While he was in complete and utter control of us, he was pretty much useless in this sort of operation. Sure, he claimed to have breezed through Ranger School and had aced the Farm during his early days with the CIA, but I had my doubts about just how well he'd done. Still, he was a meticulous planner, an organizer, and I was willing to put money down that one day he might be in charge of STFU, so there was no point in antagonizing him. At the moment he was seated comfortably in a beach chair high atop the mountain just south of the compound, undoubtedly watching this all unfold through his night vision goggles.

"Sssscales," a third voice hissed through my earpiece. Juventud was a reptoid, a giant, burly lizardman who was one of the biggest assholes I'd ever had the displeasure of meeting. He wasn't much for sneaking, or taking orders from anyone except Stricken, or even talking with us outside of the job, but he was one hell of a meat shield and tank. If shit went sideways—and with us, that sometimes happened—then the plan was simple: hide behind the giant, seven-foot-tall, nearly bulletproof lizard as it rampaged, and try not to get caught up in said rampage. He also was a lifer—he hadn't earned his PUFF exemption yet, but what kind of regular life could a reptoid possibly lead?

Plus, he had one hell of an anger management problem.

"Lovi standing by," the final member of our team checked in, her voice demure over the radio. Unlike the rest of us, Lovi didn't have a nickname given by Stricken. She was our team sniper, who worked the .338 Lapua precision rifle with the skill of a surgeon, and was Stricken's right hand on missions like this. The ice-bitch was a spirit of the forest, an *ajatar,* from somewhere in northern Europe, I think, a stone-cold killer who actually wasn't in it to earn a PUFF exemption. She already had one. Apparently she just enjoyed killing people so much that she'd stayed on after. There'd been zero complaints from our boss.

Stricken just loved dedicated workers.

The *ajatar* was also ready to provide covering fire in case reinforcements unexpectedly arrived—or to shoot one of us should we go off mission. Stricken very rarely took chances when it came to his team of monsters.

Though his fascination with that Conover dude...

"*Whenever you're ready, Fluffy,*" Stricken said over the secure comm. I took a deep breath, closed my eyes, pulled on the monster within. A snarl erupted from my throat as the neglected creature was called forth. My fingers turned into claws, and my skin shifted as fur began to grow out of the pores. Bones cracked, realigned, and organs *squished* as they moved around to support what I was becoming. We were no longer two separate beings, the monster and I.

Stricken's voice came over the radio. He was growing impatient. "*I'm getting bored up here, Fluffy. You think this is a soccer match or something? Let's go. Kill something.*"

"Execute," I managed to say through rapidly growing teeth.

Sprinting through the thick jungle, I came to the most dangerous part of the op—the open ground between the compound and the Colombian jungle around it. Jorge the Goat had done a good job to ensure that all his firing points had clear fields of fire, but unfortunately for him, while you can take the meanest killers from the streets and give them guns, you actually have to train people on how to stand watch.

A quick glance showed that most of the guards were looking toward the main gate on the east side of the compound. Thanks to their oversight, nobody spotted me as I reached the first-floor window, my planned entry point. It was slightly higher than I was tall, but with a simple leap I was through the window and rolling on the stone floor in a single movement. Popping to my feet, I took stock of the situation. My eyes shifted as they adjusted to the darkness within the building.

I was in the kitchen, exactly as planned, and nobody had seen a thing. Thanks to the late hour, none of the servants Jorge the Goat had working for him were still around. Small favors, that. The idea of murdering a bunch of innocents was not high on the list of things I wanted to do at the moment. It's far easier on the conscience to slaughter hired thugs and drug lords.

"Leave witnesses, Fluffy," Stricken warned in my ear. I snorted, both irritated and amused. Unlike the others, I wasn't about to fly off the handle and murder everything and everyone around me just because they smelled like food.

Peeking out of the kitchen doorway, there were no signs of randomly patrolling guards here. This was good. We'd anticipated none, since Jorge had his "Ghost" running around, but one never knew for certain. Moving down the narrow hallway, I heard the faint scuff of a shoe on stone around the corner ahead. Pressing against the wall, I waited to see who or what was going to appear.

It was a guard. He was tall, broad shouldered, and not paying the least bit attention as he moved down the corridor, not even keeping his head on a swivel as he roamed. If he had, he would have easily seen me. His attention was fixated on lighting his smoke. The Zippo snapped closed and the pungent smell of a cheap *cigarillo* laced with marijuana wafted filled the air as he continued down the hall. Sneaking up on him would be child's play. These guys might have been tough when intimidating innocent victims, but when a real killer shows up they're nothing more than paper targets.

Punching into his back and ripping his spine out without making a sound was a bit difficult, but I managed to do so with nothing more than a wet squelching noise and a strange little gasp from the dead man. Hearing a man die is always a little unsettling, but since this guy was probably responsible for a few innocents getting killed, I didn't let it bother me. Just to make sure he was dead, I ripped his throat out with a claw. Blood splashed onto the floor. It made more noise than anything else I'd done so far.

"Don't fly off the handle in there, Fluffy. I've seen what your kind can do when that happens," Stricken reminded me. It was difficult not to roll my eyes. The only other of my kind he'd ever run across was my mother, and she was far more in control than I was.

Outside, the guards began shouting excitedly and shooting into the jungle night. Juventud was making his move and, as usual, was drawing most of the attention. This was all part of the plan. Trigger the alarms, allow the guards time to lock the place up tight, and wait out the emergency.

After I'd slipped inside, of course.

They thought their attackers would be locked outside with Jorge and his men safely within. Instead, the cartel members would trap themselves inside with the scariest monster around.

The stench of blood filled the narrow hall, mixing with the remnants of the dead man's *cigarillo* as it burned out on the floor. There was no point in hiding the body now. There was too much blood. Besides, that would defeat the idea. Let the roving guards find him, and wonder at the grotesque manner of death. Wonder, and fear.

We had the layout thanks to a surprisingly cheap bribe to a local builder. The man had been very eager to give the giant reptoid precisely what we were looking for, and had accepted payment without complaint. He also, unsurprisingly enough, listened to Stricken's advice on moving to a new location . . . preferably a different country altogether.

The first floor was mostly guardrooms, the high-quality industrial kitchen that had been my entry point, a very fancy courtyard with a pool, hot tub, and firepit, and an armory that took up half the floor. We didn't know what was in the basement, but I was guessing money and guns. I mean, what's the point of having a basement as a drug lord if you aren't stocking it full of guns, ammo, and drug money?

Clearing the first floor was the important part. I needed to kill every other guard or inhabitant down here before searching for the target. With ruthless efficiency, I went room to room, searching. In the armory there was a single guard, so I knocked him unconscious before he could react. The next room had three guards. Killing two and leaving the third gagged and trussed up on the floor balanced things out. I may be a monster, but I can follow orders.

According to all our intel, the second floor was where I would find my true target, more than likely either cowering in a closet or hiding in his bathroom as the distraction took place outside. While the narco was definitely dangerous and was more than willing to execute whole families for more power, he usually left those killings for his men.

Two more guards were on the stairs, but looking the wrong way. They seemed to actually be paying attention, so I would have to move quickly. Sprinting into the room at full speed, I eyed the closest one as my first target. He must have caught something out of the corner of his eye, though. The guard started to turn, his AK-47 shifting ever so slightly as he moved in what seemed like slow motion to me. The faint whiff of shock and sudden fear filled my nostrils as his eyes widened, watching me leap through the air in what should have been an impossible feat for any normal man.

But I'm so much more.

Driving my knee into his neck, he barely managed a croaked warning before we tumbled into the stairs. His head bounced against one of the steps, making a loud cracking sound. The vertebrae in his neck crunched a split second later as my momentum continued to drive me through him. Just to be sure, though, I swiped a claw through his throat. Blood sprayed across the stairs and the second guard.

All of this had taken less than two seconds. The other man turned at the noise, his eyes also widening as they met mine. He panicked as he saw my changed face.

Instead of ripping this one's face off, I tripped him and sent him sprawling down the stairs. He tried sitting up, the fight apparently not quite knocked out of him just yet as he struggled to bring the AK to bear. Anatoly Kalashnikov had designed one hell of a rifle, but it was shit once someone was in close and making things very personal. I broke the guard's trigger finger, and his thumb for good measure. Then his wrist because why not? To make sure he stayed down, I drove an elbow into his face once, then again. His eyes rolled into the back of his head and he slumped back, blood and snot bubbling in his nose. He hadn't even had time to scream when I'd broken his fingers.

My forearms were coated with blood. The monster within grumbled at not being allowed to eat either one of them, but it wasn't like either of these guys would taste good anyway, so I told it to shut up. There was a job to finish first. Afterward? Maybe tacos. Or tapas. Hell, anything sounded better than the MREs I'd eaten on the flight down, or the flight attendant—which would have definitely got me in trouble.

There were no other guards upstairs. Curious, that. I could hear the continuous screams outside, but it was muted here, muffled. Our narco had invested in some quality windows to drown out the sounds of the jungle outside. Granted, we weren't too far from Camboa, a relatively quiet village alongside the Magdelena River and a few hours from Bogotá, but the jungle noise couldn't be that bad.

Then my mind wondered... what if it was designed to keep the sounds *in* and not out? The Ghost of Bogotá had yet to make his—or *its*—appearance, after all. If it was supernatural, then why let people know what was going on inside the narco's walls? Plus, garbage disposal... were we dealing with a potential ghoul after all?

Shaking away the stray thought, I checked the double doors to the suite. Focus was needed for this sort of op. Not paying attention could lead to me getting shot. I have a strong aversion to that. The doors were locked, but there wasn't any additional security device on them. I'd half expected a bar or something to help secure them from within. Very disappointed, I knelt down and peered under the door to see if there were any nasty surprises waiting for me within.

Thanks to the movies, most people would be watching for a shadow to cross the keyhole. Fortunately, things like me were natural predators, and knew just how to hunt terrified prey. Patience, intelligence, and a knowledge of the building's layout were key. Not seeing anything suspicious—which in itself was suspicious—I stood back up. Testing the doors, I noticed there was some give to them. It definitely wasn't reinforced like the plans had said.

They just don't make bad guys the way they used to. I just pushed harder and the lock on the door gave, allowing both doors to swing open.

Jorge the Goat's master suite was disgustingly opulent, with marble tiling for flooring and various types of animal skins scattered across it throughout. Three large fans hung from the ceiling, whirling slowly in the intense, humid heat. The bed was one of the largest I'd ever seen, easily capable of holding half a dozen people comfortably. There was a giant bowl half filled with prophylactics on the nightstand next to the bed, and judging by the wrappers on the ground, there'd been plenty of use. Oddly enough, I didn't see any sign of women. Maybe the party had ended early?

The briefing had mentioned stories about how Jorge the Goat earned his nickname, but I hadn't really believed them then. After all, the guy looked like someone had slapped some ears on a pineapple, gave him a '70s porn 'stache, and called it a day.

"Not fair," I muttered. Money did buy hot women and good times, I guess. My dating life could only be summed up as *complicated* ever since I'd left home to earn my PUFF exemption. And by "complicated," I mean nonexistent. High school hadn't been easier, since I wasn't allowed to play any sports. Not because my mom had been worried about me getting hurt, no. The complete opposite, actually.

I digress. The object here was to murder a drug lord, after all, and not pine away wondering why life was totally unfair.

"Hello? Mr. Goat? My name is . . . ah, Fluffy. Yeah. Mr. Fluffy. I'm here to kill you. Please make it worth my while to let you live."

Rapid-fire Spanish erupted from the bathroom. It was so much I had a hard time catching it all, but most of what I got was a grown man begging me not to murder him. There was some other stuff in there as well, including me being an evil spirit, I think, and some sort of ill-thought path to vengeance, but that was lost in the sobbing and snot.

"I have drugs! Lots of money!" he shrieked in a terrified voice, switching to heavily accented English. I was surprised. Nobody had known he was relatively fluent in English. "You're American? Americans like money, right? I give you one million dollars!"

"I'll let you live for two million," I retorted and stepped out of the way of the door to the bathroom. He was probably standing on the other side with some sort of ridiculous gun in hand, like a .50-caliber, gold-plated Desert Eagle or something similar. Being in the line of fire was not something I really wanted to risk. I'd been shot a few times since I'd joined STFU. Yes, rapid healing is awesome. Being shot still sucks, though. "You got the money here?"

"I can get it!"

"Sure you can, buddy," I murmured and looked around the room. There was no sign of a pile of money anywhere. Most narcos, from what I'd seen and heard, preferred to keep their mountains of cash close at hand, where they can have easy access to it for bribery and stuff. Plus, it's harder to freeze the accounts of a drug lord when all the assets are kept liquid.

Oh, yeah. He did have that basement we knew little about. I'd need to check it out after.

Even if he did pay, there was no way I was letting him live. Drug kingpins were nothing more than scum. But walking out with some extra cash on hand? That would *definitely* make the boss happy. While Stricken enjoyed using that government credit card, he preferred to operate off-book and without the constant bean counters breathing down his neck. While the common refrain "better to beg forgiveness than ask permission" was popular at MCB, within the even smaller confines of STFU we all knew it was far easier if we didn't need to ask or apologize in the first place.

After all, if money spent doesn't cross a bean counter's desk, does the government really care who spent it?

"So where is it?" I asked.

"In safe place!" His voice was on the edge of panic now. Good. Desperate people were more prone to making stupid decisions. I really didn't want to take a shotgun to the face, so him willingly opening the door and bribing me would make things easier. Oh, he was still going to die, but he didn't need to know that.

Looking around the room, I noticed a beam above the bathroom, about eight feet up, that appeared to be solid. There was no other vantage point that looked accessible. That would have to do.

"*What's taking so long, Fluffy?*" Stricken's voice was in my ear. He sounded irritated. "*Tick-tock. Local police are responding and while I don't have any qualms about taking them out, I have a deadline to meet.*"

"Okay. Two million. Where?" I asked Jorge, ignoring Stricken for the moment.

"The closet!" His squeals were getting rather pathetic sounding. In fact, it was almost overdone. He wasn't nearly as frightened as he was pretending. I smirked. My new friend Jorge was about to try something stupid.

I love predictably stupid people.

"Okay. I'm grabbing the money, then I'm leaving. Best of luck to you!" I called out before jumping straight up. The monster within let me do things that would make gymnasts shed jealous tears. I easily snagged the beam with my bare hands. Using pure strength, I pulled myself up without too much trouble. Crouched on the beam above the room, the only thing to do now was to stay silent and wait for Jorge the Goat to do something stupid, like come out.

It didn't take long at all. In less than thirty seconds the bathroom door slid open slowly and a pale, sweating man peeked out. Balding with a massive case of back pimples, he was not the kind of guy I'd envisioned being a chick magnet. In the photos he took great care to cover up that shiny dome, but here from above it was painfully obvious that the combover was in effect.

He looked around the room and, not seeing anyone, he must have thought it was safe and stepped into his bedroom. In his hands were a pair of gold-plated Glocks, which instantly made me want to murder him on principal alone.

What sort of deranged, coked-out motherfucker has a pair of gold-plated... I shook the rhetorical question away. Now was not the time to wonder at the sanity of man, or the eclectic tastes of a narco.

Since Stricken had wanted the message sent as loud as possible, I pulled at the monster within, inviting him to come fully out and play. Unlike werewolves, my kind can change at will because we're born like this. While it was still considered a curse, there were some serious upsides to being a hybrid monster like me.

For starters, strength and speed. And claws. Plus, we can pick and choose what part of our body we can transform.

Well, I could, at least. My mom? It's not something that's come up before.

I dropped silently from above. Jorge never knew what hit him.

Driving my claws into the back of his neck, we tumbled to the floor and rolled across one of the larger fur rugs. His blood sprayed as the monster began tearing him apart. For once, I didn't try to hold it back. I let the beast fully out. Fangs ripped chunks of flesh out from his back and shoulders. The prey shrieked in pain as my claws flipped him over and proceeded to disembowel him.

The biggest drawback, however, was that sometimes the demon-like monster within didn't like relinquishing control back to me. The blood continued to splash everywhere as the monster played with the corpse as though it were a chew toy. Struggling to regain control, it relished the warm, sticky blood dripping on its tongue and reminded me why I avoided letting it all out.

After what felt like an eternity but was probably only a few seconds, I regained control. The world around me shifted colors as my eyes—and sanity—returned. The overpowering scent of blood almost made my eyes water. Glancing down at the corpse, I grimaced.

Stricken had wanted a message sent. I was pretty sure it was delivered, loud and clear. The less said about the carnage in the room, the better.

How the fuck did I get six feet of entrails up on that ceiling fan?

During the transition into monster, I'd shredded the constricting clothes as my overall size increased and my body changed. Back in human form, I was stark naked and feeling a little exposed. Part of me wondered if I could squeeze into a pair of the Goat's pants before dismissing the idea. He was too skinny by far. I had a change of clothes back where Stricken had set up, but that meant walking around during that time as naked as the day I was born.

My mind drifted back to something Jorge had said. Had he had been telling the truth when it came to the bribe offer? With nothing to lose but time, I quickly made my way to the closet to see if Jorge had been lying in some vain attempt at survival. Inside there were indeed two large duffel bags, both zipped closed. Surprised, I took a peek in the first and blinked as a wonderous sight filled my eyes.

Neatly stacked of hundred-dollar bills filled it to capacity. It was pretty hefty, too. There looked to be a lot of fucking money in it. The other one was filled with the same. I was going to be eating Wagyu carne asada for *decades.*

I whistled. "Damn, Jorge, you weren't kidding." This would make the boss happy.

Naked, covered in blood, and carrying the two duffel bags loaded with cash, I walked calmly out of the master suite, back downstairs and past the guards I'd dropped previously, and into the foyer.

There was still gunfire coming from outside, but it was sporadic, inconsistent. There were two possibilities here: either the team had been taken down, or Juventud had managed to tear a hole in their defenses and Kenta had slipped in. My orders were to let people inside survive. I had no idea if they were under the same compunction. Probably. Stricken liked it when bad guys feared the creatures who hunted them.

A rich, spicy aroma suddenly filled my nostrils and I stumbled to a halt, one hand on the front door.

"Whoa," I muttered. The scent was intoxicating, familiar, and alluring. There was so much promise in that smell. It drowned out the blood I'd spilled, the gore covering my body. There was nothing I wanted more—*we* wanted, the monster within purred—than to find where that luxurious scent was coming from.

It felt like I was having an out-of-body experience, much like the very first time when the Herald had shown up when I hit puberty. Only this time I knew I was awake. Or at least, I think I was. With the way my mind was reacting to the smell, it was hard to say.

There was a doorway just to the left of the front door. The schematics said this was the path to the basement. It also happened to be where the scent was leading me. The smell was so inviting that I could almost hear the invitation to head downstairs, the words lingering on the very edge of my conscious mind.

I was halfway down the stairs when I heard Stricken's voice in my ear once more.

"Fluffy, you're off mission."

"Got something..." I murmured. *How the hell did he know anyway? Weirdo.* The call beckoned, pulling stronger on me as I slowly descended. It was only thirteen measly steps before I was in a cool, dark basement oddly bereft of guns, drugs, or ammo.

My eyes immediately adjusted to the darkness. The floor was dirt, which was a little surprising. The alluring smell was even stronger here, and sang the color of jade in my head. I'd almost fully shifted back to my human form, with the exception of my eyes. The monster wanted to see who offered us such promises, and I was right there with it.

"What've you got, Fluffy? I don't have time to play games," the voice in my ear said. Such an annoying thing, that. A very large part of me wanted to pull out the comm and toss it aside. In the grand scheme of things, did Stricken even matter? No, he didn't... just that wicked, wonderous aroma.

In the center of the room was a large, grave-shaped hole in the ground. While fascinating, I was still far more interested in finding out who or what had dragged me down here. The aroma remained overpowering, shoving my own wants and needs to the back of my mind as I sought out the goddess. At least, I was pretty sure that's who I was looking for. Nothing else made sense.

"You have Jorge's blood on you..." An ethereal voice floated out from the giant hole in the center of the floor. I smiled. There was a voice to the aroma. This was good. "He was weak. You are strong. You can take control. He was nothing but a puppet. You? You are so much more."

I could take over the cartel. It would be easy. The men surviving upstairs would undoubtedly do whatever I told them to. They'd seen what I could do, what I was. The idea of leaving behind survivors had indeed been a good one. There'd be no one who could stop me.

"Oh yes..." the voice purred. The monster inside struggled against that for some reason. I didn't understand. The voice was the same as the aroma. Why did the monster fight so hard? "I've always wanted a pet."

Oh. Okay. Now I understood why the monster was fighting so hard.

The spell suddenly snapped as the monster within raged at those words. We were many things, but we were nobody's *pet*. The veil that had been placed over my mind lifted abruptly as it fought for full control—not only of our body, but our very soul. Blinking, it was a struggle to shed whatever was going on with my consciousness. My footsteps staggered and I pushed myself away from the goddess—no, the damned *creature* that had almost got me—and I leaned against the wall. The cool stone of the basement wall managed to fixate me back to the now, away from the cloying scent that had very nearly taken over my mind.

"Pity. You had such promise, little pet."

She appeared out of nowhere right before me, veiled to hide from both me and the *nagualii* riding shotgun in my soul. Her face twisted and her teeth grew. Her lips twisted as fangs longer than my hand emerged from her mouth. Long, razor-sharp claws rapidly grew from her fingertips. A once beautiful woman shed the mask, allowing me to see just what had nearly led me to my doom. It took all my willpower to not recoil in horror.

She was a chkalku, a type of dark sorceress that prowled the mountains of South America. My mom had run across one once back when she'd been young. The creature was like me, a hybrid of monster and human, but unlike my kind, a chkalku owed allegiance to the dark forces that created it.

They were almost as powerful as necromancers. Terrifying

creatures, but they had weaknesses. Problem was, I couldn't remember what those were at the moment. My mind was still a jumbled mess as we struggled to shake off whatever it had done to us.

Plus, my *nagualii* was fucking *pissed.*

All this went through my head in less than a heartbeat. The primal shriek of the chkalku nearly shattered my eardrums, and caused me to wince. In that fraction of a moment she struck, her long claws raking across my bare chest. The claws were so sharp I didn't even feel the cut at first. Blood splashed against the stone wall I'd been leaning against. Looking down, I could see four perfect lines drawn on my chest. The cuts were wide and white beneath my dark skin.

Then they began to bleed, and the pain kicked in.

Gasping, I staggered back. I'd been stabbed, shot, sliced to ribbons, bit, and even drowned once, but none of that compared to the cuts that burned my skin in that moment. It felt as though the cuts had been doused in Betadine then lit on fire, just for fun. There was also the distinctive smell of poison in the cuts.

Nobody ever told me that chkalku had poisonous claws. That just wasn't fair.

"Aw . . . my little kitty figuring out that he is not the most dangerous monster in these jungles . . ."

Her taunts grated on my nerves. I was the one who talked a lot of smack when fighting. Who the hell did she think she was, stealing my bit?

"You talk a lot for something that crawls out of a child's empty grave," I snapped back. It wasn't my best, but it was better than silence. "Why don't you go take a long walk in the sun? It'll clear that complexion right up. I mean, really? All that dark magic and nothing for the acne scars? Bet that makes dating tough."

Even monsters have egos, apparently. She hissed and lunged, claws extended. This time, with a clearer mind and some warning, I was able to dodge her attack. My own claws caught flesh and I tried to pull her closer. In a fight in close, there were very few creatures in this world that could tangle with my kind and come out on top. A chkalka was not one of them.

She must have known this as well and slithered out of my grasp. Range and speed were her allies in this fight now that the stupid pheromones she'd been luring me with were no longer working. The poison was also working its way out of my system.

She had to know that the clock was against her. The longer this fight went on, the better my odds became.

She pivoted again as my claws whistled through the air, narrowly missing her. The creature blocked the exit, but seemed to be tethered to the large hole in the ground. Good to know that the information I had on these things was correct and that she was tied to the desecrated grave.

"I will feast on your entrails. I will devour your soul. I will—" She stopped abruptly, confusion etched on her monstrous features. A thin, narrow line of blood appeared on her throat. A second later, her head tumbled off her shoulders and the body dropped to the floor. The skin began steaming as the fleshy bits began to deliquesce.

"She talked a lot," Kenta whispered and flicked the monster's blood off his sword with a slight movement of his wrist. He glanced around. "I need to go get our ride. Quit dawdling, my friend."

The *tokuromubi* disappeared without another word. He'd managed to sneak up on us, avoid whatever pheromone scent she'd been infecting my mind with, and executed her without me even noticing. I blamed the poison.

Looking around, I spotted the two duffel bags I'd taken from Jorge. Sometime during my descent of the stairs I'd set them down. Funny. I couldn't remember doing that at all.

"Fluffy, I swear Lovi will blow your brains out if you've gone rogue..." Stricken's voice was back in my ear.

"Found the Ghost of Bogotá. Dead now. Kenta killed it," I said after keying my mic. For a moment I wondered just how much he'd heard of the fight before dismissing it. Stricken was a dick, but he understood. Or at least, I hoped he would. "On my way to extraction."

"About fucking time, Fluffy."

With a quiet sigh, I picked up the duffel bags, headed up the stairs, and out the front door.

The scene was utter chaos. There were bodies everywhere, with most missing their heads. A few fires had broken out somehow, and someone had *thrown* a small Chevy two-door sedan through one of the walls. Juventud and Kenta had been busy. But there were also survivors milling, just as Stricken had wanted. They looked lost, in shock at the monsters that had attacked them. They were no longer a threat.

So instead of sneaking out, I walked my bare ass across the compound and out the front gate.

It was unsurprising that none of the remaining survivors tried to stop me.

We arrived at the airfield without any delays or interruptions, the tactically acquired Land Rover handling the rough roads easily enough. Jorge the Goat might have been a despicable drug dealer who destroyed families and communities, as well as worked with a monster that he fed his enemies to, but I had to admire his choice in luxury vehicles. The interior was plush, with gold accents on random items, and some strange peach-colored leather wrapping around the steering wheel. The seats had added cushions for comfort, and the AC blew cold, which caused some shrinkage. I wasn't quite sure where Kenta had picked up the Land Rover, but I wasn't about to complain and ruin a good thing. It sure beat walking.

"I'm so glad you keep spare pants with you. I do not need to see that flopping around during the entire ride to the airfield," Stricken said as I finished pulling my sweats on in the back seat. Ignoring his jibe, I fished out a clean shirt from the backpack Kenta offered. Normal ops said not to wear any clothing that could identify us as American but Stricken wasn't the sort who really cared about our fashion sense, only results, so I would be rocking a Megadeth T-shirt. The blood on my arms and face would come off later with baby wipes and rubbing alcohol.

"Bet you're all happy to be heading home," he continued after a moment. I glanced up and looked at him in the rearview mirror. His expression was inscrutable as he drove. Having worked with him now for about a year, I had a rough idea of how his mind worked. Him suggesting something like that meant another job was in the works.

Other than Lovi, the others were all relative newcomers to the team, so they missed the subtle cue. She wasn't about to let anyone else in on the boss' little secret, though.

"So where we off to next?" I asked, instead of letting Stricken play with our hopes and emotions for a little longer. His eyes flicked back to me, and he appeared mildly annoyed at my ruining his game.

"They're headed back stateside. You and I? Something else

is going down that requires our attention. We're going to your sort of place, made entirely possible by your tax-free donation to STFU."

"My sort of place?" I asked.

"Oh yeah. You're going to love it!" he promised, then giggled and pushed his rose-tinted glasses up.

He lied, as usual.

I hated every minute of it.

MHI recruits exclusively from those monster-attack survivors. Facing evil and getting out alive is the most important thing on the résumé.

—A.L.

Land's End

Marisa Wolf

Sarah McMurray considered every stupid choice that had brought her to this moment. There weren't many, given she was days short of her twenty-first birthday, but what they lacked in volume they truly made up for in pure idiocy.

She slouched in her salt-eaten truck, hands wrapped through the steering wheel, and stared into the space above her aunt's bar.

One: Leaving the known life of her family to go west for school. Her family had never needed college before, what had she been thinking?

Two: Bonding with her party girl roommate, and letting Tasha dictate their social time.

Three: Drinking every night, running through the forests, yelling at the moon with a bunch of other young dumbasses.

Four: Going looking for her party girl roommate in the woods late at night.

Five: The fire. The burning. The...

Sarah blinked repeatedly, her eyes too dry to do anything but ache for a long moment. She'd had no business in the woods. None of them had.

The bare, scraggly trees around the bar rocked in a wind she couldn't feel, and she reached for her scarf on the bench next to her. Her coat was in the back with her bag, but if she walked in all geared up she'd never hear the end of it from whichever old salt was bellied up to the bar at three in the afternoon.

She wound the scarf loosely around her neck and slid out of the car, leaving her loose belongings behind in the vanishingly small chance her aunt didn't have room for her a few weeks early. There was hardly as much work in the offseason, but she had no interest in going home, and she'd arranged with her aunt to work over winter break and give the older woman a small reprieve from her unending routines.

"Hey, is that the college girl? Look who's back, Colleen!" the voice rumbled, familiar in its rasp, and Sarah's lips quirked in answer.

Colleen Reilly, her late father's older sister, straightened from behind the worn bar with her ready smile in place. No sign her niece was three weeks early, without any word given ahead. "That's our girl. Home to wrangle all you reprobates so I can get a little rest for once." She flapped a towel at him, then dropped it and flipped open the hatch at the end of the bar to come through and offer a hug.

Sarah accepted it, letting her shoulders ease as the scents of old cigarette smoke, bleach, and freshly drawn beer soothed a tension she'd been carrying for days.

"You getting right to work, or want to settle in first?" Colleen gestured around the open space, sparsely populated given time of day and year, and Sarah gave the collaged tables a once-over. The same local advertisements and old flyers coated by inches of epoxy shined back at her, and more tension seeped away.

"Everything's in good shape—let me drop my bag? What project do you have in mind?"

"Oh, I was going to have you sanitize the keg lines and deep-clean the fridges and coolers, but it's not the most pressing. Go tell Ronald you're not too fancy for the likes of us and freshen up. I'll find you something by then."

There were always projects at the Driftwood, and it was work she'd been doing every summer since she was twelve. Being back felt more like home than her mother's ever did, and it was almost enough to soften the ache twisted through her spine.

Greetings duly made to Ronald Deerborn, she fetched her bag, paused only long enough to separate out the faint sound of waves from the groan of the wind, then went around the back of the bar. Colleen had propped open the staff door, a habit on all but the worst blustery nights to keep the cigarette smoke cycling out and balance the buildup of heat and bodies.

Sarah walked down the left hall, away from the back room of the bar, to the small apartment at the end of the hall. She turned without thinking to the little room tucked away in the far side of the living area—her room.

It wasn't hers, technically. She never left anything behind when she went back to her mother's for school, or more recently, to the other side of the state for college.

Now and then Colleen would rent it out to someone passing through in the winter, or a local needing a temporary place to crash, but it seemed to always be open when Sarah needed it. She closed the door behind her, leaned against it, and felt her breath catch in the back of her throat. Apparently she'd been relying on the room being available for her, and the relief of finding it true nearly made her cry like the twelve-year-old she'd been the first time her mom dropped her off at the Driftwood without a word of preparation.

"No," she muttered to the memory, tossing her bag on the chair in the corner and shoving upright to pull sheets out of the dresser. Prepared for her or not, Colleen would have a list of tasks longer than her arm once Sarah emerged into the bar. After hours of driving, and hours more of scrubbing, lifting, shifting, and all the prep work in the kitchen, the last thing she'd want to do at the end of the night would be to make the bed.

There were no blankets neatly folded in the closet, so she forced another steadying breath, went out to the living room, and dug through the old steamer trunk behind the couch until she found her favorite.

It had been her father's, according to Colleen. Not something Sarah could know, never having met the man, but she didn't hate his taste. It was quilted in every shade of blue, pattern lightly suggesting waves without being held to any definite shape. It was warmer than it looked and carried a faint scent of maple that never faded no matter how often it got tumbled with dryer sheets. She gathered it in her arms, sniffed it, then marched across the room to throw it over the bed.

No reason to sit here sniffing and sniffling like a child. The forest was behind her. She didn't have to go back. Didn't have to call back the officious government man who'd invaded her dorm room after Tasha . . . after the woods . . . no. She didn't have to call him and make any kind of decision. Didn't have to do anything but scrub and clean and chop and whatever else her aunt told her to do.

Maybe she repeated that to herself twenty times while staring into the warped mirror over the bathroom sink—but so what? She was a McMurray. Took a few repetitions to get things to sink in to their thick heads.

With a quick pinch of her cheeks to force color into her face—nothing to be done about the shadows under her blue eyes or the new wrinkle in the midpoint of her forehead—she tightened her ponytail and ventured out into the fray.

The evening rush consisted of ten old fishermen she'd known most of her life, and a handful of their wives, women she'd known nearly as long. They sat in their same seats, scattered across the low tables and the high-top bar, talking over and under each other as though space and concentration had no bearing.

Mostly it was recent gossip mixed with the same old stories she'd known as long as them, interspersed with the occasional interruption to grill her about school. She slipped around and through them delivering the drinks that served most for dinner, along with a rarer cup of chowder or plate of fish and green beans.

John, the cook who'd worked for Colleen since Sarah's dad was alive, grunted fondly at her and never lifted his attention from his work. Despite the scarcity of food orders, there was plenty of fish to prepare and portion out—part of his and Colleen's payments, though Sarah always preferred her tips in cash rather than cod.

"I'm telling you!" The voice rose over the general rumble with an extra layer of irritation, and she glanced at the clock as she pushed through the swinging doors from the kitchen. A bit early for the arguments to break out, but she hadn't been back long enough to decipher if the sour mood was bad fishing or general winter crankiness, so it might be right on time.

William Pew, allegedly a little younger than most of the other captains but just as weathered, leaned far back in his chair and stretched his legs into the aisle. Sarah eeled around him and dropped off the side of corn Mrs. Deerborn had been about to ask for, but she couldn't block out William's fish tale.

"Full set of teeth, eyes in the front of its head—the damn weirdest fish I ever pulled out of the water."

"Probably a sheepshead," Matt Sanborn muttered, letting his

voice carry. A knack Sarah had yet to pick up, despite a lifetime of observation.

"You ever hear of a sheepshead in the deep water? You thinking I've never seen one'a them before? Nah sir, this thing had a face like a . . . like a person, more than a fish. Beaky front, like a parrotfish. Or a nose."

"Let's see it, then. Surely the restaurant boys didn't buy it. You holding it for the aquarium?"

"Let's see it, then," and "the aquarium's coming to get it" were the holy refrains of sea stories at the Driftwood, the bookends of conversations for the not at all rare weirdnesses that hit their local decks through the years.

"Damnedest thing. Got it out of the net into the tank, and the damn thing must have flopped out on the trip back."

"Told you," Ronald announced, elbowing Matt in his gut. "'Saw it, you gotta believe me.' Not like Sully's purple fucking lobster, am I right?"

"It was blue." George Sullivan, Sully to everyone since his sainted mother died, didn't turn from his seat.

"It was weird and had a little mutant claw, sure enough. But we all saw that one."

"Didn't believe him till we did, though, so don't take it personal, Pew."

"Not taking nothing personal. Just telling you I caught a fish with a full-on face today. Weirdest shit I ever saw. Gave me the creeps." Pew gripped his beer mug with two hands and glared at the table.

"Oh, the creeps, is it? Like when Fitz was convinced the long hair of a mermaid was tangling his motor but next day we saw it was some of that Florida seaweed, drifting the coast?"

"Yeah, Sanborn. Just like that." Pew rolled his eyes and raised his middle finger. "Maybe the college girl knows what is. What kinda fish got a face, McMurray?"

"I'm not studying marine biology, Willie," Sarah said without glancing his way. The men rarely referred to each other by first names, and she'd made a habit of using nicknames they didn't since before she grown taller than the bar. She gathered up four glasses from the bar and dropped them at their respective tables, keeping an eye out for stray limbs in her aisles.

"Nah, you don't go all the way out to the damn mountains

to study the sea, do you?" Sanborn shook his head and grunted, draining half his glass. "Marine biologists. Trying to tell us about lobsters this and cod that. Like we don't know."

"I don't know, Sanborn, that little guy who came by last year wasn't so bad. Had some good ideas about the harbor cleanup they'd been doing."

"Mark my words, boys, that harbor'll be full of California hippies once they get the jellyfish out." Sanborn gesticulated wildly, making his feelings on Californian hippies known. George Sullivan made a noise deep in his throat.

"Nah, he was all right. From Quincy or one of them damn towns. Hometown kid, close enough."

"Like our little Sarah. She's from the north shore, but we taught her all right, didn't we?" John Gorton interjected, his mouth full of chowder.

"Good enough she ran off to school." George snorted, but his smile in Sarah's direction was warm.

Sarah felt the shift coming, the next flurry of questions about what she was studying, what it was like out there, what kind of job was she going to get. The taste of charred wood coated the back of her throat and she swallowed reflexively, as though the ghost of smoke could be exorcised so easily.

"Taught me well enough I had to pass on some lessons in drinking to those other college kids." She tried to pitch it like Sanborn, something low that carried.

Old Sully laughed, deep from his gut, and even Pew chuckled. "What do they know about it, chugging instead of appreciating no doubt," Sully stated, lifting his stein and from all appearance unhinging his jaw to knock back the rest of his nearly full beer. He nodded at her to refill, and Sarah let the attention wick off her like water beading down feathers.

She woke sore the next day. It took almost a full minute to untangle from her sheets and rearrange her limbs into some semblance of order. Her father's blanket was on the floor, her pillow down by her feet.

Instead of considering what her dreams had been, she took time to stretch and then wandered down to the bathroom to take the hottest lava shower her skin could handle before joining her aunt at work.

The regulars trickled in, a slightly different crowd from the night before. Pew wasn't there to talk about his fish-with-a-face, which she wouldn't have thought anything of if Donald Freman hadn't mentioned owing him a drink. Seemed unlike Pew to pass up a free beverage, but she supposed it would taste just as good the next night.

"Storm's whipping up over the next few days," Ronald grumbled, hunched over the bar with his eyes locked into his beer. "Feels like a bad one."

"Says your knee or your hip?" Sanborn called from his corner by the door.

"Every damn hollow bone I got," Ronald replied, without so much as a grunt for the ribald add-ons that earned him.

"Nah, leave him be, boys." Sully rocked his chair back, chewing on a french fry until it couldn't be more than paste. "He's not wrong. Whatever's coming up the coast'll be nasty, but it's the time of year for it."

"Probably where Pew is. Said he had some work to do before the next big one."

"Don't we all." Meditative silence, their beers more interesting than their peers. Sarah wiped down the decorative bottles that lined the shelves behind the bar and listened more than she chimed in. Better not to remind them of any topics they'd missed the night before.

Her jumpy stomach was a result of the incoming storm, nothing more. It had been a few years since she'd spent a winter with her aunt, choosing to take extra classes over the breaks at school, and she was out of practice. Snow in the lee of the mountains was different from the midwinter storms on the coast. She just had to get readjusted.

The dinner rush, such as it was, dragged late into the evening. By the time the last patron shoved out the door, the wind had risen high enough to rattle all the loose boards in the building.

"Breakfast tomorrow?" Colleen asked, tossing a clean towel for Sarah to finish wiping the tables.

"I should be awake," she replied. The chances of Sarah sleeping in the first place were not high, but such was life. At least the wind would provide company.

"You good to finish up here?"

"Get some rest." Sarah waved over her shoulder, turned her

back to the bar, and focused so hard on each next step of the closing checklist she barely heard the occasional slam of wood at all.

The next morning was about as peaceful as the night had been.

"I talked to your mother last night," Colleen began, which was just about the worst start to breakfast as Sarah could have asked for.

She made a noncommittal noise, shoveled scrambled eggs into her mouth, and hoped her aunt would drop the topic. Unlikely, but maybe this time idiot hope would see her through.

"She seems to think your semester isn't over for a few more weeks." Colleen speared a link of sausage and held it midair, as though waiting for the response that did not come. She took a bite, chewed it, and stared at Sarah's forehead until she determined the silence would hold longer than her meat. "And also that you might leave school for a job."

"I'm not doing that." The words pushed out of her mouth the moment she finished swallowing. A chunk of egg lodged itself somewhere near the top of her throat, and she drank her whole glass of over-sweetened orange juice.

"Leaving school? Taking a job?" Colleen blew out her breath and put her fork down. "Speaking to me about important things?"

"It's nothing important." Sarah lifted a shoulder, desperately attempting to convey the truth of the statement, to both herself and her aunt. "Did my finals early."

Colleen sat back in her chair and picked up her coffee. "And?"

"And I missed you. The bar. The ocean." Some of that was true. "So I just came down."

"Sarah, she said something happened—"

Fire, creeping through underbrush. A high wailing sound, too faint to be near, too raw to be imagined.

"She doesn't know the first thing about what happens in my life." The truth of *that* burned Sarah's throat, and every half-chewed bite she'd taken threatened to climb back out of her stomach.

"I know she can be . . . a handful, but she's never been one to make—"

"And you know her so well?" Sarah tried another bite, but the formerly fluffy eggs had congealed into slime, and she managed to get it down only because of the flood of saliva that threatened vomit. Sarah pushed back from the table and kept her eyes down as she muttered, "I'll be back before lunch prep."

Her aunt didn't call her back, and she paused only long enough to grab her coat before walking out.

Exactly thirty seconds later, Sarah wished she'd been smart enough to grab mittens and a hat, maybe a few scarves, but she tucked her chin and continued toward the beach access a few blocks down.

Past the dunes, the soft dry sand was already lashing in the wind, so she turned her back to it and headed in the other direction. It would suck on the return, but that was later Sarah's problem. Current Sarah needed to walk the waterline and put herself as far from the possibility of reaching flames as possible.

Her path swerved as high waves stretched across the beach, and she held as best she could to the narrow strip of packed wet sand. The tideline was full of seaweed and debris pushed ahead of the coming storm. Plenty reason to step carefully—to keep from her boots filling with ice water, or from trodding through anything suspiciously soft.

Motion flickered in her peripheral, and she tilted her head. A bird skimming the waves? No, nothing. Probably a bit of seafoam had caught the edge of her gaze. She tucked her chin back into her coat before the wind and driving sand could rub her skin raw.

As she adjusted to the crash of the waves and the howl of the wind, smaller noises registered at the limit of her hearing. Gulls haunting the dunes, just out of her sight. The rattle of water pulling back through a rocky section of the beach. The plunk of a splash close to shore, water folding in on itself or some large fish tasting air.

Another flicker of motion, something long and lithe, and she reconsidered the source of the splashes. Seals, probably, gorging on cod.

Sarah angled as best she could to keep an eye on the incoming waves without turning too far into the wind. The weak winter sun was bright enough to sting her eyes, but barely lightened the dark water curving toward shore. Reaching strands of seaweed tangled through the rise of the waves, accompanied by a flash of movement. Had to be a seal.

Her ankle turned and she ripped her gaze from the shadows in the sea to her feet underneath her before her stumble could shift into a fall. The seaweed heaped at her feet was luridly orange, studded with barnacles that open-close-opened like gasping mouths.

Bitterness flooded the back of her throat and she swallowed, stepping wide around the mound and risking the grasping edge of a wave.

An odd shape lay in her path farther up the coast, and she squinted at it suspiciously. Too dark to be more of the gross orange seaweed. Maybe a tire? A less lucky seal, its deflated corpse pushed to shore by the high waves?

"Morbid much?" she said aloud, dropping her attention back to the sand immediately in front of her. Littered with pieces of shells and loose fronds of sea plants, it gave her plenty to distract herself with and nothing interesting enough to bend and pick up.

A shiver wrenched her spine and she realized she'd been bent forward under the wind, studying the ground. With a conscious effort, she uncurved her back, straightened until everything popped and sorted itself into its correct formation.

A flash sparkled out of the corner of her eye, but when she turned it was gone. Sea spray catching the sun, or another seal, tracking the lone human idiot wandering the land.

Before long, she was close enough to note more details of the lump ahead—and assure herself it was definitely a corpse of some kind, not a tire.

"Good enough sign to go home." Sarah stopped in her tracks, shifted her boots to sink an inch or so down into the sand, and held up a hand on the side of her face to protect her eyes as she stared off toward the horizon. The clouds piled dark down the coast, and she wondered if the storm would hit a day early, or if this was a precursor. The temper before the tempest.

Unlike her aunt, and the entirety of her father's side of the family, she hadn't spent enough time by the sea to truly understand its moods nor the signs the weather offered. Enough to know staying out much longer wasn't smart, but she couldn't gauge a storm's arrival by the tides, or measure the clouds to know the shape of the incoming squall.

With a sigh, she tightened her ponytail and ducked her head low to turn back into the wind.

Motion flickered again at the edge of her vision—sand streaming by, that same damn seal probably—and she ignored it. Nothing to do with her.

Head down, get home, pay no attention to the things beneath her feet. Focus on the burning prickle along her cheeks as her face numbed, blink her eyes clear of the protective water that rose in answer to wind and sand, one foot in front of the other.

By the time Sarah straggled into the bar, she forgot to be alert for her aunt's questions. Thankfully the beer delivery was there, so she slipped to the back for a shower without interrogation.

Lunch and dinner were sparse, and they had time to make progress on Colleen's endless list of tasks. A blessing for Sarah, meaning her aunt was too distracted to continue their morning conversation.

Conversation's a strong word for it, Sarah heard clearly in her aunt's voice. *And you can only avoid it so long.*

Sarah ducked her head and scrubbed harder. Colleen was deep in conversation with Sully, and would have laughed herself silly to know Sarah's conscience was using her voice.

"No one else is coming in," Ronald announced, balancing his chair on two legs and lifting a stein to the room. "Preparing for the storm or to take an early run before it blows in, thinking they've got control over what happens next."

"What happens next?" Fitzy took the cue, as Sully's favorite thing to do had been long established in the Driftwood Bar.

"The creatures come from the deep. The bigger a storm, the farther down it reaches, driving up the monsters we see only once in our lives."

"The monsters, is it?" Colleen played her role well, the doubting landlubber, unfamiliar with the mysteries of the sea. Joseph Abbott, newer to the area than all the natives, choked back a laugh and Colleen winked at him.

"Monsters it is. When I was young—as young as our little baby McMurray there—I caught one, tangled in my net."

"Haven't heard this one in a while." Ronald made a show of settling comfortably in his seat. Sarah rubbed her arms and grabbed her sweatshirt her next pass by the bar, shrugging it on before picking up the next round to deliver.

"Pew's tale the other day reminded me. I haven't thought of it in . . . oh, at least a few years now. Used to be I'd picture it every night, trying to go to sleep."

Sarah considered knocking back one of the full mugs in her hands, but set them all down without sloshing any excess liquid. She could only imagine the raucous response were she to take someone's beer and chug like a frat boy.

"This one I caught, though... oh it was a beast of the deep, no doubt. Collapsing in on itself in the air, once it wasn't held up by the water anymore."

"What'd it look like?"

"It was a day like this, right before the storm." Old Sully ignored the prompting, settling in to tell his story his way, as ever. "The sky was queer and silver bright, hurt to look at, but no sun to be seen. You know the kind."

Heads nodded sagely, and Sarah scooped up his empty mug as she set down a new one.

"My net was weighing heavy, so much my boat was struggling. Knew I had a good catch or was snagged, no in-between, but when I winched it up it came fast. Nothing in it but a handful of trash fish and a shadow that took me a minute to recognize. Hair. Long, dark, seaweed-tangled hair."

A small susurrus of murmurs there, as no few of the men in the room had pulled up their own corpse. Never a good day, catch cursed and tainted.

"But it wasn't a woman on the other end of the hair. I opened the net over the deck, tossed back the mess, and got to the center of the heap. Another fish—long like a seal, hair the length of its body, a face..."

He trailed off, and the room leaned toward him. Or maybe that was just Sarah, who huffed out a breath and straightened, turned away to return to the bar and whatever she had to pick up next.

"A face?" Ronald prompted, less jocular than before.

"It was a fish's face, all right, but the teeth were as human as yours." He snapped his own—dentures, for as long as Sarah had known him—and waited out the sporadic chuckle that followed. His voice softened as he continued, nearly hushed, and Sarah caught at least three of the men leaning toward him as she had. "But that wasn't the worst part. Flippers more than fins, all trailing like fingers." He waggled his own, but the motion felt less... fun than the gesture with his teeth. His eyes had lost focus, and Sarah forced herself to stop looking at him, busied herself organizing the next round of mugs on her tray instead.

"And the eyes..." He drank deeply, took a breath, and repeated the motion with his hands as he spoke. "I rolled it free of the net and its eyes opened. Filmed with death, sure enough, but no fish eyes, these. Rounded and blue and human as yours or mine."

Sarah's wrist twitched, and she steadied her tray with her other hand a fraction of a second before gravity took over. Her shoulders ached as she held her body stiff until the drinks were successfully delivered. Why she should feel out of breath, heart hammering, when this was about as slow a night as she got in the Driftwood, she couldn't say.

"I couldn't take it in, after that. Knew the Woods Hole boys would love it, but I doubted it would make it to shore, the way it deflated. Looked like it was melting more than collapsing, the longer it sat on my deck."

"What'd you do, kick it back over?"

"Wrapped it in some spare sailcloth and slid it off the back." He stared into his mug, as though the rest of them weren't there. "The way we used to send off sailors. Sending them home."

Silence held the room, and after a long moment, Colleen clapped her hands and said, "A tale like that deserves whiskey, wouldn't you say? A drop for everyone, get you home with some warmth in your chest."

Enthusiasm, muted at first but growing as they watched her pour, answered the offer.

Sarah, of course, didn't get any, and maybe that was why she lay cold and unsleeping in her bed after the work was done for the night.

She couldn't hold still any longer, and bundled up as dawn approached. Cold and miserable the beach might be, but a proper sunrise—the last before the storm rolled through—would start her day off better than the last had ended.

Tall rain boots, mittens, hat and scarf and hood all secured, she stumped out of the bar and down to the water in the dark. She'd counted on the moon to light her way, but its appearance was patchy as clouds raced across the sky. The faint lightening at the edge of the horizon and long habit served her in good stead, and she reached the edge of the water without incident. The wind was less than yesterday's. It wouldn't last, but she appreciated the moment for what it was.

She turned the other way from her previous walk, toward the harbor sheltered by a curve in the coastline. The sand was clear of yesterday's debris. She walked carefully nevertheless, her visibility only a handful of feet ahead of her in the clinging night.

Every few steps the world around her brightened, but not in the glorious golds and reds of a pre-storm sunrise. Sickly yellows and oranges streaked the sky, a shade nearer to green closer to the horizon. The clouds, probably, not so opaque to hold the darkness in place, but not transparent enough to let the sky blaze into life. Fog crept in from the water, trailing edges like the waves ahead of her.

As she rounded the curve toward the harbor, the ships were nearly clear of the cove. Fewer than she'd expected heading out, but more than was sane given the approaching storm.

Sand stretched markless ahead of her, and so she studied the boats instead of the ground, trying to place crew to ship. The red stripe was Fitzpatrick's, he was always moaning about repainting it. Blue and white was Sully, she was pretty sure, the *Idle Glass.* Farthest out was too hard to identify, even if she squinted, so Sarah focused her vision closer in. Something flashed in the water—a buoy? A marker? Lobster trap, maybe, but...

She knew it wasn't any of those.

But it couldn't have been what it looked like.

Not a face, floating in the choppy harbor waters, not when the boats continued ahead, none slewing around for a swept-over crewman.

No. It had to have been the bob of a lobster-trap buoy. Someone skirting the law.

Her heart hammered under her ribs, and she angled away, facing more fully east to watch the sun struggle above the curve of earth and sea. Her scarf slipped, chapped skin from yesterday's walk prickling in instant sensitivity to the frigid air.

Trick of the light, that's what she'd seen.

She didn't so much as glance toward the harbor again, and once the sun cleared the horizon, only to disappear into a wall of clouds, she turned her steps back toward the Driftwood. The fog thickened over the water, and there was nothing left for her to look at. She rubbed her mittened hands briefly against the small strip of skin not covered by hat or scarf, and resolved to pick up a ski mask if she was going to keep walking the beach at ungodly hours.

She didn't have time to run any errands—the moment she returned Colleen had her staking tarps over the firewood and securing all the loose material behind the building. She moved her and her aunt's cars to the slightly elevated parking at the end of the lot, rehammered loose boards, and did every small task on her aunt's list with minimum prompting. Better that than taking time to talk, and before long it was full dark outside, the wind rising.

Barely anyone came to the bar that night, only Sully and Ronald stopping by for a quick drink and carefully packaged soup to take home. Every time Colleen glanced her way as though about to say something, the phone rang, leading to one-sided responses Sarah couldn't help but hear.

"Haven't seen him all night."

"No, Pew's not here—you need me to? Yeah, that's probably where he is."

"Freman doesn't come in on his off-duty weekends. He heads up to—yeah, you know it. I'll let you know if he passes by on his way home."

"Did you know John Gorton's on the volunteer firefighter team now?"

It took a long moment for Sarah to realize her aunt had hung up the phone and had spoken to her. She'd been cleaning Ronald's table for the third time, head down, focus inward. Blocking out the high, panicked screams of...

"Is he?" Sarah pulled up a memory of the man's face. Younger, less weathered than some, but older than her father would be, if she imagined him correctly. "What if he gets a call while he's out on the boat?"

"He doesn't do that anymore." Colleen shrugged. "Got something at the market instead, so if his kids need him he's there."

"What about... um..." Gorton had a wife. She never came to the bar in the summer, but everyone else seemed to know her well, so Sarah had long assumed she wasn't a fan of tourists and just came around in the winter.

"She passed." Colleen ducked below the bar, offering no more information and little clarity, and Sarah tried to remember the woman for another handful of seconds before giving it up. Fire crackled just under her hearing, and she shoved that away, too.

"Oh." Sarah stared at the table under her cloth, finding nothing to help the awkwardness of the conversation. It was never like this with her aunt, stilted and difficult.

But then Sarah had never been like this, half burned and all the way shut down. She didn't want to remember any of it, never mind wrap her mind around how to explain it to her aunt.

Never mind she couldn't explain it. Wouldn't? Shouldn't.

She bit her lip and flinched at the sudden pressure on her shoulder. Colleen had opened the flap on the bar, walked across the room, and come up right behind her.

"Everyone is home, tucked up safe against the storm. Likely a phone's off the hook or Pew's drunk too much and passed out early."

She lifted her head enough for Colleen to register her confusion.

"I saw you tense every time the phone rang. There's nothing to worry about—it's always like this on the night of the storm, folks calling around to know where people are in case they're needed."

"No, I know." She did. Hurricanes were rare down the Cape, but not unheard of. And a nor'easter didn't have to be tropical to do enough damage to be getting along with.

"Then what is it? Expecting your mom to call?"

"I know better than that."

"She does worry about you, Sarah girl. Just... in her own way."

"Everything's in her own way." Sarah blinked, then repeated the gesture—when had her eyes filled with water? "It's fine, Auntie Coll. I just... I'm just tired."

"Go lie down, then. I'll finish up here." She squeezed Sarah's shoulder again, then dropped her hand. "And tomorrow we're talking, McMurray. Sometimes *you* can do everything in your own way too, you know, and I don't think it's any good for you."

Sarah ducked her head, turned, then spun on her heel to throw her arms around her aunt. "It'll be better in the morning." After the storm. She didn't believe it, but she tried.

"In the morning," Colleen murmured, and hugged her tight before letting go.

It was, technically, morning. But nothing was ever better at two a.m., and Sarah couldn't lay face up in the old twin bed and stare into darkness any longer. The wind had lessened, the storm blown through with all the fury of a jet plane. She slid out of bed and got halfway to bundled up before she remembered to tell herself it was stupid to go out.

But stupid she was, and out she went. A flashlight this time, in case of debris—it wouldn't be the first time power lines or entire poles came down in the wind, and that wasn't something she wanted to accidentally step into.

The sky had partially cleared, the moon heavy and bright in

the midst of a tattered display of clouds, but the shadows were untrustworthy, and she kept the flashlight on and pointed low.

She could have sworn she focused hard for the walk to the beach, but before she knew it she stood at the water's edge without a single memory of the path here.

"God, I'm tired," she said to the biting air around her, and stared at the waves that raged toward the shoreline. Her eyes were heavy despite the bracing cold, and she let them sink closed. She was far enough back from the reach of the water to stand safely and listen to the rhythm of the outgoing tide.

After a minute or ten, the pattern shifted, a double crash or a longer pull, and she forced her eyes open. Bubbles trailed away from her toes—a particularly long-reaching wave receding without sweeping her out to sea, thankfully. Didn't she know better than to lose focus in front of the sea? She traced the path of the bubbles back to the next incoming wave.

And screamed.

She didn't mean to scream. Didn't even register what she was screaming about until the sound was already scraped against her throat.

A face in the water, moon white, round, too pale too bloated too close—one of the fishermen, hadn't they said someone was missing? Familiar enough that she stepped forward, still unthinking, blindly reaching for someone it was too late to help.

The water lashed against her boots, and she moved forward, arms outstretched. Was she still screaming? Was that the echo of her roommate—no, there was no fire here. It couldn't be farther away than it was now, in the reach of the sea.

The next wave brought the face closer, and she braced herself for the cold, water tipping over her boots and instantly soaking through her socks, ice biting her skin.

She *didn't* know this face, couldn't make out more than the face, but she was committed now—some unfortunate soul, washed overboard or off an unreliable perch, and better they were identified than not.

But mid-motion, as she braced herself against the surging waves and the bitter cold, the face moved. Mouth first, opening. From the push and pull of the waves? No. Opening, wider, so wide the jaw had to be broken and fire chased down Sarah's arms, burning her eyebrows, singeing the tip of her nose, the edges of her cheeks.

No, that wasn't fire. She blinked, tried to stumble back. Flecks of near-ice ocean, the cold burning just the same. The water pushed her forward, and her hand brushed—*something.*

The face split in front of her—or was that a shadow?—seaweed poured over her, tangled her arms, blocked her sight, waves of it, undulating, pulling, and she couldn't *see.*

Fuck seeing, she couldn't *breathe.* Teeth on her arms, the biting cold gnawing her skin. Up had no difference from down, she spun. She fell. Drowning or freezing or both, her heart staggered in her chest, she was unable to focus on anything. Something deathly pale flashed before her and she reached for it—the moon, maybe, showing her the way up.

She flailed and rolled over and over again, another wave slamming her to the seafloor—wait. The sand was below her. Up reestablished itself. She shoved as hard as she could, spun once more, oriented—thank all that was good—toward the shore. She'd gone barely a handful of feet out. She didn't have to die here, but fuck her if she could feel her feet.

Moving by the faint memory of how walking worked more than with conscious effort, she dragged herself forward, water thinning around her, then farther until the sand softened underneath her, furrows dragged by her stiffened, clawlike hands.

Shit.

Shit shit shit shit.

Her mind brought her fire, which might actually have been helpful for once if it had brought any warmth with it. She tried to stand, failed, and found her face in the sand.

Crawling had worked perfectly well before. Fuck it.

She shoved herself forward, unable to feel anything until she reached the dunes, when something in her leg started to prickle, then burn. Nerves weren't dead. Good sign.

Something warm there now... blood probably. Later Sarah problem.

Past the dune line she could see the Driftwood, two lights visible—one in the parking lot, one over the door. She used the stairs and the rickety old wooden railing to haul herself to feet that still existed—were her boots gone? Probably not the worst thing she could have left behind in the ocean. At least she couldn't feel her feet to know if her socks had been replaced by something slimy and cold and awful.

One of her eyes wasn't working right, and it took three shambling, lurching steps forward to will her hand up to her face and wipe at it. Seaweed, muted in the dark but luridly orange, peeled away from her, skin burning and puckering as it pulled free.

Shock, she told herself. Nerves too battered and cold to process information correctly. She wasn't being digested by seaweed. Wasn't dying in a parking lot. Almost there.

Deliberately she summoned the last memory she had of her roommate. Tasha's face was recognizable. Untouched, pristine. Not even the remnants of her last scream were left behind, her expression more akin to sleep than terror.

The fire, eeling closer. Snuffling in the trees.

Her roommate's face was perfect, but the rest of her...

Wherever the rest of her was.

No, Sarah knew damn well where the rest of Tasha was. She brandished the burning branch ahead of her, toward the snuffling shadows, stretched up until the leaves above her caught.

They'd all burn. Sulphur and copper and smoke wrapped around her. Adrenaline and shaky intensity and she screamed as fire dripped from the trees—

Was she screaming now? Sarah stumbled against the door of the bar—*home*—and blinked between then and now.

The door was locked.

Of course the door was locked, it couldn't be later than 3 a.m., and she'd locked the back door behind her when she'd left. The front door wouldn't be open for hours.

The effort dredged a grunt from her gut as she reached into her pocket, but there were no keys there. She'd nearly drowned in the ocean. A blessing, to only lose her boots and keys.

Except... except the door was locked, and she had no keys, and her aunt had to be asleep, and she would die, on this doorstop. Quietly slip into hypothermia and shock—was she there already? Who could say—leaving fires and dead roommates and mysterious government agencies with vaguely threatening job offers to sort themselves out.

Her head fell against the door, and she crumpled into a pile on the concrete step. Summoned a hazy apology to her aunt, who'd find her body like this. She'd been dumb, and dumb things had accordingly happened... dammit. The fire didn't get her, but the water...

Sarah tipped over, the wall in front of her vanishing.

No. Not the wall.

The door.

The door had . . . opened?

She couldn't tell, then understood her eyes were closed and pried them open.

"Sarah!"

"McMurray!"

Her aunt. The cook. A rumble of concerned voices followed—Sully and Ronald and Sanborn? Why was anyone in the bar at this hour?

Thank all the goodness in the world anyone was in the bar at this hour.

She assumed they had the situation in hand and resumed the easy process of losing consciousness.

Aches everywhere dragged her back to the world. She hadn't hurt like this after her first all-day swim meet. Nor even after being thrown against every hard surface in the forest after . . .

"Wha . . . ?" she croaked, and then cut off mid-word as the memories pooled into the forefront of her consciousness.

"Idiot girl," Colleen said, tone as sharp as she deserved. But when Sarah managed to focus her eyes and find the right direction, she saw the concern dripping from her aunt's expression. "What were you doing out there?"

"Saw someone." She had, hadn't she? "In the water."

"What beach access were you by?"

"Was it Pew?"

"Shut up." Her aunt's tone sharpened, rage underlining the words. "Sarah. Can you sit up? John Gorton is here, he says you didn't break anything, but you got banged up pretty good."

"I *said* we should take her in and make sure there's no internal bleeding."

"Shut up, Gorton," Sanborn muttered in a poor imitation of Colleen. "Near-drowned, not beaten. She'll be fine once we warm her up."

"I feel . . ." Terrible. Like she'd been put into a meat grinder and extruded into a flimsy casing. "Like I can sit up."

Every muscle, nerve, joint, and bone shrieked at her, making her too aware of corners of her body she'd never, ever needed to know about before, but she managed to reach a sitting position. Only then did she take in her surroundings—a cot, in the back of the bar, right up against the wood-burning stove her aunt maintained for "ambience."

Not much on ambience in the moment, Sarah sat there, straggled and half broken on the cot, the gathered crew looming over her.

"Good job, Sarah girl." Her aunt took her hand and squeezed, then glanced over at Freman. Was he still a cop, or had he retired?

"I don't want to press you, Sarah, but who did you see?"

"Not who." Sarah flinched and dropped her eyes, then forced herself to meet his gaze. "What."

"Martin Row washed up at access point seven about an hour ago."

"Well, some of him," Sanborn muttered.

"Helpful, Matty."

"He was missing his face and package—feels relevant."

"Relevant to what?" Ronald snarled.

"We're staging here, everything closer is still flooded." Freman spoke to the air—his radio? Sarah's eyelids sank closed again before she could determine the answer.

But they struggled back up again as the words registered. Flooded? She'd gotten home without passing through floodwaters. Where . . . ?

"What time is it?" It wasn't the most pressing question—Row was dead?—but she couldn't understand when people had gotten here. Why? They'd found Row an hour ago, but she'd been on the beach not far from there. How had she missed it?

"It's almost six-thirty, Sarah girl. Sun'll be up before long."

No.

That couldn't be right. She'd been out there for . . . four hours? Impossible.

"You said, 'What.'" Freman again, attention back to her. "What do you mean?"

"It . . . it was a face. Pale enough I could make it out in the water. But when I . . . when I got closer . . ." Tromped into the water like the world's most supreme idiot. "The face . . . it . . ." Bile streamed from the back of her throat to coat her mouth, and swallowing made it worse. "It opened. Like the face was going to rip right in half, and then this . . . this weird seaweed . . ."

Colleen gestured sharply and tugged the top layer of blankets tighter around Sarah's shoulders. "You almost died, my little love. I'm sure your brain showed you all sorts of things."

"It's something to look for, anyway," Freman said, but it sounded more kind than genuine. "Fitz and Abbott haven't checked in either, Pew's MIA, and no one can remember if any of them got in ahead of the storm last night, so we're going to make the rounds. If you think of anything else, call the station. We'll call here if we find anything."

Colleen stepped away, her voice low and urgent, and Sarah stared blankly after them. Better than looking at the stove, flames growing behind the grate, crackling and stretching and—

"What did you see?"

She snapped her eyes away at the voice—Sully, who'd appeared from the side of the bar without her noticing. Her situational awareness had only gotten worse since the forest, and she wasn't sure what to do about it.

"I . . . nothing?"

"Shush with that, girl. Your aunt doesn't know everything, like it or no. Tell me again what you saw."

Sarah told all. The weird seaweed, the face splitting, the gaping mouth and the slippery feel of eldritch skin on hers. He grunted and nodded and held her gaze the whole time. For the length of time she spoke to him, she was distanced from almost drowning, and the fire, and the creature in the woods.

At the end, winded, she pressed her hand to her chest and shrugged off a layer of blankets.

"I believe you. I saw two when I was young—the story I told the other night? That was only part of it, the part I know they'll hear as another old fish tale. But after . . ." He stared above her head, gaze meditative, then blinked and focused on her again.

"I slid the body home and a moment later two faces rose out of the depths. Moon pale, fishbelly pale, the sort of white like a jellyfish glowing in the dark. They looked at me—really looked at me, like a predator. One smiled, but the smile kept growing, kept widening, until I thought the face would split in half. The other flipped right out of the water, body like a seal, like a swordfish, like nothing I'd ever seen."

She leaned toward him, mouth open, skin crawling in a not quite shiver or shudder but a wrenching combination.

"They waved. Then a cloud of seaweed passed between us.

Glowing orange like nuclear fallout on the TV. Bad color. I had to back away... and by the time I got my courage to lean over the side again, they were gone."

"I..." Real. It was *real*, what she saw. Not a lost fisherman or a washed-out tourist, but... real.

Well. She knew monsters were real, didn't she? Why the surprise?

But she wasn't surprised, she realized, taking stock of her abused body. Not after the woods.

"When I was young we had a few fishermen wash up." Sully rubbed his hand over his eyes. "No face. No... genitalia. Heard from an old-timer, then, that it had happened before. Never just one. Two or six or more, but never one. So if Row has been found, and there are more missing..."

"There are more out there." Dull understanding flooded through her. Yes, she was tired. Weary in her bones. But not surprised.

Monsters were real. She didn't need to question, not anymore.

She had to go back to the sea. To see what could be seen.

Sarah glanced toward her aunt, still speaking low to Freman. "She keeps the rifle in the back."

"I have harpoons in my truck." He didn't ask any more questions, just straightened and took a step.

"I'll be there in a minute." Change. Secure the rifle. Meet Sully.

She couldn't set fire to the ocean, but she'd figure out something.

She had the last time.

Sarah paced the dock while Sully readied the *Idle Glass*, then turned as she heard her name.

"Where are you going?" Ronald jogged up the pier, a pair of fingerless gloves flopping out of his coat pocket.

"With me." Sully leaned over the side. "Think we know what's what, got a place to look for the boys we're missing."

"Pew's boat is gone. Nobody saw him take it out, but it definitely didn't come in last night, and we've gotta track it."

"Have a signal?"

"Have an idea," Ronald shrugged, and the two old men nodded at each other.

"All right. Call up and see who else is ready to go. Sarah, you're good at the basics but it's been awhile since you've been out, and this close to the end of the storm..."

"Water's uncertain," she answered, holding her body stiff to fend off a shudder.

"If anyone can navigate us clean, it's Sully." Ronald grunted and spat off the side of the dock. "Freman has a crew at the shack, let me grab a few."

It was done by the time Sully readied his boat, fast enough Sarah's fingers hadn't even numbed in the cold. The dock receded faster than she expected, and she asked no follow-up questions when Sanborn started muttering about fickle currents. She studied the water streaming behind them, the wake folding over, shadows streaking underneath.

Dolphins, she would have said on a bright summer day.

But she knew they weren't. The boat rocked hard, listed briefly to the left, and Sarah clutched the rifle closer until her knuckles bled white.

A rifle. What had she been thinking? That she could shoot the waves?

She'd just yearned for one so badly, while she was in the woods. A gun would have made everything better. Then.

But now?

The boat leaned far to the right, bottoming between wave troughs. She secured her aunt's rifle in the closest hatch and stumbled across the rocking deck to grab one of Sully's harpoons.

Sarah turned, weighing the balance of it, and locked eyes with Ronald the moment he folded in half and flew backward. Over the rail.

Into the sea.

"MAN OVERBOARD!" she yelled, and then had no breath left as she lurched to the railing, harpoon in one hand, the other reaching for . . .

Nothing. No one visible in the dark water, not a disturbance beyond the passage of their boat.

Noise over the slap of water against the *Idle Glass*, low enough it took her a long moment to realize she was hearing it.

"Come . . ."

"Join . . ."

"With us . . ."

The words were faint, hollowed out, recognizable only once she understood they were, in fact, words. Familiar.

Had the monster in the woods—

No. There had been no voice there, only guttural growls, the snuffling of something large and furry and overly clawed trying to scent her between the smoke and the fire and Tasha's blood.

A pull, this time. Familiar like the face that wasn't a face had been. Like... a melody, on the tip of her brain, tugging so she'd follow and remember...

"Sanborn!" Sully bellowed, and she whipped around, breaking the spell of whatever had her foot propped at the bottom of the deck rail. Had she been about to—?

"He's over, he's—he's gone!" Gorton leaned over the rail, then stumbled backward, swearing, as Sarah reached him. "SHIT."

He pointed, shaking, and despite herself, she looked.

The shadows were near enough to the surface to resolve into figures. The figures were bodies, and the bodies were *looking*, were *seeing* them, the bodies were reaching—

Sarah threw herself backward, landing hard on her tailbone against the deck, panting as though she'd just pulled herself out of the waves again, clambering to shore while the weight of the ocean dragged her back.

Someone shrieked, and Gorton hauled her to her feet. They sprinted to the end of the deck, but Freman was gone, and Sully was hollering the same words over and over.

"There's one in the net! There's one in the net! Th—"

The remaining three of them raced for the prow of the boat, Gorton winching the net up, and though the boat shook as though it were in the middle of last night's gale, the net rose.

The net thrashed, like the boat, the figure contained within it shrieking, clawed hands emerging from each space, grasping. Gorton and Paulie dropped the net to the deck, still closed, and three sets of harpoons stabbed into limbs that were not fish, not human, but some unholy combination of the two.

The creature screamed and screamed and screamed, and Sarah clenched her jaw. Wetness under her ears—blood?—her eyes watered as though she were back on the beach covered in sand—but she held in there with the rest, and the boat lurched hard.

"Let me go!"

It was still a scream, but recognizable now even through the ringing in her ears. The harpoon burned against Sarah's hands but she'd felt worse and she tightened her grip, frowning.

"Not all of you. Not all! Just some! Just the old! Just them! Let me go let me go let me GO!"

Gorton staggered back, blood sheeting from his ears, from his eyes, as the creature reared up from the deck.

"Yes, go. You're not ready, you're not close enough to the sea. The old! The old! Better for breeding, better for eating when breeding is done, let me *go*!"

A wet slap behind them and Sarah pivoted, one hand twisted behind her on the harpoon, the other open, reaching for a weapon she didn't have.

"You killed the last of our males. We'll harvest what we need from you!" The new one, larger than the one pinned to the deck, slithered halfway upright, mouth wide and gaping, full of teeth.

"Better to make our children. Adapted for land and sea. We take only the old. Let me go."

"Let her go!"

The harmonics of their voices clashed, a sharp pain stabbing into the center of Sarah's brain. Paulie howled in protest, and another heavy *thwap* sounded as another wet body struck the deck.

Chaos. The boat rocked, they staggered. Bodies moon-pale and blood night-black and dark and white and slimy and wet roiled across the deck.

Sarah clutched her harpoon and swung, and stabbed, and stumbled, and screamed. Sully's face flashed in front of her, and she checked the arc of her strike just in time to miss his nose, and then he was gone and she was rolling. Like she had in the ocean, trying to reach land. Like she had down the hill, fleeing from the fire.

She launched to her feet gasping, stabbing, the background of shrieks and yells and the overwhelming *CRABOOM* of a shotgun mixing with the heavy smell of copper and salt, all adding to her disorientation.

Flash: a gaping mouth, dark like the sea, serrated and wide.

Flash: Paulie falling to pieces before her, arms ripped in two different directions, leg whipping off into the air.

Flash: Sully, diving against the hatch, reaching for something.

And then: nothing.

Quiet.

A fresh breeze, gentle, lightening the heavy brine, easing the burn from her nostrils.

The deck rocked easily underfoot, no lurching or rapid shifts.

Her hands, bloody to the wrists, a deep dark red with an iridescent slime trailed throughout, harpoon still clutched between them, buried near to the hilt in the . . . the creature. Monster. Its eyes were filmy and it hung against her. Dead weight.

Her arms shuddered, twitched, and she flung the harpoon away. Weapon and body both slithered to the edge of the boat by gravity, not any effort from the . . . mermaid? Pain, electric fast and fire deep, shot from her shoulder to the tips of her fingers and she glanced down.

A perfect oval of teethmarks, over her shoulder and upper arm, each drooling the same sort of iridescent blood as coated her hands.

It looked like an oil spill, the inside of an oyster, but ice lined the inside of her stomach. Poison? Would she . . . could she be infected? Become like them, some kind of ocean werewolf?

"Sarah, thank god." A voice, deep and reassuringly familiar, interrupted her swaying thoughts. Gorton crossed the deck and gripped her arms near the elbow, his gaze focused on her bite. "You'll be okay. Come over here, we'll disinfect it."

Everyone was gone. Sully too. Only she and John Gorton remained. As Gorton cleaned her bites, Sarah stared over his shoulder, into the water.

"Come." It was a sigh, a melody underneath the breeze. *"With us. Home. Come home."*

She could go home, a true home. Be welcomed, be safe, be warm. Never outrace fire in the forest, never be surged off her feet by the ocean. All she had to do was slide off the side of the boat . . .

Sarah bit down on her bottom lip until copper flooded her mouth, then put her hands on top of her legs and pressed until the disinfectant burned through her wounds to her bones, anchoring her in place.

They straggled home with the sun high above them, near midday, the sky an angelic blue reflected by the ocean below. Sarah almost fell onto the dock, refusing to look into the water.

The memories came anyway.

First her roommate, ripped to pieces in the woods by not a bear.

The men in suits coming to their—her room, the next day, asking questions and giving warnings.

A job offer couched like a threat, where she could work once she finished school. Monsters everywhere, a government agency set up to . . . not protect people like her, but . . . something. Punish? Make it happen less often?

Then home, her place of safety, her refuge.

But no. Monsters all over. In the forest, in the fire, in the water . . .

Colleen took one look at her, poured whiskey generously into a mug of coffee, and shoved it into Sarah's hands.

She was still sitting there, hours later, mug refilled once or five times, when the phone rang. Her aunt's voice, low and calm.

"Driftwood Bar. Yes. Yes. Mh-hm. I see. Yes. She's right here."

The mug removed. The phone pressed into her hands.

"I know you got some bullshit job offer from those pricks at the MCB." The voice was gruff, but it pulled some measure of attention from the depths of her shock. "Contingent on finishing school and keeping your mouth shut."

She made a noise, meant to be agreement. The voice on the line grunted.

"You're more than welcome to it. They could use someone with field experience. But, you want a real job—handling the monsters, rather than doing some shit back-office work dealing with the aftermath?"

Silence. Probably she should answer. She didn't.

"You don't need to wait until you're done with school. You can start now."

She opened her mouth, attempted to move her tongue, but it sat like an oyster, lodged against the rocks.

"This one's a yes-or-no question, Sarah."

The pull of the ocean surged through her veins, a wanting like the tide. She needed to run down to the beach and dive into the sea, let the freezing cold of the salt water ease the itching in her shoulder.

She needed to get the hell away from the water as soon as possible.

She needed to stop the monsters.

"Yes."

Some monsters are obvious, others are sneaky. There's nothing deadlier than a predator that feeds on souls. —A.L.

Inspiration

Kacey Ezell

Cliché or not, the dead artist's loft was gorgeous. Between the music from the jazz café drifting up from downstairs, and the rain pelting the street-lit glass windows, Siena Monroe felt herself falling deep into a noir vibe as she stepped out of the converted freight elevator and strode across the scratched hardwood floor toward the rumble of male voices over by those stunning floor-to-ceiling windows.

She threaded her way through several racks holding large canvases, her brown eyes flicking over them with brief professional curiosity before she caught sight of the man she'd come to see. She shook the wet tendrils of her red-blond hair out of her face and smiled.

"Logan," she said, pulling one hand out of the pocket of her—stereotypically appropriate—trench coat. Detective Logan James turned away from speaking to a uniform at the sound of her voice. He smiled back and reached to take her offered handshake, the ball chain holding his detective's shield around his neck glinting in those same streetlights.

"Thanks again," Siena said. "This is really helpful."

"No problem," Logan said, flattening the vowels with thick Boston accent. "Sully here and I are gonna stay with you to make sure there's no questions later."

"I thought the scene had been released?" Siena retrieved her hand and put it back in her pocket.

"The CSIs are done, we haven't given the go-ahead to the super to get it cleaned up yet. That's tomorrow. That's what you wanted, right?"

"That's actually perfect, Logan. You're the best."

"I try. I'm just surprised Catalan was insured with Hunter and Glass. He didn't seem like the insurance type."

"He wasn't," Siena said. "Jay and Melanie Andalusia, however, are. I'm authorized to share that with you—"

"Yeah, yeah, I know. Not for public consumption. Who the fuck are Jay and Melanie Andalusia?"

"Catalan's . . . patrons, I guess. They paid the bill for this place—which is generous." Once more, Siena looked around, admiring the high ceilings and open space of the loft. Her own town house was nice, but this space . . . she could see why an up-and-coming painter would find it a perfect place to create.

"It's all right. Overpriced, if you ask me. All these converted mill buildings are, and the insulation is terrible in the winter."

Siena nodded acknowledgment of that point. Winter in Massachusetts was no joke. She turned and began to wander back toward the racks of art.

"What can you tell me about the case?" she asked as she scanned the paintings in their various stages of completion. Even in the least finished works, though, Joshua Catalan's distinctive style came through. His unique blend of abstract impressionism and classical nude studies had set the art world on fire two years ago. Suddenly, owning a Catalan original was *de rigeur* for serious collectors all over the world, including Jay and Melanie Andalusia.

"No case at all," Logan said. "ME ruled it a suicide, and there's little chance of it being anything else. We got a signed note, a goodbye video on the deceased's phone, and zero indications of duress before he put a Mossberg in his mouth and pulled a Kurt Cobain."

Siena wrinkled her nose at Logan's indelicacy but nodded. "Tragic."

"Yeah, tragic," Logan said, and the still-silent Sully nodded appropriately. "So does that answer Hunter and Glass's questions?"

"Sadly, no," Siena said. "My company is a high-value collectables insurance company, they don't issue life insurance policies. It doesn't matter to me at all how Catalan died. My job is to find one of his missing paintings."

"Something's missing?" Although he worked homicide, Siena could hear the interest in the detective's tone. She forced herself not to smile as she nodded again.

"Yes," she said. "As part of the terms of his agreement with the Andalusias, Catalan drew up a will that left all of his unsold and in progress works to them on the occasion of his death. Hunter and Glass queried through appropriate channels and received the initial inventory of the loft... and something wasn't there that should have been."

Logan's grizzled eyebrows went up. "Really? What?"

"A piece called *Inspiration*." Siena turned back to the racks of art, and began idly flipping through a collection of unframed but finished canvases.

"That's a terrible name for a painting," Logan said. "Wicked pretentious."

Siena grinned. "Maybe, but Catalan turned down an offer of two million dollars for the original six months ago. It's unquestionably his best-known work, and as far as anyone can tell, it was still legally in his possession at the time of his death. Which makes it the property of the Andalusias and thus of interest to my company."

"Huh. What's so special about it?"

"It's a near perfect exemplar of his style. And like most of his paintings, it features the same model." Siena stopped flipping the canvases and pointed at the one she held. "Her."

"Ah. Yeah. His model. Helene Spitha. Nice girl. Real broken up."

"You talked with her?"

"Am I new?"

Siena smiled and let Logan's scathing reply slide. He was, as he would no doubt put it, just breaking her balls.

"Yeah, I talked to her. The video on his phone addressed her specifically, so we checked it out. Airtight alibi. She was on a Learjet to Philly at the time of Catalan's death. She'd just gotten back when I interviewed her. She'd heard the news in Philly and come home early. Like I said, she seemed real broken up."

"Were she and Catalan an item?" Siena asked, more for her own curiosity than for any other reason.

"Eh, she said not anymore. They broke up a little less than a year ago. She said it was amicable, but who knows."

Siena let her eyes roam over the woman's face in the painting, taking in the way Catalan had painted the curve of her cheek and the sweep of her eyelashes. The bold, wild brushstrokes and sweeps of color nearly vibrated with emotion.

"Who knows, indeed," Siena murmured. "I'd like to talk to her."

"I'll have Sully get her address for you."

Helene Spitha lived in an upscale apartment in downtown Boston's Beacon Hill neighborhood. Siena hugged her coat close around her as she tipped her Uber driver and ducked out into the chilly, soaking rain for the short sprint to the building's front door.

A uniformed doorman held the way open for her, returning her smile of thanks with a nod as he gestured to the reception desk just inside the door. Siena kept her expression neutrally pleasant and turned to the woman there.

"Good afternoon," she said. "Siena Monroe to see Helene Spitha, please."

The receptionist consulted her tablet and then nodded politely. "Welcome, Ms. Monroe. Ms. Spitha informed us you would be stopping by. Please go on up."

As if on cue—and maybe it was, who knew—one of the elevators behind the reception desk let out a *ding* and the doors slid open. Siena gave the receptionist a small smile and headed over to the elevator. She didn't push any buttons, because there were none. The doors slid closed and the lift started. Siena spared a brief, darkly humorous thought for all the ways this could go wrong. Would she end up in some drug kingpin's penthouse by mistake?

Another *ding* and the doors slid open again, revealing a soft expanse of warm beige carpet thick enough that Siena was glad she'd worn her Solovair boots instead of heels. She stepped off the elevator and walked into the open concept apartment beyond.

It's like a light mirror of Catalan's loft, Siena thought as she looked around. Rather than the dark industrial vibe, Helene Spitha's apartment was airy and well-lit. A sea of beige carpet stretched from one white wall to another, while large windows with gossamer white curtains let the meager light from the rainy afternoon in. Even the furniture was neutral and unassuming, using pale-colored wood and white or beige fabrics.

In fact, the whole place would have looked blank and boring

if not for the vivid art everywhere. Bold, abstract oils hung next to ephemeral watercolors and stark black-and-white photographs. Every flat surface held some kind of statuary or objets d'art. Soft jazz filled the space, low enough to be almost subliminal. Even the air itself had been curated, Siena realized as she inhaled, catching notes of bergamot and vetiver.

"You must be Siena Monroe."

Siena blinked and turned to give her professional smile to the woman who approached. Helene Spitha wasn't quite as tall as she, probably about 5′7″. She had rich dark hair that she wore in loose waves cascading down her back. Her dark brown eyes looked almost black in the dimness of the overcast day, but they were striking and fringed with lashes long enough to be fakes... though for some reason, Siena didn't think they were. Spitha had a straight, Grecian nose and full, pouty lips that currently stretched in a welcoming smile. Her skin was slightly olive in tone, hinting at some possible Mediterranean or Middle Eastern heritage, though Siena's research said that the Spitha family had been in the Boston area for generations.

"Yes, hello. Thank you for seeing me, Ms. Spitha." Siena held out her hand. Spitha took it in both of hers, clasping it warmly before leaning in to kiss Siena on both cheeks. Though she wasn't expecting such effusiveness, Siena managed to keep her reaction to a single, surprised blink.

"Of course. Please, call me Helene. And forgive my ways, I've spent a lot of time in Europe. I often forget Americans don't enjoy so much touching."

"I thought you were from Boston?"

"Oh, I am. But I travel a lot, you know, all over the world." She stopped and pointed to a watercolor on what looked like silk. "I got that piece in Kyoto four months ago, for example. Have you ever been to Japan, Ms. Monroe?"

"I've never had the pleasure. And if we're using first names, mine's Siena."

"Sienna, like the color of your eyes. How beautiful."

"One *N*, but yes. Thank you. Are you a connoisseur of art, Helene?" Siena asked as Helene tilted her head and stared at her with a peculiar kind of intensity. "You seem to have quite the eclectic collection here."

Helene blinked and then smiled as she took a step backward

and looked around as if seeing the place for the first time. "Yes, I suppose I do," she said. "I am not what I would call a serious collector, nothing like the clients your company represents. Most of these were gifts, if I'm honest. The gossip rags sometimes call me an art groupie." She quirked an eyebrow and smiled conspiratorially at Siena, as if she were amused rather than offended by the accusation.

"Are you?" Siena asked, opting for bluntness.

Helene shrugged. "Perhaps I am. I won't deny that I am attracted to artistic men. I am . . . fascinated by creativity, by the process of it. There is nothing more primal, more sensual than a man in a full, ecstatic frenzy of creation. To witness such a thing, to be a part of it . . ." She inhaled deeply, her cheeks flushing as she trailed off. Then she blinked and smiled at Siena again. "Well. I suspect you understand what I mean."

"I suspect I do," Siena said, allowing a hint of a smile to curve her lips as well. "So you prefer to date artists."

"Artists, writers, musicians, sculptors . . . the truth is, it doesn't much matter to me. I find all men equally beautiful when they create."

"And what they produce?"

"The art? It's lovely, certainly," she said, turning with a smile to look at the Japanese watercolor again. "But mostly it's lovely because of the memories of passion it brings. It's a . . . by-product, I suppose."

Siena's eyebrows went up. "A 'by-product'? That's not very flattering."

Helene laughed. "Oh, I know, I'm terrible. Please don't write down that I said that, my current love would never forgive me."

"I'm not a reporter."

"No, you're an insurance adjuster. And I understand you represent the inheritors of Joshua's estate, is that correct?"

"Well, I represent their insurance company, but yes. How well did you know Mr. Catalan?"

Helene's smile grew sad, and she walked slowly over to the beige-and-cream sofa and sat down. "Quite well," she said, gesturing for Siena to sit beside her. "We dated for almost two years. He was a beautiful, intensely creative, and intelligent soul. I was devastated when I heard the news."

"I am sorry for your loss."

“Thank you,” Helene said, blinking rapidly. “But it really is the world’s loss. He had *such* a soul.”

“I’m sorry to ask, but when did your relationship end?”

“About eight months ago. He’d hit a slump. I suspected depression and recommended a therapist, and that angered him. We argued about it for several weeks, and in the end, he refused to get help. I didn’t want to leave him, but I won’t stay in an unhealthy situation. He acknowledged that, and so we parted ways.”

“But it was amicable?”

“Oh, yes. He even sent me the most amazing gift. Do you know his work? *Inspiration*?”

Siena blinked. “I do.”

“Would you like to see it?”

“I would.”

Helene smiled again, and rose to her feet, beckoning to Siena to follow. She led her down a short hallway toward the back of the apartment and through a set of double doors into another large, open space.

Nice bedroom, Siena thought as she took in the king-sized bed with old-fashioned gossamer bed curtains and the giant bay window. Opposite the window, a gas fireplace waited for someone to flip the switch that would bring it to life. And above that...

Inspiration was a 48″-by-36″ canvas painted with mixed oils and acrylics. Critics had praised the work for its bold, slashing lines and aggressive use of color. Siena knew this. She’d even seen prints of the work, and admired the artist’s composition, and the way in which he portrayed the model’s raw sensuality.

None of that prepared her to see the original.

Siena couldn’t help it, she inhaled sharply as the sun chose just that moment to find a fleeting break in the New England weather and a shaft of sunlight speared through the room to light the canvas and the woman painted there. The wash of color that made up the curve of her hip and breast glistened in the uncertain light, giving the illusion of a snapshot in time: as if the subject were constantly in motion, and had only paused for a second, to allow the artist to worship her with his eyes before she threw herself back into movement. It felt... ephemeral. Impermanent, despite the aggressive, almost angry, brushstrokes of Catalan’s technique.

“It’s something, isn’t it?” Helene’s voice sounded softly pleased, as if she could sense Siena’s visceral reaction to the piece.

"Yes," Siena said. She blinked and refocused her eyes on Helene's face. "It is. How did it come to be here?"

"Josh gave it to me," Helene said with a sad smile. "He said it was a goodbye gift."

"Can you prove that?"

Helene's eyebrows shot up, but Siena refused to back down.

"Ms. Spitha, my company's clients believe that painting to be part of Mr. Catalan's estate, and therefore their property. If, as you claim, Mr. Catalan gifted the painting to you, and there is some sort of documentation preserving its provenance, then the issue is resolved. If, however, you don't have that type of documentation, I should warn you that my company will aggressively pursue all legal avenues to recover their clients' property."

Helene's smile never wavered, but it took on a sharper, colder edge.

"I appreciate the warning, Ms. Monroe," she said. "But, in fact, I can prove the painting's provenance and that it was a gift from the artist, a man I loved very much."

"I am glad to hear it. May I see this proof?" Siena kept her tone even and uninflected. The gloves had come off and they were now playing hardball, to mix sports metaphors, but she saw that as no reason not to remain professional.

"Of course. This way, please."

Siena resisted the urge to look back at the painting one more time and followed Helene into a room across the small hallway. This one was smaller and lined with built-in bookshelves crammed with books and small pieces of sculpture. In the center of the room, a heavy, ornate desk that looked like it was made from both mahogany and oak sat atop a plush oriental rug. Helene walked to the desk and opened one of the drawers, withdrew a file folder, and held it out across the desk to Siena.

"Beautiful desk," Siena said as she took it.

"Thank you," Helene said, her voice still cold. "It's an antique. It's been in my family for over a hundred years."

"Lovely," Siena said. Since Helene hadn't invited her to sit, she remained standing. She opened the folder and laid it down on the surface of the desk as her eyes skimmed over the documents within.

The first was a printout of an email to Helene from Joshua Catalan. It was dated five months ago, and despite Helene's story earlier, it was clear to Siena that Catalan hadn't been happy about their relationship ending. He hadn't exactly begged her to come back to him, but the subtext was definitely there. He wrote of being unable to live without her, unable to breathe, to think, to paint.

However, he *did* also explicitly tell her that he wanted her to have *Inspiration*. Interestingly, it wasn't even a contingent offer. He just gave it to her, saying that he knew in "what was left of my soul that you are the only being who should have it."

Siena pursed her lips and flipped to the next document in the file. It was a transfer of ownership signed by Catalan and the owner of the gallery where *Inspiration* had been exhibited for several months. Siena didn't have the time or the tools to do an in-depth analysis, but it certainly looked legitimate on the surface.

The next document was dated three months later, just six weeks ago, and it was a withdrawal notice requesting that the painting be returned to the owner, Helene Spitha. It, too, was signed by the gallery owner, and looked completely in order.

Siena flipped that over as well, but that was the end of the file. She raised her eyes to meet Helene's cold smile.

"You certainly keep your paperwork in order, Ms. Spitha."

"I do my best," she said. "*Inspiration* is an important piece, even more so now. I find life is easier if one is organized."

Siena let her lips curve in a small smile. "May I make copies of these documents? They will remain part of my report, which is covered by my company's confidentiality policy."

"By all means," Helene said, her smile growing.

Siena took a moment to scan the documents using her phone, and then closed the file and handed it back to Helene.

"Thank you for your time and assistance, Ms. Spitha," Siena said. "I will be in touch if we need anything else. If you have any questions, please feel free to call this number." She reached into her jacket pocket and withdrew a business card with the number for Hunter & Glass' claims department printed on it.

"You are welcome, Ms. Monroe. I'm glad to have been of assistance. If you don't need anything else, I'll see you out."

"Thank you."

It took less than an hour for Siena to write up her report. Back in her apartment, she hit SEND and leaned back in her chair. She stretched her arms up overhead and rubbed her eyes briefly before pushing up to her feet.

She wouldn't hear anything back until Monday, but Siena had every expectation that this particular case would be closed. The Andalusias were going to be disappointed, but the likelihood that Helene had somehow managed to forge all the transfer documents and appropriate signatures was just too small. All of the evidence indicated that Josh had, indeed, given her the painting before his death. Therefore, it wasn't part of the estate, and of no further concern to Hunter & Glass.

Still, something about the whole thing bothered her. Siena ran her fingers through her hair, and then fluffed it in frustration as she strode from her office to the kitchen. With quick, sharp movements, she grabbed her kettle and filled it, then set about making some tea in the hopes that it would help distract her ever-racing, circling mind.

For some reason, she couldn't get the image of Helene's art collection out of her mind. There really wasn't any coherence to it, which lent credence to her story of them mostly being gifts... but how many creative ex-lovers did Helene have? And why was she so casual about their art? It was Siena's business to know high-value pieces when she saw them, and *Inspiration* hadn't been Helene's only masterwork on display.

The tea kettle shrieked, bringing Siena out of her musings long enough to turn off the burner and finish making her tea. With a sigh of defeat, she took the steaming cup and went back into her office to fire up her computer again. If she knew nothing else, Siena knew that she wouldn't be able to rest until she answered at least some of her curiosity.

Unfortunately for her, after about an hour of internet research, she still had more questions than answers. Helene Spitha was a well enough known personality that she appeared on several gossip and society blogs with regularity. And yes, she did seem to have a decided preference for creative types. Siena scrolled back past the articles and photos linking her with Catalan. Before him, she'd apparently been spending time with a young filmmaker who died in a tragic car accident. There was a touching picture of Helene hugging the young man's mother at his funeral.

Siena pursed her lips and kept scrolling. Before the filmmaker, there was a torrid relationship with a breakout rapper who hadn't been fully divorced by the time they started dating. It hadn't stopped his album from topping the charts, however, which made it all the more tragic when he died of a fentanyl overdose a few months later. Before him...

Siena blinked, and sat back hard in her chair as another picture loaded fully. Recognition shot through her as she looked at the picture of a smiling man with his arm around Helene Spitha and a glass of champagne in his hand.

"Uncle Jake," she murmured, leaning forward. "Is that you?"

Jacob Chadvargui had been one of her parents' closest friends. He'd been her father's roommate in college at UMass, and one of the groomsmen at her parents' wedding. He'd been the one to come and sit with Siena in the hospital during the long days of recovery after cultists had murdered her parents and kidnapped her. He'd looked out for her during her own days in college, where he'd been a professor before he started writing full-time under the pen name Jake Chadwick. His mystery novels had gained a huge following, and he'd been talking to Netflix about doing a television series adaptation when suddenly everything changed. He stopped writing, stopped communicating, stopped... anything. Even Siena could barely get him to answer the phone. That had been a few years ago, before she left her old job. That job—she took a deep breath and forced herself to think about it, despite her instinctive desire to flinch away from the memories—had consumed all too much of her time, and so she hadn't pushed hard enough to keep in touch. Last she'd heard, Uncle Jake was living out in Worcester.

On an impulse, Siena grabbed her phone and pulled up his contact. Before she could think better of it, she hit CALL.

It rang several times, long enough that she was about to hang up when the line clicked and a tired female voice came on the line.

"Hello, may I help you?"

"Yes, hi. I'm sorry to bother you. I'm Siena Monroe, and I'm looking for an old friend of my family. Jake Chadvargui? This was the last number I had for him."

"Hold on one moment, please."

Siena heard the phone being muffled, as if someone had covered the microphone up with their hand. She had just long enough to wonder what she was doing when the woman's voice came back.

"Siena, hi. I'm Anabelle, Jake's assistant. He remembers you. What can I do for you?"

"Hi, Anabelle. It's nice to meet you. Jake was, as I said, a good friend of my family's for a really long time. We've fallen out of touch and I'd . . . like to reconnect, if we can. I'm up in Boston now. Is he still in Worcester? I'd love to come by and see him, and meet you in person."

"We've moved just outside of town," Anabelle said. "But Jake would like to see you, I think. I can text you the address. When do you think you might come?"

"Saturday?" Siena said, glancing over at her wall calendar. That was the day after tomorrow. "Around lunchtime?"

"We're free. I look forward to meeting you."

"Same here," Siena said. "Thank you, Anabelle."

"Thank you, Siena. Jake will be very excited."

"Anabelle" turned out to be Anabelle Suarez, according to the property tax register Siena found. She was the joint owner, along with Jake, of 2629 Barons Drive, Holden, MA. They'd purchased the property a few years ago, and it was apparently a small single-family home, about twelve hundred square feet total, with a 1/3-acre yard.

The sun was shining when Siena pulled up to the curb in front of the bungalow. The grass was overlong and dying, but otherwise the yard looked neat enough. A red Toyota Camry of indeterminate age sat under the single-width carport.

Siena got out of her Model X and walked up to the door. Behind her, the Tesla beeped to let her know it had locked itself. She took a deep breath, squared her shoulders, and rang the bell.

The door opened almost immediately.

A tiny woman in her late forties or early fifties smiled up at her.

"Siena?"

"Yes," Siena said, returning the smile. "Hello! You must be Anabelle."

"Yes! It's so good to meet you. Please come in! I've heard so much about you since your call. Jake is very excited to see you."

"Oh, thank you. That's good news, I was afraid he'd be hesitant. It's been a long time."

Anabelle reached out and patted her hand, and then pushed the door wide and stepped to the side, beckoning Siena through.

"Everyone has lives, dear. Jake understands that. I understand he knew your parents?"

"Yes," Siena said, reflexively pushing down the lightning bolt of pain that sometimes still stabbed through her, even now, at the mention of her parents. "They were good friends in college."

She stepped through the door into a small but tidy living room. An old, slightly threadbare couch sat under the window, facing an inexpensive model flat-screen TV. Around the TV, photographs and framed newspaper clippings clustered over the entire surface of the wall. Siena's eyes scanned over the collection, stopping suddenly when another bolt of agony shot through her mind.

"That's them," she said softly, before she really even meant to do so. Anabelle looked at her with eyebrows raised in inquiry, and Siena pointed to one of the photographs. It wasn't very large, probably a 5″x7″, and it hung in a cheap wooden frame. In it, Jake stood laughing in a tuxedo, his left arm around a handsome man with red hair on his right, and a tall, willowy blonde in a white dress on his left.

"Those are my parents," Siena said as soon as she could manage to speak. "That was their wedding."

"Oh, what a happy memory," Anabelle said, her voice sweet. She clasped her hands together under her chin like a child.

"You don't know what you're talking about, Ana."

The rough, slightly slurred voice came from a darkened hallway to the left of the TV, and both Siena and Anabelle turned to look as Jake slouched forward out of the dimness.

"I just meant—"

"Just shut up. Go get us something to drink or something. Hello, Siena."

"Hello, Uncle Jake," Siena said evenly. She glanced out of the corner of her eye at Anabelle, but she didn't seem to be too terribly bothered by Jake's rudeness. She just smiled at Siena and turned toward the kitchen opening that lay perpendicular to the hallway.

"Have a seat. It's good to see you. Sorry about Ana. She doesn't know what happened to your parents."

"It's all right," Siena said. She lowered herself to a seat on the couch. "I don't mind talking about them. You didn't have to reprimand her so harshly."

"Eh. Ana's fine." Jake lurched forward then, and barely caught himself before making his own unsteady way to the couch and collapsing into a seat next to her. The thick, not-quite sweet scent of cheap bourbon followed him in a cloud.

In the daylight, Jake looked old. His skin had a yellowish-gray pallor, and his hands held a fine tremor. His hair, which Siena remembered being a thick, lustrous dark brown, had gone completely gray and thinned out at the top of his scalp. He wore it long, down to his shoulders, but judging by the tangled, greasy look of the strands, he hadn't seen a barber in some time. He reached into his pocket for a cigarette, and when he lit it, Siena could see that his teeth were in just as bad shape as the rest of him.

He focused his yellowed eyes on her and blinked owlishly. He took a long drag and then exhaled, letting the smoke rise between them. Siena fought not to cough.

"So," Jake said. "How've you been? Still working for the Feds?"

"No," Siena said. "I left the FBI a few years ago. I'm an adjuster for a high-value insurance company now." The lie about the FBI rolled smoothly off her lips. That had been her cover story when she worked for MCB, and her nondisclosures kept her using it. Not that she had any desire to tell Jake—or anyone—the truth of her past employment. Or the truth about the demon cult that killed her parents. They were better off not knowing. Most days, she wished *she* had never known.

"Good money in that?' Jake asked.

"Good enough."

"Eh. Good for you." He looked up as Anabelle walked back into the room. She handed him a tumbler filled with a dark amber liquid. Then she smiled and handed one to Siena as well.

"Thank you," Siena said, taking a sip. It was iced tea. She would have bet a month's salary that Jake's wasn't. She looked up to see Anabelle nod briefly in acknowledgment before turning and heading back to the kitchen.

"So, what brings you out here?" Jake said, after draining half of his glass in one go.

"I wanted to see you," Siena said. "I'm sorry we've fallen out of touch. I'd like to remedy that. You were kind to me after Mom and Dad were killed, I've always appreciated that."

Jake nodded, his expression going solemn for a moment. "I've missed talking to you," he said, his voice low. "You were always too smart for your own good."

Siena smiled. "That makes two of us. So, tell me about Anabelle."

Jake snorted. "What's to know? She's my assistant."

"You guys own this house together. Are you sure that's all she is?"

He shrugged. "She'd like to be more, but I just... I'm not interested. We bought the house because it was the easiest way to get it done, financially. She's a good woman, and probably deserves better than a washed-up old sot like me, but I can't seem to get rid of her."

"That's a pretty shitty way to talk about someone who obviously cares about you, Uncle Jake."

"Yeah, well. I'm a pretty shitty old guy."

Siena frowned. "I don't remember you feeling sorry for yourself this much."

Jake snorted, and then laughed. The sound had a bitter, hard edge. "Yeah, well. That's because you knew me before I lost it."

"Lost what? Your kindness?"

"Funny girl. No, little Siena. My... *it.* My creativity. My spark. My stories."

"What do you mean, you lost it?" Siena frowned, leaning forward to set her iced tea on the scratched coffee table in front of them.

Jake shrugged. "Just what I said. It's gone. I can't write anymore. I'm just lucky my backlist keeps selling enough to pay for this place. Well... my backlist and Ana's alimony from her ex-husband."

"You're saying you have writer's block?"

Jake let out a growl and lifted his glass, drained it. "I'm saying," he rasped as he lowered the empty to the coffee table with a *clink*, "that I'm done. No stories. No ideas. No words. Nothing. Empty."

"Maybe if you lay off the booze—"

"Fuck you, little girl. You don't know anything. I drink *because* I can't write. It's the only way I get through the pain!"

"Okay, Uncle Jake, take it easy," Siena said, holding up a hand. "I'm just trying to help."

"You can't help. Nothing helps. Believe me, I've tried it all. I even tried to see *her* again. But she... even she had nothing for me."

"She?" Siena asked, certain she already knew the answer. "Who are you talking about?"

"No one. Never mind."

"Uncle," Siena said, pitching her voice low. "Are . . . are you talking about Helene Spitha?"

Intense longing, heartrending despair, and incandescent rage flowed one after the other over Jake's face. "She took it," he whispered, staring into nothingness. "She destroyed me."

"How, Uncle?" Siena whispered. "Tell me how."

"I don't know!" he screamed. He picked up his glass, lifted it as if to drink, and then stopped halfway to his mouth. With an inarticulate snarl, he hurled it toward the wall with the TV and the photographs. It hit one of the clusters of smaller pictures, shattering and sending shards of glass in all directions.

Siena ducked her head and then shot to her feet. Before she could say anything else, Anabelle came hustling back into the room. She rushed over and knelt beside Jake, who had collapsed into racking, body-shaking sobs.

"Jake," Anabelle said, her voice low and soothing. "Jake, it's okay."

"It's not!" he sobbed. "It will never be okay again."

"I'm sorry," Siena said, guilt soaking through her. "I didn't mean to—"

"It's all right," Anabelle said. "Sometimes this happens. You should probably go, though." She reached up to stroke Jake's bent head, as if he were a crying child and she his mother.

"I will," Siena said. "I—Anabelle, I truly am sorry."

Anabelle looked up at her with a sad smile and a nod before bending her head to whisper something else to Jake.

Feeling like the worst kind of person, Siena backed toward the door and let herself out into the incongruously bright sunlight of the New England day. She walked out and pulled the door shut behind her, but she couldn't fully shut the sound of her Uncle Jake's agony out of her memory.

Siena spent the two hours and change of her drive back into Boston with her thoughts swirling around themselves. Anger simmered deep in her belly, but she couldn't fully decide who or what was the appropriate target for her rage.

Uncle Jake had clearly descended fully into alcoholism, enabled by the besotted and long-suffering Anabelle. Siena knew enough about addiction to know that unless Jake decided to change his life, he would repeat the same destructive patterns of behavior until he died. But it had to be his decision, his choice. No one could do it for him. And while the sight of him so broken down had hurt her more than she'd expected, Siena knew there wasn't much she could do to help.

But something was off. The way he'd gotten so emotional, so violent when she'd mentioned Helene was odd. Sure, drunks were unpredictable, but Siena's gut told her there was more to this. Jake's alcoholism was just another means of self-destruction in a long line of tragedies that all had one common factor: Helene Spitha.

When Siena got back to her apartment, she treated herself to a long, hot shower and a meal. Actual food: grilled salmon and angel hair pasta with artichoke hearts and lemon butter. Quick to prepare, healthy, and fortifying enough that she felt up to digging into some more research.

She sat down at her computer and opened up her browser, then picked up her notebook, considering. Her eyes scanned the list of names and dates of the articles she'd found about Helene and the ill-fated artists she dated. Anxiety skittered through her belly as she realized that she had a pretty impressive list, certainly enough to establish a pattern. But even if she found more names, dates, and tales of self-destruction, it wasn't likely to answer her real question. Which was this: a pattern of what?

With a sigh, she swallowed back her nerves, logged in to her VPN, and typed in a web address she hadn't figured she'd ever use again.

"Hello, old friend," she muttered under her breath as the Supernatural Activity Watch Forums loaded. Back when she'd been working her old job, she'd monitored these boards closely, mostly to make sure there was no reference to any of her cases. Her job had been to turn supernatural crime scenes into mundane crime scenes, so that the public didn't ever get a look at what lurked in the dark corners of the world. If she or any of her colleagues ever slipped up, boards like SAWF were where the conspiracy theorists would have their field days speculating about what really happened. It was a point of pride with her that none of her cover-ups had ever been questioned on SAWF.

But there was always a constant low-level buzz on the boards about supernatural activity. If there was something otherworldly about Helene Spitha, SAWF might be her best chance of finding it. The only problem? Like most internet communities, SAWF was a cesspool filled with trolls, tinfoil hat fashionistas, and shitlords.

Siena rolled her neck on her shoulders, took a sip of the energy drink she'd popped open, mentally girded herself for battle, and clicked on the search bar.

"Okay, Helene. Let's see if I can comb through the bullshit enough to find a nugget or two of truth," she muttered as she began to type.

Sometime between midnight and dawn, Siena sat back in her chair and rubbed her eyes.

It had taken longer than she liked, but she'd finally found something. It had been buried in a thread started by a young man who suspected that the girl he liked might be a succubus because she made it hard for him to breathe and think every time she came around. Half of the replies blasted the kid for ignorance and naivete, and the other half defended him. It had devolved into a classic internet hair-pulling catfight, but there had been one post that had caught Siena's eye. In it, the commenter had listed the "commonly known traits" of a succubus. He was about seventy percent correct, which was high for SAWF. But he'd also written something else:

"MUSE—A muse is either a subtype of succubus demon, or something else with similar hunting modalities. The muse will attach herself to a man with great ambition and strength, and inspire him to perform even better—for a time. She will feed on the man's vitality until there is nothing left. He will then wither and die like a summer orchid left in the desert of winter."

The purple imagery had made Siena blink and reread the passage, and that's when she realized she might have found a thread of something. She looked up the commenter's other posts, but didn't find much else of use. When she searched "muse" on SAWF, she came upon one particular thread that extrapolated from Greek mythology and quickly devolved into relatively prurient fantasies about the nine demigoddesses of inspiration. Still, she'd combed through it and found a few nuggets that helped her put together a profile that fit.

Siena picked up her notebook and read what she'd written out loud:

"Helene Spitha may be a rare type of supernatural predator that feeds upon the creative energy of artistic humans. Similar to a succubus, she will engage in romantic and sexual relationships with her prey, during which time they will enter a frenzy of creation. She feeds on this frenzy, driving the prey to push more and more until they burn out. However, unlike mundane artistic burnout, this more metaphysical condition results in an inability to create ever again. This devastates the mental health of the prey, which is likely exacerbated by Spitha's inevitable departure from the relationship. Following this, the prey then descends into a spiral of self-destruction, often marked and abetted by significant substance abuse. In most cases, the prey then ends their own life, either by suicide, or as a by-product of ever riskier behavior."

Siena trailed off, then took a deep breath and closed her computer. It sounded good enough at three in the morning. She'd get some sleep and give it another read through tomorrow when she typed everything up in a report.

She pushed up to her feet, refusing to think about just where that report would go, and clicked to put her computer in sleep mode. She stumbled to her bedroom and collapsed on the bed, asleep as soon as her head hit the pillow.

The following day, Siena hit SEND.

There was more to it, of course. She'd had to log in to the specialized VPN and go through a dozen layers of electronic credentialing to even get to the portal where she could upload her report. When she'd left the Bureau, she'd been told that, as an "inactive agent," this was how she was to get in touch if there was something the Bureau needed to know. She remembered thinking that hell would freeze over before she would ever ask the Bureau for help again.

Siena shivered and glanced outside. No snow yet, but it was October in Massachusetts, so anything was possible.

Once her report was uploaded, she got up and made herself a cup of tea in an attempt to settle the restlessness that still zinged along her nerves. While the water boiled, she led herself through a series of stretches, and when that didn't help, she flipped on the TV. Maybe some mindless entertainment—

"—noted Boston socialite and philanthropist Helene Spitha, at the hotly anticipated debut of photographer Kai Schilling's new collection—"

Siena's kettle shrieked, making her jump. She let out a short, dirty curse word and turned to snap the burner off, then moved the kettle to a cooler part of the range and turned back to the local news. Sure enough, there was Helene, resplendent in a floor-length red-gold gown that shimmered when she moved. She had her arm tucked through the arm of a thin man in his midtwenties. The man wore sunglasses and had his dark hair slicked back with pomade like it was 1924. Siena watched as the two of them walked a red carpet into the Robert Klein Gallery for an exhibit opening. His exhibit, she learned. Kai Schilling, the young photographer who was apparently the new hotness on the Boston art scene.

Before she could chicken out, she turned and grabbed her phone. Though she'd deleted the number out of her contacts, she still had it memorized. During her training, they'd emphasized it often enough.

"Please say or enter your extension."

"Seven-seven-three-two-three."

"Please hold."

Siena swallowed, feeling her pulse thudding in her throat. She closed her eyes, as memories of her last job tried to rise up in a red haze that obscured her vision. Her mouth suddenly felt coated in the sweet, metallic scent of bloody, violent death. She pressed her lips together and fought to breathe through her nose, reminding herself that she was home, she was safe. This wasn't the job, and there were no half-dead monsters waiting to rise up and claw at her—

"Agent Monroe, it's been a long time."

Her eyes snapped open.

"It's Ms. Monroe. I'm inactive. With whom am I speaking, please?"

"You don't remember me? I'm hurt. This is Donovan."

Donovan. Jim Donovan. They'd been friends once. Before he declared a scene safe without fully sweeping the basement, where a ghoulish horror waited to slaughter her cover-up team and tear her lungs half out of her body.

"Are you fucking kidding me?" she found herself saying.

"Hey, you called me. What's up, *Ms.* Monroe?"

Rage flowed through her, burning away the last of her remembered terror. "I just sent in a file, on the inactive contact server. I need someone to check it out ASAP."

"Oh yeah, we'll get to it."

"I said *ASAP*," she snapped. "There's something hunting humans in the open here in Boston."

"Vampire?"

"No. I don't know what to call her other than a . . . a muse."

"Muse? Like the Greek goddess?"

"Demigoddesses, and there were nine of them. Just . . . look at the report, all right? A man's life is in danger."

"Sure, sure. Hey, Siena. I'm glad you called. I wanted to tell you, I'm real sorry about—"

Siena hung up. She didn't want to hear it. She didn't want to think about it. She just wanted to move on.

"Fuck!" she screamed, throwing her head back and closing her eyes. She held off the first racking sob for about half a second before collapsing onto one of her kitchen barstools, putting her head down on the counter and letting the grief take over.

When the storm passed, Siena picked herself up. Her water had cooled, and so she lit the burner once again, and then snapped it back off with a shrug and went to take a hot shower.

She refused to think about anything at all while the hot water pounded down on her body. Lying on the floor had made her stiff, and so she took her time, letting her mind remain empty and liquid as the water that sluiced off her skin.

Eventually, she scrubbed her hair and body, rinsed and dried off, and dressed herself. Because she still felt a little raw, she ignored her beloved Chanel suits in favor of a pair of athletic leggings and her UMass hoodie. Then she grabbed her laptop and settled in on her couch to check her email.

Sure enough, the Bureau had sent a response with a link to a secure message server. She stepped through the login pages once again until she reached the inbox and opened the message.

Agent (inactive) Monroe,

Thank you for your communication. Our analysts have evaluated your report and have not found sufficient evidence to move forward with a full investigation into your allegations. The Bureau thanks you for your continued vigilance and reminds you that violation of your nondisclosure agreement is a serious offense carrying the penalty of up to twenty years in prison pursuant to E.O. 1-TR24B.

Warm Regards,
The Inactive Agent Liaison Office
Monster Control Bureau

Siena felt like she probably should have been angry, but apparently her earlier meltdown had used up all of her strong emotions for the time being. She wasn't even really surprised, she realized. She'd asked for them to review the report as soon as possible, but the speed of their reply told her all she needed to know.

No one had read it. They probably hadn't even opened the file. Fucking Donovan had probably shunted it to the trash and triggered the standard auto-response email as soon as she'd hung up on him. He'd never liked not getting his own way, and she'd probably pissed him off.

Well, whatever. He could be pissed off. She was done with him and the entire Bureau.

Once more, Siena took a deep breath and grabbed her phone. Ages ago, on one of her first cover-up cases, she'd come into contact with one of the private contractors so despised within the Bureau. Their operative had given her their number in case she ever had to get in touch with their office to facilitate a cover-up. She'd never used it, had forgotten about it for years, and so it was still there as she scrolled through her contacts.

MONSTER HUNTER INTERNATIONAL—NEW ENGLAND

Before she could think better of it, she hit CONNECT and waited through two rings.

"MHI, Team Wicked *Awe*some. What do you need?"

"Team Wicked Awesome?" Siena asked, before she could help herself. "Are you serious with that?"

"As a fucking heart attack. Do you need something?"

"Um. Yes. Sorry. I'm . . . my name is Siena Monroe. I need to speak with one of your operatives, please."

"'Operatives'? That's good. I like that. Who the fuck are you, Siena Monroe? And why should any of our 'operatives' give a fuck?"

Despite herself, Siena chuckled. "I'm an insurance adjuster, but I'm former MCB, and I've got a line on a PUFF you might be interested in."

The line went silent, though she could still hear his breathing in the background.

"Listen," she said. "I know I'm saying a lot of words that are getting your attention. Why don't we meet for coffee and we can talk further?"

"Make it dinner," he said, and Siena could have sworn she heard a grin in his voice. "Bring your husband or boyfriend along."

"I don't have either," she surprised herself by saying.

"Even better," he said. "Pick a public place downtown. I'll meet you at seven p.m."

Siena blinked, and then let out a little laugh. "Fine. Do you know the Sullivan Circle Diner?"

"I'll find it. See you at seven."

The Sullivan Circle Diner was only about a block from Siena's place. Close enough to walk. They had a variety of dishes, everything from a delicious burger to some of the best poke and sashimi Siena had ever tried. They also had the kind of high-backed booths that were perfect for private conversations.

Siena arrived about thirty minutes early and waved to Ryohei behind the sushi bar. He smiled and beckoned her over while his wife Lisa headed back to the kitchen to get Siena's usual tea.

"I've got something special for you to try tonight, Siena," Ryohei said, gesturing for her to take her usual place at the bar. His forty-plus years in Boston had left him with a unique blend of Massachusetts and Japan in his accent. He and his wife, Lisa, were Siena's neighbors, and some of her favorite people.

"Do you? That sounds fantastic. But I'm meeting someone here in half an hour. Could I have one of the booths toward the back?"

"Of course!" Lisa said as she approached. Her blond hair had mostly gone gray, but the luminous beauty and kindness that had brought Ryohei across the world to be with her still shone in her face.

"A new friend or an old one?" Ryohei asked, sharpening his chef's knife with a foreboding look on his face. Siena laughed.

"A new one," she said.

"I will make sure he is a gentleman."

"Ryohei, Siena can take care of herself!" Lisa protested. Siena laughed.

"I can, but I appreciate the backup. Thank you both."

"You are family," Ryohei said, pointing with his large, very sharp knife. "Sit in that booth, where I can see you clearly."

Siena shared an amused look with Lisa, but she managed to keep a straight face as she nodded and proceeded to the booth he'd indicated. She'd almost finished her first cup of Lisa's tea when the door opened and a man walked in.

Siena immediately pegged him for MHI. While she hadn't worked closely with the independent contractors, she'd seen enough to know a few things. His body language was relaxed, but he walked with a kind of leashed violence to his movements. He wore a leather jacket, jeans, and a Henley. He'd cut his dark brown hair in a short military style, and his blue eyes scanned the place with a professional air before settling on her face.

"Hey," he said with a smile as he approached. "Siena Monroe? I'm Adam Leighton."

"Adam," Siena said, setting down her teacup and holding out her hand in greeting. "Nice to meet you in person."

"Likewise," he said. "This is a cool place. I've never heard of it before, but I looked up the menu. I'm excited. I haven't had good sashimi since I was stationed in Okinawa."

"Air Force?" Siena guessed. She'd dated an airline pilot who'd been stationed in Okinawa once.

"Marines."

"Fair enough. Ryohei's sashimi is the best on the East Coast. He and Lisa are friends of mine."

Adam's eyebrows went up. "Best on the East Coast, huh?"

"I said what I said."

He chuckled. "Fair enough," he echoed. "Let's get some of that sashimi, and then we can talk about how you know all those words and what it's got to do with me."

Siena nodded, and then looked up at Lisa, who promptly came over to take their order. She swapped out Siena's teapot for a full one and poured Adam a cup when he asked. He was at least polite, Siena noted with approval. She very definitely didn't approve of his strong jawline or the way his dark lashes fringed his bright blue eyes, but that was neither here nor there.

"So," Adam said, lifting his tea and taking a sip before moving on. "Tell me what an ex-MCB cleaner wants with MHI. I looked up your file."

"I have a file?" Siena asked.

"Yep. We keep them on people who have supernatural encounters in the area. So, I know about your parents, and your former career, and what happened to your team. My condolences, by the way. Losing friends sucks."

Siena swallowed hard and nodded, looking down at her tea for a moment before answering. "Thank you."

"What I don't know is why you'd walk away, get a cushy high-paying job working for a bougie insurance company, and then call us years later. So, let's start there."

Siena reached in her bag and withdrew a printout of the report she'd submitted to MCB. "Have you ever heard the name Joshua Catalan?"

"Yeah, painter, right? Sort of Botticelli meets abstract impressionism?"

Siena's eyebrows went up. Adam grinned at her. "What? Surprised the marine knows culture? I can read real good too."

"I bet," she said. "He committed suicide recently. No questions there, it was truly a suicide, but I believe he might have been the victim of a . . . a muse, for lack of a better term, prior to his death."

"A muse."

Siena nodded. "Helene Spitha. She's a Boston socialite. She also has an impressive track record of dating artistic men, who then seem to have a sudden surge of success and then burn out. Like all the way out, to the point where they can't create anymore. Then she breaks up with them, and they go on to self-destruct."

"And you have evidence of this?"

"It's in there," she said, pointing. "I tried to contact MCB, but they blew me off. The agent at the Boston field office and I . . . we don't get along."

"So why do you think she's PUFF-eligible?"

"She's hunting humans. Openly. I tracked all of that data using open-source internet. Eventually, someone's going to get wise. Plus . . . she's hunting humans."

Adam looked closely at her and then smiled up at Lisa as she delivered their plates.

"Mind if I look through this now?" he asked, his eyes serious.

"Please do," Siena said, picking up her chopsticks. "I'll be right here, stuffing my face."

Adam gave her a quick half smile and followed suit, his eyes already scanning the pages of her report.

They ate in silence broken only by the diner's background noise and other customers. Lisa refilled their tea one more time before Adam flipped the last page over and raised his eyes to meet Siena's.

"I need to check on some things," he said.

"I understand."

"Can we meet up again tomorrow?"

Siena nodded, and then prodded by some instinct she couldn't name, she went further. "Actually, I was going to attend a photography showing at the Robert Klein tomorrow. I think Helene may be there."

Adam's eyebrows went up. "What time?"

"Six."

"I'll meet you there and let you know what I find out."

For this event, Siena pulled out all the stops. She wore her very favorite vintage Chanel evening gown from the '50s. It had an asymmetrical neckline and a full, flowing princess-style skirt. She'd had it modified to include a hidden slit in the side that allowed her access to the concealed holster that held her Walther PPS. The dress would have looked better with a pair of stilettos, but she opted for a kitten-heel Mary Jane instead, just in case she had to run. She left her hair in a red-gold wave down her back and completed the look with some timeless, simple gold jewelry.

Thus armored, she called an Uber and prepared to go to battle.

She texted Adam on the way, so he was waiting by the curb when she arrived. He opened her door for her and waited while she tipped the driver, and then held out a hand to help her out of the car.

"Nice dress," he said in an undertone as she straightened up.

"Thanks," she replied, glancing sideways at him. After his crack on the phone about her husband or boyfriend, she'd expected him to be a bit more forward in making a pass, but so far, he'd been nothing but professional. It was almost disappointing. Especially because the dark slacks and sport coat he wore highlighted the swell of his shoulders and arms. And the triangle of tanned skin at his open collar kept drawing her attention the way a piece of chocolate mousse cake in a bakery window drew her attention...

Siena pushed that thought away and took Adam's offered arm as they headed into the gallery. Kai Schilling's new exhibit was in one of the main spaces, and they joined the flow of glittering bodies moving in that direction.

"So," she asked as they wound through the entryway toward Schilling's exhibit. "Any news? Are you in?"

"I'm in," he said. "And if we bring her down, half the PUFF goes to you."

"Oh!" Siena blinked. "I hadn't thought about that."

Adam grinned down at her, a dimple flashing into being in his cheek. "Being an independent contractor has its benefits."

"Apparently."

"So, where's our... oh. Never mind."

Siena followed the direction of Adam's gaze to see Helene resplendent in midnight blue, standing with her arm wound through that of a younger man wearing sunglasses and a tuxedo. He had bronze skin and sun-streaked blond hair pulled back into a man-bun, and as Siena watched, he swayed just a little on his feet.

"Yeah," Siena said. "That's her."

As she spoke, Helene turned, laughing, from her conversation and made eye contact. Her smile grew, and something dangerous flashed in her eyes for the barest millisecond before she called out.

"Siena? Darling, is that you? Come here! Come meet Kai!"

Siena squared her shoulders, lifted her chin, and pasted a polite smile upon her face. She tightened her arm around Adam's in a silent request for his support, and he flexed his bicep in response.

Or maybe that was just him being a guy. But he didn't hesitate to escort her through the crowd to stop next to Helene and her latest artistic victim.

"What a wonderful surprise, Siena! I didn't realize you were still in town." Helene said, her smile bright, but her eyes frosty.

"Oh, I live here," Siena said. "I'm based out of Boston, and I'd heard so much about Mr. Schilling's work—"

"Kai, baby."

Siena blinked. The words had been so slurred, she wasn't quite sure that she'd heard correctly. "Excuse me?"

"He prefers 'Kai,'" Helene explained, shooting an adoring look his direction. "He says it's more in keeping with the oceanic flow of life he cultivates in his art."

"I see."

"And who's your handsome friend?" Helene asked, tilting her head to look through her eyelashes at Adam. "Another art enthusiast?"

"Only if you count martial arts," Adam said with a disarming half grin.

"Oh, I *do*," Helene said, oozing enthusiasm. "What do you study?"

"Mainly Goju Ryu karate these days. Though I've done a lot of other things in the past."

"Jiujitsu?" Helene asked.

"Some."

She smiled again, satisfaction flowing through her expression. "I knew it," she said. "You stand like a warrior."

"Thank you," Adam said, his voice calm and even. Siena hadn't known him long, but she could imagine his internal monologue, complete with the appropriate profanity.

"Well, it's wonderful to meet you, and to see you again, Siena. Enjoy the exhibit, you two." With a smile, Helene turned her body just a bit to the side and addressed someone behind them.

"Let's go," Siena murmured. "We've been dismissed."

"No kidding," Adam muttered. He let her steer him back through the crowd to one of the less-occupied corners of the exhibit, next to a 5′x8′ extreme black-and-white closeup of a woman's closed eye, her mascaraed eyelashes resting on the smooth curve of her cheek.

"Did he smell drunk to you?" Adam asked. "Bro looks like he can barely stand."

"I didn't smell alcohol, no," Siena said. "But that doesn't mean he didn't consume some, or something else for that matter."

"Yeah. Or it could mean that she's feeding on him right here, right now. She certainly looks flushed and energetic. Was she like that when you met her before?"

"No," Siena said, pushing her hair back from her face. "She seemed a lot more Zen, less flirty and . . ." She trailed off, looking for the right word.

"Less predatory?" Adam said, giving her a half smile.

"Yeah, I guess."

"Interesting. Let's keep an eye on her and Ocean Flow Boy. Hey, is this one of those exhibits where they have caterers bringing around trays of tiny quiches and things? I'm starving."

Siena startled herself with a laugh, which continued as Adam spotted a young woman carrying a tray and waved her over.

Despite the excellent canapés—and yes, there were mini quiches—the evening dragged. Siena never once saw Schilling lift a glass, but he proceeded to act more and more intoxicated as the night wore on. Helene, on the other hand, never flagged. On the contrary, she laughed louder, conversed longer, and shone brighter with every passing moment. Around eleven, the crowd started to thin, and so Siena and Adam made their way to the exit and headed out to Adam's vehicle.

"Nice parking spot," Siena said as they approached the parked SUV.

"Yeah, I figured I'd park where I could see the entrance so I could catch you as you arrived. You sure they'll use the main door to exit?"

"No, but I think it's likely," Siena said. "My gut tells me Helene's not in the mood to sneak out the back tonight."

"You think she feeds on attention and adulation too?" Adam reached down and opened the passenger side door, and then held out a hand to help her in to the seat.

Siena shrugged. "Maybe. But maybe no more than any other attractive woman."

"You didn't seem to care."

Siena paused in the act of climbing in to the seat, her hand engulfed in Adam's warm grip. "I . . . was working."

Adam grinned down at her. "Focused on the mission. That's hot."

Siena furrowed her brow. "Are . . . are you hitting on me?"

His grin grew. "Well . . . not seriously. Let's call it mildly flirting. At least until we're done working together. Keeps things cleaner."

Once again, he surprised her into a laugh. He winked quickly, and then shut the door to the SUV before jogging around to get in on the passenger side.

They didn't have to wait long before Helene and Kai appeared at the main entrance to the gallery. Helene continued to talk and laugh with the few others who walked out with them, while Kai continued to stumble with nearly every step. At one point, Helene reached over and supported him with an arm around his waist as a black sedan pulled up to the nearby curb. With many waves and called farewells, Helene poured the photographer into the back seat of the car before walking around to the driver's side.

Siena's eyebrows went up as the driver exited the vehicle. Helene said something to the man with a smile and then slid into his place. The driver shut the door and lifted a hand, then walked away, pulling out his phone and tapping on it.

"Interesting," Adam said. "Shall we see where they go?"

"Yes, please," Siena said.

He flashed her that dimpled grin one more time and started the engine.

Once they didn't turn toward Helene's downtown apartment, Siena had the feeling they might be heading out of Boston. They continued past Worcester without slowing and headed down I-84 toward Hartford, Connecticut.

She and Adam didn't speak much, and eventually he turned on a soft, noirish jazz station that suited her mood.

"That seat reclines if you want to catch a nap," he said at one point. "I get the feeling we're not stopping anytime soon."

"How are you doing for fuel? I kinda don't want to lose them."

"This is my own vehicle, I put an auxiliary tank in it a few years go. I'm good for close to six hundred miles. I think they're going to have to stop soon, though."

"Don't let them see you."

"Thanks, boss. Any other hot tips? This ain't my first rodeo, you know."

"Sorry," she said, rolling her shoulders. "I'm just... what are we doing?"

"Following the target."

"Without backup?"

"My team's tracking this vehicle. They're just a call away, Siena. We can break off if you want, but I'm with you, I think this is big."

"No, I don't want to break off. It's just..."

"I know. It's okay. You're safe with me, I promise. Put the seat back, get some rest."

Siena nodded and reached down to toggle the electric seat

control. As she leaned back, the warmth of the heated leather seat wrapped around her, and the jazz filled her mind, soothing her anxiety and slipping her off into sleep.

She woke up when the car turned onto a gravel road.

"What time is it?" she asked, blinking her eyes and sitting up.

"Almost six," Adam said. "Feel better? You were out."

"Groggy," Siena said.

"There's a water in your door. I got it when our friends stopped for gas a few hours ago. Coffee, too, though it's cold by now."

"Water is good, thanks," Siena said. She grabbed the bottle and opened it with a quick twist, then guzzled about a third of it before returning it to the door cup holder. "So Helene drove all night?"

"Yeah. Sunrise is right about now, but I can't see shit in this fog."

"How are you following them?"

Adam grinned over at her, mischievousness layering over the fatigue in his eyes. "I bugged the car while they were stopped. It was so dark and foggy, I doubt anyone could see me, even if Helene hadn't gone inside the gas station."

"Did Schilling go with her?"

"No, when I peeked inside the car, he was passed out in the back seat."

"You peeked?!"

Adam shrugged. "No one saw me," he said again. "And now we can follow at a comfortable distance, though I haven't got the fucking first clue as to where they're going."

"Where are we? Overall, I mean?"

"Pennsylvania. Somewhere in the Poconos. Bug says she turned off this road and"—he checked his phone—"continued a ways. Map says this is a dead end, so she's going to have to stop eventually. Does Schilling have a place up here?"

"Could be," Siena said. "Or she could, she comes from money."

"Yeah, about that. Intel indicates that she's probably immortal. All those generations of philanthropy and shit? That was probably her. Based on your research and what we were able to find, it looks like she alternates between living here in the US and over in Europe. Probably tells people she's 'staying with a grandmother' or some shit."

"Immortal. Does that mean we can't kill her?"

"Easy there, bloodthirsty! I didn't say that... but I didn't *not* say that. We just don't know. That report you put together is the most information we've ever had on muses. Everything else is legend and conjecture."

"Well, that's comforting," Siena muttered.

"At least you know you did a good job." Adam smiled over at her, his tone conciliatory.

"I *always* do a good job. It's why I get paid so much."

"Yeah, about that. I know I said we'd split the PUFF, but you didn't even ask how much. It doesn't feel like you're in this for money, Siena, so what gives? Why do you care so much about this Kai Schilling guy?"

"I don't," she said. For just a second, Uncle Jake's haunted face flashed into the forefront of her mind. "It's just... she's hunting humanity. Besides being illegal, there's something... *wrong* about that. Humans are the apex predators on this planet. Things like Helene need to remember that."

Adam let out a low whistle.

"What?"

"That's even hotter than you being mission focused. I'm definitely going to hit on you when this is over."

Siena laughed and shook her head. She drank some more of her water and looked down at her now rumpled and slightly bedraggled vintage Chanel with a sigh.

"I don't suppose you happen to have any spare women's clothes in this car, do you?"

"As a matter of fact..."

"You're shitting me."

He grinned over again. "Nope. Scout's honor. One of my team members, Risa Comeaux, is about your size, maybe a little shorter. I have go bags for each of my team members in the back. Risa's is right behind my seat, so you can reach it if you want. If you're cool changing in the car."

"Keep your eyes on the road, marine, and we have a deal."

"Oohrah, ma'am."

Whoever Risa Comeaux was, she was, in fact, a few inches shorter than Siena, as evidenced by the fact that her tactical leggings came up to Siena's mid-calf and looked like capris. However, her long socks and ankle boots fit, so it didn't make that much of a difference. With a lot of cursing and squirming, Siena managed to get the leggings on under the gown, and then got it unfastened and pulled the whole thing off over her head.

She threw Risa's long-sleeved tac shirt on over her strapless bra, and then wiggled out of that and put the sports bra on underneath as well. Then socks, boots, and a wide belt to which she attached her Walther's holster, and Siena felt a million times more ready to go.

"Impressive," Adam said dryly when she was done and re-buckled her seat belt.

"You weren't supposed to look," Siena said.

"I didn't. Still."

She snorted softly. "Whatever."

By then, the sun had risen, giving the fog an eerie, pearlescent quality. Adam checked his phone one more time and sat up straighter behind the wheel.

"She's stopped," he said. "About a mile ahead. Just off this road."

"Can we get closer?"

"Maybe."

Adam rolled forward for a few more yards and then cut the engine and the lights. He looked over at Siena, his face serious.

"Stay close," he said. "Looks like there might be a building up ahead. Let's go check it out."

Siena nodded and followed him into the fog-shrouded forest. A surreal sensation settled over her as they picked their way across the wet ground between the tall, grasping pine trees toward a dark shape squatting at the top of the slope.

The shape resolved itself into a cabin as they drew nearer. No lights shone from the windows, and it would have looked completely abandoned if not for the black car sitting in the driveway. Adam led her in a circuit of the building, and then tried the front door.

It creaked open.

Siena drew her weapon, holding it low and ready. Adam's eyes flicked down to her hands and then he did the same. He lifted a finger to his lips and she nodded, taking up position to cover his back as he pushed open the door and slowly stepped inside.

It was a big, open-concept A-frame-style cabin. The kitchen, living, and dining rooms all looked completely deserted, as if no one had touched them for months. A rustic wooden staircase led up to a loft that looked likewise empty. Inside the kitchen, a door stood open, revealing another set of stairs leading down.

Adam glanced at her and Siena gave him a quick nod to show she was right behind him. He slowly made his way down the stairs, listening with each step. Siena followed until they stood together in a short hallway that terminated in a door with a red light above it.

Adam turned and mouthed the word "Darkroom" to her. She nodded again to show that she understood, and wondered what on earth he would have done if she hadn't.

Once again, he glided forward until he could tap lightly on the door.

No answer.

Adam reached down with his free hand and slowly turned the knob. No one cried out in outrage, telling them not to come in, and so he eased the door open.

Red light flooded the room beyond, glinting off the drying photographs hanging from lines crisscrossing the room. A long table with several tubs of liquid stood in the center of the room, and just beyond it lay Kai with his long, sun-streaked hair hanging disheveled all over his face.

Within moments, Adam had the room cleared and was kneeling next to Kai.

"He's got a pulse," he said. "But it's weak. Call an ambulance."

Siena nodded and holstered her gun to pull her phone out. She had only one bar of service, but it was enough to get the local 911 dispatcher and call it in.

They waited beside Kai for the forty-five minutes it took for the ambulance to arrive. The police weren't far behind, and Siena gave them a statement that was mostly true. She'd met Helene in the course of her work, and had heard about the gallery event where she'd met Kai. She told them that she and Adam were on a date, and had followed Helene and Kai to the cabin at their invitation. She didn't mention the weapon that she'd hidden under Risa's jacket that Adam had grabbed for her, and the cops didn't ask. They did ask where Helene had gone, and she told them the truth: she had no idea.

Eventually, the cops left, following the ambulance with full lights and sirens. As the screaming echo faded away into the stubbornly thick fog, she turned to Adam with a tired smile.

"I'm exhausted," she said. "So, I can't imagine how you must feel."

"I'm a little tired," he admitted. "Google Maps says there's a town about ten minutes from here. Wanna head there and find breakfast and some hotel rooms? In that order?"

Siena smiled, and was about to suggest that maybe just one hotel room would work when something shifted in Adam's gaze. His good-humored fatigue burned away and before she knew what was happening, he struck.

Somehow, he got her legs out from under her and she slammed down onto the forest loam, back first. Air exploded from her lungs and she barely managed to get her arms and feet up in a half-assed guard position before his weight came crashing down on her.

"Adam!" she gasped . . . or tried to. With the wind knocked out of her, she couldn't really speak.

"Inspiration takes many forms, little Siena."

Helene's voice floated out of the fog above her head. Siena craned her neck backward just in time to see the muse glide forward from between the suggestion of two trees. "You stole my most recent source, which is terribly rude, but it was kind of you to bring me this *delicious* martial artist as compensation."

"I didn't—" Siena started to say as air rushed back into her lungs. But Adam's big hands, which had been so gentle earlier, came down around her throat. She tried to use her leverage to break his hold, but it was no use. He was incredibly strong, and his fast, precise movements spoke to years of dedicated practice and training.

A martial artist, indeed.

Gray sparkles began to crowd in to her vision from around the edges. Helene started speaking again, but Siena couldn't hear over the sound of her own frantic heartbeats. She opened her eyes wide, desperately seeking eye contact with the man she'd just started to trust.

"Adam," she whimpered, the sound broken by her restricted airflow. "Don't . . . let her . . . hunt you. You're . . . apex . . . pred . . . ator."

Adam blinked, and for just a second, something cleared in his gaze.

"Please," Siena mouthed the word as the gray sparkles coalesced and overcame her vision.

She felt his hand leave her throat. Air whooshed into her starving lungs. Something tugged at her belt and her vision cleared just in time to see Adam kneeling over her, aiming her Walther at something just above her head.

"Silly boy. You can't kill me with that g—"

POP. Pop pop pop.

A high, bone-aching ringing started in Siena's ears as Adam fired four rounds from her unsuppressed weapon. He rose to his feet, stepping away from her and keeping his aim steady. Siena dragged in a breath of air and rolled to her stomach, watching as he approached the downed figure of the muse.

"Maybe not," she thought she heard Adam say. "But I bet it still hurts like a bitch to get shot in the face, doesn't it? Do yourself a favor, Helene. Stay the fuck down."

Adam's team responded faster than the EMS crews had. Siena called them as soon as she was finished securing Helene Spitha with a set of special zip-ties that Adam had in his truck. By the time they got Spitha loaded in the truck, another tricked-out SUV roared up.

"Nice jacket," a woman said as she got out from behind the wheel. "I've got one just like it."

"Uh. I think this one is yours," Siena said. "If you're Risa Comeaux, that is. Adam let me use it. I was wearing Chanel earlier."

"Chanel, hmm? Nice. Maybe I do want to be the kind of friends who share clothes. Where's Adam?"

"Watching the muse," Siena said. "In the car. She's taken a few rounds to the face and chest, so she's not feeling her best. But be careful with her. She's starting to heal and she got close to 'inspiring' him to strangle me to death."

Risa let out a low whistle, and then gave Siena one more nod as she and the rest of the team went to go help their colleague.

Siena hung back and let herself sag as she sat down on a nearby stump. The sun had risen high enough that it finally started burning off that eerie fog. Her stomach gurgled loudly, and fatigue pulled at the edges of her mind. She was close to nodding off when the sound of slamming car doors jolted her awake.

She came to her feet as Adam approached.

"You okay?" he asked.

She nodded.

"Siena," he breathed. "I'm so sorry—"

"It wasn't you," she said. "She said it herself. You're a martial artist. Your medium is violence. She 'inspired' you to attack me, and probably fed on you as you did."

"I couldn't think. Not until you reminded me of who and what I am."

Siena gave him a little smile. "An apex predator?"

He stepped closer. "No," he said. "Just Adam." He reached out and caught her fingers in his own.

She tilted her head to the side. "So, is this you finally hitting on me, Just Adam?"

"I'd like to," he said. "But I don't know if it's right, after what I did." He reached up and touched the beginnings of a bruise on her throat with the fingertips of his free hand.

"Hmm. Good point," Siena said. His expression froze, and he started to withdraw his hand from hers. She threaded her fingers through his and held tight, not letting him back fully away.

"So, maybe I'll just hit on you instead. What would you think of that?" she asked, her voice low.

Adam's eyes searched her face for a brief moment. Right then, the sun finally broke through the fog, bathing the forest clearing in light. Siena smiled, and she just barely had time to glimpse his dimple flashing into existence before he leaned in to take the kiss she gladly offered.

Some stories are hard to believe. Others make too much sense. This is one of those that covers both. —A.L.

The Hard Earth

Jack Wylder

The Cowboy stopped sawing the monster's head off long enough to look at me and nod earnestly. His voice was deep and smooth. "Yes, seriously. The world is about to end because of a jacket."

The barrel of my rifle was so hot that it steamed in the fetid air of the moonless Louisiana swamp. Dark trees covered in hanging Spanish moss, black against the darker black loomed above us as if waiting for the right moment to attack. We worked quickly in the feeble orange light of our glow sticks. Even whispering, his voice carried much more than I would prefer.

To buy myself a moment to process this, I returned to staring into the swampy darkness to watch for anything attempting to slither behind us. With a squelching noise, the head finally came free of the body behind me. I turned again to face my partner, who was casually wiping the glowing blue letiche blood from his serrated bowie knife. Most people struggled with reading a Bullman's cowlike expressions, but I had known him long enough at that point to do so easily, and I could tell he was waging some sort of internal debate. I gave him time to think while I slung my rifle and struggled to lift the severed gator-man-thing's head into the back of the van onto the tarp we had laid out. The PUFF on a letiche was almost large enough to make up for the putrid swampy smell, but Austin Bowie Gonzalez Houston was a very particular Texas Bullman, and even more so about his van since he spent most of his time in the field inside it.

He finally seemed to reach a decision and took pity on me, easily lifting the head into place with his free hand. "We need to get going—all this noise has attracted gollums and you know the local Bokor and his goons aren't gonna be too happy with us for taking away his new guard dog. I need a lift home—I'll explain on the way."

The Germans gave us the word *eigengrau*, which is used to describe the dark gray the brain "sees" in the total absence of light. I turned to peer into the *eigengrau* of the swamp and sure enough there were already the pale sickly green glows of lamplike eyes moving slowly our way and I could just hear the splashing and whispering of the swamp creatures paddling toward us. Yup. Definitely time to go. We slid the door shut, got in, and started back toward Texas, leaving the swamp in our rearview. I drove while Cowboy sat in his oversized seat right behind me, facing backward but close enough to talk. We drove in silence for a couple of minutes before he finally spoke.

"We've got company."

I looked in my rearview mirror and saw a number of red motorcycle headlights following us. It would appear the Bokor's cultists had noticed their missing letiche. I grabbed my battered aviation headset from the seat beside me and hastened to jam the U-174 plug into the van's makeshift radio as the Cowboy behind me did the same. He had specially modified his to accommodate his floppy bovine ears, of course. We had scavenged the comms system years back and I was once again grateful we had spent the time to hook it up. The headset hummed, and suddenly the world was quieter—just the Cowboy's low muttering, cutting through the chaos.

The Cowboy pushed the enormous severed head aside, slid the trick back window down, and moved his modified minigun into position. He cussed me out as I veered around a cypress that seemed to jump out onto the muddy path we were referring to as a road, a stray branch shattering the glass and creating a large hole in the windshield.

The minigun roared and one set of headlights went dark. In my head I imagined a Wilhelm scream, but the ANR ensured I couldn't hear any actual screams from the voodoo henchman. A string of erratic gunfire from behind slapped the van but with the reinforcement it didn't seem to cause any actual harm. The wind screaming through the windshield made my eyes water and even with the headsets, I had to raise my voice in order for my partner to hear me.

"So, how is it that a jacket of all things is going to cause Armageddon?"

The Cowboy let out another burst of gunfire, but my weaving around obstructions must have thrown off his aim because the number of headlights chasing us remained the same.

"Listen, Monkeyman, we've known each other a long time now and I trust you with my life, but now I'm going to have to trust you with something far more valuable—I'm going to have to trust you with some Bullmen secrets. Understand, this is classified top-secret-destroy-*before*-reading stuff that is only shared on a need-to-know basis. Unfortunately, we've hit a point where you qualify. Sorry about that. To begin with, tell me what you know about Earl Harbinger's jacket?"

I racked my brain while dodging a shape that was either a thick tuft of some tall reeds, or possibly another swamp monstrosity, but I really didn't know much.

"It's a bomber-style jacket rumored to be made of Bullman leather, right? Supposed to be pretty effective as armor. That's about it—why, is there more?"

His snort of derision came through clearly. He fired again and took out another cultist. "You have *no* idea, dude. Yeah there's more—a *lot* more. There's nothing a Bullman hates more than being indebted to someone, right? It's a weakness that can be exploited and we are not big on weakness. We always pay our debts. Always. If you die without being even, you cannot enter the afterlife, but are instead doomed to wander the midway mists forever."

He flinched as a rifle round flew past him and struck the already damaged windshield. I attempted to clear enough of a hole to see through, but it was tricky to do with one hand while navigating the swamps at full speed in the dark.

"When we die, we sometimes give our bodies as a gift, which gives us the opportunity to remove any lingering obligations so we may enter the afterlife free and clear. It isn't easy and it isn't done lightly. You think Bullmen hide is tough, just wait until you face a Bullman wearing leather armor fully imbued with active spirits."

He paused long enough to let loose with another burst from the mini.

"We've done this throughout our entire history, and it's always worked for us. Even dead, we always pay our debts. It's a point of pride for us."

I pulled the van hard to the right to run the cultist who had managed to get alongside us into a tree, but he jumped onto the roof as his bike burst into a ball of flames behind us. "Cowboy—can you shoot him off?"

"Don't be an idiot." He unbuckled, removed his headset, and shimmied partway out the side window. I couldn't see what happened but I could feel the van rock as he threw the cultist into one of our pursuers, removing two threats with one throw. He was efficient like that.

He settled back into position, buckling his harness and redonning his headset as if nothing had happened. It was impressive how he managed with his horns and floppy ears. The sounds of shots hitting the van forced him to delay, but shortly he was once again able to calmly resume the conversation.

"The craziest part of this whole thing is that I don't think Harbinger even realizes what he's got—he thinks of his jacket as just a loving, albeit odd, memento from a fallen brother. Dude doesn't even realize that he's just casually running around wearing one of the more powerful artifacts in existence."

There was another brief exchange of gunfire as we continued to race out of the swamp. I heard him breathing deeply to calm himself so I risked a glance back. He was staring at the hole in his shirt that had been caused by one of the cultist's shots. "Okay, now they're starting to piss me off. This shirt was from CPKM's first tour." The minigun let loose again and another light went dark. After a moment he had calmed himself enough to continue.

"It's not the jacket itself that makes it so dangerous. Yes it's an incredibly effective piece of armor, but it's so much more than that. When Travis Alamo Sam Houston bequeathed his skin to Earl, he effectively made him a member of our clan. That's all well and good until you remember that all Bullmen clans are a kraterocracy—we're ruled by the strongest member of the clan. And *any* member of a Bullmen clan can battle for the throne. Travis Alamo Sam Houston's parting gift has potentially put Earl Harbinger of all people in the running to be King of the Bullmen. Ooh, nice one."

I had finally caught one of the motorcycles between the van and a tree and it was every bit as satisfying as I had hoped it would be.

"The fact that a mere human is potentially even in consideration doesn't sit all too well with a lot of Bullmen purists, and for understandable reasons. We were originally created by the Fey as foot soldiers in their never-ending wars and we spent centuries enthralled to them. Once we got free, we were none too keen on being ruled by anyone other than one of our own, ever again. Bullmen only trust Bullmen. Travis Alamo Sam Houston bequeathing his skin to Harbinger was unprecedented—in all of our history no one has ever done this. Take the next left."

I pulled hard to the left and as we turned, the tires finally grabbed asphalt and surged forward. The trailing lights stopped abruptly at the edge of the path and we were clear. The Cowboy stowed the M134 and waded through a pile of spent brass to pull the tinted window back into place, continuing as if nothing had happened.

"So that text was from my cousin. Apparently the King of the Bullmen was recently killed. He had a good death, with a huge honor guard, but now we have a problem. In about forty-eight hours, each of the tribes will send their champion to compete and at the end, a new king will be named. The old king had decreed Earl to be part of the tribe and that was that, end of discussion. Whatever the king says pretty much becomes law. The problem is that there are a lot of Bullmen who still strongly feel Earl's even having that jacket is an insult. If one of them gets crowned, they plan on taking it back. I need to get home to the Labyrinth as quickly as I can."

I took a moment to consider what it would mean to have an army of Bullmen attack MHI. The MCB wouldn't like that and Earl sure as hell wouldn't like that either. I drove just a bit faster. "So where is this entrance?"

He answered and I took my eyes off the road to stare at him for a moment, trying to gauge if he was just messing with me. He must have read my mind because he nodded solemnly. "Yes, really. Now I need to rest up. Let me know when you want to switch. For now shut up, turn up the music, and drive, Monkeyman." He tossed his headset to the side as he leaned back in his seat and closed his eyes.

It normally would have taken us about nine hours to get to our destination, but I managed it in just over seven. We pulled into the huge parking lot and I saw the familiar blue-and-yellow signs with the Swedish flag flying under the American and Texas flags. I still couldn't bring myself to believe him. "You're serious about this? The gateway to your home dimension is in a Swedish build-it-yourself furniture store?"

He shrugged. "Where else? Come on, I need to get inside before they open to the public. Pull around the side to the loading dock."

I did as he suggested. He surprised me by immediately throwing open the door and hopping out—usually he was very cautious about being seen. I hastily grabbed a couple of extra mags, slung my rifle, and hurried to follow him as he stormed through the door and into the building. Normally he was the apologetic kind of tall and walked hunched over as if trying to make himself small enough not to frighten people, but now he was standing to his full height without a thought. An employee looked up, seemingly more surprised to see anyone coming in this early than he was at the sight of a Bullman. The Cowboy stalked over to him and handed him a card.

"Contact Evil Mike at Team TALON and tell him the PUFF is in the van. He'll take care of it. Whatever you do, don't let anyone else try to open those doors. It would not go well."

He handed the employee a hundred-dollar bill, grunted his thanks, and headed deeper into the store.

The employee nodded, made the bill vanish into his vest, and started dialing his phone. Judging from his reaction I got the impression that Bullmen came through here on a semi-regular basis. I wondered if that was a part of the regular corporate onboarding or if this particular store was just lucky that way. Probably make for an interesting orientation video.

I rushed to catch up with his long stride as the Cowboy stomped off into the store proper. He began to quietly fill me in without looking my way, his head moving back and forth as if looking for something. We moved from the self-serve part of the store through a jungle of plastic plants and deeper into the store proper. My partner was obviously in a hurry and was using his full stride, forcing me to trot to keep up.

"I still think taking you with me is a big mistake. Let me explain—what y'all call the Labyrinth, we call the Hard Earth. Humans typically don't do great there. Humans belong on the Soft Earth. The rules are different there since the place is composed mostly of raw chaos, so don't make any assumptions. Pretty much anything you see there might try to kill you if you take your eyes off it for even a moment. This takes that whole MHI 'flexible minds' mantra to a new level."

We turned left around the rolled rugs and then took an immediate right, headed into the lighting section.

"I will do everything in my power to protect you but understand the few people from the Soft Earth who have found their way there don't last long. Even your luck might not be enough. Are you absolutely sure you want to do this? I can't talk you out of it?"

"Cowboy, I'm not about to let you run off and have all the fun without me. I just wish I had had time to grab more ammo and hardware."

As we passed kitchen goods, he snorted. "Sorry, Monkeyman—we'll have to make do with just our sidearms and rifles. Even if the guns do decide to work in there, it's not like we've got anything that can penetrate Bullman hide. Unfortunately, we're just not geared up for this. To be honest with you, though, if this comes to combat with the other Bullmen I think we'd pretty much be screwed anyway. They outnumber us a gajillion to two."

He continued leading us through the store, going from one department to another through swinging doors and increasingly confusing point of purchase displays of housewares and furniture. "That's another thing—while you can call me Cowboy here, keep in mind that showing any sort of disrespect around other Bullman could be fatal. Use the full version of whatever name they tell you and be polite. We're an honorable people, but we're also foolishly proud, and you know how our tempers are. While we're there, call me by my full name."

I had never seen a staircase in one of these stores, but we went down a deep flight of stairs with cheap art prints lining the walls. Halfway down it turned ninety degrees to the right and continued downward. We finally came out on a lower level and continued moving across the cement floor. The displays were bizarre by this time, with products that seemed harmless enough in your periphery, but when looked at directly revealed subtle details that were just slightly off, like they had been created from an AI art program's impression of them rather than the actual things themselves. Imported directly from the uncanny valley, an assortment of chairs with too many legs, silverware with too many angles, curtains that didn't reflect light quite right—that sort of thing. The signs looked like gibberish, a random collection of letters and abstract shapes thrown on purely for aesthetics, but to be fair they had always looked like that to me. "Kinderflöopen" and "Cookenstur" couldn't really be Swedish, could it?

Each turn we took seemed to take us a little farther from logic and a little deeper into the Twilight Zone. Usually four left turns would put you back where you started, but that didn't seem to be the case here. I moved slightly closer to my companion. If I got lost here I wasn't sure I would ever find my way back. Becoming trapped in a surrealist non-Euclidean build-it-yourself furniture store would surely be an all-new, previously undiscovered circle of hell. I don't know how long we walked, my watch seemed to be acting erratically—probably needed to change the battery—but eventually we stopped in front of a swinging metal door and he turned to look at me.

"Jack, this is your last chance. Earl gave me the honor of being the official MHI envoy to the Bullmen, so I have to go in. But you are under no such burden. Are you absolutely sure about this?"

I rolled my eyes. "Dude, I was there, remember? I believe his exact words were 'Fine, whatever—you deal with it,' which is hardly the same as what you're making it out to be. But I've got your back. Less talking, more walking. Let's do this."

I pushed past my companion and opened the door. The metal door swung open easily with the slightest push. I walked through confidently, directly into an ambush.

The beast didn't seem to rise from the floor so much as it seemed to be part of it. Aside from all the tentacles and fangs, it sort of looked like a chicken/woman thing. It lashed out and wrapped my knees easily with a couple of tentacles, pulling my feet out from under me. I hit the spongy ground hard but was able to get my blade out and around to sever the appendages quickly. It shrieked at the touch of the steel and swiftly melted into the floor while I jumped to my feet, leaving behind some kind of greasy black residue.

I turned wildly around to see if it was coming from another angle so I was able to see the Cowboy as he ripped apart some *thing* that looked like a cross between a ukelele and a hyena. He turned toward me, seeming to stare at the wall behind me. I started to turn to look at what he was seeing but he stopped me.

"I need you to keep your eyes on the wall behind me, and I'll do the same for you. One of the few rules around here that seems consistent is that nothing changes while it's observed. That's a big part of the reason we usually travel in pairs. Now you're not going to like this, but since this is your first time here you need to eat some of that residue from your first kill."

"You have got to be kidding me, right? Screw you. I'm not eating that crap! It's disgusting."

"Jack, listen to me—it's important. Do it and I'll explain while we move. It will help you better understand the Bullmen. Honest."

"This had better be an ent-draught kind of thing or I'm making you into a pair of boots."

Keeping my eyes fixed on the wall behind him, I bent down and scooped up a handful of the chaotic slime. The smell was horrible and it felt disgusting, but I tentatively nibbled it. And immediately spat it out and began choking at the foulness, while the Cowboy burst out in laughter. While I continued to try to frantically spit the taste out of my mouth, I glared at him.

"Are you kidding me? What the hell, man?! That shit is next-level nasty!"

His laughter gave way to chuckling and he motioned for me to follow him as we started to walk down the tunnel, me frantically trying to wipe the goo off my tongue with the hem of my shirt.

"That nasty shit is what we mostly live on here in the Hard Earth and let me tell you, eating that your whole life doesn't improve the flavor. Pretty much the only reason we bother with the Soft Earth at all is because y'all have food that actually tastes like food. Well, that and the music. Bullmen music is all percussion. So we send a representative periodically to maintain the PUFF exemption for our tribe and in return we get barbeque and rock and roll. It's a fair trade."

The long hallway was an ashen gray color, featureless and lit by an undefinable light source. In the far distance I could just make out what seemed to be a left turn. The Cowboy stopped walking.

"Stand close, we need to get out of this hallway."

I wasn't sure what he was talking about but I moved a little closer to him so we were almost back-to-back. He leaned back until our shoulders touched.

"Okay, we close our eyes in three . . . two . . . one . . ."

I hastily did as he said but nothing seemed to happen. Within a few seconds he spoke again.

"That'll do. Open your eyes."

I opened my eyes and we were in what appeared to be an old dining room, complete with long table and chairs covered with gray dust. In the corner I saw an enormous staircase descending downward. He turned his head to see my view and nodded in satisfaction. He tapped me on the shoulder and began to walk down the steps, turning his head quickly side to side, scanning. I mimicked him, trying to walk backward as we worked our way deeper into the Labyrinth.

Time moves differently there and my watch and phone were no help so I can't say for sure how long we traveled. It felt like days but might have been hours. We fought off several more creatures, at certain points the Cowboy had us create some new paths, and we continued moving. Sometimes the hallways seemed like soaring ornate, almost baroque, spaces and sometimes they were crude and primitive passages that felt claustrophobic. Stairs, ramps, ladders, angled walls—the place was like walking through a place designed by Salvador Dali and M.C. Escher on a bad peyote trip. The only constants were that ashy dull gray and the lighting that seemed to come from nowhere. Eventually, we stopped outside a huge set of doors that wouldn't have looked out of place guarding the treasure vaults of Moria.

On either side of the door there were four Bullmen guards, paired on both sides and standing back-to-back. One of the ones facing us pointed a wicked-looking spear of some sort and bellowed loudly.

"Stop! Who approaches?"

The Cowboy stopped and held his arms out wide, still holding a large blade in each hand.

"Austin Bowie Gonzalez Houston of the East Texas Bullmen, returning from the Soft Earth."

The guard's spear tip never wavered.

"What is your business?"

"I have returned to honor our king."

I muttered under my breath, quietly enough that only the Cowboy could hear me: "And what is your favorite color?"

He made a shushing noise, but apparently there was no third question. The guard lowered his spear and nodded once, curtly.

I followed my friend and we walked past the guards and to the gates. The one on the right opened easily with the slightest push and we entered a bizarre city unlike anything I had ever seen. As we walked down the streets, the Cowboy acted as a tour guide and explained the history of the place.

"We were not created to be builders—we're warriors. Nevertheless, the earliest settlers came together and through trial and error created the Nexus to have a central meeting place to conduct whatever business we might have. It's a safe zone for our children to be born, for our warriors to recover, and for our rituals to be observed. Its random architecture was thrown up from the foundational chaos and locked into place when it was where we needed it to be. There's an entire guard unit whose sole purpose is to observe the walls and the buildings so they don't change again. Known as the Watchers, they don't belong to any of the seven clans." He gestured to a nearby guard who looked more like a yak-headed man than what I thought of as a Bullman, staring fixedly at a building. We continued walking.

The streets were wide and clean and teemed with Bullmen of all descriptions. I had never realized there were so many of them. Some looked like what I expected a Bullman to look like, but there were a lot of variations. Some looked like buffalos, some looked like great African bulls, and some even looked like Scottish highland cows. There were thousands of them moving around, but I noticed they all gave each other a respectful distance and everyone seemed to be polite to one another with none of the pushing or indifference you see in any human city. I commented on this and the Cowboy laughed briefly.

"Robert E. Howard was right about civilized men being more discourteous than savages. People tend to mind their manners when the alternative is potentially getting your skull kicked in. The clans all have slightly different rules, but there're some that don't change. Having good manners—especially in the Nexus—is one of the immutable laws of the Bullmen. Each clan has its own war leader who calls most of the shots and makes the small-L laws for their tribe, and also a shaman who is responsible for maintaining the big-L Laws of the Bullmen. Then there's the king, who lives here in the Nexus and actually makes those big-L Laws."

He pointed to a plain, utilitarian-looking tower. "That is the seat of what I guess you could call the government. The king, his immediate family, and the King's Shaman all live there. The King's Shaman is sort of the religious leader and right hand of the king. That's who we're here to see."

When we arrived at the tower, we walked straight in and I was surprised at the lack of guards. The Cowboy shrugged.

"We believe that any king that needs to be guarded isn't a king worth following."

He led me through a few twists and turns to a large plain door, made of the same ashen stuff as everything else in this place. He knocked politely and waited a moment before a deep voice like James Earl Jones waking from a pleasant dream told us to come in. We pushed the door open to reveal a modestly sized and decorated room with a large table. Seated behind the table was an enormous shaggy Bullman wearing what looked like a green kilt covered with strategically placed pieces of black leather armor. He looked at us and his furry face lit up. He stood and came around from the table with his arms spread wide.

"Austin Bowie Gonzalez Houston! You made it!"

He gave the Cowboy an enormous hug that lifted even his huge bulk from the ground. The Cowboy returned his hug with a wide smile.

"Uncle! I got here as fast as I could." They separated and the Cowboy nodded toward me.

"Jack Redacted Wylder, allow me to introduce you to Alexander Washington Hammurabi Houston—shaman of the East Texas Bullmen. Uncle, this is my battle partner and brother in arms."

The shaman looked at me appraisingly for a moment before nodding politely with a small bow. I had thought the Cowboy was a big dude but I was starting to realize he would actually be considered small for his people. Comparing the few Bullmen I've met in the world to the Bullmen in the Nexus was like comparing a German shepherd with a northwestern wolf. I mean, technically they're the same but they are definitely *not* the same. Plus, the Cowboy kept his horns trimmed down for ease of moving in the human world, while Bullmen here seemed to prefer to let them grow long which made them seem even more imposing.

"Jack Redacted Wylder of Team TALON, it is an honor to meet you. I thank you both for being a battle partner to my nephew and for coming to our aid."

I nodded respectfully. "It's an honor to meet you too, Alexander

Washington Hammurabi Houston of the East Texas Bullmen. I thank you for the invitation. How can I help?"

He tossed his head back and laughed loudly.

"Well said. You are much more polite than Earl Harbinger—you honor us with your courtesy."

Somehow I had forgotten that he had met and spent time with Harbinger. Of course. Even in another friggin' dimension, the dude was a legend.

"Yeah, Earl is a lot of things, but he's not really big on protocol. When did you two meet?"

The shaman looked somber.

"Shortly after the death of my son. Earl and I hunted down a Quilbist together. We needed its needles to craft his jacket, as they're one of the few things capable of piercing a Bullman hide. Earl taught me to shoot, and I taught him to fight with a glaive. In addition to honoring my son's request, it also gave me the opportunity to take the measure of the man. After spending time with him, I agree with the king's decree—Earl has earned his place within our tribe and I am proud to have him with us."

His face grew grim and serious.

"If we can get the new king to agree, that is. I hope you have arrived in time as the situation is quite dire. We have completed the first five of the trials, and only the tests of strength and leadership remain. It's between three champions, and none of them like the way the previous king ran things. The champion of the West American tribe has sworn to declare a war of conquest on the Soft Earth if he becomes king. Our own East Texas champion has sworn to recover the hide of Travis Alamo Sam Houston from Earl Harbinger by force if necessary. The New Zealand tribe plans to move us to the Soft Earth claiming, and I quote, 'It's more fun there. It would be a hoot.' Obviously there are no good outcomes here."

I raised my hand to get the shaman's attention. From his confused expression, I guessed that wasn't really a thing here.

"There are seven main tribes, right? So what happened to the other four tribes?"

"There are a lot more than seven tribes, but you are correct that there are seven that utilize this city. The Minok tribe, that you would call the Greek tribe, runs the city so they have no interest in who sits in the War Room. The Botswana tribe lives only for battle so couldn't find a champion willing to stop fighting and come to the Nexus for the time of choosing. The Highland Clan wanted to compete but were never able to agree on one champion. To be honest, I think they're still fighting over who to send. And the Rishikesh tribe have no interest in possessing power over others."

It sounded like those four could be removed from the mental equation. I continued to press for information in the hopes that a solution might present itself. If Bullmen were chess pieces they would be rooks—everything is a straight line. I would be less than useless in any sort of a physical confrontation, but I just might be able to bring some nonlateral thinking to the problem. Move like a knight and they'd never see it coming. But in order to think my way through this, I needed more information.

"Which candidate is currently in the lead?"

The Cowboy spoke up.

"It's not really a points system like a sport where anyone can be in the lead or in last place. All the competitors do all of the challenges and at the end of the event, the final test is a conclave with representatives from all tribes who then decide on who they believe will best lead the bullmen. It's partially a popularity contest, partially a reality show. 'Who Wants to Be King?' If you can convince enough bullmen to follow you in the Trial of Leadership, you become king. Since each tribe sends its strongest warrior, the events are all supposedly nonlethal. We don't want to deprive any tribe of its best. Accidents happen, of course, and the Test of Strength is always dangerous, but for the most part you win by impressing the other tribes."

The Q&A was cut short as the shaman stood abruptly and grabbed an enormous glaive from a hook on the wall. I had always been a fan of the massive weapon, but I wasn't sure if I would even be able to pick up that thing.

"I'm sorry, friends, but we must go now. The next event will be starting soon and I must be there. Come with me. We'll talk more after if I survive."

He led us through the door and down a series of passageways that looked somewhat inspired by Byzantine architecture. Thank goodness I had majored in art—that was money well spent. If I had gone the STEM route I might not have known what type of architecture this part of this hell dimension was inspired by.

Probably would have made more money all those years before Julie told us about PUFF bounties, too. Might not have had to clear out that shambler infestation in Tulsa to pay for my student loans. As we walked, I whispered loudly with the Cowboy.

"What does he mean 'if he survives'? Isn't he a shaman? Like, an official? Why would he be in danger? Don't priests get a pass?"

The Cowboy snorted.

"Oh no, our leaders must lead from the front—even our shaman. *Especially* our shaman. On the Soft Earth, leaders send others to do their dirty work but we would never follow a leader who hid behind us. No, Uncle has literally led the way on every challenge, as is right. He can't lead the contestants through trials he's unwilling to undergo himself."

At the end of the passage, a set of huge double doors swung open as we approached, revealing a large arena style clearing surrounded by walls that looked like stone and an enormous collection of Bullmen sitting in stadium style seats. Lit metal braziers with demonic looking faces on top of the walls cast light down onto the clearing. The fires had a weird color to them that seemed to shift subtly. The shaman leaned in toward us so we could hear him over the murmuring of the crowd.

"You two can watch the trial from over there."

With a flick of his head he indicated a sort of dugout arrangement built into the wall. We went in and shut the gate behind us. The Cowboy took a seat and looked out comfortably, but I was forced to stand on a chair in order to see.

The shaman walked to the center of the arena and the noise of the crowd swelled. It appeared Alexander Washington Hammurabi Houston was known and well regarded by everyone. He raised one of his great hands and the cheering stopped abruptly, like flipping a switch. His voice had to have been amplified by magic as there was no other explanation as to how it could be so loud and carry so well.

"Bullmen, it is time. Our three champions will now be competing in the Trial of Strength. From the West American Tribe, I give you Brigham Vegas Cody Gumb!"

Loud applause as an enormous bison-headed Bullman, wearing deep brown leather armor and carrying a long spear with feathers on it, walked into the arena floor, shaking his spear over his head and making a loud booming call. From the size of him

I guessed he probably weighed roughly the same as a midsize truck. His muscles had muscles.

"From the tribe of the New Zealanders, Āpirana Turupa Lomu Crowe!"

From the opposite side of the arena, the second champion walked out into the arena, carrying an enormous club. While the first champion had been built like a linebacker, Āpirana was built more like a swimmer. His thin frame was packed with muscle but he was built for speed and agility. His head looked more like a goat than a bull to me, with short horns that curved back along his head. I looked it up later and he actually most resembled a bull tahr covered in elaborate, intricate tattoos. I started to wonder about where they got their needles. Did they also have to hunt Quilbists? Also, what the hell was a Quilbist? My revery was interrupted by the final champion's introduction.

"And from the East Texas Bullmen, Cavelier Lorenzo San Jacinto Rusk!"

I had known a few bullmen from East Texas so I recognized the familiar longhorns, but Cavelier was easily the largest Bullman from that tribe that I had ever seen. If the first champion was a linebacker, and the second was a swimmer, he was built like a sumo wrestler. He was carrying a curved axe over his shoulder and encouraging the applause with his free hand.

All three champions walked into the center of the arena where the shaman waited for them. They surrounded him and all bowed respectfully. He spoke quietly to them, too low for me to hear, and they all nodded. He once again raised his voice so everyone could hear him.

"As dictated by tradition, this is the most dangerous of the trials and any champion is free to disengage at any point with no loss of honor. No tribe should be weakened by the Trials. Champions, do you still wish to continue?"

All three nodded.

"Very well. Release the grraahow!"

Unseen drummers began to play, a deep pounding beat with a lighter, more intricate overlay. In addition to being great warriors, it appeared Bullmen also made great drummers. The driving percussion added a tension to the show.

I immediately recognized the grayish blue creature that emerged from the great spiked gate on the side of the arena. I had never heard it called a grraahow, but I had seen one of these out in New Mexico. The beast was roughly the size of a large elephant with a mouth like a great white and tiny little eyes on the sides. It had four thick stumpy legs and two smaller appendages that looked like they came from an enormous praying mantis, with wicked sharp claws in the front for digging. The whole thing was completely covered in thick armored plates. Team Science had some big fancy-sounding name for it, but we had always just called it a landshark.

The creature turned Its enormous bulk surprisingly quickly in a circle, getting a sense of the arena. After a moment it knelt down and began to quickly burrow downward with its digging claws, vanishing from sight much quicker than logic would allow. There had to have been magic involved. Of all the things I hate about the Labyrinth, the sheer amount of magic there is top of the list. I despise magic. The champions readied themselves and tried to gauge where it would resurface.

After a short delay, the dirt beneath Āpirana exploded and the landshark's great jaws snapped where the lithe Bullman had been standing. His reflexive jump had carried him to the side and the moment his foot touched down he reversed his momentum and launched himself directly back at the beast, swinging his club hard enough to shatter stone directly into the side of its head. The shaman and the other champions charged toward its location but the creature retreated quickly back underground, unfazed by the mighty blow.

The warriors formed a loose circle, all facing outward with weapons at the ready. After a few tense moments the landshark again burst from the ground, this time trying to swallow Brigham. Brigham managed to leap clear and tried to stab downward into the beast's mouth but it snapped its teeth together, shattering the spear into splinters. The now unarmed Bullman ran a short distance away while the landshark retreated once more. I leaned toward the Cowboy so he could hear me over the roar of the crowd.

"What now? Does he have to fight it barehanded or is he out?"

Cowboy shook his head. "Nah, someone from the crowd will throw him a weapon—yup. There it is, see?"

"That's allowed?"

"Absolutely. We're brave, not stupid."

"Does it have to be the same weapon they lost?"

"Nope—any weapon is fair game."

I watched another flurry of attacks while I gave it some thought.

I could tell a couple of the Bullmen were getting close to going into a berserker rage from sheer frustration. The landshark would attack and disappear so quickly that there was little opportunity to counter, and with its armored hide, their weapons were largely ineffective. On its fifth eruption, it managed to surprise the East Texas champion and caught his leg between his teeth. The teeth were not quite sharp enough to pierce the thick Bullman hide but from our vantage I could hear the loud snap as his leg was broken. Bulletproof is not the same as unbreakable. Cavelier bellowed in pain as the monster began to pull him below the arena floor. The other champions encircled the beast and began to frantically assault it from all angles. It released its prey and sank once again beneath the ground as if it were water.

The shaman dashed over to the fallen champion and lifted him into a fireman's carry. He staggered beneath the weight but managed to work his way toward the gate near us while the other champions engaged the beast again. The Greek Bullmen opened the gates and took Cavelier from the shaman and pulled him to safely while the shaman quickly returned to the center of the ring, where the action was.

One of the most confusing aspects of the Labyrinth is in regard to time. Without a day/night cycle and with time-keeping devices that seemed to show basically random times, it was near impossible to track how long things took. How long had we been here? At a guess I'd have said not more than a few hours, but it was entirely possible that it had been days, perhaps even weeks. When we finally left, what year would it even be? And given the chaotic nature of this place, there was no way to say whether we would be forward or backward from when we left. It'd be just my luck to finally get out of this place and find out I had pulled a Rip van Winkle. All I can say for sure is that the fight went on for some time, back and forth. The landshark scored some solid hits and spilled some blood while the Bullmen beat the hell out of it, but both sides having armorlike hide prevented any real damage beyond that done to Cavelier.

Finally, when the shaman's glaive disappeared down the creature's gullet with a snap and the shaman pulled his arm out just in time, I saw my opportunity. Calling the shaman's name, I threw my rifle with both hands toward him, as flat as I could.

He turned at the sound of my voice and ran a few steps over to catch the rifle just before it hit the ground. It looked tiny in his massive fist, like a child's toy. He casually snapped off the trigger guard with two fingers to allow for his trigger finger to fit. Watching the landshark the entire time, he pulled back the charging handle on my AR, careful not to pull it apart, and flipped the safety off. He stomped heavily and rhythmically with one great foot to catch the beast's attention.

It seemed to work, as the beast's head whipped around to face him, and with a roar it began to charge, knocking Brigham aside as it did so. The shaman waited until the beast opened its maw wide to devour him to open fire, directly down its throat. Landsharks are nigh invulnerable from the outside, but apparently not so much on the inside. The shaman jumped aside as momentum carried the monster's bulk past him. It crashed into a wall and lay on its side gasping, its enormous teeth snapping at nothing and its milky black eyes staring intently at its impending end. Soon its sides fell still and the creature died. There was a stunned silence for a moment before the crowd erupted in a deafening roar of approval.

The champions raised their weapons in bloody fists and shook them triumphantly, while the crowd bellowed and stomped loudly enough to shake the ground. The shaman, meanwhile, limped his way toward the gate nearest us. I noted he maintained trigger discipline and kept his finger alongside the remains of the trigger guard—Earl would be proud his training had stuck. We came out to greet him and he handed me my rifle with a grateful thanks. I verified the safety was on and slung it over my shoulder, reloading the magazine as we followed him through the gate and over to where one of the Bullmen healers was working on Cavelier's leg using a traction box.

The shaman knelt beside them and looked at his clanmate with concern while the Cowboy and I stood over them, me awkwardly fidgeting, not wanting to look like I was staring but not sure where else to look, and the Cowboy just watching. It didn't help things that even kneeling, the Bullmen were still as tall as me. The shaman's voice was deep with worry.

"Cavelier Lorenzo San Jacinto Rusk, the beast is defeated and you remain whole. Will you be able to attend the Test of Leadership?"

Cavelier grunted stoically in pain as the healer moved the ends of the broken bone together with a loud, unpleasant pop. The sound of it alone was almost enough to make me pass out, but he took it with no other indication beyond that soft grunt. I knew from experience that he would be fully healed in a few days, or whatever passed for days in this place. Once again I admired the perfection of the Bullmen as warriors. For all their incomprehensible psychotic-ness, the Fey that had created them knew what they were doing.

"I am sorry, my shaman, but I fear I will be unable to continue in the Trials. I've cost our tribe the chance at the throne and for that I'm most sorry of all. I've failed my tribe, my family, and you."

The shaman reached out a huge shaggy hand and patted him on the shoulder.

"Rest, warrior. You have brought honor to your family and your tribe. The healers will see to this and you'll be back on your feet and fighting again before you know it. Sleep now, and heal."

The champion closed his eyes and fell into a deep sleep. Four of the Greek Bullmen picked him up and began to carry him down the hallway, probably to a recovery room of some sort.

The shaman stood and indicated with a toss of his head that we should follow him, so we did. He led us back to his chambers and absentmindedly offered us drinks from a utilitarian water urn. I politely shook my head and pulled out my pocket flask instead. I took a drink and offered it to the Cowboy, who accepted. We passed it back and forth between us while the shaman limped from one end of the room to the other. He spoke quickly, the words pouring out of him as if we weren't even there.

"With Cavelier Lorenzo San Jacinto Rusk out, there is no way forward that doesn't end in catastrophe. I'm the one who has failed my people and my king. The Bullmen leaving the Labyrinth would be an utter disaster. The ones who have never visited the Soft Earth have no idea how bad it would be for us. The Bullman love of battle works really well here, but if we were to start slaughtering humans I have no doubt we would not last long. One angry human is manageable. But when you get a bunch of them riled up, it's only a matter of time before they figure out a way. I've seen it before. Bullmen are strong, but angry humans are utterly ruthless. They would end up coming through the gates and destroying us here, I have no doubt."

He stopped abruptly and looked directly at us.

"If you leave now, you should still have time before the Trial of Leadership to warn Earl the Harbinger of the impending war on the Soft Earth. If you move quickly enough he might have time to close the gates between our worlds. Perhaps sealing us here in the Hard Earth would be for the best. If we have no path to the Soft Earth, it would take generations to find a new one. This is the only way we can prevent a war that would be too costly for both our peoples. I'm sorry, nephew, but you will have to choose between the Soft and Hard Earths before the path is closed."

The Cowboy stared at his uncle for a moment and then turned to look at me. I shrugged.

"You gotta go with your gut, man. But only if it comes to that. We still have time to look for other solutions, right? How long do we have for the Trial of Leadership?"

The shaman shook his head sadly.

"We need to leave."

Perfect. I had to figure out how to avoid the apocalypse without potentially losing one of my closest friends, in a situation with no apparent good solution. No pressure or anything.

The shaman took another glaive from the wall and, using it as a walking stick, began to limp from the room with us following him closely. While we walked, I asked him every question I could think of about the history of the Bullmen, their traditions and customs. He told me about their war in breaking free from the Fey, about their wanderings until they found the Hard Earth, about the founding of their society, and their traditions. I don't know how long we walked, but it seemed like a long time. By the time we arrived, the shaman's limp was noticeably better. I turned to look back but there was only a blank wall behind us. Stupid chaos dimension.

Before us were a pair of elaborately carved double doors in a style I was unfamiliar with. Without any fanfare or buildup the shaman pushed the doors open, revealing a large, raised dais ringed with braziers. Surrounding us on all sides was a sea of Bullmen, their faces lit by the multicolored flickering flames. Already on the platform stood the two remaining champions, hyping the crowd up. As the shaman walked in, the noise died down and everyone waited for the ceremony to begin. He raised his voice, once again magically enhanced.

"It is time for the final challenge—the Test of Leadership. Upon its conclusion, the new king will be named and we will again have a leader to guide us into the future. Remember, you are not just choosing our king—you are choosing the path the king chooses."

The thought that had been hiding in the periphery of my brain finally coalesced and the answer came to me, so obvious that I was annoyed it had taken me this long to realize it. Throwing etiquette aside, I tapped the shaman frantically on the arm until he stopped speaking and looked down at me. When he spoke, his voice was again unamplified although I hadn't seen him do anything.

I looked up at his wide, kind face.

"Alexander Washington Hammurabi Houston of the East Texas Bullmen, why can't *you* be king?"

His answer was immediate, so ingrained that it didn't require thought.

"It is forbidden for shaman to be king."

"And who forbid it?"

"The king."

"And the king's word is law?"

"The king's word is the Law of the Bullmen, barring a dishonorable command."

"So the king could reverse this decision?"

"Well... yes?"

I nodded in satisfaction and spread my hands wide.

"So unforbid it... Your Majesty."

He stared at me, momentarily dumbfounded. It was obvious the thought had never even occurred to him. The Cowboy beside me was equally shocked and for once was at a loss for words. I gave them a moment to work it out. I knew it had finally registered when the Cowboy bowed his head respectfully.

"He speaks the truth, Sire. You are the rightful king of the Bullmen, and the only one worthy of leading us. If you lead, we will follow you. You are the only one who can prevent a terrible slaughter and a war with the Soft Earth. If we attack them, we will have the combined efforts of both the MCB and MHI aligned against us. If Agent Franks and Earl Harbinger join forces, do you really want to go against them? And no matter what happens, we lose our easy access to barbeque and rock and roll. This is not a risk worth taking. I'm sorry. I know you've never sought power, but that is exactly why you have to take the throne."

The shaman's pensive expression cleared and he looked at

us, wide-eyed. He stammered for a moment before clearing his throat and starting again.

"Jack Redacted Wylder of Team TALON, you are correct . . . and you have my gratitude."

He turned toward the waiting delegates and raised his voice to be heard over the clatter. When he began speaking, the others all stopped arguing and listened respectfully.

"Brigham Vegas Cody Gumb, you have great strength and have performed admirably." The bison-headed champion stood a little taller as his followers murmured appreciatively.

"And Āpirana Turupa Lomu Crowe, you have great speed and are unmatched in your dexterity." Āpirana flexed his muscles exaggeratedly, gaining a chuckle from many of the attendees.

"But *I* have something even more important—I have great friends."

He nodded toward where the Cowboy and I stood watching.

"If you will have me, I will lead you. It is time for the final decision."

The champion of West America pushed forward and protested.

"A shaman cannot be king! It is a violation of our Law!"

The shaman raised his hand in a forestalling gesture.

"Hold that thought just a moment."

He turned toward the crowd.

"Who here will follow Brigham Vegas Cody Gumb of the West American Tribe?"

A few shouts and some clapping from the crowd.

"And who here will follow Āpirana Turupa Lomu Crowe of the New Zealand Tribe?"

Some hoots and cheers while Āpirana gestured wildly.

"And who here will follow Shaman Alexander Washington Hammurabi Houston of the East Texas Tribe?"

I was grateful that I had my hearing protection in and that it cut off sounds above a certain decibel level because the cacophony that rang out was loud enough to have caused permanent hearing damage otherwise. Every Bullman in attendance—including, to my surprise, Āpirana—bellowed their support at the top of their lungs. And just like that, it was settled. The King of the Bullmen turned toward Brigham.

"I'm sorry, what were you saying?" He looked at Brigham placidly. After a moment, Brigham bowed his head.

"Nothing, my king."

King Alexander patted him on the shoulder.

"Do not worry, my friend. I will do everything I can to be a king worthy of your support."

Brigham nodded, mollified, and walked back to join the throng of cheering Bullmen. The king turned toward us and smiled widely.

"You have solved the unsolvable and you have my thanks. Please tell Earl the Harbinger that his envoy has performed admirably. We are honored to have him in our tribe, and should he ever have need of us he has but to call and he will have an entire apocalypse of Bullmen ready to stand with him. And you, nephew—will you stay upon the Soft Earth, or will you return home to us now? You have earned a place of great honor and I could use you beside me. You as well, Jack Redacted Wylder—you are a welcome guest and we would be honored to have you join us."

The Cowboy and I didn't even need to ask to know what the other was thinking. I smiled and let him answer for both of us.

"We're honored, my king, but the Soft Earth is where we're most needed. Things are in motion there, and I suspect in the near future there'll be a need for every soldier the forces of good can muster. We've got a lot to do, but if you ever need us again you have our number."

The king nodded and reached out to shake my hand. It was more like sticking my entire forearm in a giant fist, but the intent was there. He let go and gathered the Cowboy up in an enormous hug and once again lifted him off the ground, swinging his bulk the way you would a child.

We finished our goodbyes and began the long trek back.

"You did okay, Monkeyman. It's good to know you're occasionally useful."

"Sure, Cowboy. I'm just glad I haven't had to make a jacket out of you . . . yet. You stupid magical cow."

"If my van still smells like letiche, though, you're buying me a new one."

"Can we stop by and see your mother?"

Hannah Stone was the first female employee of MHI, back when the company was called Bubba Shackleford's Professional Monster Killers in the late 1800s to early 1900s. —A.L.

Carnage at the Carnival

Hinkley Correia

Hannah crept through the trees, ducking under low branches and climbing over logs. Foliage crunched softly under her feet, made silent under the cover of wind-rustled leaves. Every single one of her senses were on fire. The barrel of her rifle snapped up to meet an unnatural movement in her peripheral vision before her brain even recognized it as nonhuman. She looked into the poor, dumb lizard creature's empty eyes for a moment before squeezing the trigger. The creature dropped to the ground with a thump, and the forest returned to its natural late-night silence.

She sighed, stretched, and tried to not knock into a tree. Jobs like these weren't quite the heart-pounding adventure she'd always chased after, jumping from show business to hunting mythical creatures, but the paycheck made it miles better than the hunting trips she took with her father as a child. Maybe she could find one of the other Monster Killers to breathe down her neck about her shot and how steady she was. Just for that extra authentic touch.

She watched the body for any more sudden movements as she made her way over to it. It was a clean kill, naturally, but to be completely honest, these things creeped the hell out of her.

The good people of Loveland, Ohio, called them Frogmen, and she had to admit it was a fitting title. They looked like the bastard love child of a frog and one of them spiky desert lizards that had grown well past an acceptable size. The smallest one they'd seen was a little bigger than a sheepdog. Most of them were closer to deer. Creepy-crawlies never bothered her much, and these hadn't either—at least until she saw them amble around on two legs, unfocused gaze drifting in two different directions. That had simply been too much for her dainty palate.

According to the locals, the Frogmen had been there for years, although nobody seemed to know exactly when they started to appear. For a while, there weren't any issues, but they'd recently started attacking the livestock. When a local teenager got a little too close to the nest and came back with broken bones and a chunk bit out of him, the mayor reached out to Bubba Shackleford's Professional Monster Killers for a proper extermination.

A few more shots rang out a mile or so away, and Hannah exhaled as she slung the rifle over her back to pick up the slimy creature. Her compatriots were still hard at work and wouldn't hesitate to get self-righteous if she lagged behind. Now if only she had one of them around to help her move the damn thing.

The Whiskey Barrel Inn was a relatively new establishment, set smack in the middle of town. It was the last stop before reaching the city of Columbus, or the first stop before setting out for a new life. The owner acted like the Inn was some symbol of hope or change, and that it was not only his job but his calling to give patrons the best possible stay. That was their first night there.

Now, nearly a week later and several days after they all thought they'd be done, the owner was clearly ready for them to go on to their next stop. Honestly, Hannah couldn't blame him. The Monster Killers were a rowdy bunch when they were content and had things to do, but with the current hunt stretching on for far longer than expected, they had to grapple with their worst enemy: boredom.

They should've been able to collect their payment and leave days ago. All the trails the Frogmen seemed to stick to were untouched and they'd already found and destroyed the nest. The infestation was dealt with, and now they were just wasting time. But the mayor was insistent that the leader of the pack had yet to be brought in. He claimed it was at least six foot on its hind legs, and smart enough to get bait out of traps without setting them off.

Hannah figured it was a swindle. Get someone else to do

all the dirty work and then complain about it not being done enough until the hunters got frustrated enough to leave without the full pay. She'd seen it plenty of times in show business. But some of the other townsfolk corroborated the story and Bubba didn't become the premier monster hunter of the great United States by doing half-assed jobs. So, she was stuck in Loveland watching Mexican George decimate Orson Pangle in a hand of cards. And here she thought lawyers were supposed to be good at lying.

Hub Bryan was the only one who also wasn't playing, on account of losing quite a bit of money the evening before. She took a seat next to him. "So, what do you think of this giant Frogman business?"

He didn't bother looking up from his drink. "I think we need to get rid of it as soon as possible or some of us aren't gonna have any money to get home."

Before she could tease him on his losing streak, the door was pushed open, and in stepped Bubba followed by Balthazar Abrams, their quartermaster. She hoped for a moment that they would jump in the game, if only to see someone else dominate. Both were scary good with numbers, and had poker faces that made statues look like clay, but unfortunately, their stony faces were in full effect.

Bubba lifted a folded slip of paper. "Got word from the Scholar."

The atmosphere in the room stiffened. The Scholar was their common contact for these kinds of jobs, with an abundance of knowledge of the supernatural. They were also a completely unknown entity who signed all of their correspondence with only the letter S. All the information they sent had been accurate so far, but Bubba's people weren't stupid enough to blindly trust someone like that. Even if they'd contacted the Scholar first.

"They got information for us?"

"Apparently. Get your Sunday best out, because the Scholar wants to meet us in person."

Buffalo Bill had performed in Columbus several times while she was with them, so she was a little familiar with the city. Granted, that familiarity ended at the tourist areas, but it was enough that she didn't panic at the sight of all the people like a country bumpkin. She enjoyed staying in cities and all their conveniences, but that was probably because she was long gone before all the annoying parts kicked in. She couldn't imagine settling down amongst city folk. Then again, the idea of settling down anywhere left a sour taste in her mouth.

All the pretty girls in her hometown left for places like this. Prospects were poor, even before all the good farmland dried up, so leaving everything behind to try to marry a banker or businessman was a better plan than staying. It's what she did after her father finally kicked the bucket, though marriage had never been in the cards. She was stocky and stubborn. Less of a prize pony and more of a workhorse. The only men interested in taking her as a wife were the kind to stay on a dying farm until they starved to death, and she had long decided that if she was to die young, she wanted it to be exciting.

At times like this, she would've liked to watch out the window to see if she recognized any landmarks. Unfortunately, she was squished between Hub and Skirmish. Her diary might've saved her from the boredom, but Skirmish had proved himself rather ungentlemanly by reading over her shoulder and teasing her about it. Claimed that it was unladylike to stretch the truth of their jobs into tall tales. The big Irishman would appreciate it in two hundred years when he was a folk hero, but in the meantime it had been mighty embarrassing. Besides, the pockets in her dress were currently stuffed with enough firepower to take down a decently sized bear, so there was no room for writing instruments. Her purse wasn't nice enough to bring to a meeting like this.

Despite all the monsters and mysteries she'd seen, the most surprising thing she discovered was that all of the Monster Killers owned at least one set of nice clothes. If she had to make a bet, she would have put money on less than half having a decent Sunday shirt, but Bubba's forethought for wild situations extended to the unthinkable scenario of the client wanting to meet them in person. They were dressed to the gills. No doubt they were armed that way as well. Naturally, she had her dress tailored to smuggle several firearms and plenty of ammunition, and she would have been shocked to find out if any of them didn't have some form of weapon tucked away.

The Scholar helped them plenty, and the information they sent was usually correct, but that was almost more worrying. No way that kind of quality came without a price. For all they knew, the

Scholar could be a nefarious demon using them to take care of the competition. Or worse, a government man waiting to take credit for all their work. This meeting might be a trap, and they might not be fully prepared, but the Monster Killers'd be damned if they didn't riddle the place with holes before they went out.

The stagecoach finally came to a rumbling stop, and all the Monster Killers piled out with a speed usually only used for emergencies. For once, Hannah was glad for the damp city air, if only to get away from the stink of cheap cologne.

The address provided to them was in a rich area. Not the ostentatious kind of rich of the South, but of the pretentious kind of rich where one pretended to be modest to appeal to the masses. Politician rich. All the neat houses guarded by wrought iron, just as sharp as it was decorative.

"Mr. Shackleford and company, I presume?"

An older man with more salt than pepper hair stood diligently in front of one of the gates. His suit was well-maintained and pressed, but still lacking some of the fancier dressings the owner of such a lavish house should possess. Hannah'd never met a real-life butler. Seemed fitting that the Scholar would have one.

Bubba tilted his hat down in greeting. "Evening. You the Scholar?"

The other man half chuckled and shook his head, maintaining a calm smile. "Scholar? No, sir. I'm simply here to escort our guests."

He opened the gate with little fanfare and gestured for them to enter. Bubba was the first through, shoulders square and confident. As if he was certain the place was fine. He hadn't been wrong about that kind of thing for as long as she worked under him, so she hiked up her skirts and followed.

The front pathway wound through an immaculate garden. Flowers bloomed from perfect bushes. A violet, exotic-looking one swayed tantalizingly at eye level, slightly out of place from its brethren. Hannah reached out to pluck it, but before her fingertips could brush the petals, the butler cleared his throat from the front of the group.

"Please refrain from touching any of the plant life. While most of the specimens in this garden are safe, a few of them can be a bit unagreeable, and we would like to avoid any unnecessary incidents."

Bubba shot a glare at her with an intensity that would make Medusa jealous. Hub snickered next to her. He stopped when she shoved her elbow into his side. So much for being on her best behavior. She picked up her pace until the front door was in sight. Much like the gate, the butler opened it for them all proper-like.

The front door might as well have been a portal to a new world with how different the inside was. While the outside was the perfect picture of order and calm, the parlor could only be described as barely controlled chaos. Papers covered nearly every horizontal surface and framed diagrams hung proudly on the walls. Where one would expect statues or precious family heirlooms, there were bones and skulls and contraptions that had purposes Hannah could only speculate.

"Excuse me for a moment while I alert my employer of your arrival. Please, have a seat wherever available." With that, the butler disappeared down a hallway.

Only Bubba and Balthazar took up the offer for a seat. The Killers spread through the room to look at all the little knick-knacks with an almost comedic speed. Hannah'd call it childish, if she weren't so busy studying one of the diagrams on the wall. It looked eerily similar to the Bear Lake Monster, cut into a labeled cross-section. Would've been impressive if it was, because the dynamite had turned most of its head into red mist. Maybe they used some fancy science to figure out what the inside looked like.

Pangle must've been the first person to hear the footsteps from down the hall, because he immediately stood up straight, setting off a chain reaction of the Monster Killers all attempting to make themselves look natural and not like they were snooping. Hannah herself froze and hid her hands behind her back, though it probably only served to make herself look guilty of theft.

The person who came down the hall wasn't the butler. It was a woman, tall and thin, with mousy brown hair pulled haphazardly into a bun. She smiled, but thick glasses made it impossible to see if it reached her eyes or not. Judging by the quality of her dress, she wasn't just some maid or housekeeper. Probably a lady of the house, but Hannah couldn't figure out if she was a wife or daughter.

The woman extended her hand to Bubba. "I apologize for keeping you waiting. I am Dr. Edith Sharpe. We've communicated over telegram, but it is nice to finally speak with you face to face."

"So you're the Scholar, then?" If Bubba was shocked that the

Scholar was a woman, he didn't show it. He just took her hand and gave it a solid shake.

"Yes, I suppose you could call me that. I'm a biologist with a specialty in cryptozoology." After a quick glance at some of her clearly uneducated and confused guests she added, "I study mythical creatures."

Bubba looked around the spacious room. "A lucrative field, apparently."

She chuckled. "Oh, not particularly. There simply aren't that many in our field. Any research is valuable research when lives are on the line. Anyway, time is limited, so we should get down to business."

Some of them had to move objects around to sit down, but Sharpe did not seem to care as to where they put the potentially valuable items. The butler returned with a thick stack of papers, which he set in front of Sharpe. She flipped through the first couple of papers, stopping at what looked like a heavily annotated newspaper clipping.

"According to my research, amphibians tend to stay in groups and fight over territory, but a so-called alpha wouldn't be likely. What I believe the locals saw was simply a larger, more aggressive member of the species. I believe it was the one that made the initial attacks."

"Does that tell us anything about where it is now?"

"No, but this probably does." She pulled a page from the bottom of the stack and set it in the middle of the table for all to see.

It was a flyer for Dr. Swan's Magical Menagerie of Mystery, in town for a few days only. Several of their most popular attractions formed a circle around a picture of the Frogman, which according to the poster was being shown off to the public for the very first time. The way the illustration was stylized, it looked like a dapper gentleman, complete with a waistcoat and hat. Nothing like the ambling, vacant-looking creatures that they encountered just a few nights before.

Of course it had to be the circus. They knew of Dr. Swan's since the Bear Lake Monster incident, but all they really knew was that he used dubious means to collect mystical, dangerous creatures. Hannah knew Bubba was trying to look into them, but it couldn't have been easy. Carnies weren't known for sticking in one place long enough to be questioned.

"I believe that he recently captured the specimen in Loveland, likely only a few days before your group arrived on the scene. Now he intends to show it off, right here in Columbus. From what I've heard, they're only in town through the rest of the week. After that, we won't know where or when they'll reappear."

The information hung heavy in the air. They'd wanted to go after the circus, but this didn't give them a lot of time to prepare. Not taking the opportunity could be worse. Her gut feeling was to go for it, and deal with the consequences when they came. And that was exactly why she wasn't the leader. This was Bubba's decision. He was studying the paper pensively.

Sharpe sighed. "Such a shame to see him stoop so low."

"You know Dr. Swan?"

"Tangentially. He used to be one of the best and brightest minds in the field of cryptozoology. You couldn't do any research without finding his work. One day, he simply disappeared. He stopped showing up to work or turning in his research. When they went to check on him, his residence had been cleared out, like he never existed. Discovering he had left it all behind to be the ringmaster of a traveling circus was a surprise to all of us."

"And nobody knew what happened to him? No assistants, or family, or anything?"

"Not that anyone knew of. Nobody even noticed he'd left until months after."

"Quite the escape artist, then."

They sat in silence for another moment, waiting with bated breath to see what the plan was.

"Well, it's obvious what we gotta do now." Bubba stood up, adjusted his jacket, and put his hat back on. "Get your stuff together. We're going to the circus."

Dr. Swan's Magical Menagerie of Mystery set up shop just outside of town. It was a good location. Just close enough to be easy to stop by, but far enough to keep someone there as long as possible. Colorful fabric tents dotted an abandoned field, trampled paths wound through the grass connecting them. They arrived shortly before dusk. Lamps hung wherever possible, soaking the area in a warm glow. To the general public, it looked like a regular circus. Hannah liked to think it was due to her naturally sharp perception, but the place felt sinister. Traveling entertainment usually was.

Dr. Sharpe had insisted on coming with them, much to Bubba's clear annoyance. She wanted to "perform some proper field research," as she put it, and absolutely refused to take no for an answer. While she promised to stay out of the way and leave if the situation became dangerous, Hannah gained a new understanding of how Bubba must've felt when she first joined. Hub, ever the gentleman, had taken it upon himself to escort the good doctor and ensure she stayed out of danger.

Hannah, unfortunately, was stuck with Skirmish again. And the big Irishman was very committed to his role of carnival goer. She followed him as best she could as he wandered from booth to booth, trying games and asking questions. She wasn't short, his legs were too damn long. Large people weren't supposed to be that fast.

Two young women, around her age, wandered by them. Barely close enough to hear. One, with an impractically large hat, was talking animatedly to her companion sporting a lacy ribbon about whatever local gossip came to mind. It wasn't something she normally cared about, but watching someone else play games could only take up so much of her attention.

"But I'm not sure if she should've come tonight, what with her constitution. If another accident happened, I'm sure the poor thing would faint dead away."

Were they talking about the circus? "There was an accident?"

The girls gave her a once-over only to sneer at her trousers and pretend they hadn't heard her. Skirmish smirked at her before stepping up to them and putting on his best Southern accent.

"Excuse me, ladies, but what did you say about an accident?"

The one in the hat gave a slight gasp, and fluttered her eyelashes at him. "Oh, the freak show closed early last night after some kind of accident. I heard from one of my friends that it was an animal attack, but she can be such a fibber."

The girl with the ribbon smacked her arm. "Sharon! It's true! I was looking for my brother, and I saw a huge animal between the tents. Other people saw it, too!"

"Really. Then what animal was it?"

"It was dark, but it had to have been a lion or something."

"Yeah, right."

"Miss Stone!" Bubba called out to her from down the walkway. Skirmish's attention was focused on the two young women trying their best to keep it. He was perfectly fine. Hannah slipped through the crowds to stand next to her boss.

"Mr. Shackleford."

"Find anything yet?"

"Just gossip. It sounds like one of the creatures got out and attacked someone."

He nodded. "Like what happened with the Bear Lake Monster. Seems like the doctor isn't very good at keeping his attractions under control. Come on, let's go through and tell me if you see anything."

"Alright, but I'll warn you, I'm no circus expert. I might know some showbiz tricks, but that's it."

"Is there a difference?"

Hannah shrugged. "No idea."

Their first stop, the freak show tent, had the somber atmosphere of a recent disaster. Perhaps that was just how it was when one's job was to be gawked at. Stages dotted the layout of the tent, forming a makeshift maze to guide any prospective visitors. Wooden bars encircled each one, designed to look like cages. She couldn't tell if they were real or decorative, but she didn't trust Dr. Swan to act humanely. In her experience, the way a person was treated indicated how they would treat people, and if he treated animals well they wouldn't be in this mess. A wooden placard with the occupant's stage name and fake backstory hung from the bars but didn't provide useful information.

Almost no one else had ventured in, leaving the two Killers surrounded by dozens of dissecting eyes. If she stepped behind Bubba at any time while they wandered through, it was purely because the path was too narrow. Certainly not because the whole area gave her the creeps.

Oddly enough, the attraction ended very abruptly, without a big finisher. There was a stage for it, visibly larger than the rest, but curtains blocked most of it from view. Hannah couldn't see the placard, if there even was one. It was either unfinished or the occupant had moved, but it didn't make sense to put the effort into setting it up if it wasn't ready yet.

The stage next to it was much smaller, hosting two occupants: a man, and a python longer than she was twisting casually around his body. The light made the man's skin appear an almost translucent green, bringing attention to the large patches of what looked like reptile scales. She didn't need to see the sign to know that this was the circus' Snake Man.

She knew the trick to this one. One of the old performers she knew used the same gimmick. Some kind of condition made their skin peel off and flake. Slap some makeup on it, and you had a human with scales. He looked at her dead on with sickly yellow, slitted eyes and gave a fang-filled smile. Of course, in her current line of business, sometimes there was no trick.

White bandages wrapped up his arm. Considering one of his biggest draws was his scaled skin, they probably only covered the bare minimum. Judging by the amount covered, it must've been a bad injury. The snake avoided the area, and she had to wonder if it was on purpose. Had the Snake Man been the victim of the attack, and that's why they shut the attraction down early?

He tilted his head at her, and she found herself mirroring him. He flicked his forked tongue at her, and she flinched more than was becoming. He kept his smile; the shaking of his shoulders betrayed that he was silently laughing at her. Hannah shoved the brim of her hat down and turned on her heels to catch up to Bubba. Maybe she needed to add snakes to the list of creatures she no longer liked after this job.

Bubba waited patiently for her outside the tent and she nearly knocked into him in her haste to get out.

"What happened to you?"

"Nothin'." She shoved her hat down more so he couldn't call her on it. "You saw that, right? I think that might've been where the accident happened."

Before Bubba could give his opinion, a booming voice echoed through the fairground. "Come one, come all! The show is about to begin!"

The crowds murmured and began to make their way to what must be the main tent. Bubba adjusted his hat and sighed. "Looks like that's next."

As the masses flowed toward the tent, the air filled with excitement. Her heart started to pound. It reminded her of being back with the Wild West Show and getting jitters before her act. Part of her missed it: the attention and praise during a performance and the satisfaction of each perfect shot. And then she thought about the long hours and never quite getting the same audience as her peers and entertaining snobs who had no idea what they were talking about. And poor Bob. The part that missed it shriveled up pretty quickly.

Eventually they made it to the main tent. Despite the size of it, there were enough people in it that it was practically bursting at the seams. Some shoved through, trying to get as close to the large dirt circle serving as the arena as they could.

Skirmish managed to save them a spot with a decent view. And by saved, she meant he was big and mean-mugging anyone who had the nerve to get in his personal space. Or maybe the normally jolly Irishman was genuinely in a bad mood. The girls from earlier were nowhere to be found, but he dodged the question when she asked about them.

Their conversation went silent when all the gas lamps lighting the room flickered off at once, leaving the audience in complete darkness. It was quiet, the anticipation like a string about to snap. Suddenly, a light beamed down, illuminating a man in the center of the arena. His costume was extremely ostentatious, a matching cape and top hat set that glittered in the spotlight. It was near impossible to see his face from where they sat, but Hannah could see an impressively styled mustache.

The man threw his arms out with a flourish. "Welcome, welcome! One and all! I am Dr. Swan, and welcome to my Mystical Menagerie of Mystery!"

That was Dr. Swan? She expected someone more mad-scientist looking, though she supposed it made sense that he was a ringmaster and would have to look the part. "We have all worked very hard to provide you with a wonderful performance tonight, so please enjoy!"

With another flourish and a plume of smoke, Swan disappeared, and the crowd went wild. The lights returned, and the show began. All things considered, it was remarkably well put together. There were clowns and contortionists, and acrobats performing tricks dozens of feet in the air. The audience gasped at every elaborate trick and near miss. Hannah even found herself gasping at some of them, even if she knew there was no real danger. Worth the price of admission, if Dr. Swan wasn't using nefarious means to do so.

The Frogman was, naturally, the last act of the performance, saved for the peak of excitement. Dr. Swan returned to the arena, an entourage of stagehands pulling a large, fabric covered box in tow.

"Ladies and gentlemen, children of all ages! Today I have the wonderful opportunity of presenting to you, for the very first time, the Ohio Frogman!"

He threw the curtain off the cage, and the crowd responded. A few people screamed and Hannah could understand why. If the regular-sized Frogmen creeped her out, this one made her want to vomit. It was far bigger than the six feet of the rumors, standing at least eight feet tall, but the extra height couldn't have been natural. It was more muscular than the others, but it all bulged unnaturally, like a costume halfway filled with water. The door creaked open, and the creature stumbled out. Its artificial musculature didn't go past its torso. Its arms and legs were stick thin, and Hannah could practically see bones through its skin. As it walked, its entire body stretched. Its throat spasmed as it inflated and deflated. She could hear its croak under the crowd due to the sheer bass of it.

The audience was enraptured. A stagehand handed a leather whip to Swan, who cracked it. Right on that cue, it leapt in the air, hanging at the peak for just a moment, before flipping over and sticking the landing. The show went on like that. Swan cracked his whip, and the Frogman performed various tricks. It was mostly acrobatics, but one of them was a little jig. Between the vacant eyes and the still twitching throat, Hannah thought the show disgusting. Eventually, the stagehands brought out a series of hoops of various sizes. Swan held them up, one at a time. Each time, the Frogman would leap through with ease. The audience went wild in amazement, growing to impossible intensities as the hoops grew smaller and smaller.

Finally, they arrived at the last hoop. Unlike the others, this one was set up upon a stand. Swan produced a match, ignited it and touched it to the ring, lighting it ablaze. The audience oohed and aahed. The Frogman would barely fit, even if the hoop wasn't on fire, and she had no idea how it would make it through this. They all waited at the edge of their seats to see the jump, but it didn't come. The Frogman froze.

Swan cracked the whip, but even that did nothing. He brought it down on the creature's back and it whirled on him. Hannah saw its neck spasm again, before it spit something slimy and green at Swan, who jumped back and brought his cloak up to try to stop it. The glob passed right through both the whip and the cloak, splattering against the floor. It steamed and sizzled, melting into the ground. The whip fell apart, one end dropping limply to the ground.

The audience exploded. Some screamed, some made a break for the exit. The stupid ones cheered, thinking it was all part of the show. Hannah grabbed one of her Colts, ready to put the creature down if need be, and she had no doubt Bubba and Skirmish would back her up. Through the waves of people, she could barely see Swan say something, though she couldn't hear through the excitement, and she'd never learned how to read lips.

The Frogman froze mid-lunge. It appeared to struggle, but it didn't move another inch. Swan whistled sharply, catching the attention of everyone who hadn't run away in the confusion. The Frogman jumped through the flaming hoop with little fanfare, before returning back to its cage. The stagehands threw their entire body weight into the door to slam it shut. and rushed to return the curtain over it. Swan threw his arms wide. "Thank you! You've been a fantastic audience!"

A few people clapped, before it erupted into rapturous applause. Those panicking just a few seconds earlier now cheered, successfully convinced that it was all part of the show. The spotlight switched off, and the house lights slowly turned back on. The audience trickled out of the exits, still abuzz with excitement. Hannah could barely see the crew cleaning the arena and readying their props for the next show. It would probably be completely done by the time the Monster Killers got a chance to move from their spot.

The Frogman was gone. Not like they could just shoot the thing in front of a big crowd like this, anyways. Well, they probably could and get out before anyone got their wits about them enough to stop them, but they were professionals, not a gang. Bubba made that very clear when she first joined up, and a couple of times after when they got a little too rowdy. All they could do for now was follow the flow of the crowd and leave. They could come back later when they had enough information for a plan.

Hannah guessed the weird thing Swan did to get it back in the cage was probably how he managed to catch it in the first place. Possibly how he had caught other monsters. Its size and acid spit were both surprises, but if she were a betting woman, that could be blamed on Swan as well. Her education mostly stopped after letters and numbers, so her knowledge of science consisted of whatever she could pick up in books on the road, but maybe Swan picked up something when studying crypto-whatzits.

The Monster Killers walked down the large dirt pathway back to the entrance, looking for their compatriots and clues. As far as she could tell, the only carnies out and about were performing for the dwindling townies. Even if they could, Hannah strongly doubted that they would be willing to answer any questions about their highly suspicious employer and how he managed to acquire an actual monster.

Something—someone, rather—slipped past the corner of her eye. The man had a wide-brimmed hat, angled a certain way to cover his face. What really caught her attention was the way only one of his sleeves rolled up, folded awkwardly over white bandages. She couldn't get a good look at his skin, but she knew she'd see scales.

If the Snake Man was injured in the attack the previous night, like Hannah was beginning to suspect, those bandages likely covered an acid burn. If anyone had more information on the Frogman, and would be willing to answer their questions, it might be him. The man ducked into a space between two tents. She needed to act fast.

"I think I see something. I'll be right back."

If they could bottle the exhaustion in Bubba's voice they could make a fortune selling it to insomniacs. "Alright, just be careful."

Hannah ducked into the same space between tents just in time to see the figure go around a corner. She followed as quickly as she could. It was much darker than the main path, the tents casting impossibly tall shadows in the dying evening sun. Soon it would be pitch black out, and then there would be no way out of the small maze.

She lost him at the outskirts, by the last tents before the fairground turned into an open field. One was smaller, and plain, but its fabric waved in stagnant air. Something had to have moved it. Seeing nowhere else the man could have gone, Hannah stepped through the entrance.

For a moment, it felt like all her senses died. The interior was pitch black, and the silence so heavy it made her ears pop. Despite all the other mysterious supernatural things she'd seen during her stint as a Monster Killer, she'd yet to see a magic spell, but that was the only explanation she could come up with. Even the nicest tents were never this quiet, especially with the crowd outside. With the Wild West Show, you either learned how to sleep through everything or didn't sleep at all. Maybe she should learn magic. She would kill for the ability to shut everything up for a few minutes.

A low, rumbling croak cut through the silence. Just a bit louder, and she could've thought it was an earthquake. In the darkness, she could just barely make out a beady black eye gleaming back at her. The Frogman had its head practically pushed into a set of iron bars, watching her closely to see if she would make a mistake and get too close.

Her eyes slowly adjusted to the darkness, and her grip adjusted on one of her pistols. The Frogman was locked in a cage barely taller and wider than it was. Hannah was pretty sure if it flexed weird the bars would pop right open. Red paint coated the bars, chipping and peeling around face height. The reason why became clear when the Frogman twisted its head and tried to shove it through the gaps, gnawing on one of the bars. The metal was slowly but surely corroding with the acid in its spit. With how bad the metal groaned with each bite, it probably wouldn't be long until it was completely rusted through.

Besides the cage, there wasn't much else in the tent, only a few unmarked crates stacked just out of reach of the Frogman. One sat on its own, and judging by the loose sheets of paper scattered on top of it, acted as a makeshift desk. Hannah plucked one of the papers to try and read it. Diagrams and odd symbols decorated the page, though she couldn't tell if it was coded or if it was just her lack of education. Maybe Dr. Sharpe would know what it was about. But how to steal it? If it was coded, it would definitely be missed if it disappeared.

The other papers looked similar. Her memory was pretty sharp, but it was already too difficult to focus. The Frogman was still chewing on the bars, and the overwhelming stench of mildew permeated the tent. She couldn't tell if it came from the Frogman or the contents of the crates.

She sniffed again. There was something distinctly smoky about the smell. At first she thought someone might've started a bonfire somewhere on the fairgrounds, before she realized it was much too close. At the back of the tent, she could barely make out a small patch where the fabric of the tent smoldered.

Did someone just try to set the tent on fire? It had to have been an accident, right? Somebody must've gotten a little tipsy and dropped their cigar. It didn't appear to be spreading, and would probably go out on its own soon, but it was producing quite a bit of smoke.

The Frogman croaked again, the deep tone rattling around in her rib cage. It was moving faster now, grabbing and shaking the bars and shoving its head against the cage with painful-looking intensity. Hannah didn't need to be a fancy cryptowhatever to tell that it was getting agitated. She didn't know if it was the smoke or what, but she was not about to stick around to find out. And it looked like she wouldn't get a choice.

With an awful gurgling noise, and the sharp smell of acid, the bar crunched open. The Frogman shoved its way through the gap, the other bars bending and twisting out of the way out of sheer pressure. Hannah shoved the notes she was still holding into her coat, and threw her hands wide, like she was trying to calm an unruly horse. "Whoa, there. Easy."

Unfortunately, the eight-foot-tall, bipedal frog was not an unruly horse, and would not be calmed like one. It made the gurgling noise again, eyes locked on her. They stared each other down as time seemed to crawl to a standstill.

Hannah had never been in a duel, but she trained for it like it was an inevitability. She'd always hoped it would've been over something honorable, but she knew it was far more likely to be her temper or her fat mouth. Against a giant Frogman wasn't any of those things, but she supposed that was just how life was sometimes.

Shattering glass marked the start. Hannah drew and fired just as the Frogman spit. The bullet struck it right in the chest. An excellent shot, if it went more than half an inch into the skin. The acid barely connected with her arm, leaving a long, wet streak. Maybe the amount of time it spent creating it correlated to how strong it was, because it didn't melt her arm off, but she could see it start to eat through her jacket.

Fire bloomed from the far wall, where the glass broke. The fabric lit, and the flames started to spread. Whatever spell cast on the tent broke, and the ambient sound of the fire and the crowd in the distance was deafening after the oppressive silence, but she didn't have time to focus on that. The Frogman was still advancing on her. She aimed for the head and fired twice, hoping to do more damage. Neither were more effective than the first shot.

The fire was spreading fast and the Frogman wasn't even bleeding. If she couldn't get this taken care of quick, she'd go up in flames with the tent. A thought flashed through her mind. If she could immobilize the monster, the fire could take care of the rest.

A burning sensation started to spread across her arm. The acid had made it through her jacket and now started to soak through her shirt. She pushed the pain aside. She had to make this shot carefully, and couldn't afford the distraction.

The Frogman started to lunge, its sinewy legs contracting. Hannah aimed at its knee and fired. The bullet impacted. It didn't go any further than the other bullets, but it didn't have to. The legs weren't as thick as the rest of its body, leaving nothing protecting the bone, crunching under the sheer force of impact.

It buckled and fell, but tried to get up again. She had no idea if it could, so she shot the other leg out for good measure.

She pushed through the flap in the nick of time, as the entire tent collapsed behind her. All the adrenaline in her body cut off at once, and she was hit with the weight of how much it carried her until that moment. All she could do for a time was gasp for air and hack up some of the smoke she inhaled. The ambient sound of talking had turned to yelling and screaming. Someone noticed either the smoke or the gunshots, and called for help.

The burning in her arm became unbearable. It took everything in her to fight the natural urge to touch it, lest she let it spread to the other hand. She holstered her pistol, grabbed a fistful of jacket, and covered it as best she could.

Her gaze met the sickly yellow eyes of the Snake Man, who just watched her, mouth agape. He looked half shocked, half apologetic. Before she could say anything, he tossed the metal handle of an oil lamp on the tent-turned-bonfire, turned on his heels, and ran back to the maze of tents.

She tried to follow, she really did. The Frogman didn't get back up, so it was probably safe to say it was dead, but she still had questions. Unfortunately, she lost the Snake Man to the quickly encroaching darkness of either the sun going down or her vision going out. Luckily, she did manage to follow him back to the main path, where the crowd was stampeding toward the exit. It was impossible to make out her friends in the chaos, but hopefully that meant she wouldn't be seen. She shoved her way through the crowd, trying to find a friendly face.

One of the women she knocked into grabbed her shoulder before she could get away. "Miss Stone?"

It was the good Dr. Sharpe, accompanied by the rest of the Killers. Sharpe's eyes locked onto where Hannah clutched at her arm. "Goodness, what happened?"

"Frogman's dead."

Bubba scoffed but grabbed her good arm to half carry her. "Damn it, girl. I told you to be careful."

"Wasn't my fault. Someone set the tent on fire and made the damn thing attack me."

They slipped out of the circus, and Bubba managed to wave down a carriage fairly quickly. He and Sharpe helped her into it. Hannah fished the loose, wrinkled, and stolen notes out of her jacket, and tried to pass them to Sharpe, who didn't even look at them before passing them to Bubba.

Sharpe, much to her surprise, pulled a knife out of a dress pocket and cut her ruined sleeve off. Angry red skin riddled with blisters peeked back at her. In Hannah's opinion, it didn't look nearly as bad as it felt, but Sharpe made a quiet noise that didn't exactly fill her with confidence. She wouldn't get a chance to figure out what the noise meant, because as soon as the doctor lightly touched the wound, everything went black.

Hannah came back to in a guest room at Sharpe's manor, several hours later, dehydrated and disoriented. According to the doctor, the acid hadn't reached her muscles, so with enough time and rest the arm should be fully functional, but the scar would likely never fade. Unfortunately, there was no saving her jacket or shirt, but Sharpe offered her some replacements for her to keep. She said that it was of no concern, since they were old and worn out, but they were still nicer than anything Hannah ever owned.

It was a good thing she grabbed the notes when she did. They were messy, but they were intact. Sharpe had never seen the symbols either, but suspected they were part of a cipher. She opted to keep them for the time being, confident that she could decode them. Now that they'd spoken in person, it was easier to communicate over letters, and their correspondences didn't have to be one-line telegrams.

When Hannah had recovered enough to travel, they returned to Loveland to collect their payment. Local newspapers made it first. The incident never reached the front page, as no one died except the Frogman. The mayor was still loath to depart from the agreed upon payment. Turned out he had intended them to give up and skip town. Newspaper clippings, Hannah's fancy new scar, and the upcoming election convinced him otherwise. Having received a sizable donation from his campaign, Bubba Shackleford's Professional Monster Killers rode into the sunset.

There is a fine line between magic and science. I would highly recommend not crossing that line if possible. —A.L.

Legacy

Robert E. Hampson

"Don't talk about this." The hulking brute leaned menacingly over Dr. Michael Fowler's desk and just . . . glowered.

The implication was clear: This was an individual who wouldn't hesitate to do violence to anyone.

"To anybody?" Mike turned to Jason Sandusky, his friend and DARPA contact. "Not even Dr. Tedd?"

"Especially not Tedd. This is his field, sure, but his health is not the best. Also, there's a family connection. We can't risk—" Jason waved vaguely in the direction of the other agent. "He can't be involved. I think you get my meaning."

Jason had arrived unannounced with several security guards, a cart full of files, and the brute—introduced as Agent Franks (although Mike couldn't help but think of him as simply "the Brute")—and the implied threat of bodily harm if Mike said anything, to anyone. The cart bore boxes labeled DECISION WEEK—HAMPSON files from a 1940s research project, allegedly a secret parallel to the Manhattan Project. An ancestor of Dr. Tedd—Mike's mentor and predecessor at the Brain-Computer Interface Group—had apparently developed something so terrifying that atomic bombs were considered the "less frightening" option to end WWII.

Jason had assigned Mike to review the material due to a troubling pattern: patients with neural implants were reporting nightmares, ghost sightings, and auditory hallucinations involving threats of madness or death. As public neurotech applications expanded, these mental disturbances demanded urgent, discreet investigation.

Mike understood the stakes. His career had been built on using neurotech to treat pain, tremor, OCD, and depression—and to preserve memory. That last focus had been Tedd's passion, achieved shortly before illness forced his retirement. The BCI Neurotech Institute stood as a tribute, especially its ethics division—Tedd's insistence.

If any lab could get to the bottom of this, it was theirs. But Jason and Franks had forbidden outside involvement.

Mike would be doing this on his own.

"Besides," Jason continued, "we don't know how much this... complication... contributed to Tedd's illness. My boss, and his boss"—he nodded at Franks—"are worried."

The Brute grunted, a wordless threat.

"You think the Neuro'face trial issues are tied to this... 'Decision Week' project?"

"Not quite. 'Decision Week' was the name given post hoc by the Occult Technologies Board of the War Department. The project's original title was 'Neurobiological Demon Bondings,' from Elmer Hampson. That's all I know. I'm not cleared for more."

"You gave me this assignment but aren't cleared?"

"All I know is the project name and its origin. Orders came from way above our heads."

"And I'm supposed to report on these... neurological demons?" Mike snorted. "Demons don't exist."

The Brute leaned onto Mike's desk, splintering its edge and jarring the heavy smart-desk inches from its spot. "Your funeral," he said, glaring at Mike.

Silence. Jason looked as stunned as Mike.

"Ah. Yeah. Okay," Mike squeaked, his voice raising an octave as he sat, paralyzed with fear.

"Look, Mike. I know your leave starts next week. You're going to have the time. However, we need this report in two weeks."

"Amy was looking forward to Hawaii..."

"I know, Patty offered you their place, since she and Tedd aren't using it. I'm sorry—we can't risk the association. This is critical."

"Sort of like the Friday five p.m. calls for Monday eight a.m. briefs?"

"Worse. Again, I'm sorry, but we need you on this. No one else. When you're ready, email me—just that you're ready. You'll get a secure drop. No names. No content. The instructions won't involve me.

"I also made a call to your institute director. He agreed to put you on sabbatical paid by our partner directorate in the Office of Scientific Integration. Handle this, send in your analysis, and then take an even longer vacation with Amy at an asset in Hawaii."

"No choice, huh?"

"No," Franks said flatly and left the room.

Mike noticed Jason relax once the Brute was out of sight. He felt the same, as if he'd just been released from a straitjacket. "Encrypted upload? What is this, the same warehouse as the Ark of the Covenant?"

"Funny, Mike. I have my orders. Now you have yours."

"And Mr. Tall-Dark-and-Murderous?"

"Pray you don't see him again."

"I'd say it was good to see you, Jason, but..."

"Me neither, Mike."

He stared at the boxes. Even in his large office, they loomed. Fowler might be Tedd's academic heir, but the only real perk was this office—big enough for secure conferences and document storage. A handprint on the desk or smartwall locked the room and activated anti-surveillance. A biometric and combination lock secured the vault.

Mike activated lockdown, wheeled the files into the vault, and retrieved a large brown envelope from the top. He shut the vault, spun the dial, and turned toward his recliner—but paused. He set the envelope on the recliner and returned to his desk.

This wouldn't be a comfortable call.

With security enabled, he could only reach Amy via the encrypted home-office line. Secure-line indicators would flash in their home, and she had the access code. It wasn't the first time he'd had to make this kind of call—but it still sucked.

Amy took the news... not well, but with resignation. Over the course of many dinners and socials, Tedd's wife, Patty, had told them about all the last-minute delays and postponements Tedd had put her through. Then there were the health issues and the time the volcano started erupting ten miles away from their vacation rental in Hawaii. Shit happened, and Patty coached Amy to just accept it, then negotiate for a longer, better vacation in exchange.

This wasn't postponement, though. This was outright cancellation, and Amy was adamant that she would get Mike for a full two-week, no phone, no laptop vacation when it was all done.

With that settled, Mike turned to the envelope. Only two signatures had ever graced its manifest: Jason's, dated yesterday, and another from 1945. Both marked CUSTODY-ONLY.

The wax seal was intact, the ribbon brittle. No sign of tampering.

Had it truly remained untouched for eighty years?

Mike pulled at the ribbon and broke the seals. He used his pocketknife to open the envelope. A large stack of yellowed paper, secured with string, slid out, the cover sheet reading:

Occult Technologies Board
File: 44—001.030—19
Project: Neurobiological Demon Bonding
Principal Investigator: Elmer Hampson
Decision No. 19—***Rejected***
Assets: ***Redacted***
Final Disposal: Quarantined, Contained
Classification: Top Secret, Compartmented, Exclusive

Following that were several lines filled mostly with numbers. One was a bunch of modifiers that meant nothing to him. "Bee-ell-zee-six? Emm-see-nine? I'm sure they mean something to somebody," Mike muttered to himself.

Next he saw the words "Cognizant Statutes" followed by a whole bunch of numbers and sections. One of them seemed familiar from the certification Mike had to sign for DARPA meetings:

"Hmm, 18 USC Sections 791, 792, 793 . . ." Mike mused, reaching for his keyboard. He typed a query and his eyes went wide.

The list basically quoted the entire Chapter 37 of Title 18 of the US Code—the compilation of all permanent laws passed by Congress. The chapter cited descriptions, laws, regulations, and penalties relating to espionage. Strangely, section 791 was redacted. Not repealed, not revised, not superseded . . . but redacted.

Mike flipped through several more pages of the US Code website. Redaction was extremely rare. In his limited search, he only came across one other redaction section of the code. Strangely, it was under the final section of the espionage and censorship chapter: 18 USC 799: "Violations of Regulations of National Aeronautics and Space Administration." There was a broken link; no content, but the hyperlink was supposed to connect to Title 50, Section 6666: "Restrictions on the Observation, Recording, or Disclosure of Non-Terrestrial, Non-Human, or Non-Euclidean Phenomena."

Non-Euclidean? What the hell was NASA doing? Title 50 was War and Defense. Were they expecting to go to war with Cthulhu?

The last line of the cover sheet was the most surprising:

Unauthorized disclosure punishable by death (18 USC § 832, MCB/paranormal)

"Well, that's not disturbing at all," Mike muttered. He tried to see what he could find out about this "MCB," but there was nothing in the US Code, the US Government Manual, or any of his usual federal contracting websites. The closest he could find was the NSF's Division of Molecular and Cellular Bioscience.

Okay, not terribly relevant... he hoped.

Mike also wasn't convinced of the supposed Hampson connection. It wasn't a common name, but over the years they'd known each other, he'd heard Tedd talk about family history a lot. He'd even met a few of them. Tedd's father was an engineer; mother an accountant. He'd had uncles that were ceramic mold-makers, brass foundry workers, a Department of Transportation supervisor, and even a statistician on some classified program at a missile base in the desert. The family history was meticulously documented in a family Bible. Mike had seen digital images after Tedd's mother passed.

Mike had known Tedd for years before he'd joined the Hampson Lab and earned his doctorate. He'd met both of Tedd's parents on several occasions, and heard many embarrassing stories about "Teddy" as well as family history. Tedd was proud of his family; his grandfather's life spanned all the critical events of the twentieth century. They traced back to the Revolutionary War, and roots in Yorkshire, England.

There never seemed to be anything dark or mysterious in the family.

So why was he admonished to not reveal any of the material to the one who should be the definitive expert source?

Still, he felt an extremely strong urge to chase down the family connection before he dug too deeply into the subject matter. It took an hour of browsing Tedd's archived emails before finding the right images—old handwriting listing names from the family Bible.

Michael & Polly Hampson.

Then: John, James, Sarah, Mary, Thomas, William, Joe . . . Later additions: Betsy, Russell (and "Russel," oddly listed three years apart), Lulabelle. James and Sarah appeared again in the next generation with a Robert, Martha and Mary. Still no Elmer. But a few cryptic initials stood alone: "M 1884," "R 1898," "E 1900."

That "E" gnawed at him. But it wasn't proof—just possibility.

The executive summary was worse than expected—like reading bad horror fiction wrapped in pseudoscience. Hampson claimed he could assault enemies through dreams: induce unit-wide fear, deprive them of restful sleep, break enemy commanders' concentration. Terminal cases would suffer endless nightmares, locked in sleep and cut off from the world.

An appendix even outlined a plan to infect Hitler with the "demon."

Mike scoffed. *Pfft. Demons.*

Enough for one day. Mike liked science fiction but had little patience for fantasy—with a particular aversion to Lovecraft's form of horror fantasy. This wasn't even that—it was delusion, masquerading as occult warfare.

He hadn't opened a single box yet, and already the executive summary ran over fifty pages. The appendices alone could be a paper. The boxes were said to hold research notebooks, correspondence with the War Department, and deployment plans.

The fact that any of this was seriously considered made him question reality.

It was evening already. He'd missed supper, but Amy was busy anyway and had expected him to be late. The twins were with their grandparents because of Mike and Amy's planned trip, and she'd be joining them in a last-minute change of plans.

Mike's eyes were playing tricks on him, odd lighting in the parking deck, constantly moving shadows, bright flashes and fleeting objects in his vision. Mike just chocked it up to eyestrain. He knew that throughout history, many incidents of "divine" and "demonic" visions could be explained by eye problems.

Mike didn't sleep well. He'd stayed up late talking with Amy as she packed. She was grumpy; getting vacation from her work was the "Take it or Leave It" kind. He'd spent a long time just holding her and apologizing. She was only partly mollified. Guilt compounded with the weird feelings about this assignment meant his brain simply wouldn't turn off and let him rest.

With Amy off to the airport, Mike headed to the office. He'd already planned his day: his brain simply wouldn't let go of guilt. They'd agreed that she should just go join the kids and her parents and take advantage of time off while he was occupied.

The drive into the office was not as quick as the night before. Just past peak rush hour, traffic was still relatively heavy. At least the extra time gave Mike a chance to plan out his day: emails until ten, a quick visit to the lab, then lock himself in the office with lunch and the files until four.

The emails took less time than allocated, but a manuscript review assignment popped up in his inbox. He could decline the request—a so-so grad student essay that wasn't a good match to the Journal. Nevertheless, it was a grad student and he had the time allocated, so he wrote a constructive review, explaining what would be required to turn it into a good paper.

The lab was running long-term durability testing in rats of the brain-to-computer interface implant he and Tedd had developed. In a few weeks they'd add rats bred to mimic Alzheimer's disease. If there was no long-term degradation, they'd move to full-up human trials next year. Mike was torn—if Jason was worried about issues with Neuro'face, his own device might gain a competitive edge. On the other hand, it could make things harder.

The lab check-in also took less time than he'd allocated. Cathe was his senior scientist, and Vinnie was a fellow—more than a resident, not quite an independent physician—in neurosurgery. Between the two of them, the project was in good shape. Cathe and Vinnie were already managing the lab with only occasional input from Mike.

Mike went back to the office, grabbed a frozen microwavable meal out of the break room fridge, heated it, and retreated to his office. Once the door was closed and locked, he sat his lunch on a table next to his chair, activated the security measures, and opened the vault.

The executive summary and appendices had been a quick read, and he'd finished those yesterday. Today he needed to open the first of the boxes. External labels helpfully numbered them one through ten, with no indication of contents. He used his pocketknife to break the seal and bindings on Box One. It contained two stacks of hardbound journals, plus several sheets of typewritten notes, stapled and placed on top of the stack. Each journal was stamped with a year, so he decided to start with the papers. He grabbed his lunch and a bottle of cold water, and sat down at his desk to eat and read the papers.

The typed list was an inventory: Box One consisted of personal journals, Boxes Two through Eight were laboratory journals; Nine and Ten contained reports filed to the Occult Technologies Board. The journals were labeled by year, and predated the lab notebooks. The final journal appeared to correspond to the OTB reports.

Mike pulled the first journal out of Box One and noticed a rectangular block of stone with slightly rounded edges. One side was engraved with an odd symbol. He had trouble focusing on the carving; he had a brief moment of double vision, and a growing sense of headache. He put the block back and went back to his desk. He quickly finished the remnants of his water and grabbed another to stave off the growing dehydration headaches.

The very first entry proved that Mike was wrong in his assumption that Tedd was not related to this Elmer Hampson. Elmer was the "E 1900" in Tedd's old family Bible. Elmer wasn't happy living in a coal town, and faked his age to enlist in the Army at age sixteen. He'd removed his own entry from the family Bible, and never returned to his boyhood home.

The initial journal described Elmer's life after the war, making—and losing—money. He'd work a job for a year at most, make some money, then cash it all in and move on. New York, Paris, Chicago, and San Francisco. England, Tunisia, Morocco, and Tibet. The final entry from 1932 had Elmer living the life of a hobo, riding the rails and working odd jobs.

The next journal was less a chronicle, but rather a compilation of dreams, ideas, and theories. Elmer had met the famed occultist Aleister Crowley in Tunisia in the early 1920s and had a brief fascination with magic and the occult. He later soured on Crowley, but still held a fascination with the paranormal—his wanderings had exposed him to different religions, cultures, and philosophies, and he began to develop his own theories that the "modern" world was missing important lessons from "the old ways."

The essays were interrupted by entries of more life experiences: operating, then owning a combine harvester. Elmer had "inherited" it from a farmer whose heirs had no interest in the farm except as property for development. No longer a hobo, Elmer had continuous work throughout harvest and earned enough to take a break and return to his essays for several months before time to harvest the next crop.

As before, the essays explored life, death, will, and the soul. The reflections were repetitive and vaguely mystical. Mike skimmed heavily. Elmer felt most people were unaware of the surrounding spiritual world, but *that* spiritual world was most certainly aware of people. Spiritual beings could be contacted if one were sensitive enough—and willing—to do so. He also speculated about whether those beings could take hold of *unwilling* hosts as well.

An alarm went off, and Mike realized that he'd been reading well past his planned schedule. His vision was blurry and he was having trouble focusing on the page. He also had a vague headache. He hadn't had water since lunchtime, and the dehydration headache had been present all along—just ignored.

It was time to head home to an empty house and cold leftovers...

...and water. Lots of water.

The next morning brought no relief. Amy texted from California: she and the kids were fine, but she missed him already. He missed her too.

He'd barely slept. His dreams were jittery, chaotic, filled with shifting lights and indistinct voices. Two cups of coffee did nothing for the headache. It felt like a hangover, despite no alcohol. Amy would've had him downing electrolytes and ibuprofen by now.

The commute was a nightmare. There'd been an accident the night before that damaged a guardrail. One lane was blocked during rush hour as crews were still clearing debris. Secondary crashes hadn't helped. Mike's temper flared more than once behind the wheel.

It was going to be a long two weeks.

While the first journal had covered the 1920s through 1932, the second and subsequent journal covered only a single year. The next was for a 1934 journal that introduced the Civilian Conservation Corps. Elmer had joined a crew building bridges and roads through federal and state lands. He'd worked on the Cedar Creek

Bridge in Arkansas and become a skilled stonemason, especially with dry-stone construction. Over the next two years, he stuck with the job—the longest he'd spent on any one job in his lifetime. He never did anything by half measures, and tackled masonry with the precision and zeal greater than the various endeavors of his youth.

He also returned to his essays, now speculating on the nature of the human soul.

By 1936, Elmer was supervising repairs to the Fitchburg Furnace in Kentucky—one of the world's largest dry-stone structures. That work brought him to the attention of Colonel Graham Abernethy of Transylvania College in Lexington.

Transylvania? Mike thought. *That's a real university?* He paused reading to check, disengaging office lockdown to access the internet.

Turned out the name referred to the "land beyond the forest"—once proposed as a fourteenth colony in what became Kentucky and Tennessee. The university had a legitimate pedigree, even founding Kentucky's first medical and law schools.

Returning to the journal, Mike read that Abernethy was a "Kentucky Colonel"—not military, but a ceremonial honor for leadership and public service. Elmer met him in 1936.

"The university needs a structure of stone—walls, floor, ceiling—no mortar, no gaps," Abernethy had said.

"Fieldstone? Cut blocks?" Elmer asked, sizing up the challenge.

"River stone imported from Germany. You'll study examples in Gard, France, then return to build a two-story dome for our Science Department. Army colleagues need it for . . . special research."

Abernethy produced photos of two structures—one square with a rounded upper floor, the other a dome. He emphasized perfection: every joint seamless, every stone marked with a specific symbol.

The journal included a drawing. Mike recognized it instantly—the same glyph carved on the block in his vault.

"What the hell?" Mike sat up and blinked his eyes. His head throbbed sharply.

The migraine came on fast—piercing light sensitivity, nausea, vertigo. He killed the reading lamp, dimmed the smartwall display, and closed his eyes.

Darkness helped. So did stillness.

✧ ✧ ✧

He must have dozed off. When he jolted awake, the clock showed he'd lost two hours. He didn't feel rested—more like something had drained him.

He remembered images: distorted lights, soundless screams, geometric shapes that hurt to recall.

The headache was lessened, and it was early afternoon. Plenty of time to read more. On the other hand, maybe he should just go home. It would be safe to drive now, the photosensitivity was gone, as well as the vertigo, although his stomach still churned. A protein shake would probably take care of that.

So would a glass of scotch.

No, that was dangerous thinking. He'd promised his family long ago not to go down that route. He'd seen it ruin too many families and end too many careers.

Besides, most headaches were just one's body telling them to restock essential minerals, vitamins and nutrients. He had "emergency" supplies in his minifridge for late nights. A protein bar and drinks for his stomach, a sports drink for the electrolytes, and *then* he could go on.

Rehydrate. Replenish. Reset.

The next journal entry was blunt: the building was a containment vessel.

In 1924, Transylvania College had exhumed the remains of nineteenth-century professor Samuel Constantine Rafinesque from an unmarked grave in Philadelphia and reinterred him in a tomb on campus.

Something else had come back with the body.

Soon after, top students began suffering nightmares. Female students reported dreams of violence, waking exhausted and pale. Abernethy, who'd spent time in Germany, suspected an "alp"—a demonic entity or revenant from folklore.

Rather than destroy or banish the creature, Abernethy wanted to study it. He envisioned a sealed dry-stone structure, inscribed with protective glyphs. On completion, it would be closed on all sides except one—plus a service entrance. He would lure the alp inside, seal the final wall, and trap it.

The alp could only exit via the route it entered. Without that exit, it would be caged.

✧ ✧ ✧

Mike stopped reading. He needed to check on the lab.

Cathe and Vinnie were surprised he was still checking in, even while on sabbatical. "JUST KEEPING MY FOOTING," he texted back.

He grabbed fast food on the way home. Once in the door, he went straight for the kitchen without even disposing of the leftovers and trash from his greasy meal. He fished around on top of the cabinet until he found the key, dropped it twice due to shaking hands as he unlocked the cabinet, then pulled out the bottle of scotch.

He didn't remember anything else until the next morning, when he awoke, still sitting in a chair in the living room beside an empty bottle of scotch.

The drive into work was miserable. He was cut off twice, and barely avoided an accident. He hated sleeping upright, it always left his throat sore, and yelling at traffic didn't help.

The 1937 and 1938 journals described Elmer's time studying drystone buildings in Gard, France, followed by a trip to Germany to study with Gerhardt Lindemann, an expert in occult signs and symbology. Lindemann was a slim man of nearly eighty with a missing hand and artificial leg. The man's hair still showed streaks of blond hair and he exuded an energy and confidence that belied his age.

Elmer recorded asking Lindemann about the injuries:

"The war?" Elmer asked.

"Hunting" was the only reply.

Elmer spent six months learning about glyphs and warding designs, and practicing his engraving skill. It was essential that every glyph was perfect. The markings on each stone would have to match perfectly to ensure a seamless warding to contain the alp—or anything else in case Abernethy's identification was wrong.

The time with Lindemann was an education all by itself, and Elmer wrote of it extensively, along with many thoughts and essays triggered by conversations with the elder symbologist. As he delved into European myth, he began to suspect that some of the horrors of the Great War had been deliberately inflicted by unearthly forces who invaded sleep. Mahrs, alps, incubi, succubi—all showed some ability to harvest sustenance from sleeping humans. While sleep disturbance was certainly expected on the battlefield, all too many of Elmer's fellow soldiers complained of nightmares and odd dreams even when they weren't under fire.

Lindemann cautioned that the words "alp" and "elf" derived from a common root, ranting that "the Oxford Professor's Book" was too kind to elves, and that Shakespeare made them playful. Elmer would do well to remember that Germanic tradition painted the supernatural creatures as magical and beautiful, but that Fey were not to be trusted—that elves and alps might as well be demons with nothing but ill-intent toward humans.

Once he had the glyphs, and keeping his mentor's caution in mind, Elmer continued across Europe in search of building materials. He evaluated stones from Ireland, France, and Norway. With his newfound knowledge of glyphs and wards, he selected Belgian Block salvaged from Cloth Hall in Ypres—destroyed in the Great War and once central to medieval demon-lore. While history reported many instances of "cats" thrown from its belfry, it appeared that the creatures weren't felines—they were physical forms of alps.

The journal contained more entries, but now they were heavily annotated with reference to the lab notebooks. Elmer had his glyphs and his building blocks. The glyphs would contain the entity. The stones themselves would repel it.

Now it was time to build...

...and time for Mike to delve into the first of the lab notebooks.

Mike was surprised to learn that the lab notes were also penned by Elmer. He'd figured the man's involvement with Abernethy would cease with the completion of the containment building, but apparently, he continued on as the professor's research aide. The professor's explicit instructions regarding the composition of lab notes were included on the first page:

"All observations and utterings within the laboratory will be recorded in the book. Entries will be made in ink with no redaction."

Mike would have been overjoyed to have Elmer in his lab, at least as evidenced by the notebooks. Sure, the first two pages showed attempts at erasure. The next few pages revealed numerous corrections, but the style changed to precise observations and declarations for the rest of the notebook: each subject on a new page, demographic details, testing conditions, and even an outline of planned testing. Each experiment had a chronological log of interactions between researcher and test subject, copious observations of the subject reactions to the experiment, and tracings of neuroelectric recordings.

Abernethy had studied Hans Berger's methods for recording "encephalo-electrograms"—which Mike recognized as a precursor to the modern EEG. While Elmer built the containment, he also recorded the first attempts to record brain patterns during sleep. Abernethy proposed that EEG-equivalent recordings would reveal dream patterns associated with demonic presence. Inspired by recent medical discoveries, he believed that those brain waves would reveal when a subject was "ridden" by an alp. His plan was to observe a subjects' sleep, record their brain activity, and use that to identify the alp's victims.

Elmer was now doing double duty—completing the containment, and recording Abernethy's experiments. Once he completed construction of the containment building, the experiments would be transferred inside the warded enclosure to isolate and capture the entity.

Halfway through the first notebook, Mike noticed a reproduced neural recording that he recognized. It was the tenth subject, the fifth reporting frequent nightmares, but the first to experience a nightmare while testing. The patterns traced into the notebook looked eerily familiar—like EEGs from seizure patients . . . but not quite.

"Vinnie," Mike asked over secure messaging, "do you remember that epilepsy patient who kept complaining about nightmares?"

"The one with the complex partial seizures? Yeah."

"Do you still have her EEG files?"

"They're in archive. Want the video too?"

"Yes—especially if it captured the nightmares."

"Okay, I'll send you the Medical Record Number. Just remember to certify the HIPAA declaration before you retrieve it."

Mike paused, fingers over the keyboard. He felt guilty. This was Vinnie's patient, not his. She'd declined memory-study participation. Mike's use was technically off-protocol—allowed, but ethically gray.

He wanted to compare the patient EEG with Elmer's drawings of Abernethy's recordings. The patterns looked suspiciously like epileptic seizure activity—but not quite. He also wanted to compare them to a non-epilepsy patient from a sleep-and-memory study years ago. She, too, had complained of nightmares. If the odd patterns were only in the epilepsy patient, then Colonel Abernethy was barking up the wrong tree.

If they were in both . . . well, he needed more data.

Mike found the tracing again—the EEG pattern from Elmer's notes. He compared it to modern records. It didn't match typical seizure activity.

But it *did* match Vinnie's patient's brain wave trace.

Not a fluke. Not just epilepsy.

Mike's stomach growled as he looked over at the rats running mazes in another part of the lab. It was odd timing, but then, he wasn't eating well with Amy gone. Between that and headaches, it was probably a good thing that his appetite was waking up. He wasn't hungry, but he needed fuel. He needed to keep going.

Mike awoke to his phone ringing. It had to be Amy, Cathe, or Vinnie—only their numbers bypassed his call filter.

His head throbbed. He was in bed, still dressed. His mouth felt like sandpaper. As he sat up, his foot knocked over an empty vodka bottle.

"Hullo," he rasped.

"Doc, sorry to wake you," said the night tech. "We have a situation. One of Vinnie's breeders had a litter yesterday. They're missing."

"What?" Mike blinked blearily.

"The Alzheimer's model rats. The pups were there when Vinnie left yesterday. Now they're gone."

"Post-partum cannibalism happens. New mothers sometimes—"

"There are no remains. And the cage shows signs of tampering."

"So, call security."

"Security says *your* badge was the last one to access the floor." Her voice held a note of reproach. She used his title this time: "Dr. Fowler."

"Check the cameras. I didn't take any rats."

"Okay. Sorry, Doc. Just thought you should know."

Mike ended the call and stared at the ceiling.

He'd just snapped at the most competent tech he had.

He should call her back. Apologize.

Later.

His mouth ached. Something sharp was pressing against his gums. He staggered to the bathroom.

A sliver of bone lodged beside a molar. Small, slightly soft. Not fully calcified.

It looked like the jaw fragment of a newborn rat.

Mike Fowler screamed.

He looked awful and knew it. He avoided being seen as he entered the office. Even the shower had hurt—every drop a hammer blow. Toothbrush: sandpaper. Clothes: fire on his skin. He settled for a loose T-shirt and fleece pants to minimize the pain.

His sleep, if it could be called that, came only with alcohol. His diet had collapsed. He barely remembered what day it was. He'd broken medical ethics, HIPAA rules, and several layers of federal law digging through restricted DARPA and IRB files to match patterns.

He *had* to finish his report so that he could get away from this . . . nightmare.

They needed to be warned.

The last journals confirmed his fears.

Abernethy had *found* the alp—or the alp had found him. A law student, aggressive during mock trials, had complained of nightmares. During the EEG recording, a shadow emerged from his sleeping body.

They had already begun testing inside the nearly complete containment dome. The student had entered through the open wall, having been told that the isolation was necessary for effective recordings but that the wall was left open for air circulation in the hot Kentucky summer.

Abernethy entered through the smaller service entrance and hooked the patient to the EEG and started the recording procedure. Elmer had hinged the segment of wall and suspended it so that one person could close the containment. Once he saw the subject begin to doze off, he stepped outside to close the wall and ensure the glyphs connected and the wards were intact. With the containment sealed, he hurried to the service entrance to check on his superior. When he got inside, he saw the shadow emerge from the student and move to the professor, who immediately fell to the floor, unconscious. Elmer wrestled his superior into a chair, attached the EEG, and watched the recordings.

The alp was trapped—but only physically.

They'd misunderstood the legends. An alp *could* escape—if it possessed a human and exited through their path.

Abernethy woke up. His eyes were pitch black.

He ordered Elmer to release him.

Elmer, to his credit, acted. He used the EEG machine to deliver electroshock. It subdued the entity—and bound it to Abernethy's body.

Mike had too much energy now. Not the good kind. The frantic kind.

He couldn't keep up. Emails poured in. Cathe and Vinnie had stopped checking in, but now the institute director was asking when he would return. Security had visited his office multiple times. The lockdown kept them out—so far—but his admin assistant warned they might return with law enforcement or engineering override.

The Compliance Office had questions. So did the Institutional Review Board. And the Animal Care and Use Committee. All while his "Out of Office" reply was active.

Journals flooded his inbox with manuscript reviews. Garbage, all of them. Grad students who thought a dissertation was enough for publication.

The shadows moved when he walked. Faces stared at him from windows. Whispers echoed in his head, low and insistent.

He wanted to be left alone. He needed to read the documents.

Something about the case was compelling him to finish reading Elmer's journals and lab notebooks. It was the only thing that mattered.

Elmer had made a bargain. He would feed the alp—feed it fear, pain, and more. In return, it would animate Abernethy's corpse, which was kept hidden in the dome. It would help with the experiments on unknowing students as Elmer worked to understand the alp.

Meanwhile, the alp studied him back. Elmer used electroshock to control the demon. It worked for a time, and the alp allowed Elmer to think that he was in control . . . until he wasn't.

Tensions escalated in Europe, Paris fell, Britain was bombed, Japan attacked Pearl Harbor, and there was a new War to End All Wars. Hampson's reports now went to a new agency, the

Occult Technologies Board, as they considered ways to use the alp to obtain a decisive victory.

The breakthrough was once again with the EEG. In 1941, Elmer learned of Wilder Penfield, an American neurosurgeon treating epilepsy patients in Canada. Penfield's papers described effects of small electrical charges applied directly to the tissues of the brain, unlike the scalp electrodes of EEG and electroshock.

Elmer found a surgeon willing to allow him to do some tests under the guise of improving EEG. A student had recently sustained a severe head injury with a buildup of pressure on the brain. Holes had been drilled in the patient's skull to relieve the pressure in hopes of saving the patient.

Elmer coerced the hospital and surgeon into letting him insert small EEG recording wires through the holes and into the brain. Waving a letter of authorization from the War Department made such things so much easier. Even moving the patient to the containment building was smoothed over by the promise that the results were for the war effort—mostly. The moment Elmer hooked up the EEG, the alp was able to switch bodies. Unbeknownst to Elmer, it was also no longer tightly bound to a single host.

The alp couldn't—wouldn't—stay in the host. The student was badly injured, and the alp begged to be transferred to a new host—one who was otherwise healthy. Elmer continued the research, and found new hosts, often by clandestine and illegal means. Eventually a young soldier, injured in North Africa and sent home to recuperate, was found. The alp was bound, and together, Elmer and the possessed soldier came up with a new plan.

Elmer wrote a report to the OTB with a daring plan: the soldier would infiltrate East Prussia. There, he'd make contact with a Wehrmacht officer named Claus von Stauffenberg, and use the bound alp to infiltrate Hitler's dreams.

It never happened.

The Board canceled the operation.

They had chosen a different path—a secret project in New Mexico.

Elmer Hampson was arrested. The lab destroyed. The soldier disappeared into solitary confinement.

Elmer, horrified by what he'd done, wrote one final journal entry.

I'm sorry.

✧ ✧ ✧

Amy returned before the kids. Mike's calls had grown erratic. She worried the project was taking too much out of him.

She decided to take the summer off. They didn't need her teaching income.

Mike didn't answer when she got home. The front door was unlocked. The mailbox overflowing. Packages on the porch.

Inside, she stopped short.

The house was a mess—trash, food wrappers, something organic she didn't want to identify. The sink was full. Bottles littered the kitchen.

She called his name. No response.

She found him in the den, slumped in a chair, mouth open, skin gray. She touched his neck. Cold skin. But a pulse.

She reached for her phone, thumb hovering over 911. Then paused.

This was *that* kind of project. Whatever had gone wrong, she couldn't let it spiral further. She dialed a different number.

"Drew? It's Aunt Amy. Case Crimson. Something's happened to Uncle Mike."

Drew Hampson was waiting in his Mike's office when the government reps arrived.

He'd hoped it would be Jason Sandusky. Drew had sent an email in Mike Fowler's name to the program manager, but the response had stated that Director Sandusky was not available. Instead, he watched the outer office camera as an absolute mountain of a man and a rather short nebbish in a poorly fitting dark gray suit walked into the outer office.

Drew keyed the inner door. It opened to admit them.

"Missus Fowler, I'm Dr. Richard Smalls, Directorate of Unearthly Containment and Security—" the smaller man began, then stopped short at the sight of Drew.

"An-drew," Franks growled, dragging out the syllables.

"DUCS? Really? Is that what you tell them before you swing, Franks?" Drew grunted, mimicking Franks' usual vocalization. He stepped out of the way, motioning for the two men to enter, then closed and locked the door behind them.

Smalls stared. "What the hell are you doing here?"

Drew gave him the once-over. Combover hair. Stained shirt. Mismatched buttons. Every inch the officious bureaucratic prick.

"Mr. Smalls—Dick, can I call you Dick? No matter, I will anyway. We're here for the same reason. Dr. Fowler had a breakdown, and you've brought the commitment papers."

"You can't be involved! This is classified!"

"I'm his psychiatrist."

"You're not cleared! Besides, treating your uncle is an ethics violation."

"Oh, I don't know, *Dick*." Drew let the word land. He reached over the smartdesk and placed his palm inside a rectangular outline. All of the backgrounds sounds quieted, and Smalls felt something akin to pressure in his ears.

"There. We're secured. No recording, no monitoring, no possibility of eavesdropping. "As I said, *Dick,* I'm his doctor; I might call him 'Uncle Mike' but it's only a courtesy. As long as my father's not involved—as I'm certain Franks ensured—there's no conflict of interest."

"You don't belong here!" Smalls protested.

Drew picked up the papers and started reading out loud: *"Axis I: Schizophrenia, ICD-10 F20.0—paranoid type, presenting with auditory and visual hallucinations. ICD-10 R44.3—hallucinations, unspecified. ICD-10 F22—persistent delusional disorder, content involving apocalyptic entities of nonhuman origin. Differential includes ICD-10 F23.1—acute polymorphic psychotic disorder with symptoms of schizophrenia, following traumatic exposure.*

"Have you heard Fowler's ravings?" Drew looked up at the two men, then shook his head. "No, you folks put too much faith in compartmentalization. Let me see, how did he say it? Oh, right. *'They whisper through the cracks in your skin. They breathe in your sleep. You've all heard them if you listen—'*"

Smalls shivered. When Drew spoke, his voice took on an otherworldly quality. Something that cause a small voice to start gibbering deep in his soul.

Drew went back to reading the papers. "Oh. Oh my. Here's a good part: '*By authority of the Directorate of Unearthly Containment and Security, pursuant to Title 18, U.S.C. Section 791, Unusual Incidents Act, and in the interest of national stability, subject [REDACTED] is to be committed indefinitely to Appleton Asylum. Records pertaining to this case fall under DUCS oversight. Unauthorized disclosure is a federal crime and a Class One national security breach.*'"

Smalls peered up at Drew, trying not to make eye contact with the strange doctor who seemed to know too much about this case. He looked over at Franks, but the agent's face only ever had one expression—disdain. Now was no different.

"I looked it up, *Dick*. Section 791 doesn't exist. Appleton doesn't exist. *DUCS* doesn't exist. You show up with paperwork to commit him to a private hospital. You bring *him* along, and you don't think his shrink should be involved?"

"Franks, do something!" Smalls barked.

Franks grunted and slugged Drew in the stomach.

Drew flew back several feet and landed on his ass on the floor. He sat for several moments, shaking his head, then slowly staggered erect. "Ooh, that's going to leave a mark."

"What *are* you?" Smalls asked.

"Not human," grunted Franks.

"Are you going to allow this?" The bureaucrat turned to Franks. "Do something!"

Franks said nothing.

Drew rubbed his stomach, and gingerly stepped back to the desk. "I'll sign the papers. Mike needs expert care, but I'll be watching. Michael Fowler deserves better than to be forgotten in some 'Arkham Asylum,' or executed out of hand."

Drew stared pointedly at Franks as he said the last. He turned back to the commitment papers and began to flip through them, initialing and signing where indicated. On the final page, he crossed out the existing signature of the medical authority requesting commitment, added his own credentials, then signed.

He passed the stack back to Smalls, who started leafing through the pages to ensure every required space was marked. He got to the last page, stared at what was written there, and gulped.

"Satisfied?" Drew asked.

Smalls just nodded.

"Good. Now, do you want Mike's report?"

Franks had been staring at a vault door to one end of the office. At Drew's comment, he turned and stared pointedly at Drew, then picked up Smalls, yanked the office door open, and tossed the bureaucrat out the door and slammed it shut.

"That was locked..." Drew said.

"Not anymore," Franks said, and leaned on the door to keep it closed.

They could hear Smalls pounding on the door and yelling something about national security violations.

Franks glowered at Drew. "Told 'em . . . bad idea."

"Wow! Four whole words. I was expecting your favorite phrase 'Your funeral.'"

When Franks said nothing, Drew continued. "This isn't an alp. The last alp was terminated years ago. You and Pitt were there."

Franks growled.

"Not my circus, Big Guy, but definitely *your* monkeys. Elmer's research found . . . an *opening* . . . and it needs to stay closed. Permanently. But making Uncle Mike disappear isn't going to solve it." Drew turned to the smartdesk and keyed a command. The vault door opened behind him, revealing only the file boxes—no stone block, no mysterious artifacts.

"Mike's burn vault. Flammable cellulose, oxygen feed, temperature containment. Fire suppression once the contents are ash." Drew held up a Zippo lighter with a grinning, horned smiley face. "Want to do the honors?"

Franks glared at the symbol on the lighter as if he wanted to crush it, obliterate it from existence.

"I'll take that as a 'no.'" Drew lit a crumpled report page and tossed it into the vault. The boxes ignited instantly, flames roaring within the sealed compartment. The design vented smoke and heat efficiently—by the time it was done, only ashes remained.

As Drew was looking at the vault, Franks smacked him on the back of his head. It was just a love tap, which was why the world went dark, and Drew woke up—alone—on the floor twenty minutes later, instead of waking to a heavenly chorus.

Drew carefully stood up, rubbing the back of his head. *Okay,* that *is definitely going to leave a mark.*

Drew crossed the now-empty office, and laid his palm on the marked space on the smartdesk.

"OSI override canceled. Good day, Colonel Hampson."

The vault door closed, system reset.

He closed the office door the best he could as he left.

As he walked away, a voice—low and mocking—echoed inside his head.

"He went easy on you. He must *like* you."

Drew scowled. "Shut up, Elmer. Just shut up."

Grimm Berlin is one of our top competitors in the monster-hunting business. The Earl Harbinger scale of monster-hunting companies is pretty straightforward, having only two rankings—they're either assholes or they're alright. Grimm Berlin is alright. —A.L.

Monsterkommando

Spearman Burke & Nick Nethery

"Why are we named Stuttgart Gruppe?" Carl Gehring wondered aloud to the van full of hunters. His Benelli M4 shotgun jostled gently between his knees as the team vehicle hit a speed bump. At least it hid his nervous foot tapping. His excitement compelled him to fill the uncomfortable silences with inane chatter. "Why not a cool name like Team *Monsterkommando*?"

"Because unlike those MHI cowboys, Grimm Berlin is comprised of consummate professionals." Luisa Fromm, the team's assistant *gruppe* leader and intel specialist, rolled her eyes as she scrolled through information on her Toughbook. "'Here comes Team Huggiepuft!' Can you imagine?"

"The death cultists would laugh us out of business, *grünjunge*." Bruno Hoch chuckled from the driver's seat. "How are you so full of dumb questions this early in the morning?"

"Jawoll, Klaus!" Gruppe leader Hauke Armburst spoke into a cell phone on the passenger side and nodded. *"Vielen dank! Tschüss."*

"So?" Luisa raised her eyebrows, her dark hair pulled back in a severe bun. Carl wondered if the tight hairstyle gave her headaches.

"We're cleared hot. Continue the mission brief, Luisa." Hauke slipped the cell phone into a pouch on his chest rig. The old wounds marking Hauke's face reminded Carl of *mensur* dueling scars, like in old black-and-white pictures of his great-grandfather.

"*Achtung*, Stuttgart Gruppe. You—*grünjunge*—pay special attention." Luisa smiled without humor from her seat and steadied herself as the van rounded a curve.

"I'm not green," Carl mumbled under his breath.

"This isn't the Bundeswehr and we're not going up against a mob of undisciplined muj." Luisa regarded him sternly, her mouth a hard line. "And dispatching a half-dead bannik in a Köln bordello does not a veteran monster hunter make."

Axel Ebner, their sniper, grunted but said nothing. His eyes focused on the floor of the van, his lean frame at rest. The old veteran's chiseled face with its walrus mustache rarely smiled, a lit cigarette almost always in his hand.

Bruno turned quickly to grin at Carl. In his case, the lines on his face were drawn by laughter, not hostility.

"Something is going on with the Ukrainian refugees at the old Grenadier Kaserne." Luisa turned her Toughbook, displaying a map of the Bad Cannstatt district with a yellow circle over one area. "They're living in the American barracks. Not very comfortable, but at least safe from the war for now."

"Not safe from other things, unfortunately," added Hauke. "Something's been preying upon them these last few days."

"'Preying upon them'?" Carl tried not to stare at the blade of Hauke's prosthetic leg extending from just below his right knee. "How?"

"Herr Lindemann passed us several reports from our contacts in the *Polizei*," Luisa continued. "Disappearances. Not uncommon with large groups of refugees and migrants. Some slip away because they dislike the camps and find lodgings and jobs elsewhere. Coupled with the information gathered from several psychotherapy notes, however..."

"Psychotherapy notes?" Bruno called from the front. "We are hacking into therapists' files now?"

"It is common for these people to receive counseling due to post-traumatic stress and grief." Luisa glanced at Bruno with a frown. Carl noticed the tip of Charlemagne's sword, tattooed on her back and neck, peeking out from the collar of her body armor. "The reports mention dreams, repeatedly. Adults, both male and female, having vivid nightmares."

"Understandable," Ebner rumbled, his eyes still on the floor.

"The dreams are all very similar, which is not. Males have sexual yet terrifying nightmares. Women dream that their men are unfaithful to them, so vividly that several have compared them to pornographic movies."

"Then there are the children." Hauke's posture tightened. He hooked his hands over the collar of his body armor, letting his arms dangle. "Until now, only adults have gone missing."

"Early this morning, a Ukrainian mother woke up to find all *four*"—Luisa stressed the number—"of her children missing." She tapped at the keyboard, and the screen displayed four children—three boys and one girl—and a pretty, dark-haired woman in her late twenties. "She thought they had gone to play or visit neighbors, but could not find any of them. No one saw the children leave. No sign of them. What they *did* find was a trail of wet footprints."

This last part finally made Ebner raise his eyes. He looked at the screen, stroking his mustache slowly, and then opened a sleeve pocket on his shirt. Extracting a cigarette, he shook his head and looked back to the floor. He lit the smoke and shifted the G22A2 sniper rifle in his lap. Luisa narrowed her eyes, but only lowered the windows a few centimeters.

"Up there, Bruno." Hauke indicated the old entrance to the base, watched by a pair of bored-looking *Polizei* who waved them through, recognizing Hauke on sight.

Luisa stowed her Toughbook as the van rolled to a stop. She opened the side door, and the team dismounted for final mission inspection and communication checks. Carl took the opportunity to take in the base. Typical Cold War-era American barracks buildings, four stories tall and beige with brown roofs, brick-cobbled streets, and the ubiquitous dual English/German signage found on old American and NATO garrisons throughout the country. Carl could see the occupants, Ukrainian refugees, moving in some of the barracks windows and courtyards. Many had laundry or Ukraine flags draped out the open windows.

"What will the refugees think we're doing here?" asked Carl.

"We have an arrangement with the *Polizei*." Hauke checked his pouches, ensuring everything was in place. "They keep civilians out and tell them either it's an anti-terror training exercise, or an actual anti-terror operation, depending on how loud we get."

Carl looked back at the gate, now being shut once more by the policemen. "Is that legal?"

"Are you a lawyer?" Luisa demanded. "Bruno, check his kit."

"Okay."

They'd parked the van in a fenced-off area with warning signs surrounding abandoned headquarters and administration buildings. These were in much worse repair than the barracks, and indeed Carl could see several with broken windows and graffiti. Empty or smashed beer and liquor bottles were scattered here and there. Clearly, the fence was not impregnable. Grass grew defiantly in between the cobblestones on this portion of the Kaserne.

Members of Stuttgart Gruppe carried either an HK417 rifle and seven magazines of 7.62x51 NATO rounds, or a Benelli M4 shotgun with side saddle and shell cards for reloads. Ebner had his G22A2 in .300 Winchester Magnum. Holstered on their gun belts were HK VP40s. They wore standard Grimm Berlin body armor and helmets fitted with noise-dampening ear pro.

In addition to their first aid kits, they carried several flash-bang grenades, a demo pouch, and other odds and ends. Carl had bolt cutters. Ebner carried his Win-Mag rounds. Carl and Hauke each slung an extra bandolier of shotgun shells.

"Do we know what it is we are hunting?" Bruno finished checking the team's comm equipment and gave Hauke a thumbs-up.

"Signs indicate a possible kikimora." Luisa drew her Eickhorn fixed-blade combat knife and turned it over in her hand. Manufactured in Solingen, Germany, of course. "Mythologically speaking, a female house spirit most often found in Slavic cultures, where folklore says they cause sleep paralysis and nightmares. The Russians have encountered them before, but Krasnov's intelligence is as reliable as it is negotiable."

"We know *scheiße*, then." Ebner polished the lenses of his Steiner rifle scope.

"They are weavers, stranglers, and drowners." Luisa set her jaw. "They can definitely get into your head. *Sein sie vorsichtig.*"

Hauke motioned for the team to circle up on him.

"The children disappeared here, in the housing areas along Schozacherstraße." Hauke indicated a position on a map board tethered to his gear and pointed to the actual buildings, in a neat row up the hill. "Footprints were found over there"—he pointed to a courtyard area leading to the unoccupied portion of the

Kaserne, then pointed up the hill to the area he'd indicated on the map—"leading toward the condemned unit buildings, but dried before anyone in authority could follow. We'll conduct an urban tactical tracking operation until we intercept the spoor and follow where it leads. Y-formation—Ebner, you're tracking. Bruno, Luisa, flankers. Carl, you're with me on rear security. Find the children, collect the bounty."

"Jawohl!" The team responded with one voice.

"Kikimora." Carl rolled the word around in his mouth, as if trying it on. He tried to remember the monster familiarization crash course that had been part of his basic onboarding. "Like a domovoi?"

"Keep in mind, monsters often present as one type." Hauke looked his team over once more. "Then turn out to be something else entirely."

"'I just need to know one thing,'" Carl said in English, pointing his hand like a pistol and dropping his thumb like a hammer. "'Where. They. Are.'"

The other hunters stared at him in a moment of awkward silence.

"Oh! Like in the movie!" Bruno smiled, pointing at Carl.

"Yes!" Carl sighed in relief.

"Shut up, Carl!" Luisa grimaced. "Bruno, don't encourage him! You boys and your stupid American movies."

Bruno shrugged as he and Luisa took their positions at the top of the Y and Stuttgart Gruppe stepped off to the last known spoor location.

"*Herr* Armbrust?" Carl glanced around at the others. "I don't know anything about tracking."

"Don't worry, *junge.* We'll teach you."

"But how?"

"Years ago, Klaus flew out an old Rhodesian SAS soldier and Selous Scout, who was one of the best trackers in the world, to work with us." Hauke grinned at the lad. "He's just passed away, unfortunately, but I think our tracking pedigree is competent enough to train you, as well."

Hauke shushed Carl with a wave of his hand before he could ask another question. The formation moved in silence for a couple hundred meters until Ebner raised a hand to halt the team and took a knee to inspect the ground.

Hauke signaled with his hands for Carl to pay attention to

Ebner, then took over rear security. The older tracker scanned the ground ahead with his eyes, then raised his hand over his head in a clawed fashion, as if he were holding a grapefruit.

"See the hand signal?" Hauke whispered. "He lost the spoor, so we'll see if we cannot cut the sign and pick it up."

They moved out in ever-widening circles. Carl felt ridiculous. They literally patrolled around for several minutes, Carl's unease slowly increasing, until Ebner called a halt and knelt again. This time, his clawed hand pointed downward toward the ground.

Ebner waved Carl to him and pointed out the wet glistening patterns indicating where their quarry had disturbed the ground in its passing. They led between two single-story HQ buildings, toward a thickly forested ravine. Visible a mile or so away on the next hilltop was Robinson Barracks, still an active US army base. In between was nothing but steep rock scree hillside with dense vegetation.

"We're on the spoor." Ebner gave a curt nod. "Now we hunt."

Carl went back to his position on rear security, and the team of hunters moved into the tree line. Deeper into the trees, it grew dark, and mist swirled along the ground. The damp fog reduced visibility and the formation closed up.

Turning to check their six o'clock, Carl saw the bright round eyes of a blond little girl in a smock dress peeking around the base of a tree at him.

"Hey, there's a kid!" Carl took a step closer to get a look.

The child giggled, then ran away, all gangly arms and legs.

"It's okay, kid!" Carl took off after the youngster. "You're safe!"

"No, Carl!"

Before he'd taken five steps, a thin gossamer line looped over Carl's head and cinched tight around his neck. The noose yanked him off his feet and steadily pulled him up into the overhanging branches. Carl's peripheral vision faded.

Shouts from his team. HK rifles barked at the darkness overhead. Hauke transitioned to his Benelli and punched a load of buckshot into the branches above Carl's dangling body. Ebner scanned the treetops, but held his fire. Carl could not tell if the shots had any effect, but he stopped ascending.

Kicking and pawing at his neck, Carl managed to draw his combat knife. Seconds away from blacking out, he sawed at the line above his head and felt it giving way. His vision had tunneled to near blackness when the thread parted with a snap. Tumbling at least two full meters to the ground, he hit feetfirst but fell hard on his backside.

The team swiftly fell into a security posture around him. Ebner focused overhead while the others provided 360 degrees of cover.

"Das Kind!" Carl choked out and pointed into the mist. He could see her just there.

"That's no kid." Hauke lowered the muzzle of the Benelli and fired.

Wounded screeching echoed through the damp trees, and where the waif had been now sneered an ancient old hag. Clammy rags hung from her emaciated frame. One hand clutched her shoulder where she'd caught a bit of buckshot. Small rivulets of black ichor dripped down her spindly arm and off the needle-like tips of long, thin clawed fingers. A massive, hooked nose jutted from between two jet-black eyes, swirling twin whirlpools of predatory outer darkness surrounding a gleaming pearl. She fixed her dread gaze on them all.

Her pupils are pure white, Carl thought, tugging at the thread around his neck.

A rolling thunderclap of gunfire erupted from Stuttgart Gruppe. Buckshot and 7.62 chewed up the trees and shredded bark and foliage, but she disappeared in the mist and gun smoke.

Luisa slung her rifle behind her and checked their *grünjunge* over.

"Glad you guys hung around." Carl coughed, massaging his throat.

"Shut up, Carl." Luisa sighed and shook her head. "He's okay." She plucked the line wrapped around his throat and handed it to Hauke to examine.

"Weavers and stranglers." Hauke rolled the thread between his fingers.

"And she can get into your head." Luisa smacked Carl on the top of his helmet. "Make you see things. That wasn't a child you saw, idiot. Stay focused."

"*Mein Gott!* My ass hurts." Carl rasped. If he broke his tailbone on his first mission, he would never live it down. "How does this monster even arrive here, anyway? Did you not say she is Russian?" He rubbed his backside gingerly. He was not sure which hurt worse, his ass or his throat. Swallowing was torture.

"Eastern European, not just Russian." Hauke kept his eyes and weapon outboard. "And it makes sense. Sharks do it. Wolves do it."

"Do what?"

"Follow their prey population's migration," Ebner muttered, lowering his muzzle of his rifle. He returned to scanning the ground, taking a few steps forward in the direction the monster had fled.

When he did not elaborate, Bruno added, "She followed her food from Ukraine. Understand?"

"Oh, yeah." Carl nodded, rubbing his sore neck.

"After charging right into her noose like you were trying to suicide, she probably thinks you're the weak link." Luisa narrowed her eyes. Every time she spoke to him, Carl could feel the temperature drop.

"If you want to die young, Carl, there are easier ways." Bruno grinned. "And more fun."

"Enough chatter." Hauke pointed a knife hand in the direction of travel. "We go."

They looked and Ebner was on the stalk again, looking down the trail and whispering to himself. Stuttgart Gruppe fell in silently and moved out.

Carl supposed the creature now knew hunters tracked her. It probably wasn't ideal to track something actively countering their efforts to nail it down. The spoor became more difficult for Ebner to find. Several old hiking trails and a larger dirt road ran through the forest, but the kikimora did not seem to be following any of them. The trail led in a meandering but definite direction . . . on down into the ravine.

Every few minutes as they patrolled, a flash of illusion would strike Carl. The first time, the same small girl beckoned to him, biting her lip and flitting from tree to tree. He wasn't falling for that one again. Now the smell of warm *glühwein* or the sound of beer tent music surrounded him, the clinking of steins and the discordant, happy roar of drunken people singing. He saw the way his teammates shook their heads periodically, as if to clear them. The kikimora wove her dream magic on them as well.

"Bruno," Carl whispered when they paused to give Ebner a moment to find the next sign. "What are you seeing?"

"My wife," Bruno replied without hesitation, his weapon on the trees.

"I didn't think you're married."

"I'm not." For once, Bruno didn't smile.

"Ah." Carl cleared his still-burning throat, trying to be quiet but earning a scowl from Luisa. He hesitated but asked her. "Luisa! What does it show you?"

The second-in-command seemed about to snap at him, then bit her tongue and looked away. "Never mind. Keep silent and do your job." Carl couldn't help but notice that she blushed furiously, her neck and cheeks turning bright red.

The afternoon sun dropped quickly and the valleys between Stuttgart's many hills and ridges already grew dark. Soon, Carl knew, the temperature would fall, and although it was barely September, it would get cold down in the dark ravine.

They moved out again Carl noted they paralleled a stream that ran down the bottom of the gorge. Game trails led down to the water here and there. Ebner stopped at one to assess some of the same silky threads that had looped around Carl's neck earlier. They fluttered loosely in the air with the gathering mist.

Ebner crouched to poke with the tip of his knife at the collection of wispy strands. Between a pair of fallen logs, he found a child's red shoe. Carl watched as Ebner craned his neck about, gripping his weapon and peering upward. There was nothing but waving branches and leaves. Beyond them were the gray rock walls of the next hill.

Ebner stood, holding the small shoe in his hand.

"*Bedammt* animals!" He gripped his rifle, the shoe tumbling to the grass. His unfocused gaze stared out into the woods.

"Axel?" Hauke approached him. *"Alles gut?"*

"They're just babies!" Ebner's nostrils flared. He raised the rifle. *"Ich werde euch alle töten!"*

"Axel!" Hauke smacked the man on the helmet and shook him out of the creature's illusion.

Ebner's eyes refocused on his team leader.

"Sorry, boss." Ebner shook his head. "She took me back to Mali for a moment there."

"*Achtung*, Stuttgart Gruppe!" Hauke spoke calmly, but the tension on his face caused the scars to contract into deep creases. "Stay sharp! I'm tired of this creature's mind games. Remember our mission."

The hunters nodded. Ebner got back on the spoor and the team again moved out.

Carl glanced about to check his bearings, then resumed following the team as rear security. He promptly tripped and fell face-first into the grass. Fumbling to get up, he saw a strand of the sheer filmy line stretched between the trees where he'd tripped. The kikimora wasn't only a kidnapper, but a mischief maker. Carl plucked bits of grass and dirt from his gear.

Luisa stood watching him. Expecting another reprimand, Carl prepared to apologize, but then she dropped her rifle to the grass. He blinked in confusion as she unclipped the strap of her M4 and dropped that, as well. She then ripped open the belly straps of her body armor, shrugging out of it.

Bewildered now, Carl watched as she smiled at him. *She's really very pretty when she isn't angry at me,* he thought dreamily. His heart skipped a beat when she plucked up the bottom of her tank top from where it was tucked into her camo pants.

"*Was machts du?*"

"Shut up, Carl." She grinned at him and raised the shirt over her head, revealing a taut tummy and a sports bra. Luisa tossed the shirt at him, giggling, and pulled one of the bra straps off a shoulder—*Wait a minute.* Luisa hated his guts. *And where are all her tattoos?*

"This is bullshit." Carl took a knee and raised his rifle.

His head jerked to the side with a smack as someone slapped his helmet. Carl looked up, startled, and blinked hard as Luisa glared down at him where he knelt. She stood completely dressed in full battle rattle. Not giggling. Not smiling, even. Not one bit. Yep, he knew it had been a dirty lie even as it happened.

"What are you doing?" she hissed.

"Oh, thank goodness it's really you!"

"What?" A strand of Luisa's brown hair had come undone from the bun and wisped down beside one ear.

Carl looked back to where illusion-Luisa had just been disrobing a few feet away and now saw nothing, just two or three sickly-looking pine saplings clumped together. "I, uh . . . nothing. I thought I saw something. More . . . more tricks." He shook his head.

"Really." Her face softened somewhat. "What did you see this time?"

"Uh . . ." Now it was Carl's turn to blush furiously.

Luisa may have guessed. She watched him for a long moment, one eyebrow raised, and then jerked her head.

"Come on." She stepped off. "Ebner found some abandoned buildings the trail seems to lead toward. Not on any of our maps."

"Oh?" Carl forgot his embarrassment—for now—and perked up. "What kind of buildings?"

"Old American military," she said. "Possibly part of the base we didn't know about."

"That's not good."

"No," she agreed. "It's not. *Kommen sie.*"

When they caught up, they found the team squatting by an old kayak trailer, with two rotting kayaks still strapped to it.

"A recreational area?" he whispered.

"A base on either side." Hauke nodded. "And another across the highway. Twenty years ago, this is where the Ban Cannstatt urban district ended, and there weren't any houses up that way. This must have been where the Americans could rent canoes and kayaks, and we've already seen hiking trails. My guess is, there are also the remnants of old camping cabins around these hills."

"And when the American *soldaten* were done hiking or kayaking, they went to have beer and schnitzel there," Ebner added, pointing.

A large run-down old hunting lodge commanded the clearing, one large dining-hall style room with two wings jutting out at opposite ends, like outstretched arms. Though it looked like a traditional forest lodge, little things like the large brown numbered signs on the corners gave it away as American construction. It must have been quite grand when it was still in use and well-maintained. Now Carl could only see the disrepair, the heavy moss covering the roof and some of the walls . . . and thick clumps of the shimmery threads. The filaments hung over the entire structure as if it were Silly String or bunting.

Carl's skin crawled. The lodge stood near the stream—a small river, really, Carl reasoned, and tried to remember the name. *The Neckar? One of its smaller tributaries?* Though it wasn't too cold yet, curls of fog pushed lazily from the river's surface up into the clearing and around the lodge. Down the incline abutting the water was an old boathouse that Carl reasoned once contained canoes, kayaks, life preservers, and other water sport accoutrements. He could almost taste the earthy loam of the clearing.

Hauke fished the buzzing cell phone out of his pouch. He checked the text message and swore.

"Grimm Research Gruppe advises not to look the kikimora directly in the eyes." Hauke stared at the phone, as if considering throwing it into the woods.

"*Herr* Armburst, I totally looked that thing in the eyes." Carl closed his eyes and took a breath to calm himself.

"We all did, *junge.*" It might have been the nicest thing Luisa ever said to him. "No wonder she's been in our heads this whole time."

"When we engage," Hauke suggested, "use your peripheral vision to track it as much as possible."

"And be careful where you step." Ebner held up a length of the thin glossy line the creature wove. "I've disarmed two snares already."

Stuttgart Gruppe indicated they understood. They slung their rifles and took up their shotguns.

"Movement in the main room," Ebner murmured from where he crouched behind one of the trailer's wheel wells, looking over one of the disused kayaks. The old sniper held a monocle to his eye and pursed his lips as he peered through the large windows fronting the building. "Looks like at least one, an old lady, and possibly several others."

The team shared glances with each other, a mix of cold and flinty looks. Carl looked down at the growing amount of swirling haze around his boots. *This fog is really building up.*

"Movement in that wing, as well, on the far side, *nach links.* I'm . . . not seeing any movement in the section on the right," Ebner added. He looked at Hauke. "Sweep the building?"

"*Genau,*" Hauke nodded. "We'll go in the right side, closest to us. Ebner, provide us cover as we move to that side. We'll clear from end to end."

"*Jawohl.*" Ebner moved to the other end of the trailer and braced the G22 on the kayak.

"Sixty seconds, team. Stand by."

The other members stacked up, Bruno on point, Luisa, Hauke, then Carl. Weapons held at the ready.

"Thirty seconds." Safeties clicked off.

"I can't see her anymore." Ebner frowned behind his optics.

"Ten seconds."

And all hell broke loose.

The kikimora burst out of the murky shadows near their lone

team member. A slash of her claws across the back of Ebner's legs sprinkled warm droplets of blood across the rest of the team. He roared in pain and went down under the kayak trailer.

Carl placed the optic reticle on a mass of twirling rags he hoped contained something vital. Thick tendrils of mist rolled in and obscured the shot. He held his fire.

"Axel!" Luisa bent to work on Ebner and opened her medical kit. Hauke, Bruno, and Carl took hasty overwatch positions.

"Vollidot!" She threw a pack of cigarettes she found in Ebner's med kit over her shoulder and removed the pressure bandages. "How many times now?"

"Mein Go—" Bruno's feet left the ground as a filmy noose yanked him kicking into the air. Somehow, he'd managed to put his hand up to his face and the thin line bit into his wrist instead of his throat. Above him, the kikimora appeared, clutching at his struggling body. Her ancient mouth opened impossibly wide, revealing jointed chelicerae within, a squirming horror like a spider's maw. The creature clamped down on his trapped upper arm with her articulated fangs. Bruno screamed. She released him and he fell into the rotting kayaks with a splintering crash.

Carl fired two rounds into the branches where Bruno had just been dangling.

"Grab him!" Hauke put a hand under Ebner's shoulder as Luisa helped him on the other side. "Over there!"

Carl snatched Bruno by his drag strap and hauled him up the slope closer to the building. There were no overhanging trees or brush there to give the creature concealment.

Aggrieved screeching reverberated through the mist. Hearing Bruno's VP40 bark, Carl turned to see the vile scarecrow charging at them from the tree line. He dumped three more rounds at the thing, aiming between her knees and waist to avoid her gaze. She disappeared in a swirl of damp rags and roiling fog.

The other two assisted Ebner and laid him down on his stomach, his torn trousers slick with blood. Luisa applied pressure dressings to his legs. He grimaced and put his rifle to his shoulder.

"I can't feel my... I can't feel..." Bruno's pistol fell from his slack hand.

"Bruno!" Carl tore open the shirt sleeve where his teammate had been bitten. Awful swollen puncture wounds throbbed with corruption. The man's eyes fluttered.

"Likely a paralytic veno—" Luisa slammed flat on her back as a gossamer snare snatched her feet out from under her and pulled her back toward the fog-banked tree line. She cursed the entire way.

Without thinking, Carl charged after her into the mist and trees. He followed the sound of her yelling and the muzzle flash of a VP40 until he found her on the ground. Carl stood over her and emptied his Benelli into a fleeing shadow. He bent to assist her.

"Reload first, *backpfeifengesicht*!" Bleeding, she got to her knees, helmet gone, armor shredded, her weapons torn away.

"Shut up, Luisa." Carl scooped her up into a fireman's carry and ran for everything he was worth. She could slap his face all she wanted if they made it out of here. Probably would.

Luisa screamed another curse and her pistol boomed again, accompanied by the enraged screech of the monster from directly behind him. Thank goodness for ear pro. He felt something smack against his back, but it only caught a bit of his jangling gear. He kept sprinting.

"There!" Hauke spotted them as they emerged from the misty tree line. He pointed back the way they had come, and then advanced, raising his shotgun. He only got off one round before a loop of the monster's fiber whipped closed on his prosthetic. Hauke fell, skidding on his back until the prosthetic popped off with a snap. He swore unintelligibly, using his free hand to brace himself as he hopped up on one leg.

The blade, yanked around several intervening trees by the thread, sailed through the air into the talons of the waiting kikimora, squatting on a broad hornbeam branch just past the edge of the clearing. Another arm—*a* third *one?*—jutted from beneath her ragged cloak and wrapped around the tree's trunk. Despite her inhuman features, Carl thought he discerned an air of befuddlement from the monster. Her beaked scarecrow head with its black eyes cocked to one side, and she clicked and burbled as she held up the prosthetic to examine.

Then her head came apart as a .300 Win-Mag round passed through it. The *thump-crack* of a G22 rifle echoed down the ravine, rebounding off the sheer scree hills on either side. The false leg fell from her now-limp clawed fingers. The body tumbled backward, smacking hard on a lower branch before landing with a dull thump.

"Bitch." Ebner chambered another round, and then laid his head in the grass, sighing heavily.

The echo of the shot rolled between the two hillsides and faded, and then a heavy silence settled over the little camp, an eerie contrast to the last few seconds of ferocity. Carl lowered Luisa to the ground. She slapped him on the helmet—*there it is*—and swayed unsteadily, sinking to sit on the ground. A laceration on her scalp ran from her forehead into the hairline and bled into her eyes. The white bone of her skull peeked through the ugly gash. Carl knelt and dug through her med kit for some gauze. Bruno still breathed, but his head lolled insensibly.

"Die kinder!" Hauke growled, hopping over to him on one foot. Carl almost grinned at the sight, but his was not a time for comedy. "I'll tend to the team. Go find the children!"

"What about *that*?" Carl asked, pointing to where the kikimora's body lay in the brush below the hornbeam. "Did we really get her?"

"No more visions." Hauke grunted and dropped down to his knees. The fog seemed to be dissipating as well. "She's gone. Get to the children."

"What about your leg?"

"One problem at a time!" Hauke pressed a pressure bandage against Luisa's scalp. "Go! *Mach schnell!*"

By myself? He nodded and snatched up Hauke's bandolier of 12-gauge and shouldered his M4.

Carl followed their original plan and jogged to the end of the wing on the right. Approaching the door and peering through the glass, he saw the silky threads glistening all over the floors and walls. Some strands hung from the ceiling. Other smaller ones drifted lazily in the air. Clearly the kikimora had spent enough time to turn the place into a nest.

Nests, Carl realized, are for birthing young. He screwed his eyes shut and shook his head. His eyes snapped open, and he kicked the door in.

"Making entry," he reported over the team frequency.

"Be wary." Hauke's voice came in through the comms in his helmet. "If this is her lair, there may be snares and such waiting on you. And mark your trail."

True to Ebner's estimation, this wing seemed unoccupied. Eight small but well-appointed bunkrooms and a common bathroom across from an alcove with a sink and ancient refrigerator filled the space. Gossamer threading covered everything. The rooms laid empty other than the old furniture, all covered with a thick layer of dust.

Carl snapped a chemlight and dropped it to the floor. He repeated this every few meters as he progressed.

Here and there in small mounds on the wood floors and rugs sat piles of . . . *something* brown-black and reeking. Viscous black ooze ringed the floor around them. When he approached one, a cloud of fat flies leapt up angrily and whirled around before settling back down. A fecal stench filled his nose, and he could taste it. Carl suppressed his gag reflex. Bile rose and he tried to swallow, but his throat still burned from being strung up by a noose earlier. He hurried on.

As he neared the main room, he thought he heard a faint, high-pitched keening. His skin crawled at what it might be. He put his shoulder against the doorframe and peeked around the corner. Typical hunting lodge furniture. A slew of couches, several long tables, and a bar against the front wall, adjoining the main doors. Along the back wall an enormous window looked out onto the river. Two staircases, one on either end of the large hall, ascended to a second-story balcony overlooking the lower room.

Carl paused a moment, verifying where his extra shotgun shells were, and took a deep breath. He reminded himself to be alert for trip wires.

"Clearing the main room balcony now," he whispered into his mic.

Two clicks came back in acknowledgment.

Sending one final glance skyward—*Please, just let me find those children unharmed*—he rounded the corner and dashed up the stairs, M4 pointed. When he cleared the stairs, he swept the muzzle around the banister. This floor also featured a large glass rear wall looking out at the water. There were low couches and easy chairs, shoved into one corner in a haphazard jumble. Other than the ubiquitous silky threads, there was nothing up here.

Carl keyed his mic and reported what he saw. He tossed a chemlight to the floor.

"Clearing the far wing now." He descended the staircase. At the doorway to the last section of the lodge, a large mass of woven strands turned the hallway into a gray weblike funnel.

Moving down the hall, he cleared rooms as he went, mindful

of trip wires. The tubelike tunnel interwoven around him gave the young hunter the impression of walking down something's throat. Carl shook off the thought as he came upon a room half-way down. He looked through the door and swallowed a loud exclamation. More of the gossamer thread covered every surface, including the windows, although they were sufficiently translucent that the waning daylight outside shone through. A wide threaded, bowl-like nest lay a meter and a half across. Was this its den? He cleared the room and moved on to the next door.

He paused. Strung across the doorframe, about ankle height, a taut slim line waited to trip an unwary intruder. Carl stepped over it and into the gray darkness of the room beyond.

A high clicking squeal filled his ears and he dodged in a panic, shooting a glance upward. A *thing* about the size and shape of a rugby ball dropped from the ceiling, all pale segments and legs like a giant tick. Carl batted it away with the barrel of the M4. It bounced to the deck with a squeak. Three more of the creatures charged him with multiple appendages, brownish-white skin papery and translucent. Each wore a tiny version of the kikimora's face: sharp beaklike noses, scarecrow-stitched mouths opened to reveal chelicerae, and eyes of jet black with bright white pupils. They screamed and charged.

Carl gripped the stock so hard it creaked in his hands. Screaming back in revulsion, he kicked the nearest one with the toe of his boot, punting it into the wall. He stepped back in the face of their assault, only to trip over the wire he'd previously avoided. Carl's back slammed into the deck in a cloud of dust but he tucked his body, using the momentum to roll over backward and onto his knees. The shotgun came up smoothly, just like on the range at Grimm Berlin's training center in Fullendorf.

The Benelli roared twice, turning the two remaining mite-like creatures into a semitransparent phlegmy mist. Carl stormed to his feet and strode back into the room. The last two baby moras lay stunned, but moving. Carl stomped them both with the cutting edge of his bootheel.

"Can't collect a bounty with a cup full of slime." He put a hand to his mouth and shook the snotty gunk off his boot.

"Carl!" Hauke's voice came over the radio in a burst of static. *"SITREP!"*

"I'm good. Came across some of its larval spawn. They were

light work." Carl hoped against hope that no one outside heard him screaming like a teenaged girl that whole time.

"Very well, proceed. We'll bag the bodies later."

He paused for another moment to listen for any more stalking claws clicking across the wood floor. He fed more shells into the M4 and moved back into the room. Something odd caught his attention. He keyed the microphone again.

Carl held for a beat and peered at two oblong objects stuck to the wall, resembling misshapen cantaloupes and tethered in place with multiple silk strands. They appeared to be composed of tiny woven threads, like lint from a clothes dryer. They were split down the middle. Using his flashlight, he saw the sacs were empty. Maybe the larvae he'd encountered had gestated here?

"I can see . . . they look like . . . fuzzy balls? Like cotton balls, but the size of melons? Two of them in this room."

A pause. *"Egg sacs, maybe,"* Hauke came back over the net. *"Is that all you see?"*

"No."

Two corpses, both apparently those of adult human males, lay at his feet. They looked desiccated and dried out. Drained, maybe. Small puncture wounds dotted the bodies here and there.

"Moving on."

Two clicks in reply.

In the bunkroom across the hall, he found a cage-like bubble woven into a latticework enclosing a small space in the corner. Four little bodies laid in a neat row within, eyes closed and breathing raggedly. They were bound, ankles and wrists, with the thread. The smallest, a little girl, moaned softly in her sleep. Deep frown lines marked her face.

"I've found the children!" Carl almost forgot to key the mic.

He grimaced. Drawing his knife, he approached the makeshift holding pen. Several strong strokes parted the strands. Some of the filmy threads touched his skin and he cringed, half expecting another hallucination or some other horrible thing. The eyes of the oldest, a boy of about thirteen, snapped open wide and staring. The poor kid started to shiver. Carl cut him loose.

"I've got you," Carl said to him in English. "Do you speak English?"

"Yes." The boy nodded and rubbed his arms, sitting up. "Little bit."

"What's your name?"

"Bohdan."

"Bohdan, I'm with the police. Help me wake up your brothers and sister, and we'll take you to your family."

The lad clawed at the threads binding his siblings with his bare hands. The kid would probably have an iron constitution after this.

Carl gently shook and patted the other children awake; they moaned blearily and scowled, their eyes still screwed shut. The boy spoke to them, but Carl couldn't tell if it was Russian or Ukrainian. Bohdan gathered them to him, staggering and bleary-eyed.

"Bohdan, my friends are waiting for you outside. Follow the lights on the floor! Go on! Go!" Carl keyed his radio and let Hauke know they were on their way out. He followed them to the hallway and kept an eye on them from the doorway until they disappeared, hand in hand, around the corner into the big room.

The mass of threading grew thicker back down the hall. Carl caught sight of another large spherical web sac, split open along one fuzzy side. No movement for the moment.

"We see the kids!" Hauke radioed. *"But Carl, we're not getting paid by the hour. Get in there and take care of that nest!"*

Carl moved down the hall to clear the next room.

He found three more human bodies, recently dead and intact. They laid beneath an enormous clutch of egg sacs in the far corner, past a dresser and a big-screen television that had probably been expensive when installed years ago. There were dozens of the podlike capsules spread around the room. Carl stared, mouth open, and felt his stomach turn as he observed the larger sacs very slowly, but noticeably, pulse with life.

"There's . . ." He cleared his throat, keyed his mic again, and described the scene to his team. "It's her nursery," he concluded. "There's maybe forty or fifty of the egg sacs here."

An avalanche of German swearing came over the net. Hauke could be prolifically profane.

"I'll clear the rest of the wing." The sight still nearly overwhelmed him. "Then I will come back and take care of the eggs. Maybe I can put a shotgun blast in each one."

"Do you have enough?" asked Hauke. *"Forty or fifty? I don't think you do."*

"Fire?" Carl suggested, his forehead wrinkled.

"We're in the middle of the forest and it's been a dry summer." Hauke sighed deeply. *"And we don't know what effect fire would have on them. Make them all hatch at once? The last thing we need is a few dozen baby moras running around a refugee camp."*

"We also may not have enough time," Ebner broke in. *"Some already hatched. The ones you dealt with."*

"'I say we take off and nuke the site from orbit. It's the only way to be sure.'" Carl did *not* say that over the net.

"Demo," Hauke came back on the radio. *"In your kit, you have two blocks of Semtex, time fuse and initiators already set up and ready to prime in. You're going to blow the nursery."*

"Will that kill them all?"

"You can finish off any of them that are still squirming."

"Jawohl." Carl took a big breath.

"Take pictures for the bounties before you blow it!" Hauke reminded him. *"Burnt ashes and piles of Scheiße don't pay the bounty."*

Carl cleared the wing, but found no more people, alive or dead. He quickly dragged the three bodies out of the room, panting with effort and trying like hell to be quiet.

With Hauke's guidance, he taped his blocks of Semtex together and primed it with a blasting cap. Holding the little coil of time fuse, he stepped forward and gingerly wedged the charge in between two sacs in the center of the clutch. He started to uncoil the fuse and paused, his stomach knotting again as he looked down and realized he had a problem.

The time-fuse coil was neatly sliced through in several places. Carl checked the demo pouch and found ragged vertical slashes in it, probably from one of the kikimora's sharp talons. She'd punched right through and snipped his time fuse. Even from beyond she was making his life miserable.

What to do? There were now multiple short pieces of time fuse, all just a few centimeters long. He reasoned there must be a way to splice time fuse together, but he was no demolitions expert, time was a factor, and the thought of those pulsing malevolent sacs bursting open at any moment . . .

"I guess it will have to do." *Scheiße.* Carl unscrewed the endcap on the igniter enough to remove it. "I understand hearing aids are very stylish these days," he said to nobody, sliding it onto the piece of fuse running to his blasting cap and the Semtex. The fuse was woefully short. He pulled the safety pin on the igniter, then twisted the pull ring.

He crouched and dialed the noise-cancel feature on his headset to maximum, then keyed his mic. "Ready to fire."

"Go ahead when ready," Hauke sent back.

Carl keyed the mic. "'This aggression will not stand, man.'" He couldn't resist.

"What?"

"Nothing. Fire in the hole!" Carl released his mic button. He yanked the ring. "It's probably fine."

Nothing happened at first. He opened one eye, then a faint wisp of smoke emanated from the igniter and the time fuse started to blacken as the flame ate through. Carl turned to run. He made it to the door and around the corner, and—

A massive pressure smacked him all over. His hearing fizzed into a high whine.

Eeeeeeeeeeeeeeeeeeeeeee!

It wasn't fine.

He came to with his helmet askew and down over his eyes. The Benelli stock jammed him painfully up under his body armor and Carl thought he might have broken one of his lower ribs against it. It hurt terribly. He rolled onto his side, crying out without hearing himself. Whenever he turned his head, it sounded like he'd gotten water in his ears from too much time in a swimming pool. He pushed himself to his feet and, holding his side, stumbled back toward the main room.

Slipping on something, Carl braced his hand on the wall as he tried to walk. A viscous, phlegmy fluid dripped off his arm in thick ropes of snot. It oozed down the walls. His boots slid all over. He tried to wipe it out of his eyes, but that just made it worse. Were those sirens he heard? He couldn't see.

Luisa shook him. He looked around and realized he was sitting on the front porch of the lodge, looking up at the forested hillside. Luisa held a fire extinguisher, dripping residual fluid from its nozzle, a hastily wrapped bandage wound around her head. Blood seeped through it and a trickle of it had dried on her nose. Her mouth moved.

How did he get outside? Three of the children sat with the team. The eldest, Bohdan, trotted up to Hauke with the team leader's bladed prosthetic in his young hands. Hauke slipped the boy a folded bill. Bruno sat leaning against an old refuse bin and looked like Carl felt, but at least he was alive. Ebner drew deeply on a cigarette, nodding at Carl. Most of the old soldier's trousers were cut away, his legs covered in pressure dressings.

Carl prodded hesitantly beneath his armor and decided no ribs were broken, but he would still have a hell of a bruise. It even felt painful to blink.

Luisa smacked him on his helmet and yelled again. This time he could just hear her.

"WHAT?"

"Are. You. OKAY?"

"'HE SLIMED ME!'" Carl gave Luisa a salute, sending a sticky string of phlegm into the air.

"You're an idiot!" Luisa smirked. "But that wasn't too bad for a *grünjunge*!"

Carl spat a thick gob of unwholesome ichor onto the grass. He rolled his tongue in his mouth and promptly vomited all over his boots.

Oh, that hurt all over.

"Well done, Carl!" Hauke snapped a photo with his phone. "Now *that's* a real live *Monsterkommando*!"

MHI encountered the ghost of the legendary Roman monster hunter Sextus Bassus, during the events of Operation Siege. This historical record is on loan from the Oxford Supernatural Archives. —A.L.

Pater Monstrum

Mike Massa

Sextus could tell the rich kid was dead meat, no matter how flashy his swordplay. His finery would soon join the bloody rags on the bodies scattered about the wagons. Sextus' expert gaze also detected the fatigue of the veteran by the boy's side, desperately fighting to cover his master's flank. Both would die before the orange-red sun, just touching the horizon, fell much farther. The green-skinned urks surrounding them would see to it.

Sextus hadn't planned for a fight on Emperor Vespasianus' road during the march south, so he'd ordered his cohort to sling most of their kit. Iron-gray hair was all that covered his head, and his thick, five-and-a-half-foot frame was protected by no more than a red woolen tunic and dun breeches. Sometimes, like today, duty demanded you work with what you had.

Sextus knew from duty. He made a snap judgment, and put the spurs to his latest charger.

"Shit, boss—wait!" came the resigned plea from over his shoulder, followed by Cato briskly delivering familiar orders. "Lancers up and abreast! Archers—saddle fire, independent fire, now! Gracos, get your century moving! None of the fire grenades this time or I'll shove one up your ass! Everyone else, follow me!"

As familiar as the bone-handled *spatha* he drew in a slither of steel, Sextus heard the clatter and jangle of his cavalry *ala* as it began to shake out into hasty fighting array, emerging from around the base of the hill obscuring them from the fighters ahead. It would take them several moments to self-organize and the Romans on the road ahead didn't have that long. Besides, experienced hunters didn't need orders, they just needed targets.

Ahead, the urks remained oblivious for a few more precious seconds. Only two were crossing blades with the travelers, a shorter fighter with a sword in each fist, and a giant of an urk swinging a huge hammer. A loose semicircle of a dozen or more tusked humanoids, wearing mismatched black leather armor, bits of mail, and other castoffs, was intent on the fight, hooting and gesticulating. Several more picked desultorily through an overturned wagon partially blocking this offshoot of the *Via Traiana*. Sextus preferred to attack without warning, but a half-ton warhorse galloping down a paved road did not a stealthy attack make. An urk archer, close enough for Sextus to count the blackened iron rings on its vest, jerked its head upright. Shiny black eyes peered from under a ragged hood. The bandy-legged humanoid spun to face the new threat, knocked a shaft in a single, continuous movement.

Too late.

Sextus leaned forward in the saddle and, with a smooth forearm stroke, slashed at the *urk*'s unhelmeted head. It ducked with the preternatural speed of its kind, sacrificing the bow to the keen edge of the Roman's weapon. The next urk wasn't as lucky, falling to Sextus' backhand.

The roan warhorse turned inside its own length to the measured pull of Sextus' hand on the reins, and kicking forehooves kept three urks at bay, even as they menaced Sextus with short, leaf-bladed throwing spears, quite unlike the longer, pile-headed *pilum* his infantry carried. Other urks quickly formed a line to meet Sextus' attack, one staggering as a red-fletched arrow struck home. The others flinched away from the resulting head-high spray of blood. Behind Sextus, a signaler was blowing his *cornu*. The measured blasts from the curved Roman trumpet ordered infantry to advance rapidly. Another, taller urk raised a twisted horn and blatted a battle-call in response.

Bronze Roman ranks were decisive, but brains won battles. Sextus took a breath for a second or two, surveying the action.

Round urkish shields snapped up, and the urks regrouped as neatly as any Roman *decurion* could hope. They began to move backward, disengaging over the rough ground between the road and a nearby thicket. Archers hidden there began shooting, and urkish arrows fell among the charging lancers, confusing their advance.

The paired duels in the center of the road hadn't paused, though. The guard was nearly down, and the nobleman's strokes were faltering.

Sextus whirled his sword and drove into the fight. The taller of the two urks pressing Sextus' countrymen was an absolute giant whose eyes weren't far below Sextus' own, even mounted. Sextus got a good look at its bestial face. Ivory tusks gleamed, and hot foam sprayed as the urk roared a challenge, spinning to face the new threat. His battle hammer was easily as long as Sextus was tall, and the ogre-ish foe directed his next looping strike with skill. Sextus hooked a heel under his saddle and leaned way over, ducking under the swing. The hammer's business end clove the air with a *wheeting* sound.

Sextus cut the urk across its leather-armored shoulders to no effect. Without warning he found himself flying, his mount's death scream blanketing all other sounds of combat. Airborne, he caught a glimpse of the smaller urk recovering from the strike that had buried a short sword in the belly of Sextus' horse.

The ground came up to meet him, and Sextus landed hard enough to cost him a moment of coherent thought. Reflex drove him hastily to one knee, and he raised his long cavalry sword to block the inevitable follow-up.

A deafening roar from the tall urk arrested the movement of the shorter, its remaining sword suspended over his head. It shuffled back several steps, and instead held the weapon in readiness over the two Romans in the road. The guard was face down, and kneeling boy was conscious, cradling his side. The giant green-skin approached short of striking range, and gestured abruptly for Sextus to stand.

He did so, definitely not wobbling upright. Sextus looked around for reinforcements and took stock of his injuries. His back and shoulder felt truly wretched. The burning sensation from several denari's worth of hide scraped from his face, legs and arms in the fall was a distraction he didn't need. His right forearm was bleeding freely.

The tall urk grunted with disdain, upper lip curling away from jagged tusks easily longer than Sextus' fingers. He grounded the hammer with a thud and wound the weapon's leather thong around one thick green wrist. The big urk glanced at the fallen Romans and then stared at Sextus. The challenge was clear.

You want 'em? Come take them. Just you.

Sextus turned an inner ear to listen. If the Many-Winged god had words to share, this was the moment. Instead, his right palm, fitted against the *spatha*'s grip, began to itch. Sextus had come to learn, in the years since the god had taken an interest, it deigned to speak but rarely, as though silence was all most mortal matters deserved.

So be it. On the other hand, this isn't where I die. Probably.

His squadron of lancers had arrived, weapons bristling as their mounts shifted nervously. The tall urk seemed indifferent. At close range, Sextus could see a heavy iron necklace descending behind the urk's leather tunic. Its breastplate was decorated with a few arrows, including one with red fletching, standing proud in the center. The thick leather backed by a mail shirt had been penetrated by the light projectiles. Heavy lances would be another matter. Sextus sensed the tall urk was relying on Roman honor.

Damned and thrice damned.

"Back," he ordered, turning away from the urks and waving both sword and his free hand at the lancers as his bodyguard finally reached him. "Stop!"

"'Ware arrow!" sounded as a scowling Cato reined in alongside.

With a casual motion, the scarred veteran interposed his shield between his master and the source of urkish fire. Simultaneously, the shield jerked in concert with a loud *whack!* Sextus had an excellent view of the cruelly barbed arrowhead newly decorating the inner surface of laminated wood.

The tall urk faced the tree line, bellowing. It pointed at Sextus and slammed the hammer against the road. Sextus felt the impact through his calcei.

"Single combat?" Cato sputtered, dismounting. The stout-legged, barrel-chested centurion, who'd watched Sextus' back since before Judea, was shorter than his master by a handspan, but nearly as wide as he was tall. "That thing? Are you mad?"

"The gods must think so, else I'd be reclining on pillows, eating pears and drinking chilled wine in Jerusalem."

"At least put this on, sir!" Cato said, extending Sextus' helmet, smeared with horse blood.

"It's not my destiny to fall today, Cato," Sextus said, peering around the edge of Cato's shield. Sextus' first century of infantry had trotted around the bend, and Gracos was fanning them out from a column into a double rank. They'd discarded all the gear they carried on the march, save for their tall red shields, a single *pilum* per trooper, and the swords that hung high on each man's waist. The grunts dressed their line and began traversing the plowed field. Apparently the big urk's cease fire only applied to Sextus, because one legionnaire fell, clutching his leg. The ranks closed up and continued toward the archers.

"Tell the *cornicen* to bring the boys back to the road."

"I suppose the voice in your head has guaranteed your life against your stupidity, honored Sextus?" Cato said, lowering the shield. He sheared off the black shaft, and relayed Sextus' order to the signaler before reversing the shield, allowing the golden gorgon snarling from its face to catch a bit of the fading light. The she-monster decoration screamed defiance, dagger-teeth and blazing eyes menacing the cohort's enemies. The maws of her serpent hair gaped, matching the fury of the monster, forever raging.

Not unlike Cato's sarcasm.

His faithful subordinate continued, "Did the voice of the gods have any advice on how to beat an urk with twice your reach and three times your weight?"

More followed. Sextus sighed at the jibes as Cato continued, alternating between pragmatism and business advice.

"You know, if you wait just a bit, the kid might bleed out, and then we'd have some legitimate salvage, as well as whatever the Navigatus will pay for a half dozen urk heads."

"We don't do this for the gold, Cato." Sextus overrode the angry protests from the centurion, who by then was buckling the last strap on a cuirass of banded steel he'd slipped around Sextus' torso. "Or we don't do this *just* for the gold."

"Honor buys no remounts," quipped his trusted first spear and bodyguard. "Certainly not as fast as you go through horses. Or decent food, and more incendiaries for Gracos."

"*Pax*, Cato," Sextus said, working on getting his breathing even. "Keep the boys back and give me room."

The urks' main party was well across the field now, retreating in remarkably good order. Even if any of his lancers dared chance the uneven ground, the urks were moving almost as fast as a horse cantered. It was clear to Sextus they'd reach the shelter of the trees before his cavalry, let alone the infantry, could intervene.

"Right," he said, taking the proffered shield. He rolled his shoulders one at a time and winced, before stepping toward the waiting giant urk. "Let's do it."

As he strode toward his opponent, the tall urk grunted happily. It kicked the grounded hammer head, driving it forward unexpectedly. Sextus dodged, carefully guiding the hammer past with his shield edge. The impact was stunning, and the brass strip guarding the shield edge was dented as deeply as if he'd caught a full-armed axe blow.

In a blink, the urk withdrew its hammer and cocked it across his body.

Jupiter's cock, he's fast. But not as fast as a Chosen. And fair fights are for the arena, not the battlefield.

Sextus had always been a good swordsman. One didn't survive leading from the front when crossing blades with the wild painted men of Brittania unless you were competent with a blade. But Sextus had something extra. Something better than luck. He drew up all the control he could muster, and carefully tapped a portion of the tightly sealed reservoir of hot energy, deep in his chest. It was the unexpected gift from the uninvited god who rode his shoulder, intervening just often enough to disrupt Sextus' life.

Hungry fire spread through his limbs. Molten energy swelled his chest, and the pain from his injuries faded to insignificance. Sextus bounced lightly on his toes, vision sharpening, hearing becoming so acute he heard the creak of the big urk's bloody leathers, and the rasp of its unclean breath.

The urk paused, cocking its head to one side, like a wolf confused by a rabbit suddenly producing fangs and claws.

Sextus struck.

The lunge was so fast Sextus marked his target before the urk could react. He pinked the urk in one thigh, the tip of his cavalry sword finding a gap in the rough armor. Like lightning, he withdrew, waited a quarter beat while the urk belatedly parried downward, and repeated the strike on the urk's forearm. The urk jerked the hammer up, so Sextus stepped sideways and struck yet again. With the gift burning through him, he was faster than water through a millrace, and more unpredictable. Each lick of his blade found unprotected flesh. Anywhere the mail and hide armor left any opening, Sextus painted his red anger on dark green urk skin. Sextus struck, and struck again, dipping inside the massive urk's reach before dancing away from each counterstrike. Speed would be no protection if the hammer landed. Sextus drew a bit more on the god's power, trading future cost against current danger.

His hands and feet tingled. He could feel every pebble underfoot, the grain of the bone in his sword's grip, and felt burning energy coil tightly in his muscles.

The urk, goaded by his attacks, finally committed to a charge. Pounding footsteps brought the enormous urk close enough to swing.

The big hammer swept toward Sextus' torso, as fast and implacable as stone shot from a siege engine. Deflecting such a massive weapon would break his arm, shield or no. Sextus instead skipped lightly to the side, drawing on the power to reverse direction, and carefully cut behind the swinging deathblow. The draw stroke pulled the blade downward and back as the urk thundered past.

A cry went up from the audience.

The giant urk stared stupidly at the spurting stump of its right arm, which now ended at the elbow. Thicker than Sextus' thigh, the urk's forearm lay on the ground. The urk still had a grip on the shaft with its left hand, but the hammer head wavered.

Ave, nice weapons retention!

The clamor of voices, full-throated yells of excitement, grew louder, threatening coherent thought. Roman short swords rang off shields decorated with gorgon heads, and the *cornicen* tortured his instrument with a single, screaming note. The remaining urk flinched, sword drooping dustward.

Sextus strode forward to hamstring his maimed opponent, but as he advanced, the big urk fell to one knee, releasing the hammer to arrest its fall with its remaining hand. It sank even further, sitting back on its hams, trying to squeeze the huge wound shut. The smaller urk darted toward Sextus, but its fallen comrade growled, forestalling the attack. More grunts in their incomprehensible language drew Shorty closer, and Sextus watched as the downed urk shrugged off attempts at aid. Brushing away assistance, the mortally injured urk tugged a leather amulet out of its tunic with its remaining hand. The smaller urk, bowing, tried to intervene. The argument was brief and one-sided. With a yank, the big urk pulled the necklace off and slumped the rest of the way to the road.

The smaller urk straightened, swaying, and wound the amulet's chain around one forearm. At close range, Sextus could see it was female. The she-urk knelt, reversing the sword tip carefully onto the flagstone road. Then she looked directly into his eyes and spoke, the words incomprehensible, but possessed of a meaningful rhythm.

What the hell do I do with you?

"That creature killed Arnis!" a shrill voice whined as Sextus, staring at the kneeling urk, began to force the heat from his limbs. The familiar pain was unpleasant enough. Every time he called on the strength of the Many-Winged, it was harder to compel the gift back to silence. Unseen, unheard by any others, horns trumpeted, and a wordless paean filled his ears, celebrating battle glory, inviting Sextus to let go completely, to fight and slay until there were no enemies at all.

Sextus Lucilius Bassus was a Roman, before Mars and Jupiter. He was no one's puppet. Even as the chorus sweetened, promising power and freedom from care, he successfully locked the gift away, drawing on a lifetime of discipline and pure will. The effort left him trembling, as though a deep bruise lay on every part of his body. His very bones stung with a heat like the first kiss of a red-hot brand. Painful, purifying.

"He killed Arnis!"

Somehow, the approaching voice was even more irritating than Sextus' sudden weariness, like lemon juice on a cut. Unnecessary and distracting.

The high-pitched complaint was repeated.

Sextus identified the source. The young Roman he'd just saved had reclaimed his sword. A gold bracelet, a gold ring, and an ornate, jeweled scabbard spoke of wealth. The rich cloak decorated with a narrow purple stripe was a daring—or stupid—statement of political power. With blood on his face and one hand still on his ribs, the teenager stalked toward the kneeling urk, raising his overdecorated blade.

"That creature killed Arnis!" he repeated again, and swung if not well, then at least earnestly.

The urk never took her eyes from Sextus.

With a flick of the *spatha*, Sextus blocked the noble's blow.

The young man recovered, his eyes a bit too wide, and raised his sword again. This time, Sextus batted it out of his hand. It probably stung a bit.

Oh, no, not that.

Low hooting was audible in the distance, but his own troops were silent.

"My prisoner, youngster." Sextus felt the heat in his heart surge, but fought it down, back where it belonged.

"Do you know who I am?" the noble demanded. "I'm—"

"Damned ungrateful, is what you are," Cato said, collecting the sword from where it lay. "Time to see to your man, young master."

"Who are you to stop me?!"

Sextus let the process go, ears still ringing like they always seemed to do afterward. He ignored the disarmed noble, but spared a grateful glance for Cato. Then he heard his long-time comrade running his mouth. Again.

"Well, sir," Cato drawled, unobtrusively keeping the sword out of the young man's reach while leading him toward the prone guard. "I'm Centurion Cato Sallus, late of the Tenth Legion, *Fretensis*. That right there is Bassus, ex-commander of the Tenth, ex-legate of Judea, and now on the emperor's personal service."

"Ex-what? What *is* he? I've never seen a man move so fast! What army unit is this?"

Sextus continued to meet the flat, hooded stare of the kneeling urk, but he heard Cato's chuckle, and dwindling reply.

"We're not exactly in the army, see? We kill demons and evil spirits, boyo. We're monster hunters!"

Sextus emptied his wine cup, and sat it down with a will. A small piece of ceramic chipped off the flared base. He squinted angrily at the mutinous cup as the surface of the wine stilled. Momentarily, the surface rippled anew at another minor tremor, common in southern Italy this season.

About the large, leather command tent, flickering lamps provided a warm, glowing light that turned everything shades of amber and orange. Enough were placed about Sextus' pavilion to light the long wooden camp table filling most of the chamber, though dark shadows lingered in the corners. The light gleamed from the small silver mirror and brass wash basin perched on a tripod just inside the entrance, as well as from the back plates of the loricated steel armor worn by the legionnaires standing guard just outside.

Small luxuries and guards came with being the commander. Those, and respect.

He ignored the incipient smile on the beautiful woman tending his wounds. Estella had never been one for hierarchy.

Sextus returned to coping left-handed with the scrolls he'd allowed to accumulate. His right arm, radiating a constant pain, lay on the table, clear of the scrolls. Sextus was accustomed to ignoring the minor bumps, scratches, and aches that always seemed to appear after a fight. Of course, such disregard presumed he wasn't dealing with the cohort's healer, whose tender mercies would test a Stoic.

A sudden, fierce burning sensation on his injured forearm made him jerk.

"Minerva's bleeding sheath, did I owe you money and forget?"

"Watch your mouth," the robed woman said, sponging the surprisingly deep cut on Sextus' forearm. "If consigned here I must be, at least I can tease out the answer to the puzzle of how I came to be bound to a human who enjoys tallying sums, and do so without enduring Roman crudity."

"You like puzzles, Estella?" Sextus replied, setting his jaw against the next swipe of the bloody sponge. He reread the same sentence a third time, before laying the scroll down, making a top layer across the wax tablets, slates, and other records used to manage the business of his cohort. Then he abandoned what was becoming a heroic effort to remain impassive by glaring at the physic who'd attached herself to his band not long after the business near Masada.

"I adore puzzles, Sextus," Estella said, admiring her handiwork. "Bleeding humans are just puzzles who happen to scream."

"I am," Sextus said, clenching his free hand. "Not. Screaming."

"I hear you screaming on the inside."

The open smile she now wore marked her as beautiful as Sextus was blunt and worn. The deep, hooded cloak she habitually wore was thrown open, and her marching pack sat open next to her stool, revealing a score of small sacks, tiny boxes, and a selection of folded leaves, each twisted tight. Her bow case and quiver leaned nearby, the red fletched arrows providing a bit of color to her dun traveling outfit. Though blond hair in Grecian ringlets framed her blue eyes, and several waist-length, honey-colored braids complemented the cream-colored skin of Gaul, Sextus knew damn well she didn't have a drop of northern blood in her.

"Is this really necessary?" he asked, when she switched from her sponge and began industriously applying a stiff boar-bristle brush to the red wound.

"It's only necessary if you want to avoid blood sickness, or gut fever from unclean urk steel," she replied. "Not to mention whatever foulness accumulated on the road. I'm well aware your... gift will heal you. Eventually. Cleaning the cuts speeds the healing, and slows your steep slide into the debt of your tame god."

"The Many-Winged isn't *my* tame god, he's just a nosy and insistent task master," Sextus protested, and then indicated the cluttered work surface with a lifted chin. "Whereas this work is for the very short-tempered man who's my master every day."

"Should not the commander of this warband assign such labor to a menial?" she asked. "Surprising that your king-father requires more than simple results. Roman preoccupation with ledgers is a mortal plague."

"We've been over this,'" Sextus replied, running his free hand over his face. "This isn't a 'warband.' I command the Fraternitas Monstrum, a proper, independent auxiliary cohort. And second, Romans don't have a king, we have an emperor. Titus Ceasar Vespasianus doesn't know I exist—I hope. I work for his spymaster, the chief of the Frumentarii."

Sextus tapped the ruddy wax seal on the opened scroll. The true name of the Roman head of secret police, the Navigatus, was a state secret, but his personal mark was the curling sternpost and jutting rudder of a trireme, the three-banked, rowed warship that anchored Rome's naval might. Any Roman officer or bureaucrat would recognize the imprint, and think twice before impeding Sextus in his duty.

"I respect the Navigatus enough to ensure what I give him is right and true. He has enough to do, watching every crooked noble who would try for the purple. It wasn't long ago Rome had four emperors in a single year. Not to mention the raids in the north from our so-called allies, or the fucking *Gypos* who muck about with the grain ships that feed much of Rome. Navigatus rightly expects an honest accounting."

"Oh, is that all?" Estella's eyes twinkled, and Sextus realized she'd once again been twitting him. He awaited her riposte.

"Is there not something about killing monsters?"

"We protect the empire from blood-eaters, sirens, harpies, every sort of undead, and keep the roads safe from marauders and nonhumans, yes."

"Am I not included in the tally?" Estella asked, adding a white powder from the open box on the table to the basin. She held her hand over the bowl, concentrating for a moment. The water bubbled. Then her brush went into mixture, and she stuck the damn thing back into Sextus' cut again.

"Surely I qualify?"

"No!" Sextus answered, perhaps bit more decisively than he intended. It definitely wasn't because the damned brushing hurt.

He waved to the guard, who had turned at the sound of the loud denial. Sextus controlled himself, ignoring the scrubbing on another cut. "No, a true Roman can tell a basilisk from a ballista, and an ally from a monster. Even when the ally is slowly sawing off his arm with the bristles from a diseased Gaulish boar."

Estella rolled her eyes and laid the brush aside. She dropped a linen rag into the bowl and added water from a steaming kettle. Then she gripped his forearm more firmly, and carried on.

"How fares the young one you rescued?" she asked. "Not your preferred human maiden, alas."

"Cato's getting a skin of wine into the lad as we speak," Sextus answered. "Easier to manage that way. If looks can be relied upon, his father will have a heavy purse. A reward would gladden the men, particularly since loot has been seldom of late. The boy was on his way to his father's seaside villa in Campania, so we'll head there."

"What of your captive urk?" Estella said, raising one eyebrow. "Will you slay your prisoner?"

"The urk surrendered under honorable conditions." Sextus rolled his neck from side to side to distract himself. "It stares, and speaks, but I can't make out a word."

He drained his goblet and listened inward, fruitlessly, for the Many-Winged remained silent.

Don't the Greeks say the gods help those who help themselves?

Estella met his eyes, and Sextus decided.

"Guard!"

The guard captain stepped into the tent, slapping his armored chest with a closed fist.

"Bring the prisoner," Sextus ordered.

"Say this much about Sextus Lucilius Bassus," Estella pronounced. "No one will accuse him of overthinking a matter."

A few moments later, two legionnaires walked the short urk, hands bound behind her back, into the main chamber. A wave from Sextus forestalled their move to throw their prisoner to the carpeted floor. They settled for flicking the urk's hood onto her shoulders.

Sextus regarded the urk's remarkably unlovely face. Her brow ridge was far less prominent than a male's, but the beetled and slightly bloodshot black eyes had the universal malevolence of her kind. A flat nose, spiky hair, and small gleaming ivory tusks completed the urk's mien.

The she-urk twisted each shoulder, wresting her arms free of the guards' grasp, and muttered something needing no translation. She stared angrily at Sextus, and when that yielded no response, she glanced at Estella. She sniffed, stared at the healer, and then deliberately sniffed again. The double take that followed spoke volumes.

"*Ssstheno*," she said, ducking her head and adding an unintelligible but rhythmic phrase.

"I have become too accustomed to being around your soldiers, Sextus," the healer said, arching one fine eyebrow. "The young urk seems to know who I am, which could be inconvenient. She is quite upset at this treatment after giving her blood parole. A vassal, even a temporary one, expects better treatment—"

"By Juno!" Sextus interrupted, using his good hand to lean back. "You speak urkish?"

"I do not speak urkish, Roman drudge," Estella said, effortlessly tugging him back into position. There might have been a touch of frost in her voice. "There is no such thing as 'urkish.' Rome tells time by the kalends. I count the centuries during my exile here, and I happen to understand Scythian."

She patted the cased Scythian hornbow and quiver of red-fletched arrows that never left her side.

"Yon she-urk speaks a nearly extinct variety. I recommend you cut her bonds. Or will you torture information from your newest vassal?"

Sextus ordered the guards to remove the leather straps binding his shiny new vassal, and dismissed the men outside. The urk rubbed her wrists and warily took stock of her surroundings. She ignored the wine cup Sextus pushed across the table, and after another long look at Estella, fixed her dark gaze on the Roman.

"Ask her why urks are here, not a week's march from Rome," he ordered. He might be a stripling compared to his healer, but he understood the futility of arguing with feminine pique. "What brings them so far south?"

Sextus listened to a longer exchange. The urk repeatedly bowed toward Estella, though the motions began to seem perfunctory. The conversation sounded like a gurgling river of algae being slapped by an ancient waterwheel, while the millstone gears clashed.

Typical barb language.

"Her name is Wurzzibythnappat," Estella finally reported, winding a bandage into place. "It means She Who Spins with Two Swords. Her tribe was raided by a great evil, and several urk children were taken. Their clan chief marshalled the entire sept, and they have spent half a season tracking. At the cost of a river of their own blood—these urks do go on, so dramatic—they followed the raiders to the shore of *Mare Adriaticum*. Last full moon, those urks who survived took ship in Illyria and landed a few days' march north of here. They tracked the remaining raiders this far, but their quarry moved farther west."

"Tell Wurzy here attacking Romans on a Roman road has fuck all to do with urk children. Why did they take arms against Rome?"

Estella and the newly christened Wurzy appeared to argue. There was more shallow urkish bowing. More phlegm on wet millstones.

"They do not seek war on your master's house," Estella said, continuing to listen. She asked some questions of her own, some quite sharply. The dialogue between the healer and the urk grew hotter, and louder. A final exchange of monosyllables left Estella red-faced, and the urk's eyes even more bloodshot.

"Sextus, I advise you drop the matter."

"Well, now I'm curious, Estella." Sextus scratched his scalp. "Does she know who took the children or not? And if the chief was their tracker, how can they continue, now that I've killed the big fellow?"

"They attacked the caravan because it is where the trail led.

Their clan chief detected the taint of dark magic somewhere in the convoy, but found nothing. Yet, they cannot stop until the evil is purged and the souls of the children are freed."

"Awfully convenient."

"Sextus, I recognize this tale." Estella began bundling her supplies back into her pack. "The children are likely dead, or will be soon. Such souls are used to fuel dark rituals. The power of any being which can accomplish such sorcery is beyond your—admittedly considerable—capacity for simple, bloody violence."

"That's not what I asked, princess." Sextus drained his goblet and let the silence stretch. "You underestimate our Roman capacity for *simple bloody violence.*"

"Down this road lays only pain, suffering, and regret, Sextus." Estella folded the top on her pack and tucked the straps into the sides, securing the contents. "But you ask. Bound, I shall answer. The urk has a talisman. It can lead a bearer toward a destination. She says her chief recognized you as Chosen. His final order was to give it to you, to continue their quest."

The urk had been fiddling with something as Estella spoke. As the healer finished, the urk completed unwinding the necklace the chief had given her. Wurzy held it up so the stained, brown leather amulet fell free of the iron links. The urk opened the cover, revealing a small, silver ring.

"Well, give it over, Wurzy," Sextus said, leaning forward in his seat and extending his arm.

"Sextus, no!"

Sextus froze at Estella's call. Her eyes were round and staring, her grip on his forearm an iron shackle, right across his wound. Her warning carried not just to his ears, but reverberated in his chest, much like the trumpet of a war elephant just outside your shield wall, waiting to smash it to kindling.

The guard *tesserarius* was inside the door in a flash, sword clearing the scabbard.

"Explain," Sextus said, feeling Estella's grasp weaken, then tremble. He waved the sentry back.

"My father set my sisters and me against this evil, Sextus," Estella said. She swallowed and released her grip. A spot of red seeped through the linen bandage. "Despite my family's sacrifices, we have done no better than a draw. The ring has power—it can guide you to your heart's desire, or to your heart. But the very name is a terrible warning. A dark god, a god of gods, will take notice if you wield the ring. Better to let it pass. These are not Roman children at stake. Dismiss Wurzzibythnappat. I will away to attend the other wounded and ret—"

"TAKE IT."

Almost without volition, Sextus jerked his hand toward Wurzy, who flinched away, deaf to the voice in Sextus' head.

"Yours is a cruel god, Sextus," Estella whispered, bowing her head.

"Maybe, Estella," Sextus replied, shaking first his head, then his wrist, before reopening his hand palm up for the silver token. "Probably. The *matula* likes his little games. But I've been living on borrowed time since the right bastard saved my life. In exchange, I was made to leave my command in the middle of night, a stranger's mutilated corpse left behind for my legion to burn. All I have is my duty to fulfill my bargain: follow the orders of the Navigatus and kill monsters where I find them. And when the Many-Winged says the ring is mine, then that's how it is."

He took the ring and turned it in his hands. Unadorned, silver-white metal shone cleanly in the lamplight. He looked up at Wurzy. She nodded, eyes serious, mouth closed so her small tusks overlaid her upper lip, dimpling the skin there.

He slid it on. Nothing. He waited a bit. Nothing.

"Well, so much for the ring of great power," he said, standing up. "Tomorrow, we'll head west to return the young fool we rescued. We'll look along the way for this *great evil.*"

As he said it, he felt the slightest pull, like a longing for something he didn't know he was missing. He glanced up sharply, to the southwest, beyond the tent walls.

Huh.

From their expression, neither of his companions missed the movement, one with sharp interest, and the other with regret.

"What's this thing called, anyway?"

"I call it our doom, Sextus," his healer replied very softly and stepped to one side. Set on his finger, the ring tugged in her direction, and Sextus darted a hard look at her. Before he could turn his look into a stare, she'd raised her hood, set her shoulders, and turned to the entrance. Pausing, she said over her shoulder:

"You could call it the Ring of Obligation. The urk name is tied to their quest: *Cruthu An Asag Shedu.*"

"*Curuthuu!*" Wurzy howled, shattering the quiet. "*Curuthu arg bythcrzzz an hwalla an Asag Shedu doost!*"

Sextus looked to Estella for more translation, but she'd already slipped into the darkness beyond the tent.

The late fall sun beat down, warming the steel-and-brass armor that Sextus wore. No breeze stirred to cut the dust or cool the men. Behind the command party, the even tramp of iron hobnails made a comforting sort of marching music against the good stone Roman road. The column had been passing small farms and settlements all morning, and they were approaching a typical example. Ahead lay a paved square, surrounded by several small brick-and-wood huts centered on a well and watering trough. A nice tavern of white plaster took pride of place. Oversized barns lay beyond. Far to one edge, the village funeral grounds were an ashy-gray counterpoint to the low, rolling hills covered in the golden stubble of last month's harvest. Sextus decided the tavern looked like a good spot to rest.

He turned in his saddle to see how the column was spread out. Immediately behind his horse, Estella rode. Her features were invisible in the deep shade of a heavy, hooded traveling cloak. Beside her, Wurzy perched uncomfortably on a mare, escorted by a single legionnaire whose eyes rarely left the urk's form. Sextus had ordered all her weapons restored to her, and the urk bristled with matched pairs of dirks, knives, and wickedly curved daggers. Behind them, the ranks of the first century, nearly a hundred strong, marched confidently. The hospital wagon, the portable smithy, and several others followed, then a second century of infantry, mule-drawn battle engines, and more wagons stuffed with provisions and camp followers. On *their* heels came a third century of infantry, then finally Sextus' German mercenaries. The column was long enough to be mostly hidden by a low rise, but Sextus was confident his centurions would be keeping the remaining troops in good order.

"So you got a magic ring for rescuing the young fop, eh?" Cato asked, swaying easily as his mount paced alongside Sextus'. For all that he had come up through the infantry, the seasoned centurion could ride. "I'd prefer a few talents of gold and a pretty maiden. Say, two maidens, both wet as October!"

"Maybe you should settle for a grandmother in drought, Cato,"

Gracos said, matching the position of the first-spear position on the other side of Sextus' horse. "Old infantrymen should know their limitations. Any engineer would know to ask for a shipload of Falernian red."

The artificer and officer for Sextus' siege train scanned ahead, his eyes and deeply pitted face shaded by the brim of his black-crested helmet. Underneath, he was as bald as an egg, courtesy of a naptha accident.

"But I don't see the *ala*; how far ahead did you send them, sir?"

"I ordered Severus to screen south, just in case there's another surprise off the road," Sextus replied. "Pass the word we're stopping here. Let the men get some shade. Water the animals."

"Uh, sir," Gracos said, coughing into a gloved fist. "As you ordered, I spent some time with the rescuee, as it were, pouring some wine into him last night while the Lady Estella tended the hurts of his soldier. Good lad that, ex-Legio IX, back from Egypt."

Sextus gestured for the engineer to continue.

"He told me his family is rich as Crassus," Gracos said, speaking a bit faster. "So, I might have talked you up a bit, friendly-like, to make sure his master was proper grateful. You know, so's he understood how things lay."

"And how do things lay, Gracos?"

All Sextus received in reply was a brief sunny smile as Gracos turned his horse to canter back to the column. Sextus caught Cato's meaningful glance and sighed. A moment later, the rescued noble slid into Gracos's spot. His wardrobe had been refreshed from the wagon they'd added to the column, and the youngster's sword hung in its garish scabbard. Red eyes and pale cheeks hinted the previous evening's wine was still making itself felt. Since Sextus was planning on using the man's family estates to replenish his supplies, a modicum of politeness was in order.

"*Legatus*," the young man said, bringing his fist to chest, legion-fashion.

Sextus gave him a nod. It was simpler—and more advantageous—than correcting the boy.

"Know that I, Marcus Istacidius Zosimus, am most grateful for your timely assistance," he declaimed, shoulders thrown well back. "You saved my life, and perhaps my companion, Arnis. My father will be most grateful."

Sextus remained impassive. A quick glance toward Cato's

carefully schooled features suggested he, too, recognized the name. The Istacidius gens had profited from sale of grain, oil, and beasts to all sides during the unpleasantness of multiple civil wars in a single year. The cadet branch, Zosimus' family, had senators in their pocket and extensive lands south of Rome. Fabulously wealthy, they might be persuaded to use their wealth to reward the return of their scion.

Which would help refit the cohort.

Sextus essayed the briefest bow toward Marcus.

"Arnis can't yet rise, but he's most grateful, Your Excellency," the young noble went on, plummy tones ringing a trifle too loudly. "Your healer isn't just a most beauteous goddess, she's a miracle worker! She spent hours during the night, ensuring what blood remained in his body stayed where it belonged! How she saved him I don't know, for his wounds were most sore, but we owe her thanks. I will sacrifice a choice bull to Apollo, and two rams for Ascelpius in her name!"

"Spare the beasts, kind Marcus," Sextus replied, raising one palm placatingly. "Like this cohort, Estella does her duty as she finds it. If it's thanks you seek to offer, perhaps your father would allow us to camp near his estate, to rest the horses, and repair our equipment? In the while, Estella rides behind us, and you can thank her yourself."

He watched as Marcus twisted in his saddle and bowed with practiced elegance toward the healer's hooded form. Sextus narrowed his eyes at the smoothness of the maneuver.

"My father will insist on a banquet for you and your officers," Marcus said. Beaming, he turned back to face Sextus. "Of course, you must come to rest and celebrate your great victory! Naturally, make good any damage your valiants suffered saving me! You must tell my father of your duel with the giant. I saw only a part of it, but your sword was like living quicksilver. Truly, you are touched by Achilles!"

"You flatter me, but I and all of my men merely labor in the emperor's service," Sextus replied, pulling off the road. The command group, as well as Marcus, followed, making room for the infantry to march past. "It's our duty to ensure you are both returned safely to your families."

"Sir, your centurion told me you are the commander of the Tenth Fretensis," Marcus said, gesticulating at the column behind them, eyes brightening. "And in addition to the glory you earned crushing the Jewish rebellion, now you've been given a magic ring by the gods!"

"Cato has misinformed you." Sextus glared in the other direction, but his aggravation slid right off Cato, if the centurion's smug look was any indication. "I command an auxiliary cohort for the Navigatus, honor enough for any man. As to a magic ring, I claimed a token on behalf of my master. We hunt monsters to protect Rome, but honest steel and Roman discipline have more to do with our victories than magic and the whim of the gods."

Sextus heard a snort from behind, where Estella sat.

"Your lady mocks you?" Marcus said, frowning over his shoulder. He followed Sextus' lead and dismounted in the courtyard. A groom hustled up to collect reins. The usual commotion surrounding a break in marching order began. The wagons holding the ballistae and scorpions creaked past, drawn by sweating mules.

"She isn't my lady," Sextus said, dusting off his lorica with both hands, and removing his helmet. Sweat had darkened his hair. "Estella is a master healer, and tends to our wounded, and such victims as we can rescue."

"Your pardon, sir," Marcus bowed. "I didn't realize she was simply the *therapeutes*. I thought her claimed."

"Claimed?" Sextus couldn't quash a guffaw, and the men nearby showed toothy grins. "No, Estella isn't mine to claim."

Marcus bowed fulsomely and stepped away.

Before Sextus could act on the impulse to address the gleam spied in Marcus' eye, Cato was introducing the innkeeper, and then Gracos wanted to discuss the state of the siege equipment. By the time the tedious business was finished, Severus reported from his scouting, and the taller cavalryman opened a leather cylinder, extracting a scroll decorated with a familiar deep red seal.

"*Salve*, Legatus," the cavalryman said, bringing his fist to his chest.

The horses entering the corral neighed nervously.

"Well?" Sextus said, hand outstretched for the message.

"Ran into a messenger looking for us, sir," Severus replied. "His horse nearly foundered."

The ground very gently shifted, and both men reflexively controlled their mounts.

"Damned earthquakes." Sextus began quickly skimming the

note. "Hmm. Navigatus has learned a section of Praetorians has been dispatched from Rome."

"Those assholes," Cato said, gesturing rudely with his thumb. "Chosen of Mars, that lot. Just ask 'em. Think they're hot shit in their fancy armor."

"The best Senatorial bribes can buy," Severus laughed. "What's the emergency, sir—is there an orphanage in need of a good terrorizing?"

"No," Sextus said, annoyed. He flipped the scroll over to continue reading. "Suspicion of usurping imperial honors on a coastal estate in Campania. We're to render aid if needed."

"That's weird, sir," Severus scratched his chin. "Is—"

"You dare!"

On the heels of Estella's exclamation came a wordless yell, but the bestial screech that followed arrested Sextus' attention, and the bustling activity about him paused.

"Legatus!"

Sextus trotted toward the commotion, automatically joined by his officers, and a pair of Severus' cavalrymen.

A frozen tableau met the party as they pushed through the ring of villagers and the cohort's servants.

Estella was sprawled in the hard dirt of the square, one arm shielding her face. Her hood remained barely in place, perhaps stirring slightly in the breeze they'd been missing. Marcus stood frozen above her, a hand held to his own cheek. The other arm was outflung, as though he'd just thrown a stone across his body. The reason for Marcus' immobility was obvious. Wurzy, standing within half an armspan from the noble, had her twin short swords around his neck, scissor fashion. Anyone who'd ever crossed blades with an urk knew of their great strength. A simple twist of the wrists would send his head on a bloody arc.

"What in Pluto's flea-infested crotch is going on?" Sextus demanded. "Wurzy, swords down!"

"*Stheno ash furzn negryxxzny?*" The she-urk looked to Estella, and jerked her head toward Sextus.

Sextus didn't speak urkish, but he recognized a question when he heard it.

Take this one's head or listen to the big man, lady?

Estella nodded, the motion clear through her hood, and in a blink, Wurzy sheathed her swords over her back, the blades slipping into the twin scabbards as though they had eyes of their own. The little crowd took a half step back and Marcus sidled a bit farther to one side.

"What's the meaning of this?" Sextus demanded. Inside, the urge to spill blood stirred, like a serpent uncoiling toward a tasty morsel.

"The fop propositioned me, Sextus," Estella said as she was pulled to her feet by Wurzy. From the shadow of her hood, her voice grew louder. "Then laid hands upon my person. Since his action lacked honor, I marked him with my hand, but the oaf dared to strike me in return. I was so surprised, I fell over my own feet, but I am unharmed. As your vassal, Wurzy did no more than what she thought was appropriate."

The legionnaires within hearing began muttering.

"Lies, honored Legatus!" Marcus exclaimed, lowering his now clenched hand. A delicate pink handprint was already blooming on his cheek. "I no more than offered to bed the wench—she isn't yours. Unclaimed, you said! Besides, she dared strike me! A servant, even one with healing skills, should be gratefu—"

Simultaneously, a few legionnaires drew, Wurzy's hands blurred back to her swords, and the god's power surged, fighting for release.

Sextus would control it all.

"Hold!"

Sextus' bellow stopped all motion.

"Marcus Istacidius Zosimus, I don't know how you treat the workers on your estates," he said. He took a deep breath and permitted it to slowly trickle out his nose, knowing his example could serve others. "But in this command, no one lays hands on the servants of others. Worse, Estella is no servant."

The circle of muttering, armed men around them thickened as whispers spread the tale. Their anger was palpable. In a land where an infected battle wound usually meant death, most of the legionnaires had been saved by Estella. They looked at the armed nobleman like a pack of wolves considering how to divide a lapdog.

Marcus' eyes darted side to side, and he paled.

Sextus took another deep breath, put his hands on hips, and kept his right hand well clear of the hilt of his *spatha*.

Estella was standing, apparently unhurt, Wurzy at her elbow. The urk stood calmly, arms held slightly away from her torso, not looking at anyone in particular, and yet watching everything. Any veteran would recognize the quiet signature of dangerous competence.

"A terrible misunderstanding, entirely my error," Marcus said, possibly intuiting the urk's stance as well. He sketched a bow toward Estella, and looked for an opening to escape the circle, finding only hard looks. One hand twitched toward his marked face. "Whatever I may do to apologize, I will surely do."

"Perhaps we should step into the cooler tavern to dispel ill feeling over shared wine," Sextus said, gesturing toward the nearby building. "Apologies could be tendered, and amity restored."

"Acceptable," Estella replied from within her hood.

"My d-deepest apologies, honored Legatus," Marcus said. His eyes darted from side to side. "I'm very sorry for my boorish actions. I find need for reflection, pray allow me to return in a short while, and we can repair inside."

At a gesture from Sextus the circle opened toward the corral, and the young man not quite ran in that direction. A minute later, fading hoofbeats suggested he was not going to return very soon, after all. The faintest tug on Sextus' ring finger suggested his hope of restoring this cohort's fortunes was receding as well.

Sextus looked to Estella, who shrugged. The soldiers and servants dispersed. The excitement was over.

Sextus sighed, and realized he was still holding the forgotten scroll.

The fucking work never ends.

"Well, that didn't go so great, sir," Cato said, looking to the west as Sextus read to the end of the message. Cato turned around when heard Sextus' grunt of surprise. "You'd need an urk tracker to follow the boy now. Any point in going on? I was all set to wrap myself around some of that high-class wine, but now I wouldn't bet a clipped denarius against daddy's gratitude."

"Are we going on?" Sextus replied, raising his eyes from the scroll in the direction his rescuee had fled. "By Dis, yes! The name of the estate where the Praetorians were sent? Same as the place I hoped to refit. Villa Istacidius. The young fop's father. A bit of luck and we can beat the Praetorians there. Either he'll give us the refit, or we can help ourselves after his arrest."

"So now we're the broke legionnaire asking an Aventine madam for a leg over on credit," Cato snorted. "And as welcome."

✧ ✧ ✧

"Please, enter, and be welcome to my home!" the short, robed man exclaimed. "Rest your horses and men, most noble Sextus Lucilius Bassus! Hero of Herodium! Master of Marchaerus! Savior of my only son, foully attacked on the emperor's own road!"

Sextus didn't break stride, despite the embarrassing praise. At least the greeting removed any doubt of Zosimus the Elder's identity. A rich, ankle-length linen tunic, edged in purple and gold left short, spindly arms bare, and failed to conceal a fat belly. Zosimus' face was pale with makeup, like a Roman street performer. Carefully pressed ringlets were plastered to his forehead and temples. Zosimus' personal decoration was of a piece with the surroundings.

To each side of the deeply carved and gaudily painted stone arch, wings of servants bowed in their festival best, and a band of horns and drums was banging on in the background. Brilliant, brass-backed torches illuminated the paved lane onto the estate and blazed a welcome visible for the last league of the two-day march to the Istacidius estate. The face of a two-story manor rose at the back of the courtyard, and Sextus glimpsed an outdoor, curtained pavilion, also brilliantly lit, to one side.

The elder Zosimus waved imperiously, and a pair of servants trotted up, one bearing a tray of finely wrought glass stemware, and another a silver ewer. Behind them, more staff were drawn up in a long line leading to the stairs of the pavilion, inside which low tables, couches and more servants waited. Apart from the considerable armament of Sextus and his three hundred, there wasn't a weapon in sight.

Better, Sextus had arrived in advance of the Praetorians.

Sextus swung down, hiding his grin and handing reins off to eager hands. Boots thudded behind him as his immediate officers dismounted. Crisp orders swung the infantry past into the courtyard.

"Greetings, guarantor of my family!" The little, oily man minced right up to Sextus, and seized his hand, kissing it. "A toast to the noble Roman legions, and wine for all your men! Then we feast!"

Sextus accepted a glass, not quite pulling away from the man's soft grasp. Carts, laden with racks of wine amphorae, were drawn up to one side, and as he watched, yet another pair of servants were lifting a full amphora and trotting after the first century, which had stamped past and was grounding arms.

Excited murmurs were audible from the ranks.

"I, Decimus Istacidius Zosimus, father to Marcus, whom you rescued at the peril of your own life, welcome you to my Herculaneum estate!" Zosimus exclaimed, flinging his arms wide and sending a splash of wine into the neatly swept flagstones. "We've eagerly awaited you, to give thanks for your protection. Marcus has not ceased singing your praises!"

The scented oil Zosimus wore was bearable at this distance only because of the sea breeze gently stirring the crest on Sextus' bronze helmet.

"Salve, most honored Decimus," Sextus said, trying to keep his eyebrows from climbing any further up his forehead. "Is young Marcus well? He left in a bit of a h—"

"Yes, yes," Decimus replied, airily waving both hands, as a richly garbed servant tried desperately to match the arc of his master's empty glass with a serving jug of wine. "He told me all about his mistake. A young man, eh? All piss and vinegar and the excitement of living through his first real fight! Still, he's quite embarrassed, and wanted to wait to see if you remained angry with him before he apologized."

The portly man waved one hand and Zosimus the younger emerged from the pavilion. The youth bowed from the top step.

"It can happen like that," Sextus said, nodding in return before sipping the unexpectedly good wine. "No further thanks or apologies are required, kind Decimus."

"Please, refresh yourself as we go into the feast," the short man said, waving forward a very pretty attendant whose thin, white tunic was cut to emphasize, rather than conceal. A brass plaque hung from her throat. The menial immediately began gently wiping Sextus' forearms and brow with a damp, scented towel. "I have wine and roast pork and mutton on the way to all your men as we stand here."

Gracos' wagons creaked past as Sextus waited with his beaming host. More servants appeared, cleaning the travel dust from the officers as they dismounted. Sextus again glanced through curtains into the richly appointed pavilion. It was a permanent structure, obviously meant to entertain. Figures inside stirred, Zosimus' other guests, perhaps. Behind him he heard Severus slurping wine, and the distinctive tread of Cato's hobnails.

"This must be the most revered Lady Estella!" Sextus heard

Decimus exclaim. He turned to see Estella approach, lowering her hood in the evening darkness as Zosimus burbled on. "Your healing talent is eclipsed only by your beauty, most honored lady! Marcus insufficiently described your splendor and grace!"

"This one lives well, Sextus," Estella said as an aside, before meeting Zosimus' gaze, and surveying the riches on display. Her waist-length braids swayed as she nodded in approval. "I wager you don't waste time with the work of administrators and functionaries, Decimus Zosimus.'"

"Bureaucracy is the bane awarded by the Fates to those who rise too far," chuckled Decimus, moving to her side, and settling her hand on his forearm. Servants pulled the curtains open, and Sextus noted a handful of civilian men. Some stepped out, softer versions of their host, if that were possible. Sextus' officers straightened. Servants descended from the pavilion steps with platters of delicacies.

Introductions proceeded, and while the younger Zosimus remained in the pavilion's doorway, the elder introduced local landowners whose paint and perfume aped his own. Cato grunted appreciatively, mouth full of sweetbread. Severus just nodded, waving the wine bearer forward for a refill. Wurzy, her face covered in wrappings that left only her eyes visible, took her recently self-appointed station behind Estella.

"Lady Estella's personal servant," Sextus said in reply to Zosimus' suddenly wrinkled brow. "A pet of sorts."

"Indeed, Sextus, you're quite the mystery," Zosimus said, replacing his frown with a twisty sort of smile. "When Marcus reported he'd encountered the legatus of the Tenth Fretensis, I said, 'Impossible!' *That* Sextus Lucilius Bassus died from illness, on campaign, a few years ago. When he claimed you have a magic ring taken from a giant urk warlock, I said, 'Nonsense!'—good Romans don't traffic in magic, especially not a man of the Frumentarii. Yet, I spy it on your finger. When he related that even though he'd laid hands on your lady, his life had been spared, I said, 'Never!'—Legatus Bassus, who destroyed the Jewish army, is renowned for many things, but not mercy. Yet, Marcus lives. Such innovation suggests a new way to be Roman, no?"

Sextus stiffened a trifle.

The Navigatus had lectured him on civility. Even the Many-Winged, so enamored of violence, had on occasion rewarded a more politic response. Sextus would do politics, if it meant refitting his cohort.

"Your pardon, kind Decimus," Estella said, smiling a bit more broadly than usual. "I do recall Plato said something about need being the true creator. Rome has prospered by taking the best of every land and making it her own. And, as I told your son, I am the healer to the cohort, not lady to the legatus."

Sextus regarded his wine, considering answers short of tossing the glass in Zosimus' face. Anything he told this fool would be buried in Vespasianus' dungeons soon enough. Thus, the commander of the Fraternitas Monstrum drained off the last swallow of wine in his glass and extended it for a fresh pour.

The wine bearer swayed, spilling a few drops, as the pavilion shook briefly. Shadows shifted minutely as the hanging lanterns swayed back to stillness.

Who said he couldn't do politics?

"Even the mountain itself wants to hear the tale, Sextus," Zosimus said. "Please?"

"You seem to have the shape of the matter already, kind Decimus," Sextus said. "Maybe I've invented a new way of being Roman. What matters is we live and serve at the will of the emperor. What Ceasar Vespasianus needs, our cohort provides, so yes, necessity is the mother of invention. I obeyed our master and brought Judea to heel, perhaps too well, for a god changed the nature of my service, plucking me from my legion. But my duty didn't change, and duty is father to destiny. Now I serve Rome by killing monsters. If it was the intent of the Many-Winged to change the destiny of Masada, it mattered not at all, because the defenders did for themselves in any case, and Roman rule again stretches unchallenged from Asia Minor to Aegyptus. As for the rest, I answer to the Navigatus, not to a merchant, even one so esteemed and considerate of his guests."

Decimus stiffened a bit. For a moment, only the restless stamp of a horse could be heard. Sextus watched his host's face harden. A decision reached, then.

"The bluff soldier makes too little of his fame," Decimus finally retorted, eliciting polite titters from his coterie. Partially concealed by the extra flesh on his face, piggish eyes shone in the lamplight, and settled on Wurzy. "As for duty, if you hunt monsters for the Navigatus, why bring one to my home?"

Everyone within earshot, from the enslaved to the battle-hardened Roman soldiers, understood the preamble of questions, rudely stated in the courtyard without pretense of privacy, before a meal, was Zosimus' calculated declaration of his low regard for Sextus, his men, and their master.

Sextus' expression never changed, but the stem of his glass snapped, a spot of blood appearing on his calloused fingers.

No man who'd fought Vitellius, then on his way to becoming a second Nero, in battle after bloody street battle, and then turned about to single-handedly demolish a pack of flesh-tearing nymphs while armed with nought but a simple *pugio,* felt a need answer to a *merchant*, however wealthy. Sextus wasn't of a mind to indulge a man already under investigation by the emperor's personal guard, let along subject himself even to casual questioning, refit be damned!

Decimus had not yet made a move to the open pavilion, moistly stroking Estella's hand instead. Estella's features were frozen, braids hanging absolutely still. Cato dropped the rest of whatever he'd been stuffing in his mouth, and Severus discarded his glass as well, dispensing with the nicety of a tray. The tinkle of broken glass brought the Romans to the quivering edge of action.

Fuck politics.

"What of giving yourself imperial airs, Decimus Istacidius Zosimus?" Sextus said, moving his hand closer to the hilt of his *spatha*. "Even now riders come here, to demand answers for Rome—perhaps to questions related to your purple and gold."

"Oh, dear," Zosimus simpered, eyes locked on Sextus. "Riders, whatever will I do? Do you mean these?"

With that, six additional figures, big men, emerged from the pavilion. The black-and-white dorsal crests adorning their brilliantly gilded helmets were unmistakable. Each was in full armor, polished brass and tinned steel gleaming. All wore full cavalry masks, the features of each rider completely covered by idealized, armored likenesses, leaving only holes for the eyes and mouth. Swords as long as Sextus' own were sheathed, and every rider carried a tall, hexagonal shield. The only surface not covered by steel bands, silvered-scale armor, or leather were their hands. Sextus didn't need to check the unique, gold-enameled scorpion sigils on their shields.

Praetorians.

Self-styled bully boys who served themselves as much as they served the empire. Officially assigned with the security of the emperor's household, the Praetorians worked in concert with the Navigatus' spies and special teams. In practice, however, the Frumentarii and the emperor's personal guard worked at cross-purposes as often as they cooperated.

"They're not here for me," Decimus said, backing up the steps. "They're here for you."

The six approached closely, and Severus began to speak, but the leader of the Praetorians descended a further step, until he was face-to-face with Sextus. The tall man paused one step up, placing his eyes well above Sextus' own, and within Sextus' personal space.

This probably worked to intimidate some people. They liked their theatrical touches, the Praetorians.

"Sextus Lucillius Bassus?" he asked, voice as raspy as a farrier's file.

"Who asks?" Sextus replied.

"The Emperor's Guard, Bassus," the man replied. The extra emphasis on Sextus' *cognomen* carried an audible sneer. "Relinquish your cohort to your first centurion, surrender your sword, and come with me."

A ripple of reaction radiated away from the command group. Sextus could hear the distinctive sounds of his men preparing for battle. Gracos had faded back and begun marshalling the nearest engineers. Cato was quietly chivvying the first century into ranks. Severus ordered his *ala* back into the saddle, remaining himself at his commander's side.

Servants vanished, and the grossly cherubic Decimus had mounted the steps, clear of any pending action. The other five Praetorians descended all the way to the courtyard, standing in echelon from their leader, facing the hundred or more men of the cohort, which had already filed into the courtyard. Encouragingly, no one on either side had yet reached for a weapon. Behind Sextus, the sound of a horse adjusting position appeared to catch the Praetorian's attention, and the man's steel-masked visage turned to orient on someone behind Sextus.

Sextus risked a glance.

Wurzy was mounted behind her mistress, sniffing. She pulled her face wrappings away and snuffled again. Quicker than an ordinary man could move, she drew her swords and screamed a challenge.

"Rlurrrrrghazzbl!"

Estella stared at the Praetorian whose face remained hidden behind the impassive silver faceplate.

The slap of palms against sword hilts throughout the cohort was unmistakable. The metal-masked Praetorians remained still.

"Boss, are we really going to do this?" Severus asked, his perfectly level voice an indicator of stress. "Maybe we wind down Lady Estella's pet, and not fight the pretty boys?"

"You will surrender your urk prisoner as well," the Praetorian officer ordered, still looking over Sextus' shoulder. "Now."

"You have an arrest decree from the Senate?" Sextus asked, using formal language and otherwise carefully remaining motionless. "Or a signed order from the Chief of the Frumentarii?"

"Praetorians like to act tough behind that fancy armor, but you'll bleed like anyone else if you try to arrest our commander," Severus said, raising his voice unhelpfully.

"Arrogant fool," the Praetorian pointed at Severus, and finally laid hand to his *spatha* hilt. He pivoted back to Sextus. "You know my authority. If you come with me quietly, perhaps I will spare your woman."

Severus released the reins to his mount, which was standing patiently behind him.

"The six of you plan to . . . what's the word . . . discipline a Roman cohort?" he asked, bridling. He showed a couple inches of steel, matching the Praetorian. "I'd like to see you try!"

"Done," the Praetorian said, drawing and cutting in a single motion, moving so fast the sword simply appeared on the far side of the Praetorian's target. Sextus watched, disbelieving, as his cavalry leader was cut down. Severus wasn't beheaded, so much as his arm, shoulder, and head exploded free of the bloody trunk that remained, making the nearest horse shy and plunge. A fan of blood showered the scout adjacent, blinding the man to the return strike of his murderer.

Chaos reigned as the other Praetorians drew steel and attacked the closest legionaries, every bit as fast as their leader, and with similar results. Screams of shock reverberated from the battle-hardened legionaries.

Without hesitation, Sextus drew upon his gift and attacked

Severus' assailant. Sudden, familiar heat flared through Sextus, but the Praetorian parried the strike.

The Praetorian's first cut at Sextus was nearly as strong as the hammer stroke of the tall urk, and every bit as fast as Sextus. The Praetorian whirled and delivered another terrifying blow, this time catching the horse of Severus' *decurion* across the neck, wholly decapitating the hapless animal. The headless trunk collapsed to the ground as fast as a curtain yanked off a window by a strong man. The Praetorian's return stroke cleaved the falling rider from forehead to navel, and fresh offal spilled steaming onto the stones of the courtyard. The mounts of two of Severus' riders began plunging as they scented the sudden, overwhelming amount of their fellow's blood, ignoring the riders sawing at their reins. Fighting for control, the riders were borne away on terrified horses.

Urkish screeching in the background suggested Wurzy was entering the fray.

"Sextus, duck!"

He didn't argue and followed the example of the surviving riders, evading to one side in a hasty roll.

"THROW!"

Fully forty javelins, enough to momentarily shade the torchlight, sleeted past and crashed into the Praetorians. The impact made them reel. Most of the thrown weapons glanced from the steel armor or were caught by the hexagonal shields. Three of the fully armored men had javelins stuck in shoulder or hip joints. The far Praetorian had a red-fletched arrow in the eyeslit of his cavalry mask, which should have dropped him to the ground. Sextus watched from his back as the man ripped the arrow free, the slender shaft bending as the wicked point emerged in a welter of black blood.

Black. Blood.

"UNDEAD!"

Sextus couldn't have said if it was his scream of caution that rang across the courtyard, or another's. Perhaps it was everyone who watched as all the javelins that had found flesh were torn free and dropped to the flagstones. Wurzy screamed again.

"*Rlurrrrrghazzbll*"

Then the command from Cato: "THROW!"

A second flight joined the first. Most of these missed, deflected by Praetorian shields or armor. Then the Praetorians yanked javelins from their bodies again and closed the distance, resuming the carnage.

The cold voice reverberated in Sextus' skull, as unwelcome as it had been infallible.

"DO NOT TOUCH THESE. KEEP ONE ALIVE. FIRE FOR THE REST."

"Gracos!" Sextus yelled as loudly as he was able. "The grenades!"

In three seconds, he rose, parried, dodged, struck, and parried again as the Praetorian undead used the same blinding speed, trying to close and destroy its target.

Namely, Sextus.

He gave ground again, remaining in contact with the leader. Sextus shut his mind to the screaming in the courtyard. He could do nothing about his men dying as they tried to overwhelm the other five Praetorians.

"On line, on line! Close up!" an unknown file closer bellowed at the survivors. Measured, synchronous hobnails announced the vanguard of the second century as they used overwhelming numbers against their foe.

"Light!" Gracos' voice echoed, even as Sextus drew farther back, trading lighting strokes with the Praetorian. "Cast!"

The unremarkable tinny crackling of the glass shells belonging to Gracos' specials breaking against their targets sounded. A few seconds later, the characteristic *whooomf* of the pitch, honey, and twice-distilled brandy igniting followed, as the new fuses that were Gracos' invention touched off the incendiary payload, creating five human-shaped torches. Another salvo of grenades burst alight as soon as they broke against the Praetorians, ignited by the armor already aflame. The undead continued to fight, keening eerily. The second century advanced, using their shield wall and pila to hold the flaming Praetorians at a distance, while probing their armored legs. A few of Sextus' men were also alight, and ran screaming into the night.

The keening caused the undead Praetorian officer to hesitate, just for a moment, leaving Sextus with the briefest window of opportunity. He fully loosed the heat in his breast, and struck with all his might. A full overhand sword stroke hewed downward, unstoppable by any living man. The lack of peripheral vision caused by the Praetorian's armored mask should have been lethal, but the Praetorian flinched away at the very last instant. The helmet's neck flange caught the full force of the blow. Sextus's augmented strength staggered his target, and the speed of the Many-Winged sang through him, as he hewed even more. The Praetorian was impossibly fast, and overwhelmingly strong, but artless. Sextus' second cut on his momentarily stunned opponent was a disarm, and the Praetorian's sword flew into the air. Sextus' final strike connected with the impassive features of the mask, hammering the man's face to one side, the silver covering falling free.

The Praetorian turned back. Red eyes, like burning rubies, met his own, and the man's misshapen face twisted in hate and rage. Gray skin was exposed under the mask, and the yellow teeth were pointed and sharp, like a dog's.

Wurzy blurred into the fight, yelling, repeating "*Rlurrrrrghazzbl*!" and shoving Sextus rearward several steps.

Ah. So "rlurrrrrghazzbl" means wights. Good to know.

"Wights!" Sextus bellowed. "Don't let them touch you!"

The legionnaire across from Sextus drove his gladius into the Praetorian's armpit. Without breaking its gaze from Sextus, the wight grabbed the legionnaire's bare arm and the man dropped, motionless.

Wurzy's twin swords fanned in a complicated pattern ending when she took the wight's hand off at the wrist, and it fell to the ground, fingers twitching. The wight hammered her with its shield, and she flew back, as one of the Praetorian's red eyes sprouted an arrow with familiar red fletching. It ignored the shaft, batting a javelin from the air.

"Down it!" Sextus yelled, keeping the Praetorian undead's attention.

Gracos trotted up, holding a grenade in one hand, and a red-hot glowing ball with tongs, but before Sextus could order him not to throw, the Praetorian took another shaft, this one finding a small gap along a greave. Sextus collected a discarded pilum in his left hand and threw at point-blank range. The needle-sharp point found a gap beneath the damaged helmet and the weapon sagged downward as it stuck in the unclean meat. Gracos used the javelin shaft to lever the armored figure face down, and Sextus helped keep it there.

"Estella, order her to cut off the feet," Sextus said, focusing on the wriggling undead, hoping his healer would be within shouting distance. A phlegmy exchange in the background later, the urk reappeared to helpfully remove the undead's remaining hand and both feet. It fought mightily, but to no avail.

"CALL FORWARD THE FEY CHAMPION."

Sextus jerked again, but this time it was indistinguishable from the movement of the *pilum* Sextus was using to hold the Praetorian still.

Three sentences in three days, that's a record.

"Another champion?" Sextus yelled, jerking his head left and right. "Whose, now?"

Nearby, Sextus could see five dwindling pyres, undead figures still moving, each pinned to the chinks in the flagstones by several *pila*.

Estella was alongside, bow in hand.

"Roll it over," she ordered, poised with an arrow nocked. "Hold it still."

Sextus gestured, and Gracos, with the help of a few legionnaires, turned the mightily struggling wight on its back. Another man stepped on the creature's forehead with his iron-hobnailed boot, fixing it in place.

Estella leaned forward, staring intently into the wight's remaining red eye, braids slowly stirring of their own accord. Gracos noticed and leaned back instinctively, shooting a glance of unmistakable concern at his officer.

"Gracos, minutes ago, a rich man offered you as much free wine as you wanted," Sextus said, winking. "Now you're astonished by a little hair moving around?"

Estella addressed a single word to Wurzy. A moment later, the urk struck the wight's head free, but all the separated parts continued to spasm. Wurzy hawked, spat, and stalked toward the legionnaires pinning the remaining undead to the ground.

"About this one, lady?" Gracos inquired, stepping on a detached hand that was alternately stretching and clenching.

"Fire will purify the unclean bodies and release the captive spirits within."

"You know my policy on monsters that don't have the good grace to die when we take their heads," Sextus said, nodding to Gracos. The artificer promptly emptied a bottle of lamp oil on the dismembered wight, while Sextus used the borrowed pilum to hold the trunk in place. One soldier helpfully donated some burning wagon debris while onlookers stepped back a pace or three. The separated parts began to wiggle more intensely in the spreading flames.

Sextus savored the sight for a moment, and then began the familiar drill of containing the power within. Legionnaires began returning order to the bloodied courtyard, which was filled with their dead. Uncharacteristically, Estella wasn't already helping the littermen sort the wounded.

"There was little of the original mind left," Estella said, ignoring the activity building around them. "Yet, I could see fragments of memory and purpose. These creatures were made, and recently. Fashioned to protect something specific. A gate, like the great arches of Roman cities."

"A gate to what?" Sextus demanded. "Where?"

"The gate is not yet open," she replied. "Such gates allow passage between worlds, between gods and men, if you will. The stronger the guardian, the more dangerous the portal. Six wights, so rapidly turned and yet so strong? The corresponding danger is very great. We need the dark wizard responsible for making the wights. He will know where to look for the gate, and how to close it."

"Pardon, lady, but how great a danger are we talking?" asked Gracos, speaking for every Roman in earshot. He nudged a flexing foot and ankle back into the oil fire. "Danger like another bunch of these things, or are we talking about civil war-type danger?"

"Great danger, as in the sinking of Atlantis described by Plato."

"That's a fable," Gracos said. "A Greek fever dream."

"Sail beyond the Pillars of Hercules, boy, and tell that to the Atlanteans," Estella said, closing her eyes. Behind her, Wurzy was back, wiping one of her swords. "The Greeks made many errors, and where they did not, the fictions served the politics of their day. But Atlantis was real, and it was destroyed by infernal forces. We need Decimus Istacidius Zosimus, but I spy him not among the dead or the living."

Cato stepped forward, joining the little group gathered among the impromptu bonfires, in which the dismembered corpse were still twitching. The first spear was holding another figure bent at the waist, one arm levered upward painfully in an iron grip

"Gots a present for you, sir," he said cheerfully moving into the orange-blue circle of wight-fueled firelight. Cato stood his prisoner up abruptly. "Daddy ran like a quail, but Junior was hiding in a corner. I think he's ready to talk, pretty-like, if you want."

Sextus stared into the terrified face of Marcus Zosimus.

Estella eyes narrowed, and Wurzy snarled, the tusks forming an intimidating display.

The interrogation wasn't difficult. Cato wasn't even required to pull the usual number of fingernails.

Sextus had watched as Estella leaned so close to the cringing youth her hood hid both their faces, and muffled her speech. One set of urine-stained trousers and some persistent whimpering later, Sextus had the information from the noble-born youth. It led them up the slopes of Vesuvius, which was smoking more heavily than before.

Nearer midday, a pair of cavalrymen were waiting at the top of a steep ridge, just below the last line of trees, beyond which blasted rock led upward to the smoking mountain peak.

"Legatus, our path is blocked," one reported. "The wizard's shrine is ahead, and a line of undead more than a hundred strong bars the way."

Estella, riding behind Sextus, spurred forward a few paces.

"*Tempus fugit*, Sextus," she said, swaying in her saddle as her horse shifted its weight. "Zosimus the Elder will be preparing the ritual, and once begun, stopping it will be much more difficult."

Sextus glanced at her, and then at the strangely overcast sky. He tilted his helm to the rear and mopped his brow. The scrap of linen came away smudged with a fine gray ash.

Enough.

"Take the rest of the *ala* and screen us as we prepare," Sextus said to the centurion, taking care to keep his voice even.

The rider brought fist to chest and cantered off, shouting orders, leaving Sextus and his healer alone.

"I need more, Estella," he said, meeting her eyes. "You have power, and your magic has saved Roman lives. The value of your service to my cohort, to me, can't be summed and I know it. Yet, you hold your secrets like a miser hoards coins. But now I need more. What are we fighting and if matters are so dire, if your family has sacrificed before, why do you stay?"

Estella lowered her head, and tugged her cowl further over herself.

"Duty," she said, her voice low and clear. "Assigned by the duke of a far realm. He fought invaders, sent by one who would feel at home in your Roman underworld. Asag Shedu."

"The same name from Wurzy." Sextus raised his hand and regarded the plain silver metal. "And?"

"Asag triumphed, and we fled. Our new home can be reached by gates which are made here, in your world. The duke-my-father set three daughters as guards. The eldest stopped the adversary long ago, though it cost this world a nation. The youngest sacrificed herself to stop Asag, and the Greeks made a myth from an overweening would-be hero. I alone remain. I will show you how to stop the ceremony, and keep the gate closed. It is my duty, and I will not fail. Telling more would only lead to further questions, and time is very, very short."

The ground shook again, enough to make Sextus' mount plunge, though he quickly controlled it. He eyed Estella again, who had laid her hand on her horse's neck, keeping it immobile, if trembling and sweating.

Sextus put aside the secrets Estella continued to keep close. He knew enough and could guess most of the rest. Instead, he focused on the battle ahead, refraining from rubbing his hands in anticipation. His cohort, though battered by the surprise encounter with six wights, was designed precisely for this purpose. Even with the losses in the first century, Sextus remained confident. The dark wizard might have additional tricks, but Sextus had dealt with worse. He was ready.

"You are clearly unworried," Estella said, interpreting his silence as assent to continue. "Is this a particularly good situation?"

"It's about as straightforward as I could hope for," he replied, surveying the level field which was slowly filling with undead. "Clear away the rabble, kill Zosimus, wreck the empire-threatening ritual. Simple enough."

"It won't be simple. A necromancer with access to infernal power sufficient to raise wights in mere hours will have additional resources."

"Perhaps, but in daylight, the little perfumed bastard can't surprise me, and murder thirty of my men," Sextus answered, his voice rough. "Gracos! Deploy your engines in the center! Cato, get the infantry set, two up, one back, with the Germans and the First in reserve."

Sextus scanned the massed of men about him, frowning. The cavalry screen was unevenly split, something which would never have happened under Severus. He waved forcefully at the decurion in charge, and pointed at the problem.

The protection afforded by the modest cavalry screen went unneeded. The undead stayed put just beyond bowshot, arrayed along the opposite, wooded side of a small meadow. Now numbering a few hundred, many were naked. Sextus thought he could make out some finer clothing on some, likely on former ranking servants of the Zosimus estate.

Gracos' hoarse yelling produced good progress as the engineers mounted the mule-drawn wagons and rapidly set about assembling the scorpions, smaller and more accurate cousins to traditional *ballistae*. Horizontal crossbow-like arms were powered by twisted sinew, driving oversized arrows with finger-thick shafts and steel points capable of passing through two armored men at a time. Two stone-throwers were also being staked to the ground, improving accuracy against the kick of the wooden-framed devices. The artificer's epithets drove the crews to a frenzy of hammering, as mallets were used to drive stakes deeply into the black, rocky ground.

The Second and Third Centuries had drawn up in ranks two deep, to either side of the artillery. The cohort's standard and cornicen fell in behind the command party, where Sextus was joined by Estella, her urk guardian, and a few others, including their bound prisoner. Eventually, flagmen raised red colors by each scorpion and stone-thrower, signaling their readiness.

Sextus pointed to Gracos, who loosed his machines upon the undead. A pair of stone balls nearly half as heavy as a man, flew into the crowd opposite, knocking down several. The scorpions fired, and the stabilizing vanes on each missile made a whistling sound before passing entirely through their targets, disappearing into the woods. The undead howled, and screamed, but didn't advance. A second flight of projectiles arced out, and a third. The cacophony didn't quiet at all, as still more undead filtered out of the trees to join their fellows, in some cases walking across wriggling bodies pinned to the ground by the scorpion bolts.

"That's a lot of fucking undead, sir," Cato observed, kneeing his horse to remain still. "Don't think I've seen that many in one place before."

"The boy's father has been busy," Sextus replied, sparing a glance for Marcus Zosimus' slumped form. "We don't have a lot of time, and this lot isn't charging the way I'd hoped. Let's hurry things along. Get the infantry moving after the next volley."

Cato trotted away to warn the officers in each century, the cornu sounding again. The serried lines of Roman infantry stepped forward, advancing with the surety born of grinding opponents to dust on every battlefield in the Empire. The men stayed in contact with each other so shields could form an interlocking wall over which javelins could be thrown, and through which swords could saw their unarmored opponents bloody. Sextus tracked the motion of bobbing brass helmets, and the horsehair crests of the officers to mark the leading edge of the cohort. They were nearly halfway to their foes when the undead reacted. Perhaps the motion of the cavalry streaming to the flanks set them off, or perhaps the mind driving the undead became impatient, but the dead surged forward, their numbers seemingly unaffected by the bloody tax levied by Gracos' engineers and their projectiles.

The forces collided, the staccato succession of bodies rebounding off plywood and brass shields sounding just like washerwomen beating their rags clean. Short Roman swords licked out through narrow gaps the shield line and began threshing their unprotected enemy. The stream of possessed bodies emerging from the woods seemed endless at first. A minute passed with any slowing, then another. The wall of undead actually impeded the progress of the horde.

Whistles ordered the lines back a few steps, and more undead filled the newly vacated space, while tiring infantry renewed their red harvest. It's what Roman infantry was designed for, and the formation worked like a machine, chopping adversaries into bloody, waist-high walls before withdrawing a few steps and repeating the process, leaving the undead in scarlet windrows.

"Where did they all come from?" Sextus asked no one in particular. Cato was forward, and Estella was silent. "No matter. When Zosimus runs out of undead, we will advance farther and murder the little shit."

The avalanche slowed, then trickled to a halt.

A bit of cheering was audible, quickly squelched by the centurions.

"Well, *that* seems to be th—" Sextus was interrupted by a

wailing sound that began somewhere above the upper limit of his hearing, and deepened slowly. Bass drums sounded from deeper in the wood, deep booming percussive impacts accompanying the high-pitched wails filling the now bloody meadow.

"Sextus, ready yourself!" Estella said, stiffening. "Those drums are known to me. They come."

"Who comes?"

"The servants of Asag prepare the way. Each of my sisters heard those drums before they fell."

"Now you tell me!"

"Pull your men into the strongest defensive position you can!" Estella said, pleading. Sextus noticed Wurzy was again sniffing the air suspiciously. That wasn't good.

"Bring 'em back," Sextus ordered the *cornicen*, who nodded, spat, and applied himself to the curved brass horn, blowing the message across the field.

Second and Third Centuries continued to face front, stepping back carefully, and maintained their dressing. Sextus nodded approvingly at the steadiness of his men. The formation split again, unmasking the artillery.

"Signal, prepare to fire," Sextus ordered, and the cornu blew.

Sextus watched Gracos' head jerk upward. He looked a question at Sextus, just as hell opened the door and the first demons appeared.

They might be slightly smaller than men, but their hunched and asymmetrical build made it difficult to discern their true height. They resembled nothing so much as the spawn of a Nile crocodile and a cockroach. Pebbly, orange-streaked hide stretched over insectile limbs. The faces were horror incarnate, with pairs of interlocked jaws set below vertical rows of red eyes. Their arms ended in wickedly curved black claws. But worst of all, they were swarming in numbers to match the cohort.

Cato's leather-lunged call was audible over the entire battlefield. "Prepare to throw!"

Sextus could see the legionnaires step back, planting their rear feet in readiness, arms cocked.

"THROW!"

The first flight of *pila* sank home, tearing holes in the demons leading the charge. Where the spears penetrated a demon's thorax, black fluid spurted out, as though under pressure, and the stricken creature would drop. The second rank repeated the maneuver, then the first again, and still the demons came on, perhaps a hundred now, moving as fast as a man could run.

Gracos' order was followed an instant later by the slapping sounds of the scorpions. The stone-throwers launched incendiaries, great glass jars trailing a line of gray smoke against the blue sky. They burst on contact, engulfing the nearest demons in fire. The affected enemy roared, spinning to bite the flames, and then, maddened with pain, their fellows. The two blooms of fire hollowed out the demons' rush, but did not stop it.

"Prepare to receive!" Cato yelled, and his call was echoed down the line.

The legionnaires steadied. Sextus gave thanks for every Roman centurion with a throat of brass and balls to match.

It nearly wasn't enough. Demons hit the shield wall much harder than the undead. Sextus saw a few men fall as demons pulled their shields down, accepting lethal sword thrusts that burst the internal reservoir of ichor, drenching the legionnaires to each side even as subsequent demons exploited the gap to reach inside and kill. But the same shield wall and stabbing swords that had put paid to the undead worked nearly as well on the unarmored, unshielded demons.

He called the reserves forward, even as the *ala* guarding their flanks were pulled down and torn apart. The screaming of horses was deafening, overwhelming the roars of the enemy and the screams of their human victims. First Century steadily tramped forward as the wings of the engaged infantry bent backward like a seawall.

"*Porca mater* to Jupiter's bleeding arse!" Sextus exploded as the German mercenaries turned as one and sent their horses galloping to the rear. An arrow buzzed past, and he realized that Estella had been shooting the entire time. At her knee, her quiver was nearly empty.

The scorpions kept up a steady fire, men sweating to turn the twisted sinew and punch through several demons at once. Sextus saw Gracos personally load a stone-thrower with a bundle of almond-shaped sling bullets, then leap from the dangerously poised throwing arm to yank the trigger rope and send its bucket of lethal payload in a rapidly spreading cone, leaving several orange insect-enemies reeling.

It still wasn't enough. Immediately to either side of the cohort's standard, Sextus' men were refusing the center, defending the artillery and his person. Every few breaths, another infantryman was torn out of formation, or shredded where he stood. His troops were halved, and shrinking everywhere he could see.

Cato appeared next to him, his right arm black to the shoulder with ichor, and splattered with red blood everywhere else. His crest and his trousers were singed, perhaps courtesy of Gracos' fire-specials. One cheek-guard was missing from his helmet, and a wicked slash down his exposed face exposed red-rinsed teeth.

"Hot workth, bosss," he shouted over the din, spraying a bit of blood. Both men ignored the little extra that hit Sextus. "Maybe we try to make like those German pussies?"

"Well, Cato," Sextus replied, looking at the carnage, "I don't think we have the time."

Before Sextus could add to his answer, a shrill warbling rose above the din. Even the orange demons paused, uncertain, as the otherworldy sounds grew in volume.

Wurzy sprang forward, her sword blades already black with her enemies' lifeblood.

"*Curuthuu!*" she screamed into the sky, tusks bared. "*Curuthu arg bythcrzzz an hwalla an Asag Shedu doost!*"

And she leaped forward, seemingly alone against the orange horde.

"Shame, that," Sextus said. "She's lost her mind."

"Maybe not, Sextus," Estella said, cocking her head and glancing toward the flank where the warbling seemed loudest.

From Sextus' left side, a motley group of urks burst from the hillside brush, loping forward determinedly. The oncoming group was smaller than a Roman century, and entirely without formation. But their blood hunger was plain, and in the last few yards they accelerated, crashing into the flank of the orange demons, whirling and cutting, stabbing and killing in an orgy of revenge.

"Her clan comes for their children," Estella said, watching with the rest. "They will free the spirits or die here."

"Where th'fuh did tha' bunsh come from?" Cato said around his bleeding facial wound.

"The urks are famous trackers," Estella said, pulling a linen pad from her saddlebag and pressing it to Cato's face. He held it in place. "But skill is hardly required to follow the trail of lazy Roman soldiers."

Sextus picked out Wurzy as she used her two swords to slash eyes and sever claws. She tumbled forward like an acrobat, using the sagging corpse of a demon not yet aware of its own death as a springboard to leap head high and decapitate yet another orange enemy, sending black blood upward in a grotesque fountain.

The line of orange demons turned as one to crush the much smaller figures that fought individually. Immediately, Sextus exploited the mistake.

"First Century turn, right up their backside!" he screamed as loudly as he could. Standards waved furiously.

In half a minute, the depleted First Century passed through their fellows and took the demons from behind. The fight was hard, but the conclusion foregone. Pinned between two groups who sought not safety but retribution, the remaining orange demons were cut down, and the surviving urks and soldiers stood side by side, chests heaving.

Urks employed their jagged axes to begin methodically chopping the heads off downed demons. The crunch of the axe blades against demons' spines was a grisly counterpoint to the screaming humans who'd been struck down. Their hale fellows checked the fallen, dragging back those few who might survive, and gave mercy to the rest. Sextus assessed the wreckage. He noted Marcus Zosimus lying among the dead, victim of a demon that had broken through before being slain in turn. More critically, Sextus had fewer than a third of the men with whom he'd begun the battle with.

It still might be enough.

Then the fucking drums began beating again.

Wurzy stopped in mid-wipe of cleaning her swords, and raised her head, sniffing.

I wish she'd fucking stop doing that.

Down the field, a dozen tall orange shapes lurched out of the tree line, moving in time to the booming drum. They walked on two legs, but each was half again the size of the previous batch. Worse, these bristled with spines. As the first rank stepped fully into view, the trees rustled again. More were coming.

"Gracos, consolidate into two centuries!" Sextus said. "Cato, get that properly bound up. Take Estella to the rear. If we hold, I may need you both, yet."

A firm tug on his hand grabbed his attention, but none had touched him. Forgotten in battle, the ring tugged again, straight toward his healer. Inside her hood, he could see her blue eyes, but not much else.

"Estella, flee while you can!"

She shook her head, but he didn't have time to argue. Cato would see to her safety. Fortuna knew those who escaped would need her services.

The scorpions and onagers loosed their lethal payloads. The rocks tumbled two of the giant demons to their knees. Scorpion bolts feathered more, but those didn't stop their forward advance. The monsters reached his shield line and began crushing the depleted Roman ranks.

He didn't bother to consult the god riding his shoulder. This was a commander's affair, a soldier's business, a Roman's duty, and the Many-Winged could serve him this time.

Or not, if it chose. No matter.

Looking to the front, he released the control he'd maintained every moment of nearly every day, excepting those times he'd carefully meted out anger and violence. Closing his eyes and throwing his arms wide, he let the heat loose, holding nothing back. In a flash, it uncoiled again, a last time, filling every fiber with strength, purpose.

And rage at what was happening to his men.

Time slowed as he spurred forward. Sextus snatched an upright *pilum* that had been thrown short. He cast it, pinning two demons together and opening a path for his charge. The *spatha* simply appeared in his hand, and he swung, faster and faster, removing horned heads and elongated arms before their owners could even register surprise. To his right, he saw a clawed hand reach for another Roman shield, pulling it down and scarring the snarling gorgon decoration. The *spatha* licked out like a living thing, cleaving the front of the demon's rough carapace. Sextus saw hot, black fluid sheeting outward, each gobbet of poison glistening in a dark fan. He watched a scorpion bolt pass, each detail of the thick shaft and needle-sharp point distinguishable before it struck yet another orange enemy.

A demon raked his mount across the face, and before the animal could throw Sextus, he leaped free, using the fall to target yet another enemy, cleaving downward through a shoulder and torso. He saw a demon sever the neck of one of his centurions in a single slashing bite, shaking the man like a terrier shaking a rat, sending the brass helmet with a traverse crest slowly spinning across Sextus' field of vision.

An incorporeal wave of black fear washed across the battlefield, staggering Sextus, and every living thing still upright. Monsters reeled, and the close-packed shields of the legion clattered together. With a popping sound, movement all about him sped up to normal, and the battlefield clamor returned. Moaning wounded, screams of fear, the hoarse commands of the file closers filling holes in the thinning ranks, the rasping breath of the demons that momentarily stood still, facing Sextus.

His left arm hung useless; the gods alone knew how he'd been injured, for Sextus had no memory of a blow. His cuirass hung from one shoulder, the straps and hinges torn. He'd fought into a little empty space, forward of the wavering line of infantry, which had retreated past the abandoned wagons. He reached for the anger, and it answered, but his limbs felt heavy and his left knee oddly loose.

In more than one tight spot, Sextus had suddenly felt he—he specifically—was being watched, and he'd better look to his own safety. It had saved him in every instance because he listened. That feeling was back, and strong. He could see no new danger, however.

Before him, a score of the spiked demons remained, some visibly injured, all of them heaving and snorting, but not advancing. He watched their insectoid jaws grind hungrily as they eyed their still-standing prey. One leaned down and casually tore a red mouthful from a Roman corpse.

Yet they still didn't renew the attack.

"Maybe life is still on the table?" he asked rhetorically, for the Many-Winged had remained mute all this time.

Well?

Sextus didn't really expect a reply.

Naturally, now the Many-Winged elected to do so.

"SERVE MY PURPOSE, SEXTUS LUCILIUS BASSUS. A CHAMPION TO CLOSE THE PORTAL."

So, this time he could die. Good to know. Slaying demons and shielding his men was a worthwhile death. A Roman's death.

Amazingly, the demons continued to pause their attack, and behind him, Sextus heard Cato ordering the remaining ranks. Maybe they had a real chance. Estella could guide the next legatus better than he. As long as there weren't any new enemy.

Again, Sextus renewed his faith in the gods' sense of humor, for at that moment, a fresh wave of demons emerged from the tree line, many yards ahead.

He shrugged. A man could die only once. Sextus flicked his *spatha*, sending black droplets to the ground. He flexed his left knee experimentally, preparing for the orange avalanche.

"Lady Estella!" Sextus heard a despairing shout from his first spear, in exactly the same tone reserved for Sextus' historically bad decisions.

He turned, and saw Estella sprinting forward on foot, her mount trotting riderless back down the road. Estella was moving so fast her hood flew back. Her cloak billowed wide before tearing free, and Sextus saw her face in the daylight for the first time.

As he watched, Estella's glamour dissolved. The northern features he knew blurred, and her blond braids, whipping with the speed of her advance, began to change. Her shin-length gown and sandals likewise wavered and shifted. Her lightly tanned skin turned dusk gray, and her hands and feet, bone-white. Familiar lips thinned, and a mouthful of ivory razors shone under the Roman sun.

Her eyes widened impossibly, distorting the width of her skull, though not unrecognizably so. The glowing embers of her eyes had always before been safely banked, but now the bellows of rage blew them past red, orange, until, like twin suns, they grew too bright to gaze upon. Her braids moved independently, a slithering corona of scaled malice, each tentacle terminating in gaping, toothy mouth and jet eyes, indistinguishable from a quartet of living snakes. The flared hood of a cobra, the triangular wedge of a viper, the arrow-shaped desert krait, and the blunt, black-banded sea snake wove about her shoulders, swaying and hissing.

Sextus knew her as a friend, and still his guts went watery.

Estella skidded to a halt alongside. She was still somehow female, but her skin shone with fine, closely fitted gray scales covering every visible inch from her wide, angled cheeks, down her chest, and past her groin and down her legs.

A taloned hand cupped Sextus cheek for a moment.

"Look away, noble Ssextusss," Estella said, her voice still her own despite the sibilance. "My father callss, and it is my turn to answer."

"You are ever beautiful, my lady," Sextus said, the onrushing horde nearing. "But the Many-Winged has spoken. This is my destiny."

"Look away, Sextus," she repeated. "Asag faces more than one Chosen today. Destiny will await its turn."

She stepped past him toward the enemy, deliberately giving him her back.

Sextus clapped hands over his ears as Estella howled, high and piercing, an eagle's scream that trampled other battlefield sounds flat, and with that, the air began to sizzle as translucent lighting played upon the onrushing hoard. Its origin hidden from Sextus' sight by the curve of her face, and the coils writhing over her head, ethereal energy shot forth, like tiny, twining, glacial streams. Clear rays of energy played over the advancing horrors. Everywhere the energy touched, orange hide darkened, and demons began to claw their own bestial faces. In mid-stride, their motions slowed, then froze, the dark stain spreading across stiffening bodies. Estella's scream never ceased, lasting as long as a calm man might hold his breath. The register climbed impossibly high, and the demons in the rear brushed past the statues of their leaders, crumbling them in their haste, before meeting Estella's medusan gaze and freezing in turn.

Every last demon slowed, froze, and died under the gaze of Sextus' protector.

Could it be?

Sextus absently noted the handful of remaining urks kneeling, then throwing themselves forward on the torn, bloody ground, prostrating themselves over and over toward the Tenth's very own monster.

Could it really be? Victory?

The damned drums beat again.

Estella still faced outward. She cast about, searching for something. Sextus watched as the bone talons on her feet flexed in and out, like a great hunting cat seeking purchase on unknown ground.

"Whath's next, shir?" Cato slurred. "Fukkin' devil elephants?"

"Consolidate the line!" Sextus ordered, using his good hand to gesture with the blackened sword. "Wurzy, put your urks on the flanks!"

He watched Wurzy sniffing, and decided he didn't give a shit. Whatever came from the tree line would die.

"He comes!" Estella hissed. "Asag has found a mount!"

"Steady, steady!" an unknown file closer ordered from behind.

Sinew creaked as Gracos readied the remaining artillery. A single red flag snapped.

And a solitary, dumpy little man emerged jauntily from the trees. Sextus exchanged a confused look with bloodied Cato.

"Well, hello, Stheno," an impossibly loud voice boomed from the painted lips of Decimus Istacidius Zosimus, who continued to daintily pick his way through the carnage. Despite the distance, his words were perfectly clear. "How did I not recognize you? It's been a while since I dealt with your sister. The saucy bint cost me quite a bit of time, but I'm back."

"That's him?" Sextus asked, his brow wrinkling. "That's the terrifying god? The little pimp?"

"No," Estella said, the snake's heads mirroring her quick, sideways glance toward Sextus. "His Voice. The ritual to fully open the gate requires sacrifice, and an invitation. We must give him neither and destroy the portal."

"Be a good little Fey, Stheno," Zosimus' voice spanned the shrinking distance between them. "Hasten back to your plane; leave the mewling human Chosen and his bauble to me. I'll even let you depart in peace. Stay, and I'll perch your skull on my throne."

Estella open her mouth to scream, her snake-hair lashing in fury, but before she could utter a sound, Zosimus casually waved a hand. A wall of superheated air tumbled Sextus backward, blasting his sword away. He lost sight of Estella. Struggling to his feet, he ignored the heat radiating from his armor and stumbled toward the now visible gray form of his healer, lying on the flattened grass. A more violent temblor complicated his stride.

"Pathetic," Zosimus observed, easily keeping his feet despite the earthquake. "Two mortal Chosen, and neither worth my time. There won't be a grand, final battle. I will simply open the gate and step through, and this world will be mine."

Sextus ignored the self-important little shit. He reached Estella, and half collapsed against her body. The finely scaled skin was blistered, and some of her joints had burst under the direct impact of a strike from a petulant godling. Her braids were entirely torn away, leaving obscene gray stumps drooping from her skull. One ruined eye was dark, smoking, but when he gently turned her head, the second opened, a calm golden gaze, entirely detached from the ruin of her body.

"It is time for you to flee, Sextus," she said. "The gate must be destroyed."

"*We* can flee, Estella," Sextus said. "We can fight after you heal."

He cast about desperately for option. A horse, or a wagon perhaps . . .

"No, Sextus, you must away while you can," she said, shaking her head minutely. "When you called me princess, I would have bet my hair you knew my secret. You were right from the start. Duty first. I would stay with you, but I must call on Father, while I have the breath to do so. I will send you and the others as far as my remaining strength permits, and still destroy the portal."

"We can run together," Sextus said, shaking off the hands reaching for his shoulder. Around him, the few dozen legionnaires were clustered, as were bare handful of urks, who hooted defiance at the sky. Sextus looked up. It had begun raining gray grit.

"We don't need your father, whoever the hell he is!"

"We do," she said, spitting ash. "If a mortal heard my father's true name, they would succumb to madness. The Greeks, damn their self-serving histories, called him Hephaestus. Your lot name him Vulcan."

"Your father—"

She began to laugh, but starting coughing instead.

"Asag created a gate on an island; Medusa foiled him. Before, he tried for a continent and Euryale sank it beneath him. This time, the fool is trying for a gate atop a mountain already spitting fire."

"We can fight again." Sextus held her even more closely, and her eyes began to glow fiercely. "We can go!"

"Asag still doesn't understand, because all he serves is himself," Estella said, voice firming. "We understand, you and I, Sextus Lucilius Bassus, because we serve something bigger."

Unseen hands pulled Sextus back an arm's length, at which point Estella cleared her throat, drew a deep breath, and opened her mouth—to scream, Sextus supposed.

Instead, a sound like a swelling chorus, accompanied by instruments he'd never before, heard filled the clearing.

Nearing the tree line, the stumpy little silhouette of Decimus spun and raised both hands.

"Noooooooo!"

The very air squeezed Sextus from all directions, and the ground shook wildly enough to knock him flat, yet he remained suspended in an invisible cocoon. Then all the light in the world turned white.

"Helluva thing, sir," Gracos said, handing a wooden bowl of water to Sextus. "You don't suppose there's any chance the lady got out?"

"Look," Sextus replied, never lifting his gaze from the scene he'd been watching the last hour. Behind the ship, dirty gray and brown clouds stretched across the horizon, thinning overhead. No late afternoon sunshine penetrated, leaving the crew and passengers of their galley in a smoky twilight. Other refugees on the ship spoke of a wall of fire and ash burying the closest coastal cities, including Pompeii and Herculaneum.

"I suppose not," the artilleryman said, shoulders slumping. "We're lucky the *praefectus* happened along with his ships, or we'd still be on a Stabiaen beach, waiting to die."

"Where's Cato?" Sextus asked, his gaze still fixed astern. After he'd gotten the legionnaires and urks aboard, he'd left the details to his centurions.

"One of the urks is a medicine woman," Gracos explained. "She's fixing his face for him. Smells like a cesspit, but since we don't have the lady anym—"

Sextus jerked his head over to stare at Gracos. The centurion dropped the subject abruptly, and for a few moments, only the sound of the ship's wake could be heard. Sextus knew the silence was temporary. Wanted it to be so. Gracos was a Roman centurion who'd just fought waves of demons. His armor was still soiled with the blood of his enemies. Pissed-off commander or not, duty would come first.

"So, where to next, sir?"

Sextus echoed the question mentally, but the Many-Winged had remained silent since the abrupt translation from the field of battle to the beach. Sextus didn't have the energy needed to curse the silence.

The small silver ring on his finger tugged gently northward. Destiny lay that way, it seemed.

"We hunt monsters, Gracos. It's what we do."

ABOUT THE EDITORS

Larry Correia is the *New York Times* best-selling author of twenty-five novels. He's best known for his Monster Hunter International urban fantasy series, the Saga of the Forgotten Warrior epic fantasy series, the Grimnoir Chronicles alternate history trilogy, the Dead Six military thrillers, the sci-fi *Gun Runner*, and the progression fantasy novel *Academy of Outcasts*. He's also written over sixty pieces of shorter fiction, many of which are included in his Target Rich Environment collections, and he has edited five anthologies. He lives in Yard Moose Mountain, Utah, with his wife, children, and fearsome Krasnovian Waffle Hound.

You can follow him at monsterhunternation.com.

National best-selling author **Jason Cordova** is both a John W. Campbell Award and Dragon Award finalist. He is the author of *Mountain of Fire*, *To Tread Obsidian Shores* (with Melissa Olthoff), and *Monster Hunter Memoirs: Fever* (with Larry Correia), as well as the editor of *Chicks in Tank Tops*, *Dancing with Destruction*, and the forthcoming *Chaos and Consequences* anthologies.

Along the way, he has had novels published in multiple languages around the world and is currently an Associate Editor at Baen Books. You can find him at jasoncordova.com.

ABOUT THE AUTHORS

Melissa Olthoff is a sci-fi and fantasy author, a military veteran, and a self-proclaimed mocha addict. In 2023, she took second place in the Baen Fantasy Adventure Award and has won the Imadjinn Best Short Story Award twice. She is published by Baen Books and CKP and is best known for high-stakes adventure and sneaking romance into everything she writes.

Steve Diamond is a horror, fantasy, thriller, and science fiction author for Baen, Aethon, Gallant Knight Games, and numerous other small publications. His most recent works are a collection of short fiction, *What Hellhounds Dream*; a dark fantasy/horror novel cowritten with Larry Correia, *Servants of War*; and the supernatural thriller novel *Residue*. He is also the cohost of the writing advice podcast, *WriterDojo*.

Brad R. Torgersen is the 2019 DragonCon Dragon Award winner for Best Science Fiction Novel (*A Star-Wheeled Sky*). His award-winning stories have appeared in numerous magazines and anthologies. A veteran and chief warrant officer in the United States Army Reserve, Brad has also served in half a dozen different countries. Married for 25 years to his very first audio narrator, Brad lives with his family in the Intermountain West. He can be found most often at his Facebook page, and occasionally writes nonfiction for both his personal blog, and the Mad Genius Club group blog. A political classical liberal, Brad believes in having an open mind—so long as you don't let your brains fall out.

Ian "LawDog" McMurtrie was born on the island of Malta to American parents a long, long time ago, and lived in Africa and the Middle East before relocating to the US as a teenager.

In 2017 his first book, *The LawDog Files*—a collection of humorous stories from his law enforcement career—made it to #82 on all of Amazon, and convinced him that maybe there was something to this writing thing.

Eight years later, he is CEO of Raconteur Press—which should be proof that he isn't exactly right in the head.

He currently lives in North Texas with a very patient lady and their dachshund overlord.

Marisa Wolf writes SFF that ends with hope, no matter how hard the circumstances. She has a number of coauthored novels in shared universes, solo novels in her own worlds, and a plethora of short stories. All contain various levels of snark.

After several years living on the road in an RV, Marisa, her husband, and their high-maintenance rescue dog are currently based in the woods of New England—but it's anyone's guess where in the country she is at any given moment. More at marisawolf.net.

Kacey Ezell was born in South Dakota in 1977. Her parents joined the US Air Force in 1984, and she grew up around the world on various military bases. When she was seven, her mother gave her a copy of Anne McCaffrey's *Dragondrums*, and shortly thereafter, Kacey decided that she wanted to be a dragonrider when she grew up. In 1999, she followed her parents into the "family business" and graduated from the United States Air Force Academy before going to pilot training. As dragons were in short supply at the time, she reasoned that flying aircraft was the next best thing. She earned her wings in 2001, and has over 3,000 hours in the UH-1N, Mi-17, and EC130 helicopters. From the time she was a small child, Kacey made up stories to tell to her friends and family.

Kacey writes science fiction, alternate history, fantasy, horror, noir, romance . . . etc. fiction. She lives with her husband, two daughters, and her cats, Atlas and Birch.

The mysterious **Jack Wylder**, producer and co-creator of the *WriterDojo* podcast, has made a career of working behind the scenes. In his 25+ years in the marketing field, he's worked with huge names while mostly avoiding attention to himself. He's worked as an artist, bass player, blacksmith, gunsmith, carpenter, convention organizer, editor, private investigator, writer, and has a bunch of interesting stories. Wylder is a Texan living in an undisclosed city with his wife, son, two cats, and two heelers.

Hinkley Correia's debut story, "Blood on the Water," first appeared in volume one of *Target Rich Environment* and starred Hannah Stone. In the time since it was published, she has appeared in several anthologies and edited *The Super Generation* for Raconteur Press. She is currently working on a full-length military sci-fi novel, and enjoys playing video games in her free time.

Robert E. Hampson, PhD, is a national best-selling author and world-class neuroscientist whose stories traverse science fiction, military adventure, postapocalyptic scenarios, and hard-SF-style urban fantasy. Drawing from more than 40 years in scientific research, he crafts universes filled with carefully constructed ecological, technological, and political systems, infused with rich character dynamics and moral complexity.

After retiring from a globe-spanning career of swashbuckling adventure in the US Marine Corps, **Spearman Burke** tried his hand at this GI Bill thing he'd been hearing about. He earned an interdisciplinary degree in English Literature and Creative Writing with a minor in Theatre. Interestingly, he learned more about storytelling in theatre than in all of his writing classes combined. That, and how to apply his own makeup, which was in utter contrast to the whole Global War on Terror thing he had going on before. Now a writer/editor with Raconteur Press, he is the only person in his circle astonished that his first major publication is a children's book titled *Giant Counting Robots*.

Nick Nethery is a writer of science fiction and fantasy, including *Relics of the Fallen*, a near-future military SF novel. Also an editor with Raconteur Press, he has curated several collections of short fiction.

A retired soldier, Nick is now a full-time dad and trophy husband. He has worked as a bomb technician, teacher, sandwich artist (Go SU!), dishwasher, and caterer, among other jobs. In the army, Nick earned his jump wings, Air Assault wings, Explosive Ordnance Disposal badge, and other uniform candy.

If Nick had free time, his hobbies would be hiking, foreign films, and gaming. He enjoys playing tabletop, roleplaying, and video games with his sons.

Mike Massa has lived an adventurous life, including stints as a university researcher, a tech entrepreneur, an investment banker, and a US Navy officer (1130). In addition to the usual military deployments, he has lived outside the US for several years as a civilian, mostly in South America and Europe. Mike is married and enjoys the challenges of three sons and a growing cohort of grandsons, all of whom check daily to see if today is the day they can pull down the old lion. Not yet...